Dreamcatcher: Fortunes

To Kaye from Donna –
Blessings –
KCPearcey

KC Pearcey

For my literary midwife, Anne.

Birthing books feels quite a bit

like birthing babies.

The pain, the patience, the persistence –

the praying through –

and the peace when it's over.

Thank you for being there

through it all.

Three is a beautiful number.

Welcome back!

We're glad to see you've come for a visit!

Balfour's been pretty busy since we saw you last,

but one fact never changes –

life in the South may appear to slow down to a country crawl

but there's always a story to tell,

even in a fictional place inhabited by make-believe people.

This is your friendly reminder that the new folks

who show up between these pages aren't any more real

than the ones you've already met.

Truth.

Believe me, it would be easier to write about some of you,

but I can't afford the lawyers.

Just saying . . .

Chapter 1

The First Day: Sunday

The dream was back, in stark black and white and all the shades of smoke and gray between.

The soft, well-worn rag rug beneath her bare, cold toes felt deceptively safe and understandably familiar, especially when accompanied by the soothing warmth of the hot, soapy dishwater that entombed her slender fingers up past her wrists.

The reassuring emotions were short-lived.

Cora was in her grandmother's kitchen. Again.

She trembled with equally familiar apprehension, determined to be thoroughly peeved with any ethereal messenger who had invaded her peaceful earthly existence.

From behind where she stood she heard the scraping legs of the wooden ladder-back chair on the linoleum floor, the creaking of the woven cane bottom beneath a substantial weight, and she knew without a doubt that the past three short months of peace were about to be shattered into a thousand pieces. Maybe more.

Much like watching a cut glass goblet slip from clumsy fingers and fall in painfully slow motion, Cora knew there was no reprieve. Only shattered shards from which she'd be expected to find meaning.

James didn't wait for her to turn, his shuffling footsteps making their way across the protesting floor to her side. His wrinkled, age-spotted hand rested lightly on her slight shoulder, the grandfatherly warmth of his touch moving through the thin cloth of her shirt.

"Please breathe," he said reassuringly. "The journey is long, but there can be joy along the way. You know the verse I mean. The songs too. The night is long, but there's joy when the light is revealed."

Joy, she thought, refusing to be placated, her heart sinking with the warnings she knew were certain to come. *Joy comes in the morning. If only it were morning and this could literally be just a bad dream.*

The elderly preacher shook his shaggy head and chuckled into her ear as he hummed—a rusty, graveled sound that carried the time-worn tune as a bachelor uncle might attempt to rock a crying baby suffering from colic.

Broken melodies became broken song.

"Trials dark on every hand, and we cannot understand . . ." James began singing. Then the singing stopped as he waited for her to join him with her warm contralto, coaxing the words from her with a nod of his head and an ever-so-gentle smile.

"All the ways that God would lead us," she recited, refusing to sing, the words of the old hymn wrenched from her memory to her tongue.

You're not leading me, she thought. *You're pushing me. Stop pushing me.*

The fingers that gripped her shoulder tightened and then released.

"I'm sorry, Cora," he said, peering over the top of his horn-rimmed glasses and clearing his throat. "I'd forgotten that you never really liked to sing. Or to be pushed."

She shrugged his hand away and turned to the stove, but James simply shook his head again and sighed.

"Suffice to say," he said, "you and I are once again on our way. Shall we have some fresh, hot coffee and discuss the next leg of our journey together?"

Cora snatched the woven cotton dishcloth she found conveniently draped over her left shoulder and roughly dried her hands.

I knew you'd be back, she thought irritably, her face a mask of discontent. *Last time it was for Christmas, and now you're here for Easter.*

"You really should talk out loud," he said, taking his milky, translucent mug from the Formica counter and holding it away from him as he gingerly poured the rich brew. "I don't feel quite polite reading your mind, you know. Invasion of privacy and all such stuff and nonsense."

"Sorry," she said involuntarily.

"You don't sound very sorry," he grumbled good-naturedly, shuffling back to the table and lowering himself with a pained groaning sound that harmonized with the equally complaining chair. "You aren't this irritable with anyone else are you?"

She had no answer for that. He was right. He was usually right. She scolded herself for forgetting, for being so selfish.

"I am really sorry for sounding like a brat," she said. "You wouldn't be here if it weren't necessary."

Cora brought her own filled cup to the table and sat down at his suit-clad elbow, studying him. She should know better than to let herself be controlled by her feelings. She knew perfectly well what was going on.

There was a reason he'd appeared—clues he was sent to deliver. Clues which could, and would, appear anytime and in any form in the next few minutes of dreaming.

"You're thinking about Charlie, aren't you?" he said.

"No," she said. "Quite honestly, no. I wasn't. But I am now."

Charlie.

Three months since she'd heard that name—even in the deep recesses of her mind. Now James was back and Charlie was strolling through her thoughts as though he'd never left. As though he belonged—as though he'd never divorced her and tucked her away in Balfour to go off and solve mysteries and murders in New Orleans.

She was happily married to Thomas now. She had a new life. Charlie Abbott wasn't entitled to take up temporary residence in his old room, behind a door somewhere hidden and locked in her heart and head. All because he was the one James always meant the dream clues for.

Well, almost always.

Stop it, she thought, chastising herself. *This isn't Charlie's fault any more than it is yours. You're just the messenger.*

Cora wasn't the blaming kind of person. She was the doing kind. So she did.

She forced herself to pay attention to what she knew: the words to an ancient hymn, an unidentified scripture verse, and ambiguous references to morning.

And joy.

She stifled a yawn, covering her mouth with her free hand, inexplicably tired before the ordeal had even begun.

Another random thought skipped through her head, and she wondered if the coffee in her dreams might help her stay attentive the way actual coffee kept her alert when she was awake.

"You're distracted tonight," he said, sipping at the hot, fragrant liquid, the expression on his weathered face impish and amused. "Am I boring you? You're very pale, and you look quite troubled. You need to get out more. Sunshine and exercise would do you wonders."

Cora felt the illogical need to defend herself.

"I've been going to the front porch every morning for coffee with Thomas before he goes to work and to the back yard every afternoon with Marjorie and Jane to plant spring flowers and vegetables in the raised garden," she said petulantly. "If you're suggesting a world tour, I'm not quite up for that yet."

"Tsk, tsk, I seem to recall you went all the way to your husband's office just before Christmas, and that worked out well," he chided, picking up a rose-handled silver spoon and dipping it into the crystal pine cone sugar bowl. "That's quite the mood you've got there, Cora."

"Yes, I'm in a mood," she admitted, taking a cautious swallow of the steaming coffee and trying not to be appeased by his continued tolerant humor. "You know exactly why. Every time I think my life is getting back to normal, you show up with puzzles to be solved. I'm frightened and confused by the things I see. And then there's Charlie. Come on, James. I'm only human."

She held her grandmother's floral cup slightly away from her face, ignoring his reproving stare, inspecting the inside of the delicate porcelain, full of tiny spiderweb cracks and faint stains from the years of loving use.

The cup was always old in her dreams, as it had been in life.

She felt a sudden longing to see her grandmother again.

"Why must you come when things are going so well?" She knew she sounded like a cantankerous child. "I know you've got your reasons, but right now my life is so peaceful."

"Maybe that's the problem," the preacher said, adding a first, a second, and then a third heaping spoonful of snowy granulated sugar before he stirred. The metal spoon clinked against the sides of the translucent mug in an odd melodic rhythm.

Another hymn perhaps. She couldn't tell.

"So many people think that their lives are going well when in reality they're not," he observed sagely. "Or sometimes the exact opposite. People can be despondent and depressed when there's everything in which to hope. We're deceived in so many ways, perceiving life through such a dark, dark glass, and with such human frailty and foibles."

He removed the dripping spoon and placed it on the faded oilcloth before sampling the coffee, a tiny drop of black liquid pooling in the shiny bowl, reflecting the lamplight like a bright dot of white.

"*For now we see through a glass darkly, but then we will see as we are seen,*" he recited with practiced ease, the thick study Bible he always carried on the table between them. He gave the tome a firm, friendly pat. "*Then we shall be known even as also we are known.*"

Cora felt more than the usual confusion about what the preacher meant. The words seemed directed at her personally, but there was something odd about the translation. The words seemed patched together.

Maybe I'll ask Marjorie to help me look it up later, she thought. *She knows her Bible far better than I do.*

"Is this your obtuse way of telling me that I need to be worried about something?" she said. "Because if you're going to warn me that something terrible is about to happen, I'd think that would be obvious by your mere presence. You certainly haven't given me anything to tell Charlie."

James threw up his hands, laughing out loud, his sides shaking, creating ripples in his checkered vest beneath the folds of his ample suit jacket—a human volcano spewing glee.

"My dear girl, you should learn to have more faith," he managed, choking briefly over a few drops of coffee that had detoured into his esophagus. "I'd never try to frighten you with all sorts of unnecessary concern. On the contrary, I'd suggest you don't bother yourself at all with worry, but that goes against our human nature now, doesn't it?"

He cleared his raspy throat, regained his composure, and made another unsuccessful effort to sing more familiar words set to a faltering, discordant tune.

"Tis so sweet to trust in Jesus—just to take Him at His word . . ."

"And you, James, are a tuneless conundrum," she said sternly, interrupting the moaning melody, not at all amused by his glib response to her mounting fears. "Should I also put my trust in you?"

Eyes twinkling, he ceased his noise-making and took a full swallow of coffee, brandishing the translucent mug like a tankard before he returned to humming the first tune, in a slightly different form, though still quite horribly off-key.

"James," she said as sweetly as she could, "you never sang on Sundays, for goodness' sake, why are you singing now?"

Pointedly setting down his empty cup and picking up his Bible from the table, he studied her frowning face, tucking the bulky volume in the crook of his elbow and standing with a faltering wobble.

"*By and by, when the morning comes,*" he sang, more vigorously, the corners of his wrinkled mouth creasing like a Cheshire cat and his portly body swaying to tune. "I know what you're thinking, Cora. I can't and shouldn't sing. I'm only doing what I've been told to do."

She lifted her cup and made a valiant attempt to control her mounting agitation.

"That's the chorus to the first song you were singing," she said. "Am I supposed to remember the words to the chorus? I barely remembered the first verse."

He gurgled with amusement, patting her hand to the rhythm.

"*We will understand it better by and by,*" he sang. "You *will understand it better by and by . . .*"

"I'm trying so hard to understand," she said. "Truly I am. I just wish I could."

The last notes drifted away, and James and her grandmother's kitchen were gone as quickly as they had come.

And Cora was awake and staring at the ceiling in her bedroom—4:48 a.m. Thomas lay curled on his side away from her, sleeping in blissful ignorance, unaware of this most recent disruption to their tranquility.

Her long-suffering husband would be as dismayed as she was by the long-dead preacher's unforeseen nocturnal visit. She certainly couldn't blame him one bit.

For a moment she was too irritated with the reappearance of the dream to be concerned over much of anything else but solving the puzzle as rapidly as possible.

But what *was* the puzzle?

After all, he'd only told her some disconnected lyrics to two hymns she'd learned when she attended church as a teenager. Then something about joy and mornings.

Yes, she thought, more than a little confused. *And singing the hymns himself. What was that all about? Church? James was in a remarkably cheerful mood for a messenger who almost always brought somber, depressing news.*

Despite her bewilderment, Cora knew at least one thing she needed to do.

Calling her ex-husband could wait until she knew what to say. Writing down what she'd seen needed to happen immediately.

She swung her feet over the side of the bed without waking her dozing husband and made her way downstairs to her office. In a burst of optimism she'd moved her dream journal from the bedside table and needed write everything down before she forgot.

Because there was one thing she did know for certain. The dream she'd had was an indication of the immediate future.

Death was involved.

When and where that death occurred was out of her control, but the clues she'd see in her dreams would be the only hope of finding out what really happened.

The clues . . . and Charlie Abbott.

Chapter 2

Preacher Evans had been up since before dawn, methodically pacing the hardwood bedroom floor of his modest ranch-style home and muttering to himself about the text of his Sunday sermon. Much to the concern of his long-suffering wife, he was also absently rubbing the decades-old throb in his left shoulder blade.

Not that Ginny minded being awakened at all hours of the day or night, that was part and parcel to life as a minister's wife. She was simply befuddled. This agitation was noticeably uncharacteristic behavior from her well-disciplined, military-minded husband.

She hadn't seen him quite so distracted since the early years of their marriage.

Andy relished preparing ahead of time, keeping current in his topics, avoiding the obvious and the trite. To the untrained eye, he might seem to be in a constant state of flux, but his wife knew that any outward sign of nervousness was only on the surface. At the core he'd always been settled, calm, and confident about the pastoral process. She could only surmise that this increasing conflict was due to something else entirely.

She considered that perhaps this change in the status quo was a behavior linked to some sort of holiday phobia her husband had developed. He'd had issues writing the Advent services at Christmas, but had found his proverbial feet and recovered beautifully by New Year's.

At least, she thought so.

Now he seemed to be exhibiting the same lack of confidence over his Palm Sunday and Easter sermons that he'd had in December.

For a fleeting moment she wondered if his inability to focus had anything to do with the recent return of their only child to Balfour, but she dismissed the thought. Andy had been more willing to talk openly with her, and with Jack, in recent weeks, so she was almost certain that their prodigal son was not at the root of his wakefulness.

Although as she considered her husband's odd behavior, nothing was out of the question at this point. Not even the three years of his military service before they met.

By the time Andrew made his exodus into the bathroom for a shower around five o'clock still muttering, mumbling, and moaning, she resigned herself to rise and make a pot of strong coffee, preparing a batch of homemade buttermilk biscuits for the oven.

Experience with her spouse's moods had taught her well that there'd be no further sleep in the Evans house for the morning.

As the timer clock on the stove buzzed, the preacher made his deliberate way into the kitchen. Nothing bothered him in his present state of agitation quite so much as noisy electronic devices. She silenced the offending warning, grabbing two potholders and removing the heavy-laden aluminum baking sheet from the oven.

There was no point in making only a few buttermilk biscuits at a time. Andrew liked them as much when they were cold as he did when they were warm. He loved bread in any form.

"Do you want jelly with your biscuit?"

Andrew hesitated, his hand on the back of the nearest chair for support, and considered his waistline where his starched white shirt was tucked into his pleated black slacks. He'd obediently put on the clothes she had laid out on their bed, knowing that, as always, he could depend on her color choices.

His socks would match his shoes and each other, and his tie wouldn't clash with his shirt. Some days he allowed himself to forget that he was completely color-blind, and thanks to Ginny, today was one of those days.

"Maybe just a pat of butter this morning," he said, frowning at his expanding midline as he pulled out the chair to take his seat. "Thank you for getting up with me. You don't have to do that, you know."

His wife put a cup of steaming coffee at his elbow, the teaspoon protruding from the rim like a sterling silver flag, her lips pressed together in a thin smile.

"Do I have to remind you how long we've been married?" she said. "That will bring up a totally inappropriate discussion about how old I am, and it's too close to my birthday for that."

"Your birthday?" he said, looking up. "Oh no, Ginny!"

"You can forget pretending to be surprised," she teased. "Being born on April Fools' Day means no one ever forgets my birthday. You've said it often enough."

Andrew gave the liquid a quick swirl, testing the flavor with the tip of his tongue and grimacing. With the spoon balanced expectantly between his fingers, he reached across the table for the sugar bowl.

"I've already sweetened that," she said, taking the silverware out of his hand and lifting the bowl from his reach. "The last thing you need this morning is more refined sugar."

"You were offering me jelly," he protested. "That's full of sugar, isn't it?"

"Point well-taken," she admitted, feeling guilty about treating him like a child. "Sugar in fruit is not the same thing. But do as you will."

Ginny handed him back his spoon and replaced the sugar bowl, peering at him fondly over the top rim of her glasses. She was still curious about the source of his erratic, grumpy attitude.

Andrew Evans sighed in resignation, his gaze full of patient adoration for his wife.

"I can't win, can I?"

She turned to get her own coffee, refusing to answer the redundant question.

"In that case," he said, stirring his cup and scraping at the bottom for the last bits of undissolved sweetness, "I believe I'll have jelly on my biscuit."

Virginia returned and stood behind him. She held her cup out to the side with her right hand while she absently patted the back of his head with her left hand and combed down his unruly hair with the tips of her fingers.

I might as well ask, she thought. *He won't tell me, but I might as well ask.*

"Do you want to talk through what's bothering you?"

"Not really," he said not unkindly, taking her hand from his head and kissing the center of her palm. "You needn't fret, Ginny. I'm fine. You're probably right about too much sugar. I'm just hungry."

"Biscuits it is, then," she said, extracting her hand and putting down her cup.

Stubborn man, she thought. *You are an adorable, lying, stubborn man.*

Removing two plain white Corelle plates from the cabinet, she placed a fluffy brown biscuit in the center of each.

"Careful," he warned unnecessarily. "They're hot."

"Indeed." She put their meal on the table and looked down at him, hands on her hips, unable to contain herself. "You're a well-spring of wisdom this morning."

He picked up his coffee and sipped.

Apparently, he thought, *I'm not the only one who's moody this morning. Ginny's being sarcastic, and that isn't like her at all. Wonder if the Wilton House opening has her nerves on edge. She's been working so hard lately. I should have let her sleep.*

"Only one butter knife?" he asked, lifting the utensil into the air, waving it as he had his spoon. "Don't you have one?"

"It's called *sharing,* Andrew."

She took the knife out of his hand, split his biscuit horizontally into two steaming symmetrical pieces, and tossed a thick square of butter between the halves.

So much for not treating you like a child, she thought. *Oh well.*

"The jelly and jam jars are in the refrigerator door," she added, performing the same procedure on her own flaky biscuit. "I'm not having any, so you need to make your own selection this morning."

"Is there any muscadine left over from Christmas?"

Ginny gave him another pointed stare over the top rim of her glasses.

"You aren't listening to a word I'm saying," she said. "Maybe there's something else you'd like to talk about. For example, what's your sermon topic today?"

She replaced the halves of her biscuit and took a sip of her coffee while she waited for the butter to melt and for her husband to respond.

"The joy of serving others," he said absently. "I thought I'd talk about the man who provided the Upper Room for the Last Supper meal for Jesus and the disciples. I thought it would be an appropriate topic for Palm Sunday leading into the Easter sermon next week."

He had made no move to check the refrigerator, still sitting motionless in his chair, staring at the food in front of him as though he had no idea how it had come to reside on his plate. He gazed at the biscuit on her plate with the same childlike wonder.

"Did you say there was or there wasn't any muscadine?" he asked innocently.

She took a deep breath and reminded herself that he'd always been a bit absent-minded and hadn't been sleeping very well. She resolved to give him the benefit of the doubt.

She just wished he would confide in her what was really bothering him. He'd never liked to talk about his feelings, especially about his life before they met. He was a strong man with strong convictions. Ginny had been drawn to the determination in him as much as it had sometimes taken her to her knees in prayer.

"Would you like me to check the refrigerator for the jelly?" she said patiently.

"Would you?"

Ginny pushed her plate back and got up.

I love you, you adorably annoying man, she thought. *You don't get your own socks from the sock drawer—why would I expect you to get the jelly from the refrigerator?*

The distinctive jar was on the center shelf between the ketchup bottle and the Tupperware container of chicken salad she'd prepared last night for today's light lunch.

There was a scant tablespoon's worth of deep purple muscadine jelly in the bottom of the container, Darcie's Christmas label stuck prominently to the side, fading red and green ribbon decorations on the top of the screw top Mason lid.

I'll have to ask her for more at the Wilton House opening on Saturday morning, she thought, placing the Mason jar and a long-handled iced tea spoon on the table beside her husband's plate. *It really is Andy's favorite.*

"There's just a bit left," she said. "Maybe this will let you reach the bottom without getting jelly all over your fingers."

"First-rate plan." He picked up the second spoon, gripping the slender handle like a shovel and scratching at the glass bottom with noisy enthusiasm. "Thank you, Ginny."

"You're welcome," she said.

Outside the bay window of their modest kitchen she could see the first rays of early morning light, the song of a mockingbird in the distance calling to its mate.

Spring. Life. Change.

The mother in her wondered what Jack was doing and if he'd be in the services this morning, hoping he'd be in church somewhere even if not with them.

She looked across at her husband, a thin streak of purple jelly creeping from the corner of his mouth, his smooth-shaven chin littered with bits of biscuit crumbs, and her heart felt a surge of protectiveness.

Reaching over, she absently brushed the bottom half of his face with the corner of her napkin.

Whatever is going on, we'll get through it together, she thought, her heart at peace. *We always do. I've great faith in you, Andrew. Past, present, future.*

Then her mind moved on to what she was going to wear to church and the upcoming meeting with Linda about the Wilton House opening.

After all, there were things to do. It was Sunday. Again.

Chapter 3

Marcie Jones lay the practical bamboo placemats on the handmade wooden table in her kitchenette, silverware clutched in her chubby hands, and surveyed the results of her effort with pride.

A knock on her apartment door alerted Elvira, who perked up her velvety Plott hound ears, drooling, her pink tongue hanging from the side of her ample brown jaw.

The landlady knew without looking that it was Marjorie, ready for their usual Sunday morning breakfast before heading out to Emmanuel Baptist Church for services. Since they'd established their routine not long after Marjorie had moved into the Piney Woods, they'd missed this weekly meal a mere half dozen times. Since Marjorie's recent kidnapping, the Sunday morning routine had taken on even greater significance.

Marcie was more than ever a guardian of their friendship and time together.

Neither woman attended Bible study classes nor volunteered

to work in the children's department, although each had her own reasons.

As the one-woman owner and caretaker of the Piney Woods, Marcie had never been able to carve out time for anything other than the weekly Sunday morning service. She had her own personal daily devotionals, as well as discussing spiritual matters and prayer requests with Marjorie, but Marcie simply had no free time for volunteering.

On the other hand, Marjorie would have loved to work with the children on Sundays, especially when she and Cora weren't fostering during the week, but that would have meant giving up these breakfasts with Marcie.

Many people spoke kindly about Marcie, but Marjorie had noticed that although her landlady was respected and well-liked, she didn't seem to have close friends.

Her relationship with Ben Taylor and his weekly visits to the Piney Woods, however, were the stuff of grocery store gossip. Publicly they feuded like cats and dogs, so naturally people wondered why they would voluntarily spend so much time together.

At any rate, Marjorie decided that Marcie's private life was none of her business, and she was determined to cultivate this particular friendship no matter her own personal wants or opportunities. It just seemed the right thing to do.

"Right on time," Marcie called from the kitchenette. "Have a seat while I turn off the oven."

Elvira stood with a full-out shake of her ample torso, greeting their visitor with a muffled half-yowl yawn.

Marjorie, dressed in one of her traditional cardigans and neatly tailored slacks, ignored the dog hairs and slobbering. She leaned down and stroked the dog's huge ears with affection and hugged her canine head.

"Haven't we had the talk about locking your door?" Marjorie chastised. "Good morning, Elvira."

"I've got a guard dog," Marcie said, appearing in the doorway with two plates filled with crispy homemade waffles topped with blueberry compote. "Pour the tea, please. We're having chamomile this morning."

"This looks lovely, as always," Marjorie said, seating herself and removing the quilted tea cozy from the pot. "But you keep promising to let me cook every now and then, and you never do."

"That's because you cook all week for Cora," Marcie said, putting the plates down and returning to the refrigerator to get a well-worn ceramic pitcher of concentrated orange juice. "The only time I get to cook for anyone else is for you on Sundays and when Charlie decides to grace me with his honored presence."

At the sound of her master's name, Elvira's ears perked up and she lifted her head, her round brown eyes eager and expectant.

"Sorry, dog," Marcie said, settling herself at the table and digging into the waffle with enthusiasm. "He's in Memphis for another conference, and I don't expect him anytime soon. You know how he is when he's working. He misses you too."

"You're awfully kind to take care of his dog," Marjorie said, picking up her own fork and plunging through the thick topping. "You've got a generous heart."

"Shhh," Marcie said, holding her index finger against her lips. "No one needs to know that. You're no friend of mine, spreading vicious rumors."

Marjorie knew her friend was joking, but good-natured

bantering aside she also knew that there was a grain of truth in what Marcie said. She knew that more than one person in Balfour had taken advantage of the landlady's kindness and generosity.

"So how's the house coming?" Marcie asked between bites, pausing to lick a smear of thick compote from her fork in most unladylike relish. "The formal gardens must be gorgeous this time of year. I hear Deborah's Daughters have been hard at work for months now. I wish I had the time to come out and look before Saturday's opening. You know I can't abide crowds."

"Well," Marjorie said, her own fork suspended over the break-fast plate, "the whole project seemed impossible at the beginning, but Virginia Evans is a miracle worker if I ever saw one."

Marcie nodded, her loose gray curls bobbing around her cherubic face as she took another bite of waffle and spoke through the chewing.

"It takes a miracle worker to keep Stewart Wilton in line, that's for sure." Marcie's voice was full of warmth and admiration. "I know you've done more than your fair share of the work with the Daughters. You're a saint."

Marjorie blushed. "Now who's spreading rumors?"

I don't feel like a saint, Marjorie thought. *I'm just another thankful member of Deborah's Daughters. Blessed to be part of an ever-growing community of women who make a difference in people's lives. No credit. No names. Just acts of kindness done under the cloak of secrecy and coordinated by lavender envelopes. Thank goodness and the good Lord for Virginia Evans.*

"Are you okay?" Marcie's voice interrupted Marjorie's musings. "Aren't you hungry? You've stopped eating."

Marjorie looked up from her plate and realized that she had

gotten lost in thought and contemplation.

"I'm sorry," she said. "I was just appreciating the delicious waffles."

"You are a terrible liar," the landlady said. "I know you don't want to talk about the Daughters. I'm sorry I put you on the spot. Finish your breakfast, and I'll try to restrain my curiosity. I guess I must think I'm talking to Charlie."

At the second mention of her master's name, Elvira lumbered over to the table and parked her broad head on Marcie's knee, gazing up soulfully. Marcie patted the dog's velvety fur and affectionately tugged at one of the drooping ears.

"Okay, dog, apologies to you," she said. "I'm apparently not as gifted keeping my mouth shut as I think I am."

Marjorie scraped the last of the juicy blueberries from her plate onto the edge of her fork, verifying the time on her wristwatch as she took the final bite.

"I hope you don't stop talking," she said, teasing. "Where else am I going to get the latest gossip? We'd best be washing up, though. Don't want to be late for services."

"That's why I love sitting on the back pews," Marcie said, taking both plates as she stood. "The preacher's too near-sighted to see me come in and too vain to put on his glasses so he can tell who's late."

"Andrew doesn't wear glasses," Marjorie said.

"Well, that's just what I mean," Marcie said pointedly. "Alice and Donna say he should. Virginia's been nagging him to go to the optometrist in Griffith for weeks now."

"See there—that's what I mean! Where else am I going to get that kind of news?"

Marcie laughed out loud.

"Please finish the orange juice," she said. "There isn't enough to save."

Marjorie obediently emptied the remaining liquid in the juice pitcher into her glass, drained it quickly, and followed her hostess into the kitchenette with the used silverware and cloth napkins.

"It's my turn to wash the dishes."

"Is not," Marcie corrected. "I distinctly remember you washed the dishes last week."

"A gossip and a liar." Marjorie smiled. "No wonder we're friends."

"Two of a kind," the landlady admitted. "Now grab a dish-cloth, or we'll miss the prelude. I heard Lavinia's been practicing all week with some new worship song, not to mention you know how irritable she gets when someone walks in while she's playing the organ. I heard she's been getting migraines lately. Pain does all sorts of things to people's temperaments. Besides, I get enough preaching from Evans. I certainly don't need lectures on behavior from the musicians!"

Chapter 4

Thomas had dressed for church with the hopeful expectation that this would be the Sunday that Cora would decide she was coming with him to the services. His hopes were dashed, however, when he came downstairs at a quarter till ten to find she was still wearing her comfy clothes while Jane was dressed in a fluffy pink sweater over a rose-colored smocked dress. The outfit was completed by a giant bow on her head.

Thomas had difficulty understanding many feminine behaviors, however the concept of big bows fell into a category all its own.

The little girl's bright, dark eyes watched him with quiet antici-pation, the stuffed kitten sister wearing the pink bow that matched her sweater tucked securely in her arms. She'd left the other kitten sister keeping the Cabbage Patch doll company in her bedroom.

Jane was never without one or the other of the stuffed kittens, and more often than not she insisted on carrying both. Cora some-times thought she should ask Charlie where he got them so they could find a replacement if something ever happened to one of them, but she never remembered to ask.

Taking better care of the stuffed toys just seemed easier than talking to Charlie.

Cora watched as Thomas handed Jane a tiny white New Testament from the bookcase and collected his own leather-covered Bible.

Since the first time Thomas had taken her to church, Jane appeared to love the time they spent together, chatting constantly, skipping the entire fifteen-minute walk in sunshine or rain, taking the car only when absolutely necessary.

Many downtown Balfour residents and visitors to the B&B took the same walk, taking in the seasonal scenery and greeting each other on their way to either the Baptist or the Methodist church.

Every Sunday morning since Jane had come to stay with them, Thomas had considered broaching the subject about church attendance with Cora.

Every Sunday morning he reconsidered that decision on his way down the stairs.

Once had he even brought the situation up with her Atlanta psychiatrist, Ted Floyd, who told him to be patient and wait. Floyd was an avowed atheist, so Thomas took the advice with a rather large grain of salt, but in his heart he knew that pushing Cora to do something she wasn't ready to do was wrong.

Besides, Cora had insisted she didn't need to continue her medication past the early stages of her depression, and she'd stopped making regular appointments with Dr. Floyd after Marjorie came. Cora confided in him that she called Floyd from time to time, but she insisted that those were professional conversations about the children she treated. Thomas had no reason to doubt what his wife told him.

Cora seemed so much better. First with Marjorie. Now with Jane. With him too.

Thomas held fast to his hopeful expectations. This morning was no exception.

"Ready?" he asked, quite unnecessarily, absorbing the beauty of the moment.

Cora and Jane stood together in the double French doorway to the sunroom, light shining in behind them in bright halos highlighting their dark hair and outlining their slender forms. The little girl's big bow set upon her head like a crooked hot pink crown. Thomas felt a swelling lump of emotion in his throat.

Jane shyly offered a tiny hand, taking a step toward him. She looked back over her shoulder at Cora.

"I'll walk you to the door," Cora said reassuringly. "And I'll have lunch ready when you get home. Tell Morrie that I said 'Hello.'"

Jane nodded solemnly.

At the door, Thomas kissed his wife tenderly on the cheek and looked into her eyes, uncertain of what he hoped to find. She seemed troubled in some odd way he couldn't quite identify.

"We'll be back by twelve thirty," he said. "Even on Palm Sunday you can depend on Evans to be punctual and to the point."

"Yes," she said. "At least he's that."

She stopped and felt momentarily ashamed of her attitude.

"I didn't mean that the way it sounded," she said. "He's a decent man. I enjoy watching the church service videos with Marjorie, although how she sits through his sermons twice is beyond me. I just wish every once in a while he'd break out of his trained seminary shell and find something really relevant to talk about."

"I'm sure he's trying," Thomas said, not sure at all what his wife meant. Evans sounded like every other Baptist preacher he'd ever heard, and for Thomas that wasn't a bad recommendation. The way Thomas saw it, predictability was a positive character trait.

He and Jane reached the corner of Main Street and Maple, the barrels and flower beds along the sidewalk already blooming with early daffodils and the expectant buds of azaleas, and were about to cross in front of City Hall when Bill came ambling up from his apartment over the nearby Simmons' Restaurant.

He was wearing his customary Sunday attire—a starched, long-sleeved shirt and a modest blue and green striped necktie. His graying hair was combed back, gathered at the nape of his neck and braided, resting like a second spine against his back and ending just below his waistline. From the expression on his face the tie might as well have been a silk noose and his easy stride the long walk to the gallows.

Bill never looked really relaxed or at ease except when he was wearing his faded Levi jeans and plain white T-shirt under a spotless canvas bib apron, and even then his weathered face was a stone-cold neutral.

Thomas refused to waste his time formulating any opinion about Bill, knowing that what anyone might think mattered little to Bill. The silent, stoic man had been a fixture in Balfour for too many years to be questioned.

Bill was an accepted enigma in more ways than one.

Thomas had noticed on more than one occasion the puzzling effect Bill had on the children who came into Sam's restaurant, which would have mattered little to him except that he was witness to the same reaction in Jane.

For reasons known only to the child and the other children with whom he came into contact, Jane was inexplicably drawn to the towering goliath. All children, from babies to toddlers, appeared to adore him. Babies gurgled joyfully at his presence. Toddlers reached up for his reluctant embrace. Jane herself never failed to greet him with a smile, often laughing while crossing the street to join him, dragging a doubtful Thomas in her wake.

From the first accidental Sunday morning walk together, they formed a comic trio as they sauntered to church on Sundays—the cook's broad stride adjusting effortlessly to Jane's skipping steps, moving in tandem down the sidewalk.

They almost never spoke, choosing a companionable silence over the slightest conversation. A silence that Thomas was reluctant to break, believing his own presence in the threesome to be superfluous.

This morning as they arrived on the front steps of the church in their usual state of quiet calm, Sam was standing just inside the church vestibule having an animated discussion with Ellie Sanderson.

"Good morning, beautiful," Sam said to Jane, who had slowed her step at the sight of Ellie, whom she did not know. Jane retreated to a position under the lawyer's elbow, clutching his arm. Only the oversized pink bow revealed her hiding place.

"Hello, Sam," he said, patting the child reassuringly on her hand. "Good morning to you too, Ellie. How's college life?"

"Busy—I'm glad for the break, even if I'm spending it working two jobs."

She turned to Sam, indicating a flowered backpack at her feet.

"Can we talk about this later, please?" Ellie said. "I'll see you after church. I brought a change of clothes, and I'll be there as soon as I can."

Sam frowned and turned to acknowledge Bill with a nod of her head. Bill, who had been waiting patiently for the cluster of people in the doorway to clear, waved at Sam and Ellie before he continued into the church, the salt and pepper braid swinging rhythmically between his broad shoulder blades.

He stopped at his familiar place at the end of the third pew and nonchalantly took his seat, folding his arms across his chest and resting his gaze on the distant empty pulpit as if in thoughtful meditation.

"Thomas," Sam said, grabbing Ellie's elbow before she could walk away, "maybe you can settle an argument here. I was just saying—"

"I don't work on Sundays," the lawyer interrupted, sliding past them easily into the main auditorium of the church building, maintaining his own firm grip on the shy Jane who seemed almost glued to his suit jacket.

"Besides," he called back over his shoulder. "I'm not qualified to pass judgment in the church. Maybe you should consult the preacher. Or check with Candler when he comes for lunch."

"Come on, Thomas," Sam protested as numerous heads turned to see who was causing such a commotion in the doorway to the sanctuary.

"I told you so!" Ellie said, her enthusiasm tempered with the knowledge that she was talking to one of her employers. "No one wants to get involved—not even Thomas. I've got to get to Darcie's. I'll see you after church."

Thomas, satisfied that he had avoided a conflict he could not win, searched the gathering congregation for Marjorie and Marcie.

Jane spotted the duo first, dropping her guardian's hand without ceremony to abandon him for the housekeeper's side. She settled into the pew with unabashed joy, snuggling under the second safe and secure arm of the morning.

Assuming his most neutral courtroom expression, Thomas took his seat at the opposite end of the same pew, balancing his Bible on his knee.

His second disappointment in less than an hour was no easier to handle than the first had been, but he was a pragmatic man and prone to optimism, although experience often taught him the folly of his belief.

The organist struck the first chords, and the crowd drifted into the rows like grains of sand seeking the base of an hourglass and coming to rest in a mound.

As the music swelled, he bowed his head and prayed.

Thomas Stone knew he had much for which to be thankful, but he wasn't so foolish to believe that everything he loved might not disappear in a heartbeat.

Chapter 5

Naomi Balfour had prepared a cartoonishly grinning plate of fried eggs and strips of turkey bacon for her father's breakfast—two shiny yellow eyes ringed in milky white with a pair of wrinkled brown lips beneath them. Beside the plate she had also placed a mug of freshly brewed coffee with three creams and extra sugar, just the way he liked it.

Zeke sat down at the table and watched his daughter as she relocated the step stool she needed to reach the upper shelves in their country kitchen, realizing that she hadn't even reproved him about the added sweetener or the calories in the heavy cream.

Her silence was Zeke's first clue that Naomi was up to something.

His preteen daughter was vocal in her concern about his health and his weight, although no one else could have criticized the forty-two-year-old's athletic physique.

She would deny any ulterior motive—deception with villainous intent had no part in her eleven-year-old nature. Indeed, she was a direct child. One who assumed quite logically that obedience and hard work equaled her father's favor.

This particular morning, however, she wanted something from her father and had what she believed was a worthy goal. Knowing her father's nature, she had no intention to share until her father was in the proper mood to be approached.

Naomi enjoyed watching her father try to figure out what she was thinking, and his confusion at her kindness and thoughtfulness amused her.

Which, in turn, amused Zeke, who doted on his only daughter. His wife left him when Naomi was only two years old, declaring that she could not and would not make her home in the desolate hill county of Georgia among the wild critters of the woods and mountain streams.

She didn't care that it was his family's home, his inheritance and legacy. She wanted a better life for herself—or so she said.

Zeke forbid her to take their child with her, not that her new boyfriend was keen on children anyway, and Balfour chose to offer his former wife her freedom and his last five hundred dollars in exchange for her signature on the divorce papers.

When she agreed, Zedekiah Balfour proceeded into the town that bore his name, sought out Thomas Stone, and made sure the divorce agreement, along with the custody arrangement for his only child, was airtight. Thomas agreed to take his fee out in stonework in the form of an exquisite carved granite angel that graced the headstone marker over his parents' grave.

Then Balfour and his daughter retreated into congenial solitude, surrounded by the Mountain River Christian Church and a diverse community of believers who refused to judge him for his former life choices.

In the intervening nine years, Zeke brought up his daughter as both mother and father. Privileged that his widely respected skill as a stonemason and blacksmith allowed him the freedom to stay at home, he kept Naomi at his side while he worked carving statues, engraving monuments, blacksmithing for the locals who kept horses for nearby horseback riding venues, and doing whatever repair work was needed on the ancient plows and equipment many of the farmers still used.

He was always patient. Always talking. Always instructing her in life.

Together they'd created an idyllic routine that included the best parts of country folk and country living. They had no need to venture into town for anything. The community in which they lived was close-knit, self-sufficient, and fiercely independent.

Well aware of his daughter's need to socialize with other children, Zeke had arranged for frequent playdates with friends from the rural Mountain River Christian Church that they attended on Sunday mornings and Wednesday nights.

The church, like many rural churches, had a welcoming and diverse membership made up of those who preferred mountain life over the more settled and predictable life in an incorporated town. They resembled a human quilt of humanity who liked their privacy and jealously guarded the privacy of others.

The congregation ranged from retired couples looking for peace and quiet to several young families who were looking for land and space to grow. Pottery makers, painters, and writers found inspiration and calm.

There were the standard occupations too.

The Mountain River Community boasted a service station with two pumps, a volunteer fire department with the fire truck parked in an old barn, a general store whose sign read simply "Mountain River," and a vet clinic with one veterinarian and a vet tech who were kept busy taking care of the riding horses and local farm animals, goats, cows, pigs, chickens, as well as cats and dogs.

In addition to the white clapboard church located at the four-way stop that defined the center of the community, there was also an antique store and a thrift shop.

Never a particularly religious man, Zeke tolerated the sermons and the evangelistic parishioners for the sake of Naomi's mental health and well-being. He sat politely in the same back pew nearest the exit every Sunday, no matter the weather. He never opened a Bible or a hymn book, never joined in the greeting time with more than a polite nod of his head, and listened dispassionately to the pleas and proclamations of the young zealot pastor to make a decision for Jesus.

His daughter made ready friends with everyone from the newborns to the aged, sang all the hymns with passionate zest, and spent time reading the Bible on her own.

In time, she came to radically different conclusions about the Creator than her father held and was politely but firmly vocal about her opinions.

With some guidance from Naomi's Sunday School teacher, who styled hair in her home salon during the week, he learned to comb and braid her unruly hair into neat cornrows, securing the bottom with ribbons she provided from her own daughters' supply. Naomi was never wanting for lovely hand-me-down dresses and suitable shoes—though Zeke often suspected that the gifts were new and that calling them donations was simply an attempt to spare him the embarrassment of charity.

He wanted nothing for himself—but they knew he could not refuse a gift for her.

At night he showed her how to cook the fresh vegetables they grew in their small garden plot and how to keep a tidy house. He read to her from all kinds of books the local librarian recommended on their sporadic trips to town, and from those, he taught his young daughter to read and write. By the time she was five and the local truant officer arrived to inquire about her public school attendance, the man was met with an articulate and petite preschooler who invited him inside to a fresh pot of coffee, served him homemade molasses cookies, and entertained him with summaries of her latest literary adventures.

The official left her father with detailed instructions about how to register a letter of intent to homeschool in Georgia and went on his way, confident of the child's future education and wholesome upbringing.

This particular morning she was waiting with eager anticipation, already dressed in her favorite ankle-length green corduroy jumper and long-sleeved plaid shirt for their morning trip to the little church. A large white cotton apron protected her clothing and a considerable portion of her small frame. Her hair was neatly combed and corralled into two dark brown puffs, one over the top of each delicate ear.

Zeke knew there was something afoot, but he hadn't a clue what it might be, even knowing his daughter as well as he did.

"Thank you for breakfast," he said. "The eggs are perfect."

"You're welcome," she said, placing her own last bite of egg into her mouth and gracefully wiping at her lips with the tip of a paper towel.

Okay, he thought. *I'll play. I guess I'm supposed to ask questions until I find out what you want. Here goes.*

"Is there a social today after church?" he asked. "Or dinner on the ground?"

"I don't think so." She placed her fork across her plate and stood, deliberately avoiding her father's eyes.

"Another book you want from the library, maybe?" he persisted. "Or a dress you saw the last time we were in Griffith? Maybe a pair of fancy overalls?"

"No," she said, making a polite but disapproving face at her father's outdated suggestions. "I don't need anything, thank you."

Standing at his elbow, she picked up her glass and downed the last of her milk, stacking everything neatly in the center of her plate.

He eyed her suspiciously.

"Naomi," he said, using his most serious parental tenor.

"Yes, Zeke," she replied, taking his empty plate and then her own from the table in one efficient swoop.

He grunted, his brow wrinkling in a frustrated frown.

"You know I don't like that."

"Well, Zedekiah sounds too formal," she responded blithely. "You've said you don't like it when I call you that either. Daddy just sounds so childish."

Zeke realized that he'd made his own problem. He treated her like an adult, so he shouldn't be surprised when she acted like one.

His annoyance turned to pride as she placed the dirty dishes on the countertop and paused to unbutton her sleeves, rolling them neatly out of the way before turning the white, cross-handle faucets.

"You're being rather saucy for someone who wants something from me," he said.

The sound of the running water drowned out the muffled sound of her denial.

"I don't know what you mean," she said, her capable hands swirling the bright pink dish sponge in a circle under the surface of the suds. "What could I possibly want that I don't already have? You should learn to be more trusting. Preacher said just last week that suspicious minds breed discontent."

Zedekiah Balfour chose to ignore the rebuke and finished the last of his own coffee, delivering the empty cup and his fork to the sink.

He found his father's love overcoming his irritation at her antics, bending his dark head and delivering a resounding kiss to his daughter's temple.

"All the same, young lady," he said, trying to sound stern. "I'd appreciate it if you'd remember to call me Dad at the church this morning. Maybe you've also heard somewhere that familiarity breeds contempt."

"Of course . . . Dad," she said, her eyes twinkling playfully. "I'll just need another minute or two to wash up the rest of the breakfast dishes, and then I can get my Bible and be ready."

"Thank you," he said. "I'll go put on my necktie with that suit jacket you expect me to wear."

"Thank you," she said.

Amid the clattering of the pots and pans in the kitchen came the lilting sound of Naomi's voice and an awkwardly childish rendition of a chorus the minister of music had introduced to the congregation the previous week.

The song was full of repetitious lyrics interspersed with words of love and Jesus.

Yes, he thought. *Sing, beautiful daughter. Be happy. The biggest mistake your mother ever made was not staying to watch you grow up, and my greatest joy is that I did.*

Chapter 6

Dinah Browning placed the oversized faux leather purse she had purchased on the padded pew beside her, unopened. The broad brass zipper at the top was firmly secured, the strap twisted loosely around her wrist. In her lap was a black large print King James Version of the Bible. It was well-used, but only because she had purchased the oldest, cheapest one she could the day before from the book section of a Goodwill store several neighborhoods away.

She glanced through the worn pages briefly this morning while she was waiting for the services to begin, but the words all seemed blurred, jumbled, and confusing, so she gave up. Both her head and her heart were pounding, and she felt a bit breathless and faint.

Her medication wasn't due to be taken until noon, but that didn't matter. She wouldn't be taking it anymore anyway. Not after today.

All she needed to do was escape detection as a counterfeit church member until the invitation was given.

Dinah's thoughts turned to her extensive preparation for the day and her mental checklist. Her modestly tailored dress, the artful cut of her hair, recently styled by an enthusiastic young woman at a generic walk-in beauty salon, the sensible low-heeled shoes.

Nothing unique or out of the ordinary. Nothing to distinguish her.

She hadn't been in a church in years, and she felt like a hypocrite. A deceiver. Her mother had taken her to services many years ago. Her mother said her appearance was important, and she wanted to look like everyone else even though she couldn't relate to the peaceful spirits around her.

This book is only a prop anyway, she reminded herself. *A way to somehow look as though I belong in one of the scattered groups within the congregation. An homage to my mother—God rest her soul—and my father.*

Her aching heart beat with an unnervingly irregular rhythm at the thought of her father, but she refused to have second thoughts.

It's because of my heart that I'm even here, she thought. *It's only a matter of time anyway. No one cares. No one ever cared except my mother—and she's been gone for two years.*

The preacher's voice droned rhythmically around her, waves of sound parting as they reached the row where she sat, about halfway back on the right piano side of the sanctuary. The words drifted over her like rushing, rapid water over stone.

Somewhere to her left a cranky toddler protested and was tenderly shushed.

A teenage boy on the second row crumpled a bulletin while his younger brother constructed a paper airplane.

Deacons, their faces alight with well-rehearsed greetings,

walked down the aisles carrying round wooden offering plates.

Dinah kept her head down, pretending to be absorbed in the crinkled pages of the book she held, and they passed by without disturbing her.

If she could have risen to her feet without attracting undue attention, she would have moved after the choir's presentation and made her way to the balcony seating. That was where she'd planned to be this morning, but someone had roped off the staircase, and the entrance to the upper level was being guarded by a well-dressed and much too friendly female greeter.

Dinah didn't want to speak to anyone. About anything.

It was too late for talk now.

She settled instead for the end of a pew near a stained glass window, the pattern one of grape clusters in varying hues of purple, red, and green. A brown vine heavily dotted with thick green leaves twisted around and through the grapes, allowing a few stray tinted sunbeams to illuminate the carpeted floor at her feet.

The preacher continued speaking, prattling on and on, while she gathered her courage. She told herself that she wasn't having second thoughts, that she just wanted one more song. She liked the music. Beautiful harmony. Sweet words.

She understood the meaning of the words they sang, the lilting optimism, the joyful thankfulness, although she felt none of it and believed none of it.

She once had. As a child with her mother.

But hopefulness and assurances were not possible today.

No, today was a day of decision. One of her own choosing. Time was passing quickly, her heart and her head in a struggle for ultimate control.

Dinah Browning sat desperately alone in a sea of friendly faces.

A young couple sitting two pews ahead of her silently leaned their heads together in romantic conspiracy, their shoulders touching. The wisps of the woman's hair clung to the static of the man's white linen shirt.

Dinah closed her eyes. She wasn't going to be distracted. She knew what she had to do. She wished she could be anyone else, anywhere else.

But that was not the way it was meant to be.

Voices in her head spoke to her, reminding her of her promises. Reminding her of the cruel fate that awaited her. A familiar female voice echoed in her head, bringing memories of long afternoons filled with fragrant tea, consultations, and commiserations.

She took her cell phone from her purse and slid it beside her on the covered pew, securing it under the edge of her thigh.

The number Dinah wanted to call was on her speed dial.

She'd debated letting someone else tell him what had happened, but even in her depression she knew that she should let him know herself.

He'd be hurt, perhaps, but he'd understand. He might even be relieved that she hadn't contacted him and involved him before the fact.

She hoped so.

She didn't want to make him feel guilty. Not really.

After almost forty minutes, the preacher closed his Bible with an audible thump and lifted the bound volume easily with one hand, gesturing toward the congregation with upraised arms.

The organ music lent undertones as he continued to speak.

Imploring. Pleading. Waiting.

When there was no obvious response from anyone in the congregation, he grudgingly tucked the book into his well-clad elbow and against his right side and gestured to the hovering choir director.

The pianist played the introduction to the closing chorus as the director ascended the platform and pivoted. With a wave of his hand, the choir and the congregation stood.

Dinah remained seated.

With a purposeful yet trembling hand, she reached over and unzipped the purse, pulling the base against her leg, reminding herself that the cell phone was still there.

She'd tried to prepare herself for this part in her mind, and she thought she was ready, but she hadn't counted on the music. The music was too distracting, too loving, too hopeful.

She steeled herself. There could be no hesitation. No mistakes. The preacher resumed pleading with his flock as she took a tissue from the bag and wiped the hot perspiration from her fingertips and then her quivering upper lip.

The music stopped. The preacher offered a closing prayer.

The time had come. At last.

She reached under her thigh with her left hand and pressed the only icon on the home page of her Android phone.

A little over four hundred and fifty miles away, a cell phone vibrated insistently before going almost immediately to voicemail.

I didn't expect an answer, she thought, willing the call's recipient to hear her thoughts. *I knew you'd be in church. That's the one way you were always like Mom. I just wanted you to know I didn't forget you. I want someone to let you know I'm gone.*

In a fluid loop, her clammy right hand slid down her body and into the mouth of the wide zipper, emerging with a small, bluish-gray steel pistol.

I'm so tired, she thought. *My chest hurts, and I am so very tired.*

Dinah Browning inserted the barrel between her dry lips, took her last breath, and pulled the trigger.

Chapter 7

The astonishing pop of the single gunshot echoed in the sanctuary, the sound ricocheting from the sides of the pews and against the upper level of the balcony.

A chorus of gasps and muffled screams erupted, rippling outward, followed by shouts and the sounds of scurrying feet and hysterical fear, members and visitors alike in state of panic, dashing, crowding toward the exit doors. Others stood frozen, frantically searching the crowd for the faces of loved ones, pressing back against the wall of human fear and simultaneously reaching out and pushing away to find and console each other.

Within seconds, two church-appointed security guards dashed in, impelled through the masses, rushing from the vestibule where they had been standing sentry.

The older guard, a white-haired police officer, was the first to reach her, his service revolver gripped securely between his two hands and aimed at the floor.

The younger man, a volunteer firefighter and EMT, was directly behind him, one hand on his own personal weapon still safely holstered underneath his navy-blue suit jacket and the other carrying his emergency tactical bag.

Both experienced men recoiled at the shocking sight.

Dinah's body was slumped sideways in the now-vacant pew, her right hand resting in her lap, still clutching the gun. The gaping purse sat accusingly beside her as the maroon tweed fabric that covered the pew rapidly absorbed the life flowing out of her limp body. Her remarkably calm face and staring eyes were mercifully obscured by the fringe of hair that had fallen over in a stained curtain.

The EMT dropped his bag on the edge of the seat and took out a pair of blue latex gloves, pulling them on but already aware that any efforts were futile.

The exit wound in the back of her head left no question. She could not be saved.

On the floor near her right foot was her fallen cell phone, released as her body shifted after the single shot.

Mark, the older guard, holstered his weapon, thankful he had once again found no need to use it for its intended purpose, and removed a handful of white tissues from the box at the end of the pew. With practiced intention, he methodically extracted the revolver from her stiffening fingers and laid it on the rapidly staining bench the required distance from her lifeless form.

Part of him hated that he knew exactly what he needed to do.

The EMT turned from the hopelessness of the woman in front of him to survey the frightened congregation, assessing the need for further action.

Neither of the seasoned men had ever seen a church scene quite like this one.

The young couple had huddled together in the doorway where they had entered only an hour before, the wife sobbing and trembling uncontrollably into her husband's shoulder as he attempted to console her. He gazed over the top of her head, his eyes darting from one side of the room to the other as he surveyed the space in terrified disbelief.

The pair of subdued teenage boys, devoid of their recent animosity for each other, paper airplanes still in hand, had been retrieved and dragged across the room by their hysterical mother and were being unceremoniously hugged and slavered with multiple random kisses.

"Friends," the officer announced, "if I could have your attention please."

All over the sanctuary the mass exodus was suspended while groups assembled, whispering and praying in hushed fright, uncertain if the danger was over as they murmured concerns and questions.

The murmuring ceased immediately and an eerie silence fell.

"There doesn't appear to be any current danger," he said. "This is a crime scene now, and investigators will be here shortly. If you could all please assemble in the fellowship hall, that would be helpful."

The senior pastor, who'd been standing inside a protective circle of suit-clad deacons to one side of the platform, moved out to help supervise the transition. The choir, along with their director, had fled through the side doors of the choir loft at the sound of the shot, robes and white satin stoles flowing around them. They rejoined their family and friends lining the outer aisles of the sanctuary.

A dozen or so of the middle and high school youth and their interim minister, a fresh-faced intern from the local college, had assembled in the hallway leading into the education building. Cell phones in hand, they were told to text their parents to let them know that they, too, were moving with the others.

Someone must have called 911 because moments later the scream of the sirens pierced through the cool spring air and mingled with the chiming of the church bells sounding the noon hour.

Inside the walls of the sanctuary, the hushed human voices fell silent.

One of the choir ladies from the alto section left her family group and reappeared from a supply closet, one of the long white linen cloths used to cover the communion tables pressed against the crimson red of her choir robe like a bandage over a bloody stain. She hesitantly approached the paramedic and the security officer, solemnly holding out the snowy offering.

"Poor soul," she said sadly, her gaze steadfastly focused on their faces and away from the macabre figure on the pew between them. "I don't know who she is—but I thought maybe she should be covered."

Mark reverently took the folded square and handed it to the paramedic, who was doing his best to block any casual view of the deceased.

"That's kind of you," the older man said, turning to acknowledge the commotion at the front doors and the arrival of the additional paramedics and police. "Very kind. We'll have to see what the officer in charge wants us to do, but thank you all the same."

"I just wanted to do something," she said, her voice breaking and tears flowing. "I didn't know what else to do . . ."

Chapter 8

Simmons' Restaurant had become a customary local destination for celebratory occasions and events every Sunday, opening promptly for lunch at one o'clock.

Most of the entrée selections on the limited menu were prepped ahead of time, either late on Saturday night or before services the following morning, and there was always a fresh salad full of local produce or some hearty homemade soup to keep the customers satisfied until Bill could complete his culinary main course magic.

Sam, ever the attractive hometown busybody, filled and refilled Mason jars with sweet tea and tart lemonade, exchanged pleasantries and good-natured bantering, and danced more or less discretely between the tables with theatrical flair.

Most of the clientele were regulars, a harmonious mingling of both Emmanuel and the Methodist congregations, along with the intermittent day-trip visitors thrown in for good measure.

Today's boisterous crowd was no exception.

Susan and Harry were seated in what had become their habitual spot at a front window booth, engaged in an intense discussion about the movie they had seen in Griffith the night before. Judge Candler and Linda were joined by the Reverend and Betsey Anne in the back corner in the Judge's routine lunchtime booth, their conversation dominated by the latest community service projects and improvements to be brought before the town council in the coming week.

Darcie Jones was without boarders at her bed and breakfast for the weekend except for the Senator, who had flown in on Friday afternoon. Wilton had invited his hostess, along with Katy, little Elizabeth, and Amy for the afternoon to share Sunday dinner and discuss plans for the Wilton House opening scheduled for the following Saturday, the day before Easter.

Ben Taylor, a towering Jim Smith in tow, had made his habitual Sunday after-church appearance on his way to the police station, picking up takeout for the dispatcher on duty as well as Jenkins, who was pulling a double shift for the weekend.

Sam's local regulars had been joined by an older couple and their grandson from nearby Griffith who were celebrating a birthday and a middle-aged couple from Atlanta who were just out for a day trip to the country.

Ellie Sanderson, who had reached a truce in her discussion with Sam, had just delivered two plates of prime roast beef with glazed carrots and tiny new red potatoes to the couple when there was a disturbance at the front booth where Susan and Harry sat.

Ben Taylor stopped mid-stride on his way out the double front doors, his ample take-out bag in hand, Smith awkwardly bumping into him from behind.

"Is something the matter?" the chief of police asked, taking a second step closer to the booth where Susan sat ashen-faced. Harry was holding his cell phone to his ear, his face cherry-red as his breath heaved in and out audibly.

"It's a detective with the Germantown Police Department, just outside Memphis," Susan said, her voice cracked and unsteady. "They've just called Harry on his sister's cell phone—it looks like she's shot herself."

Ben turned to the officer at his back and thrust the containers of food into the younger man's ample arms.

"Deliver this to the station and come right back," he barked. "Don't stop to gab, and certainly don't try to explain anything. I may need you here."

Jim didn't ask questions.

Judge Candler and the Senator got up in unison from where they were sitting, the Judge waving to his wife and the Johnsons to remain where they were while joining Ben in a half-circle around the front booth.

The three exchanged concerned looks without speaking, waiting, although none knew precisely what they were all waiting for—simply watching as Harry Halstein's flushed face drained of color as he listened to the officer at the other end of the line.

Finally the startled businessman found his voice.

"Yes," Harry managed, unsteady but bringing his breathing to a more normal rate. "I think I understand. Of course you'd like to go over all the details in person. I suppose I'm the next of kin. I can make arrangements to be there tonight."

He threw an inquiring look at Susan, who offered him a

tremulous smile.

"Yes, I can definitely be in Memphis tonight." His voice had returned to its customary steady, strong rhythm. Harry had overcome the initial shock and was back in charge of his emotions. "Can you tell me exactly what I need to do?"

"Can I be of assistance?" Ben interrupted, closing the remaining gap to the table. "Do you want me to talk to the detective for you?"

Harry looked up, noticing the police chief for the first time.

"Could you speak to the Balfour Chief of Police? He's here with me at lunch," Harry said into the receiver. "I'm still somewhat in a state of shock, you understand."

He listened for an answer, then held out the phone.

"It's a Detective Davis."

Ben took the phone.

Harry, hands temporarily freed, reached impulsively across the table for Susan, gripping her fingers as though he were drowning and she was his only lifeline.

"Chief Ben Taylor here, Balfour PD," he said briskly. "What's your situation?"

As Ben listened, Harry quietly addressed the small group huddled protectively around him.

"It's my half sister," he said. "She's shot herself. She's just outside Memphis, in Germantown. She doesn't have anyone else. They want me to go handle things."

"That's where you and your mother lived," Susan said, not knowing what else to say. "Of course you should go."

The man nodded.

Just as Harry's face had gone from red to stark white, Ben's normally ruddy color also drained, leaving his complexion splotched as his jaw tightened.

"I see," he said, measuring his words with restraint. "I can't say I've ever dealt with anything quite like that. I can offer Mr. Halstein one of my men to escort him to your department."

Ben paused to listen to the response.

"No," he resumed, nonplussed, his confidence returning. "Nothing of the sort. I've no doubt Mr. Halstein is perfectly capable of coming alone. He's free to make decisions for himself, of course. Under the circumstances this would be quite a shock for anyone."

Ben paused and looked to Harry for confirmation, who nodded his assent.

"Then it's settled," Ben said. "Mr. Halstein will be in touch."

He handed the phone back to Harry, who let go of one of Susan's hands, persisting in holding the other.

"That's generous of you to offer someone to go with me to Memphis," Harry said, replacing the cell phone in his inner suit pocket. "I need to go home and throw some clothes in a bag and leave directions for my foreman."

"Not at all," Ben replied. "I didn't mean to presume—even though I did. We're a family here in Balfour. If you've got someone else you'd rather have, a lawyer maybe, or a close family friend."

Everyone standing around the table knew he meant Susan, but Harry shook his head, his eyes never leaving Susan's face.

"I don't know why I'd need a lawyer," he said, sincerely puzzled. "And I don't really have any family I could call. Who were you thinking could go with me?"

"Jim Smith could go," Ben said.

Harry tried not to look surprised that the Chief could so casually requisition one of his men for such a private matter.

"Are you sure this will be okay with Officer Smith?"

Ben pictured the eager young officer's face and his enthusiastic affinity for novel cases and firsthand experiences. No one had appreciated the details of solving the Steve Wilton murder more that Smith—or taking part in the investigation into the Chen murders in Savannah. In truth, the young officer had seemed a bit melancholy since Charlie had gone back to New Orleans and life in Balfour had returned to its normal boredom. Another atypical case might be just what he needed.

"Smith's got a good head on his shoulders, and he's dependable," he said confidently. "He'd be the first to volunteer if I didn't do it for him."

Harry looked at Susan, who nodded in agreement.

The garrulous rookie officer had garnered a number of fans in Balfour with his ready wit and easygoing disposition.

"Well, now you and Smith need a means of transportation," the Senator interrupted, his impatience at being left out of the conversation glaringly obvious and mounting. "I've got my private plane at Anson's. The pilot's visiting an aunt in Griffith, but I can have him at the airport within the hour if necessary. Flying is your best option."

When no one countermanded him, he continued.

"I'll call ahead and tell Mike to fuel the plane, do a pre-check, and have the pilot get a weather briefing and file a flight plan when he gets there. The plane can have you and Jim at the General DeWitt Spain Airport outside Memphis in just over three hours,"

Wilton said, his voice taking on an irritating tone of pompous, patronizing generosity. "I've used the airport several times, and the pilot knows it well. There's a Cessna service center for the plane, and he can lay over there until other decisions are made about when you're returning."

"I've flown into that airport," Harry said quietly. "The Halstein Group corporate jet has been landing there since we opened for business in Memphis in the 1970s. The airport itself experienced several years of stagnant growth, but it's still the closest to Memphis proper and most convenient for our purposes."

The Senator had the decency to look embarrassed. He'd obviously misjudged Harry's silence for ignorance and was suddenly regretting his assumptions, adjusting his estimation of the unassuming Harry Halstein.

"Harry is a prominent real estate investor and developer in Memphis," Susan interjected proudly. "He has an extensive portfolio of commercial properties in Tennessee—specifically Germantown, Collierville, and Bartlett—where he's been involved in all the planning and construction of multiple subdivisions and industrial properties and office spaces since the 1980s."

For a moment, Harry was taken aback and flattered by the intensity of Susan's defense of his feelings and his business acumen.

"Thank you," he said. "Remind me to add your name to the PR department roster and put you on the payroll."

"I didn't mean to be insulting," the Senator said, his mouth drawn and his face flushing at his error in judgment, embarrassed, searching for a polite way to excuse himself from the awkward conversation and go back to his lunch.

Ben slipped his stubby thumbs through his belt loops and

tried not to look too satisfied that someone had the gumption to put Stewart Wilton in his place. He hadn't seen anything this gratifying since the last time Charlie was in town.

"Not at all," Harry said graciously. "You had no way of knowing. I'm still relatively new to Balfour, and we haven't had the opportunity to socialize. Susan will tell you that I'm something of a recluse. I do appreciate your offer. Thank you. You're generous to suggest your plane, and I accept with gratitude. I'm still in shock."

"Understandable," Ben said sympathetically, his admiration for Harry Halstein increasing by the moment. "Are you sure you wouldn't rather go on your own?"

"No, Chief." Harry released Susan's hand and pushed away the uneaten half of his plate. "I'm looking forward to spending time with one of Balfour's finest."

"I'll call and have a rental car ready for you when you land," Susan said, pushing away her own food and reaching for her handbag on the bench beside her. "I'll reserve it in your name. I'll drive you to your house so you can pick up your things and then get you to Anson's."

She looked up, her bright eyes sparkling defiantly at the sheriff and the Senator, who were standing over her with smothering, brotherly concern.

"Don't look at me like that," she said firmly, fluffing at her spikey white hair with her flame-red fingernails. "I'm fine. I'm not some silly emotional woman. Besides, Harry and I need to talk about what to do about the farm while he's away."

Harry gave her a grateful, affectionate smile.

"Then it's settled," Ben said decisively. "Senator, you make your calls. I'll wait here for Smith to get back and then take him by his place to pack a quick bag so I can drop him off at Anson's within the next hour or so."

Ben took a quick look around and spotted the Reverend Johnson, seated in the back and waiting expectantly to see if he might be included in the preparations.

"And you there, Reverend," he said. "Didn't mean to leave you out. Maybe you should start a prayer chain or whatever it is you do."

"Yes," Reverend Johnson said wryly. "Whatever it is that I do. I'll get right on that now, Ben."

"Excellent," Ben said, rolling his eyes at the sarcasm. "You know what I mean."

"Unfortunately," he responded evenly, "I know exactly what you mean."

Chapter 9

"Explain to me again how the Germantown Police Department knew to call you about your sister's death," Susan said, trying to keep her eyes on the winding country road and her mind on her driving instead of the present crisis. "I didn't think you had the same last name. Were you in her cell phone as her next of kin?"

"I don't think Dinah ever considered me her kin," he said, "much less her next of kin. We shared the same mother but different fathers."

"How have you never told me this story?"

Harry reached over and squeezed her hand apologetically.

"We've only known each other for about a year, Susan," he said gently, "and I know there are personal parts of your life that we haven't discussed, by mutual agreement. I'm good with that. You'd be surprised how much we don't know about each other because it just hasn't come up in conversation."

"That's true," she admitted, realizing that most of their

discussions had centered around old movies, classic books, views on religion, and his business dealings. For all his interest in buying her sequined clothes, she hadn't realized just how private Harry was until now and how little she actually knew about his personal life. Not to mention how very little he knew about her first husband simply because Harry hadn't asked and she had avoided the subject entirely. "Go on. Different fathers, same mother."

"My father and hers were business partners in Memphis in the early 1950s in real estate and development. Housing boom and rapid growth. They'd served side by side as commissioned officers in the Navy during the war. My mother was married to Dinah's father at the time. Mom had been a secretary for a rival company, and he fell in love with her at first sight, or so she said. Dinah was born shortly after they started the company."

He stopped talking, his glance off into the thick stands of pine trees that lined the road, their yellow pollen dusting the underbrush and passing bushes. His mind drifted, divided between relatively insignificant concern over his present allergies and painful memories of his childhood past long buried.

Susan let him wander, waiting wordlessly until he spoke again.

"Dinah was only fourteen years old when her father committed suicide. My mother never talked much about that time of her life. I knew only the basic facts, mostly from coworkers when I started at the company years later. She'd married Browning when he was in his early thirties and she was twenty. From the beginning, he'd had problems with drinking and he was a heavy smoker, although neither of those were the actual cause of his death. He had heart disease and suffered from deep depression most of his life, though if you asked my mother she'd say he was a faithful husband and they had a happy marriage."

"Until he killed himself," Susan said, trying not to judge and failing. "What happened to Dinah and your mother?"

"Life went on. My mother had more than a working knowledge of the real estate market, and she inherited Browning's share of the company. In time, she took over his duties as partner, which meant close contact with my father. When Dinah turned eighteen and was about to go off to college, my mother and father announced that they were going to extend the partnership to include marriage."

"How did Dinah take that?"

"She didn't like it, to say the very least," he said. "Relations were even more strained when I was born three years later. I don't think either of my parents anticipated me—my father almost sixty and my mother in her late forties."

"That's not so old," Susan said. "I'm glad you were born."

"I'm happy you're happy," he said, almost laughing. "Anyway, Dinah insisted on the inheritance she would have received from her father when she turned twenty-one, and my parents complied. They paid her quite generously for her share of the company, and she went off to live her own life."

"Didn't she keep up with her mother?"

"I don't think she ever forgave her for what she saw as a betrayal of trust."

He sighed.

"I know that after my father died of a sudden stroke, my mother tried reaching out to Dinah, but nothing ever came of it. She never said so, but I know it must have hurt her deeply to be rejected by her only daughter."

"Of course it did."

Susan was finding it difficult to focus on the road with the unexpected tears that gathered in her eyes. She removed one hand from the steering wheel, brushing them roughly away. Only five minutes to Harry's house.

After you drop him off at Anson's you can break down and cry, she thought. *You can hold yourself together for the next hour—for Harry's sake.*

"You haven't explained about the cell phone," she said.

"It seems that Dinah's last call was to me during the church service this morning. I've no idea how she got my cell phone number. I give out business cards all the time, and the company knows I don't mind if they give it out. Maybe that's how she got it. I did give her a quick, impulsive call the last time I was in Memphis, but I had to leave a message when she didn't answer. She never called me back, but she could have saved my number."

Susan saw a fleeting look of sadness throw its shadow across his face.

"I suppose when the police saw that she'd made a final effort to reach out, they called the number back to see who would answer. I always turn off the phone between ten thirty and noon, something my mother insisted on when we went to services together. She said it wasn't quite respectful to let other people call in on God's time."

"I wish I'd known your mother."

"I do too," he said. "She'd have liked you, and I think you'd have liked her. She was a lot like you . . . independent, strong, kind, lovely in appearance and spirit."

She blushed, the roots of her spiked platinum hair going bright pink.

"I'm just wondering," he said, "what would have happened if I had answered the phone when Dinah called? Or if she'd answered me when I called her and we'd actually talked. Do you think Dinah would still have . . . I mean, could I have convinced her not to shoot herself? Did she want to tell me something important? I can't help but feel responsible."

"You aren't responsible for this, Harry! Listen, do you want company in Memphis? I could volunteer to come with you instead of Jim," she offered shyly. "Thomas would understand."

"You're kind," he said, "but no. I don't know what I'm getting into or how long all this is going to take. I'm hoping to find some answers to all my questions. There's so much going on here that I'm a little concerned about leaving without someone I can trust implicitly in charge."

Susan blushed again. Harry had often complimented her capabilities, but never with such blunt praise. She pulled the car deftly into the driveway and parked.

"Well," she said decisively, removing the key from the ignition and dropping it into her purse, "thank you for that resounding vote of confidence. I'll just get a pad of paper from your desk in the den—I know where you keep your office supplies. You can dictate what needs to be done on the farm while you are packing."

Chapter 10

Susan efficiently ticked off all the items on Harry's list while curled up on the sofa with a pillow and a book on decorating, resigned to waiting for Harry's eventual call.

For Harry and Jim, the flight itself was uneventful. Neither Harry nor his sturdy sentry found much to say to each other. Harry was deep in thought and Jim, respecting the severity of the situation, chose not to carry on attempts at idle conversation, struggling with his urge to comment and fill what felt to him like uncomfortable silence.

The Senator's pilot, an experienced veteran, was courteous and professional, keeping his own counsel as well, giving only the essential information his passengers needed during the flight.

A midsize rental car was waiting for them, exactly as Susan had promised. Harry could have been comfortable in his usual economy car, but she knew that with Jim along the smaller car might be a rather tight squeeze.

Harry made a mental note to thank her for the additional kindness. More and more he noticed her thoughtfulness, wondering if he should have included her in the trip and if he might have inadvertently hurt her feelings by not asking her to come along.

His self-reflection was interrupted when the pilot asked for a cell phone contact number in order to schedule the return trip.

Harry and Jim settled their bags in the trunk of the rental car. Harry put the key in the ignition but didn't start the car immediately, first contacting the Germantown PD to notify them of their arrival.

Harry didn't feel like eating, but Jim could hardly contain the rumbling sounds of his empty stomach as they pulled out of the airport on the ride to the police station.

"Are you going to be okay?" Harry asked, amused at the officer's inability to keep from grimacing. "We can stop and get you some food. You haven't had a proper meal today."

"I'm okay," Jim lied. "I can wait until after we meet with the detective."

"I'm sure you can," Harry said. "But I'm not sure whether or not I can concentrate over the noise your digestive track is making."

Jim's face reddened.

"I'm sorry," he said. "Maybe a convenience store or something. It's already late."

"There's a McDonald's," Harry offered, flipping on the turn signal. "Let's get you a couple of cheeseburgers and fries for now, then we'll have something substantial after our interview. Won't take a minute."

Jim nodded gratefully and reached for his wallet.

"Nonsense," Harry said. He waved the young man's hand away and pulled up to the speaker to order. "You wouldn't be here if the Chief hadn't volunteered your services."

Jim nodded again.

Harry rolled down the window and was greeted by the cheerful voice of a female employee.

"I'll have three double cheeseburgers, a large fry, and a chocolate shake—upsize that, please," he announced briskly, then glanced at Jim. "Wait, add two apple pies."

"Thank you," Jim said sincerely. "That's a lot of food."

Harry chuckled.

"Let's just say your reputation has preceded you," he said with a sidelong glance. "Balfour is a mighty small town, and there's not much to talk about most days of the week. Besides, I owe you."

Harry pulled up to the window, handed over his credit card, and passed the paper bag of food to the hungry officer, who politely opened the top and began devouring the contents.

"I appreciate it," he mumbled between mouthfuls, wiping at his face with a paper napkin. "I'm not sure what you've heard about me—but this is great."

Harry looked both ways for traffic before pulling back onto the main street. "We can consider it a down payment. You decide between Mexican and pizza and you can feel free to tell me everything I don't know about Balfour. Fair enough?"

"Fair enough." Jim finished the first cheeseburger and started on the second. "More than fair enough."

Thirty minutes later, thanks to the GPS on the cell phone, they were sitting in the precinct interrogation room across the table from the detective assigned to Dinah Browning's case.

Jim wondered why they weren't being seated in the detective's office, but he had little experience with other police departments and thought perhaps they might be joined by other people and the office might be too small. Much like the station in Balfour, this station seemed the same inside except for more rooms. The outside, on the other hand, had better signage, a bigger gate-enclosed parking lot, and quite a few more uniformed officers.

The coffee was better too, although the young officer was already considering whether or not there would be a waffle maker at the complimentary breakfast bar in the morning and if he should get a couple of quarts of chocolate milk for the hotel refrigerator.

Harry seemed tired and tense, rubbing the back of his neck with his hand as though he had a headache. Jim decided that was probably normal under the circumstances, and he didn't give it too much thought. His own stomach had stopped rumbling again, although his questions about what was going on grew. This didn't seem like the way the Chief would handle things.

At any rate, no one seemed inclined to ask him to leave Harry's side in the windowless room, so he stayed as quietly and as unobtrusively as a man his size could stay in the corner of a twelve-by-twelve-foot confined space.

Both of them noticed the two-way mirror on the wall across from where they sat and wondered who was watching on the other side. And why.

But Harry was a patient man, and he knew he had nothing to hide.

He'd come for the answers to all his questions about what happened to Dinah, and if this was the means by which he would find answers, then so be it.

Chapter 11

About an hour into the standard questions, the detective excused himself and took his manila folder of notes with him. Instead of returning, he was replaced by a tall, unsmiling Native American woman in a gray suit wearing an official-looking badge and identification tag on a lanyard around her neck.

Her smooth hair was pulled severely back into a tight bun, exposing her high cheekbones and the delicate sculpted contour of her attractive face.

Harry and Jim stood immediately as she entered.

Jim, who recognized a federal agent when he saw one, felt the cheeseburgers shift in his stomach and his creative mind went in all directions of possibility, none of them positive. No wonder they weren't in a detective's office.

Harry decided he might have needed to invite Thomas Stone along in addition to Jim.

"I'm Agent Walker," she said. "Please sit down."

"FBI?" Harry said sharply, reading her identification tag. "Was Dinah under investigation? What's going on?"

"Please sit down," she repeated. She surveyed Jim's looming form. "You too."

"Yes, ma'am," Jim said obediently, clearly intimidated as he lowered his long form into the chair, leaning back against the wall in an effort to melt into the corner of the room.

She waited for Harry to sit, but his innate male chivalry refused to surrender. After a moment she relented and sat down first.

"So," Harry said, taking his seat, "why is the FBI interested in my half sister's death, and why are we being interrogated? I came here of my own volition."

"I'm accustomed to asking the questions, Mr. Halstein," she said, opening a folder and removing an ink pen from her bun, where it had been hidden for convenience sake. "When was the last time you spoke with your sister?"

"My half sister," he corrected her evenly. "We shared the same mother but little else. My father and hers were business partners."

"You took over the business after her father died," the agent said, still writing.

"How did she feel about that?"

"I wouldn't know her feelings," he said. "After I was born, my father gave her half of the company—her father's half plus the interest that had accrued—and she took the substantial funds and reinvested the money to create millions more."

"You're rather well-known here in Memphis," she said.

"Are we talking about me, or are we talking about my half sister?" he asked, the agent's attitude reminding him unpleasantly of his recent encounter with Senator Wilton.

"Then you are her only close relative?" she persisted.

"Her only relative, as far as I know. She never married. If your implication is that I'll inherit from her, I'm quite certain that I won't. We weren't close, and I don't need her money."

"Why would you assume I'd ask about her money?"

"Well"—Harry leaned forward and tapped the file in front of her with his index finger—"that's the only question the detective didn't ask me. Agent Walker, I'm not answering any more of your questions without my lawyer present. This whole process seems unnecessarily accusatory."

The agent's eyebrows arched as though she'd been stung by a wasp and was refusing to acknowledge the pain.

"There's a great deal of money involved here," she said.

"It's more than that." Harry pressed on, sensing he'd opened a crack in the agent's cold professionalism. "The FBI doesn't involve itself in simple suicides, even of wealthy socialites. Why are you treating me like a suspect?"

The agent leaned back, tugging down the hem of her suit jacket. "So you haven't had contact with your sister? What did you speak about the last time you talked?"

"You are avoiding my question," he countered. "I was in Memphis for a business meeting the first week in December. I was feeling especially guilty because I hadn't reached out in years, so I looked her up to see how she was doing. To wish her Merry Christmas."

"And how was she doing?"

"I don't know. She didn't answer so I left a brief message. She may have gotten my number from her caller ID. Dinah was never a talker, and she certainly never shared personal information with me. I decided if she wanted to talk to me, she'd call me back."

"Were you surprised to learn that she'd shot herself?"

Harry hesitated. He looked at the two-way mirror and wondered if someone was watching from the other side and whether he was being recorded. Then he glanced over at Jim, who appeared to be soundly napping in the corner.

"I'm not sure how to answer that," he said flatly. "Her father shot himself when she was young. I'm sure that had an effect on her, but she seemed to have adjusted in her adulthood. She volunteered and contributed to all sorts of charitable groups—abused and missing children, injured veterans, abandoned cats and dogs. She especially loved cats."

"Do you know why her father committed suicide?"

"My mother said that he was despondent over a heart condition that became debilitating in his final years."

"I see." The agent closed the folder. "Did your sister share this condition?"

"I don't know," Harry said. "She wouldn't have told me if she did."

The businessman pulled at the knot of his necktie and sank back in his chair, his face a mask of fatigue and frustration.

"Look, I've answered every question you've asked, and now I'm ready for answers. You can easily determine that Dinah's money is going to numerous charities, and I'm fine with that—"

"How altruistic of you," she interrupted dryly. "You're quite the philanthropist."

The crow's feet around Harry's eyes deepened, but his voice belied his irritation.

"Why are we in an interrogation room?"

She looked at the two-way mirror and shrugged.

"No one's watching," she said. "Would you believe we're in here because none of the detectives wanted to give up their personal spaces for my exclusive use? Fancy that. Seems they find me a tad bit overbearing."

"No," Harry said sarcastically. "Really?"

The agent leaned forward, almost confidentially out of character.

"We were also told that you'd be bringing an officer with you and didn't know how long it would take to get background information on your sister. Someone thought you might be more comfortable in here."

She looked pointedly at the corner where the effects of a twenty-four-hour-long shift had finally caught up with Jim, who'd begun to snore softly, his chin resting on his broad chest and his muscular arms folded, hands tucked neatly under his upper arms.

"And you couldn't just tell me this?" Harry said.

"No," she said bluntly.

"I can see that," he admitted. This woman didn't make excuses or give explanations, that was abundantly clear. "What else did you need to know about Dinah?"

"Statistically speaking, women do not use guns to commit suicide," she said. "Do you think it's odd that your half sister used a gun?"

"Yes, I find it very difficult to believe that Dinah committed suicide with a gun. Because of what her father did, she despised guns. She wouldn't have one in the house. That was one of her major bones of contention with my mother, who was an expert shot."

She tapped her pen against the table, her expression unchanged.

"You've no doubt checked my background," he continued, propping his elbows on the tabletop and folding his hands, the fingers loosely laced together. "So perhaps you'd like to tell me exactly why the FBI is investigating Dinah's death—and how you think I may be able to help."

"Who said we need your help?" she said sharply.

"We're having this conversation," he said. "You must want something."

The slightest twinge at the corner of her mouth hinted at a sense of humor, but her next comment was interrupted by an insistent knock at the door.

"Enter."

A close-cropped dark head appeared and a hand motioned for her undivided attention. After a brief, whispered, one-sided conversation, she turned.

"You are free to go," she said, ignoring his curious look and pointing instead to the sleeping mammoth in the corner. "Please wake Officer Smith and take him with you. He looks like he could use a satisfying night's rest in something other than a chair."

"Is that all?"

She picked up the folder from the table.

"I assume you're staying in Germantown for the next several days to make arrangements for the funeral," she said.

He stood and stretched the muscles of his neck and shoulders, buttoning his suit jacket and straightening his tie.

Unexpectedly she rose and strode around the table, thrusting out her right hand.

"Inola Walker," she said. "Thank you for your cooperation, Mr. Halstein. I'm sorry for your loss."

He shook her hand and was not at all surprised at the strength in her slender fingers and her crushing grip.

"I still have questions," he said when she released him, hoping that her rapid shift in attitude would hold now that he'd been cooperative.

"And I will be forthcoming with answers," she said, "as soon as those answers do not imperil the ongoing investigation."

Jim made groaning noises and shifted his body in the chair, his legs at all angles and his head flopping against his chest.

Poor guy, Harry thought kindly. *You didn't sign on for this. Sent to babysit a grown stranger, throwing clothes in a duffle bag on a moment's notice, flying out with no idea where you are going, eating cheap fast food, and now napping in a hard chair in an unfamiliar police station. You're a sport if I've ever seen one.*

The last thing he wanted to do right now was rouse Jim from his first semirestful moment, but the agent was right. The dedicated officer did deserve to eat a real meal and rest in an actual bed with clean sheets and pillows.

There was nothing else they could do tonight. Walker had made it plain that she wasn't ready to share more information, at least for the moment.

"I'll be expecting your call then," he replied, but he'd waited too long to comment.

The agent was already out the door without looking back.

Chapter 12

The Second Day: Monday

Cora heard the creaking complaints of the antique rocking chair before she realized that she was dreaming again. She turned from the sink, half-expecting to see James, and saw Gramma Crawford's diminutive apron-clad form.

She was struck by the contrast between how she felt about seeing James and how she felt now. She wanted to rush to her grandmother's side and embrace her, as though a missing piece of some long-forsaken puzzle was about to drop into place and the picture would finally be complete.

But she held back, wondering what possible meaning there could be and what she would be expected to see.

Pleasant warm sunlight flickered from the windows behind where the country woman sat, a round enamel dishpan in her lap and a paper grocery bag on the floor by her right knee. The dishpan was filled to overflowing with unsnapped pole beans, the ends curling about each other, hugging with tiny stick-like arms.

She was rocking slightly, balancing her work as she did her life—with serenity.

Cora thought how natural it was to see her grandmother like this, in the kitchen preparing the season's food to be canned or stored in the oversized chest freezer in the back corner of the kitchen.

Cora felt something was off, but she couldn't quite identify what it was. When James visited, he came with a message. Gramma Crawford appeared to be busy about her normal, everyday life. Almost like she didn't know she was there to meet Cora.

Is this the past or the present? Cora thought. *This certainly looks and feels like the past, but what could that mean?*

Wisps of gray-white hair had escaped from the loose bun at the back of Gramma Crawford's head, the simple white collar of her calico printed day dress peeking out from the bib of the apron. Her gnarled hands were busy at work, her expression pleasant but intently absorbed with her task.

"Pull up a chair, sweet girl," the woman said warmly. "You've arrived just in time to snap a mess of beans for our supper and hear the latest gossip about Aunt Phoebe."

"Aunt Phoebe?" Cora said, pulling a ladder-back chair from the table, where a second large aluminum roasting pan sat.

This is the past, Cora realized. *What kind of dream is this? Have I just stepped back in time? Is this a day I've lived before or one that might have been?*

Either way, memory compelled her to take up her role in the scene.

Reaching into the overflow bin her grandmother held, she scooped out several handfuls of beans, seated herself next to the paper bag used for discarding the broken stems, and began method-ically snapping off both ends of the beans just as she had been taught so many years ago.

How odd that this feels so peaceful and yet so confusing, she thought to herself, the long stems fitting neatly into the palms of her hands as she snapped, her fingers remembering the rhythm and unconsciously measuring the optimum length for breaking off without losing the precious edible center.

"Now, tell me about your classes." Her grandmother's voice was reassuring and gentle. She pushed her rimless glasses up to the bridge of her nose with the back of her hand. "You're a senior this year, aren't you? I'm so proud of you. Exams next week. Won't be long until you're out on your own."

A senior, Cora thought, searching back through time. *She must think it's the week before the fire. The weekend I didn't come home from college to see her. This is the conversation we never had. I was studying. I should have been here. I might have been able to get you out of the house.*

A tidal wave of regret swept over Cora, her throat tightening and her heart aching, but she knew there was nothing she could say. Nothing that would change the past.

"Let's put the bowl between us so we can both use it for the snapped beans," her grandmother said, moving the stool and bowl together across the floor. "There now, that's better."

An oppressive pause hung in the air like a woolen blanket on a chilly night, oddly uncomfortable, irritating, and scratchy, yet necessary.

With dogged effort, Cora forced herself to resume breaking the beans, resolved to be thankful for sweet memories that in-cluded a woman she'd loved so dearly.

76

Gramma Crawford was a pragmatic farm woman. Birth. Life. Love. Pain. Death.

All holding hands and dancing together in one enormous circle with God in the center.

The past is in the past, she'd say. No point in trying to live there. Life's a cycle. Live. Learn. Love. Move on.

Except for tonight, when the past and the present inexplicably came crashing into Cora's dream.

Cora realized that she'd almost forgotten why she was here in the kitchen at all.

"You said there's gossip about Aunt Phoebe?" she prompted.

"Dear me, yes, child!" Gramma Crawford took another handful of beans and leaned forward, relishing the juicy tidbits of news like hard candy sweets. "She's gone and found another man who's foolish enough to marry her."

Cora counted mentally.

"Doesn't that make four husbands?"

"Five total," the older woman corrected her. "She was only sixteen when she married Stan—he died in the Great War. Then she married his younger brother, Ed. He was closer to her age. He died of consumption after the Spanish flu came through around 1919. She waited about a year before she married Walter—he sold shoes over in McComb at one of the department stores there on Beulah Street. We thought he'd be a survivor, but then he went and joined the second war effort in 1942 and got himself buried in Flanders."

She stopped to take a breath, drop a handful of snapped green beans, and push up her glasses again, magnifying the deep creases and wrinkles around her bright eyes.

"Let's see, that makes . . ."

"Three," Cora said. She knew this part of the story well. Aunt Phoebe's romantic life was well-documented by the gossips and family historians. "Stan, Ed, and Walter."

"Yes, she waited almost five years after Walter before she took up company with Farley. He was a dairy farmer almost twice her age. We knew he wasn't going to last long. I swear, Phoebe went at life with more enthusiasm than anyone else I ever knew. She ran through husbands like butter on hot biscuits—and never stopped long enough to have any young'uns either. Despite our worst fears for Farley's health and safety, he lasted almost ten years."

"And that made Aunt Phoebe . . . ?"

"That made your Aunt Phoebe old enough to know better than to get herself another husband."

Gramma Crawford continued to alternately sigh and snap.

"Poor George. There wasn't a soul at the wedding who didn't try to talk him out of it, including Phoebe herself—but he wouldn't hear of it. Odds are he won't make it more than a day past their tenth anniversary."

"So that's the fresh gossip about Aunt Phoebe," Cora said flatly, trying not to sound disappointed. Cora hadn't come home for the wedding either. She wondered idly what else she'd missed that semester by not coming back, and what any of this had to do with her current life or clues for Charlie.

Cora gathered more unsnapped beans and decided to be patient, pushing the practical aspects of the visit aside. She was thoroughly appreciating the moments of memory with the woman who had cared for her so tenderly after her own parents died.

"I suppose sooner or later Aunt Phoebe will run out of

surprises," she said, unable to see any relevance to the present in her great-aunt's erratic life story.

"Heavens, I don't expect that will ever happen!" The old woman tossed another handful of stems into the paper bag and adjusted the pan in her lap. "That's just the *old* news—the *new* gossip from this morning is much more interesting."

Cora found the revelation promising. Her grandmother's baby sister had lived many fascinating years and was the source of countless wild and entertaining stories.

There had to be a clue in the dream somewhere.

Something besides recently harvested pole beans and multiple marriages.

"Everyone knew Phoebe was into potions and concoctions."

The wisps of white hair danced as Gramma Crawford continued, her voice dropping to a conspiratorial whisper, pausing only to refill her container with beans.

"You know the stories about her home-brewed elderberry wine. I'm sure she enjoyed the congregational trouble it caused for the Baptist preacher, who favored it over traditional Welch's. She did a steady business with the Methodists too. They weren't so particular, and their preacher ordered a gallon or so every month for their communion services. More in the winter cough and cold season."

"Gramma," Cora said tolerantly, "Aunt Phoebe was eccentric, but preachers and wine are mild news compared to her escapades with the menfolk in her life. We've all had our fair share of her famous elderberry on Christmas Eve."

"Well, the wine isn't the newest dilemma."

The gnarled hands snapped along, engrossed both in her work

and the joy of retelling her story.

"This is still a dry county, though she's escaped legal trouble with the revenue agents because she's related to half the population by marriage. No, the real problem is much more serious. Phoebe's added black licorice plants to her herb garden."

Cora frowned.

"Isn't that used to make candy?"

"Yes, dear," her grandmother said pointedly. "Sometimes it is, and sometimes it isn't."

Gramma Crawford's strong, wrinkled hand reached out and took Cora by surprise, squeezing her upper arm with an urgent insistency that stopped just short of pain.

"Your Aunt Phoebe decided to use the plant for something else entirely."

"I don't understand."

"Charlie will," her grandmother hissed, her bright eyes darkening like black fire magnified by the lenses of her glasses. "The fool woman's gone and made tea for the wrong person."

In an instant, Cora was roughly dragged back into the present. *Charlie?*

Her mind reeled at the realization that her grandmother knew—about the dreams, the clues, the time.

Her head filled to the brim with confusion as she tried to piece together what it all meant. She felt a slipping—she knew the dream would end soon. She had to know more.

"I don't understand," Cora repeated, dropping her handful of stems into the paper bag, the bony, gnarled fingers around her upper arm tightening. "What does that mean? Tea for the wrong person?"

"Tell Charlie, sweet girl," Gramma Crawford said, releasing

Cora's arm, thrusting it away roughly. "She didn't mean to do it. She didn't know it was poison. It doesn't matter that she didn't know, she should have known."

Cora was horrified.

"Aunt Phoebe poisoned someone!" she exclaimed. "Who? What happened? Did someone die?"

"Oh, never you mind," she said. "I'm not talking about your Aunt Phoebe. The family put a stop to that craziness before she went that far. But no one stopped that other woman. She's as much responsible for murder as if she'd pulled that trigger."

"But what do I tell Charlie?" Cora said. "What was the poison?"

"Black licorice," her grandmother repeated. "Tell Charlie it's all about the black licorice. Except for the tea, that man's poor sister wouldn't have died."

And Cora was awake.

Chapter 13

The spacious meeting room at the Hyatt-Regency was filling with uniformed officers and an assortment of detectives. The crowd was made up of all shapes, sizes, and ages wearing a wide array of sports jackets, slacks, jeans, and polo shirts.

The ten o'clock Monday morning session was a scant half-hour from beginning. Cushioned metal chairs were lined in neat rows in the center of the space. Pressed against the two side walls, eight-foot folding tables were laden with tubs of iced bottled water and matching silver coffee services, flanked by trays of assorted fresh donuts and prewrapped pastries.

Charlie Abbott was eagerly anticipating the training session. He'd flown in on the red-eye from New Orleans International and landed at Memphis International, preferring to begin his day before sunrise rather than waiting for the business traveler crowds to form. After renting his usual economy car, he found the hotel without much ceremony and stored his luggage in the corporate-rate room where he was spending the night before taking a return flight the next day.

Although the locales frequently changed, he knew the routine well.

The Germantown PD had graciously contacted a local audio-visual company who sent a team to set up the system. Two highly efficient young techs had just completed troubleshooting Charlie's laptop, making absolutely sure that he would be able to click through his prepared PowerPoint presentation on the white screen with the greatest of ease. The wooden podium and the microphone with the connecting cords and remote speakers in the four corners of the room had been tested and retested with calm precision.

Charlie sat on the high-backed swivel stool someone had borrowed from a supply room somewhere and sipped his coffee, twisting agreeably from side to side like an overactive toddler. He wondered, as he did from time to time, what he really knew that made other policemen come to hear what he had to say.

He'd been personally involved in interesting cases and caught elusive criminals, of course, and his methods were widely applauded and accepted. Innovative ways to investigate, ground-breaking forensics—but all in all, Charlie doubted that his experience was more worthy to tell than any other detective from another major city.

Maybe, he thought, looking over the gathering group of uniformed officers and plainclothes detectives, *they just want a break from their own routine. Maybe they just want reassurance that we are all in this together and we can catch the bad guys no matter the odds against us.*

A random, runaway thought of doubt traipsed through his head.

Or maybe it isn't me at all they come to see—maybe they hope I'll say something about Cora. Maybe it's just curiosity seekers hoping to hear stories about her.

Even before Maclin and the Savannah PD had contacted him about the Chen murders, asking him to take the child witness to Cora, he'd wondered how much people knew about his relationship with the arguably brilliant child psychologist. She was a rising forensic star when he met her in New Orleans. Six turbulent months later they were married.

Charlie had always been a loner. He'd never seriously considered marriage. But there was something about Cora that didn't leave him any other option. Neither of them would have settled for less. Even after Cora lost the baby and he moved her to Balfour, he refused to regret their time together.

Only a year and a half as a married couple established their reputation as a team. A team able to solve the most difficult puzzles, find the most incredible clues, and dig out the deepest secrets in the darkest hearts.

Then their careers and their marriage had crashed in one evil, vicious act of revenge, and life together was over.

Just the thought of Cora brought all the emotions back in a torrential flood.

A devastated, broken Cora. Her hope and faith shattered.

He'd done what he thought was best for her, and she hadn't protested. He told himself that she knew as well as he did what would happen if they stayed together.

Now Cora was well on the road to a new life with Thomas and Jane.

Charlie refused to wallow in regret. He was right back where he started. He loved her, and he'd had his chance to protect her in the past, and he'd failed.

He wouldn't make that mistake again.

The noise level in the room increased, hauling his attention back to reality. He thrust away the memories that still lingered too close to the surface and looked at his wristwatch.

Almost nine forty-five a.m. Ten minutes left to prepare.

He opened his three-ring binder of notes, flipping through for the first page of the day's session, feeling confident about the material. He'd done this particular seminar several times since Christmas, and the content had begun to feel like an old friend.

The hotel liaison, an attractive young blond in a crisp pink cotton blouse beneath her navy-blue uniform jacket, walked over and smoothly replaced the empty cup in his hand with a full one.

"Did you need anything else?" she said, smiling a practiced, professional smile, her too-white teeth gleaming between pink lips that matched her shirt.

"No," Charlie said politely. "Thank you."

He balanced the dangerously full cup on the outer edge of the table, well away from his paperwork, and audibly exhaled.

A chill ran up his spine, and he felt suddenly, inexplicably drained of energy, the tips of his fingers cold and tingling and his backbone on fire.

He'd never put much store in those people who claimed to sense omens about the future. He lumped premonitions, deja vu, rabbits running over random graves, and the like into the same category as Ouija boards, palm reading, and the boogeyman. People who believed such things were crackpots and crazies who insisted they knew vital facts about impending events that could not be verified by logical, rational means.

Charlie the detective had never held with such malarkey.

But Charlie the man was conflicted. He'd been given hunches from those who called themselves legitimate fortune tellers. He'd seen the accuracy in what they said.

His logic insisted that Cora belonged in the category he denied, but his heart knew that as confusing and inexplicable as her information was, she'd never been wrong or led him astray in an investigation.

This contradiction vexed and frustrated him, but never more so than in the ten minutes before he was about to give a lecture on police procedures that didn't rely on hunches.

He felt safe discussing solid investigative work with concrete evidence and verifiable proof. The kind of proof that could stand on its own in a courtroom and withstand vigorous cross-examination. He relished detailing the step-by-step techniques and practices that could be studied and reproduced in the field.

His mind unwillingly returned to Cora and his last seminar.

An overly enthusiastic and eager rookie had asked one question about Cora's involvement in the Ed Brackett case in New Orleans. The case that had brought both of them national attention. The case that ended their marriage and Cora's pregnancy.

For the first time in his life, Charlie stood tongue-tied, stumbling through an awkward explanation about the virtues of profiling.

He cursed himself for not being prepared. He should have known. The case had gained national notoriety, involving sensational details about serial killings in multiple states with both local and national agencies involved. The FBI had been stymied for months when Cora was asked to come to New Orleans to profile a totally different case. Together, he and Cora discovered Brackett's involvement and were able to tie him to the FBI's case. Charlie tried, but no matter how diligently he strived to move on and downplay Cora's part, the whole sordid issue was fodder for every hotshot who delighted in going over high-profile cases.

On the other hand, Mark Maclin had been able to keep a tight lid on Cora's involvement in the Chen murders. At least he hadn't been asked about that yet.

On this day, the prospective questions hung over his head like the branches of an ancient weeping willow tree, portending gloom and inescapable doom.

Charlie had practiced a canned response to any inquiry about Cora, praising her as a brilliant profiler, listing her degrees in child and forensic psychology, and naming her books, articles, and accomplishments.

He would give her credit for her insight and ability to read the criminals as well as empathize with the victims of the crimes they had investigated together.

He knew there was always the possibility that someone would take the questions deeper. Press harder. Bring up some personal aspect of their relationship. Charlie's heart pounded uncomfortably in his inner ear.

Another chill ran up his spine.

A man who believed in premonitions would have known what was happening.

The light touch of the hotel liaison on the sleeve of his jacket brought him back from his troublesome concerns.

"Are you sure you're okay?" she said, her smooth, youthful face darkening with obvious anxiety for his state of mind as well as for her job as his assistant. "I can get you some bottled water or some orange juice if you'd rather that than more coffee."

"Just lost in thought," he said truthfully, then added less candidly, "There's quite a bit to cover, and I don't want to leave anything out of the presentation."

"Ah," she said, relieved. "That's okay then. You ought to have a bottle of cold spring water. Too much caffeine makes anyone jumpy."

Charlie objected to her assessment of his mental state, but this was hardly the moment to tell her so.

To his relief, the eager blond dashed off.

His glance followed his provisional keeper to the door and into the corridor where his attention was caught up short by a statuesque woman whose appearance temporarily drove from his mind all thoughts of self-serving assistants and any memories of Cora.

She was standing to one side of the entrance into the room, all alone.

The detective took rapid inventory.

Her stance was military, or at least highly trained.

She looks federal, he thought.

Her lanyard was tucked under the lapel of her nondescript gray pantsuit. The bottom of the pants covered the tops of her serviceable shoes, and a bulge implied a shoulder holster under the jacket. Her sleek, dark hair was pulled back. No makeup. No jewelry—not even simple studs in her exposed ears or a plain wedding band on her left hand. Close clipped nails. No nail polish. Tall, athletic, chiseled facial features. Native American.

The information performed dizzying somersaults inside his brain.

Her aviator sunglasses made him wish he could see her eyes.

She's not here to listen to a lecture about investigative procedures from some hotshot police detective from New Orleans, he thought. *She's got better things to do with her time. She's on a case.*

"If you'll all please take your seats so we can begin," the blond assistant drawled pleasantly into the microphone. She waited for the undercurrent of friendly conversation to stop and deftly stepped aside to allow Charlie to resettle himself on the stool.

"Good Monday morning," he said aloud into the microphone, willing his mind to concentrate on the task at hand. He clicked on the title slide and the screen behind him came to life.

"I'm Charlie Abbott, and we're here to talk about improved methods in criminal investigations and their application to cold case files. Grab another cup of coffee and hang on."

Chapter 14

Susan stared at the silent desk phone to the right of the neat stacks of manila folders containing Thomas's recent clients, mostly people who were interested in writing and rewriting wills and one or two with ongoing property disputes. Each was labeled along the outer edge in a bright strip using her own color-coded method.

She had laid her own cell phone face up beside the sleek black handset and answering machine, as if somehow putting them together would increase the probably that Harry would call with an update.

He'll call when he calls, she told herself firmly. *Don't be such a worrier.*

His call last night around nine had been short and to the point, the information minimal. He'd arrived at the airport with Jim and the midsize car she had reserved was waiting. His polite "thank you" seemed stiff and formal, although she told herself that he was still adjusting to the news of his sister's death. Plus, Jim was probably at his elbow listening to the mostly one-sided conversation.

Harry told her they were going to the police station to meet with the detective and promised to call her when there was news to share.

Susan had tormented herself for the last half-hour, arguing back and forth with herself about how she should have handled the whole situation. Should she have been more sensitive? More sympathetic? Asked more questions?

She inspected the sequins curving down the sleeve of the bright floral sweater, Harry's most recent gift. The brilliant flowers in flamingo pink, burnt orange, and crimson red on a lime green background formed a wild, chaotic pattern that came shockingly close to illustrating her present state of mind.

Stop, she ordered herself, the running dialogue persisting its trek through her mind. *Stop acting like some moonstruck adolescent. Harry will call when there's news and not one minute sooner. You've checked with the foreman on the farm. He's got the list of chores for the morning, and you'll talk to him again this afternoon. There's nothing else to be done. Harry goes on business trips all the time. He's a grown man who knows how to handle himself. All this worry is ridiculous.*

She'd decided to get up and clean out the office refrigerator, a minor job she despised, when Thomas arrived in the office a little after nine and refused to comment on her unconventional behavior.

Politely overlooking the gaudiness of her newest ensemble, he deposited a white bakery box with a half dozen cream-filled donuts next to the coffee maker.

"I'll be fine if you want to go home today," he said. "There's not much on the schedule that can't wait until later this week."

Susan shook her head.

"Thank you," she said. "But at least at the office I can find something to do while I'm waiting for an update."

She eyed the white bakery box.

"Besides," she said pointedly, "can't leave all those innocent donuts alone in the same room with you."

He chuckled. He'd hoped Harry's absence wouldn't damper Susan's spunky spirit and clever comebacks, and he was pleased to see she still had her sense of humor.

"Well, the offer is open anyway," he said, resisting the urge to prove her right and take a donut for himself. Instead he ambled into his office, leaving his able assistant to her own devices.

Forty-five minutes later, Susan had made a pot of coffee, watered the recently acquired houseplants, unnecessarily dusted the bookcases, typed two memos for Judge Candler's office about recent property settlement issues, and reorganized her desk for the third time.

She felt fully justified sitting down to eat her second donut of the morning.

Despite her efforts, she was seriously questioning her ability to think clearly or to be genuinely productive. She also wondered what other busywork she was going to find to do for the rest of the day because she had no intention of going back to her house for the day and staring at the walls there alone.

A male voice interrupted her musings.

"How are you holding up?" Thomas said from the doorway. "If you aren't going home, do you want to talk about what's going on?"

Susan jumped noticeably at the query, fluorescent light reflecting from the myriad sequins in her heavily decorated sweater like tiny sparks of electricity.

"I'm fine," she lied. "Harry said he wasn't that close to his half sister, so after the initial shock, I'm sure he's okay emotionally. He said he would call when there's news. I'm just a bit anxious. You know how I hate being in the dark about anything. What can I do for you?"

"Are you sure you wouldn't feel better if you talked?"

"I'll know more what to talk about when Harry calls," she said. "Thank you for asking."

She saw he was holding an oversized manila envelope.

"I'm heading over to the courthouse to talk to Jenny," he said, answering the question on her face. He checked his back pocket for his wallet, opening it slightly to determine the current state of his finances and to avoid a second question in her eyes. "Then I'm having lunch at Sam's."

"Why are you talking to the deeds and records clerk?" she snapped with a hot flash of unanticipated anger, her eyes sparking like exploding fireworks against the iridescent shadow on her delicately painted lids.

"I've spent all morning trying to find something to do and you had something all along," she said, giving full rein to her emotions. "What's the matter with you?"

Thomas found himself speechless under the onslaught of words. He couldn't remember the last time she'd been so furious with him, if ever.

"You're the lawyer, and I'm the paralegal," she continued crossly. "It's *my* job to go over to the superior court and interrogate the clerks. I'm still capable of doing *my* job, thank you very much."

Thomas swallowed hard at the level of emotion in her protest and regrouped.

"I apologize for stepping on your toes," he said quietly. "Jenny's just going to point me to the computer terminal, and I'll sit down and look it up for myself."

He placed his hands on the desk and leaned down.

"I had no idea you were so possessive of your time with the clerks. I thought you might have other things to think about this morning."

"I'm going to repeat myself." Her voice rose, the volume and the octave going up with her vexation. "Why are you doing *my* job?"

"I know how to read a plat, Susan," he countered, feeling defensive. "If I don't get this filing issue settled between Bill Dawson and Tommy Hightower over the easements to the proposed subdivision, Balfour may just have another Hatfield and McCoy feud."

The final reservoir of her patience broke over the dam of restraint. "Well! We can't be having *that*, can we?"

"Oh my goodness, Susan," he exclaimed, his hands in the air in mock surrender. "I've never seen you like this. You know perfectly well that I respect your abilities. I'm trying to be considerate of your feelings. I can't decide if you've had too many donuts, or if you really need to polish off the box before I get back from lunch."

The cell phone on her desk buzzed.

"It's Harry," she announced, unnecessarily holding the phone out for him to see the caller ID.

"Then I strongly suggest you answer him," he said wryly, backing toward the door. "I'll give you some privacy."

She nodded, still staring at the phone.

"Answer the phone, Susan," he said. "I'll be back in a couple of hours. Text me if you want me to bring you something different for lunch from Sam's, otherwise I'll bring your usual."

Chapter 15

Andrew Evans arrived at the church almost an hour before the secretaries and settled into his cluttered office surrounded by a vast array of theological texts, a legal-size pad of yellow paper, and a substantial army of his favorite fine point pens, lined like soldiers in their parade day best.

He'd left the house exceptionally early, refusing his usual breakfast, sparking his wife's curiosity and some mild concern for his general health and well-being. He parked his compact car in its reserved spot in the vacant church lot under the shade of a trio of blooming dogwoods at the far left corner, away from the outer office door.

Alice's husband, no great fan of Evans or his policies, was not impressed when he pulled into the lot at seven forty-five to deposit his wife for work.

"About time he decided to come to work before you get here," he said snidely. "Wish he'd acknowledge that you and

Donna pretty much keep his boat afloat. Don't know after that last sermon on Sunday morning what the man does with his time. It's not preparing sermons, that's for sure."

"Now, dear," his wife said, wagging an index finger, "let's be charitable."

"Oh, he's no charity case," he continued, pointedly ignoring her meaning. "I know his salary, Alice. I'd say it's time he earned that too. You may need to be civil with him, but I'm one of the deacons. It's our job to hold his feet to the fire. We are called to make certain that the church is getting its money's worth."

Alice sighed.

"Yes, dear," she said, changing the subject and snugging up her purse under her arm. "There's a pot roast on low in the slow cooker for supper. I've already added potatoes, onions, and carrots, so you don't have to do anything. Just let it go. I'd appreciate it if you could pick up some brown-and-serve rolls on your way home."

He wrinkled his nose in distaste.

"You aren't making biscuits?"

Alice sighed again, this time more forcefully.

"I made biscuits for breakfast," she said, affectionately patting the bib of his overalls and tugging at one of the shiny galluses. "We've leftover green beans, corn on the cob, and sliced tomatoes from yesterday's dinner. Let's just be thankful for what we have."

He made a grumbling, incoherent noise and stopped abruptly at the end of the sidewalk that led to the door, pulling up at the emergency brake to prevent the car from rolling.

"If you say so, Alice," he said. "Watch your step."

She pulled the handle, pushing firmly outward, hugging her purse, and smiled sweetly at him over her shoulder. The sharp scent of the freshly planted marigolds along the walkway drifted into the open space along with the musty smell of earth and fertilizer—the world still wet from the morning dew.

Alice saw her husband smile too. The smell of blooms and rich soil did that to farmers, as well she knew.

"Yes, dear," she said, "I do say so, and I certainly will. Remember that Donna's offered me a ride home this afternoon, so you don't have to hurry back. Take your time visiting your mother. Give her my love."

"Yes, Alice," he said, waiting for a moment after the car door closed to drive away without looking back.

Alice unlocked the main door and went into the office area, calling out briefly to announce herself, but there was no answer. She looked around the room and saw why.

The door to the preacher's office was uncharacteristically closed.

For all his faults and foibles, the preacher had made every attempt to connect with his two-woman office staff. Unlike previous ministers, Evans insisted that his door be left open unless he was in a private conference, yet absolutely never closed when the private conference involved a woman. Even when he worked on his sermons, the door generally remained at least partially open, a standing invitation to interrupt him for any church business they deemed to require his input.

The two women tried not to bother him with trivialities, but he made it clear that they could if need be.

Alice was momentarily taken aback by the suddenly secretive behavior, but she recovered quickly and proceeded to make the coffee and to water the African violets and the succulents, working steadily until Donna came in fifteen minutes later.

Alice was wound up and coiled to pounce on her unsuspecting coworker.

"Did you notice the door to his office is closed?" Her intense voice was barely above a whisper. "What do you think he's doing in there? Do you think he's working on the Easter sermon? I can't say I've been impressed with his recent ramblings. This is the first time he's come into the office before us since he's been here."

"I don't know," Donna returned, draping her dark green cardigan over the back of her office chair and tucking her purse into the desk drawer. "He's been acting oddly since Christmas when his son moved back to Balfour. I've been wondering if things are okay there. This isn't the first time he's struggled with writing his sermons."

"That's true." Alice's eyes widened. "He didn't even get upset on Friday when the bulletins weren't back from the printer until after five. He nearly bit my head off the last time that happened."

"I know," Donna agreed. "He usually proofs them himself, and he didn't seem to care. I don't think he knows about the Easter music for the choir, or he'd say something about that. Even the altos are in open revolt against Frank's arrangement, unbearably high and more chant than real music. Remember the song that repeats the chorus twenty-two times? Like that."

"I try to forget. It isn't my favorite either."

Donna came around her desk, drawing Alice aside to whisper confidentially into the other woman's ear.

"Do you think he's having a midlife crisis?"

Alice rolled her eyes, her lips pursed in a sour frown.

"Who knows what is going on in that man's head."

"Exactly what I thought," Donna agreed. "Where does he get those fifty-cent words he uses? I don't remember having to use a dictionary when he first came."

Alice sat down and took a box of multicolored, plastic-coated paper clips out of her desk drawer, spread out a rainbow mound, and twisted them together, forming a delicate childish chain. Donna perched on the edge of her coworker's desk and watched in mild fascination, amused at Alice's preteen response to stress.

"What are you doing?" she asked, trying to keep a tone of judgment from her voice. "I haven't made one of those things since middle school."

"He's making me nervous," the secretary admitted, staring at her hands and sliding two of the small wires artfully together. She continued to add paper clips one at a time until she had used two dozen or more. "I saw this on the internet the other day. Someone said it could keep your hands busy and help you concentrate. Besides, I'd look silly with one of those fidget toys the children use when they can't keep still."

"Indeed," Donna said, doing her best to sound supportive. "If it helps."

"Do you really think this has something to do with his son?" Alice said, adding the clips one at a time. "Maybe he's looking at other churches. Do you think he wants to leave?"

"You're just worried that if he goes, Virginia's going with him."

"Of course I am." Alice shook out the paper clip chain, admiring the eight-inch length. "Don't pretend that you're not fretting about that too."

The coffee pot gurgled, forestalling the obvious answer to the question.

"Should I offer to take him a cup?" Alice said impulsively, raking the clips, chain and all, back into the open drawer. "Or do you think he'd want tea?"

"Just take a breath," Donna said. "You know he likes to get his own coffee unless Virginia comes into the church office, and then that's her prerogative. Don't be a nervous Nellie, Alice. Have a little faith."

Alice stood and smoothed down the waist of her modest pleated cotton skirt.

"Have you called Susan this morning to see if she's heard from Harry?" Donna said casually. "I was just about to check the answering machine to see if there's a message."

"Harry?"

"There was a Calling Post. Harry Halstein had to go to Memphis last night to see about his sister," Donna said. "Word has it she killed herself. I heard Ben Taylor sent one of the officers with Harry to talk to the police in Tennessee."

"Why in the world would he do that?"

"I haven't the foggiest idea."

"Did they drive?" Alice tugged at her cotton skirt again, momentarily regretting the vanilla ice cream she'd had on her apple pie after supper the night before, and sat back down. "Memphis is a long way."

"I heard the Senator sent them in his private plane with his personal pilot—called the pilot back from his aunt's in Griffith and they flew out from Anson's late yesterday."

"I'll bet that cost a pretty penny."

The exterior door opened with a warning beep, and the

secretaries fell silent. Virginia Evans's cheerful greeting resounded from the outer hallway, preceded by the delightful aroma of vanilla pound cake.

"Good morning," the preacher's wife repeated, coming into view, a bright white Tupperware cake carrier cradled in her hands. "How's everyone doing?"

"Fine," Donna said, cutting Alice off before the other secretary could express her concerns about the preacher's behavior and shooting her a warning scowl. "We're both just fine. Any news about Harry's sister?"

"Not yet." Virginia put the cake on the side table next to the coffee maker and took the top off of the plastic container. A second wave of vanilla drifted through the room.

"I didn't have time to slice this at home," Virginia apologized. "It was still too hot when I took it out of the oven. Isn't there a knife in the office somewhere? A plastic one will do."

"I'll check the kitchenette off the conference room," Alice offered, popping up, glad for the opportunity to expend her pent-up energy. "Someone left a nice stainless steel one at the last dinner on the ground and hasn't claimed it. Be right back."

The inner door to the preacher's office swung open.

"I thought I heard your voice," Andrew said. "Come on into the office."

"In a minute," his wife said. "I want to slice the cake first."

Andrew's eyes crinkled lovingly at the corners, and he went back to his desk, leaving the door open behind him.

Donna could clearly see that the room was in more than its usual disorder, the preacher's suit coat flung carelessly over the side chair and stacks of books scattered about on every available flat surface.

Crumpled balls of yellow tablet paper were strewn about like tiny spiked tennis balls around the writing pad and circling the bottom of the trash can where he'd tossed and missed the mark.

Some of the myriad books were open and others had bright slivers of paper marking the edges like multicolored budding leaves peeking from fanciful trees.

Donna didn't know why he bothered with the colors. He'd tried to hide it, but they all knew he was color-blind. Virginia had gone out of town unexpectedly one weekend right after they'd come, and he'd had to dress himself for church services without her. Everyone in the congregation talked for weeks about the outrageous color combination he'd worn in the pulpit as well as the fact that he'd worn one black shoe and one that was brown.

It was behavior that might have been endearing in someone more well-liked.

The secretary's attention returned to the chaotic office.

The disorder extended to his apparel too.

He'd taken off his necktie and that too was draped over the back of his high-backed leather chair along with a scarf he'd wrapped around his throat to protect his voice from the early spring air.

All in all, what Donna witnessed were the marks of a mad writer in pursuit of a narrative—or a desperate preacher in search of a scripture. From the looks of the study, they were one and the same, at least at Emmanuel Baptist mere days before Easter Sunday morning.

Alice came back with the hastily washed knife, wiping it dry with a paper towel.

"I'll take care of this," she said, patting Virginia on the shoulder and taking the lid from her hand. "You should go in and see what's going on with Pastor. I'll bring slices of cake and some coffee."

"Thank you," Virginia said, "but I really can't stay. I've got appointments about the Wilton House opening on Saturday. So many details. I'd love to chat for a minute, but I know you both understand!"

She saw the women exchange looks of concern not unlike her own when her husband had decided to alter his morning routine.

"I'll speak to him for a moment before I go," she added. "And I'll see if he'd like cake and coffee."

Donna had turned on her computer, waiting for the menu to appear. Her hand hovered over the answering machine, about to check for the overnight messages, when she deliberately met Virginia's eyes.

"Thank you for always thinking of others first," she said, indicating the open Tupperware container. "Alice and I agree that you're the sweetest, most considerate person we know. This church and the people in this town don't appreciate you enough. You're doing an amazing job with the Wilton House. Everyone knows who is really in charge, even if you don't want anyone to know how much you do."

Virginia Evans blushed to the roots of her white hair, her eyes misting over and her lips trembling ever so slightly.

"Nonsense," she said, embarrassed by the praise and seeking refuge in the partially open doorway to Andy's office. "We all do what we can for others. Balfour's a family."

The church phone rang.

"I'll let you get back to your work," the preacher's wife said. "I'll just have a quick word with Andrew and then I'll be on my way. Have a lovely day."

Chapter 16

Jim was enjoying his third waffle and had poured batter for the fourth onto the sizzling griddle of the hotel's waffle maker when the call came from the Germantown Police Department.

Harry had showered and dressed early, unable to sleep, and was drinking his second cup of heavily sweetened hazelnut coffee and eating a salted boiled egg. He'd commandeered a table near the front window in the hotel's breakfast nook, finding it difficult not to be amused at his traveling companion's bottomless appetite.

Outside, the thunder clouds had obscured any hope of sunshine, and, except for enjoying Jim's gastric antics, his mood was as dark as the impending weather.

In the back of his mind there were too many unanswered questions about Dinah. Had she been involved in some sort of criminal activity? Why would the FBI be investigating a suicide? What did her heart condition have to do with anything? What did they want from him? He felt badly about dragging someone else into this mess, though the bright spot in the trip was getting to know the young officer a little better.

The memory of Jim seated at a table in Papa's Authentic Italian Pizzeria from the night before was etched indelibly on the businessman's mind. After consuming a sixteen-inch pizza with extra pepperoni and roasted green bell peppers, an order of cheesy breadsticks, a garden salad with extra dressing, and four large fountain drinks, Jim still asked politely if they could stop at a convenience store on the way back to the hotel to get snacks to make it through the night until breakfast.

Jim emerged from the QuikTrip with a half dozen Yoo-hoo chocolate drink bottles and two supersize bags of barbeque pork rinds.

Harry had been more than satisfied with his own simple garden salad and sweet tea, and more than happy to foot the bill for the entire meal including the snacks. Having the young detective along was proving to be just the distraction he needed, and he made a mental note to thank Ben Taylor.

"When do we need to be at the station?" Jim asked, mopping the last of the maple syrup from his Styrofoam plate with the crispy edge of his waffle. "Do I have time for some cereal?"

"Cereal?" Harry said, mildly bemused. "You want cereal?"

Jim made an effort not to look sheepish and failed.

"The dispenser is out of waffle batter," he explained. "And they have fruity crispy cereal. I haven't had that in years."

Harry checked his Rolex watch, a gift from his mother for his fiftieth birthday.

"We're supposed to be over there by noon," he said. "Shouldn't take more than forty-five minutes or so, even with traffic. Sure.

Enjoy your breakfast."

"Thanks," Jim said. "I hate to be a bother."

"That's not a word I'd use to describe you at all," Harry re-assured him, wondering idly if someday all the food would catch up with the young man's metabolism. He looked down at his own ample midsection and considered his personal craving for sweets, hoping the officer would escape the same pancreatic fate he'd had to endure.

"I'm going up to my room to give Susan a call," Harry said. "Just knock on the door when you're ready if I'm not back down by the time you've finished."

"Yes, sir," Jim said, balancing an overflowing bowl of sugar-sweetened breakfast cereal in one hand and a carton of skim milk in the other.

The irony was not lost on Harry. He gave the young officer a vigorous thumbs up and made his way to the elevator. Whatever lodgings and food might cost, having Jim Smith in his corner was certainly a blessing he could not have predicted or anticipated.

Chapter 17

Cora spent the better part of her morning with thoughts of Gramma Crawford, Aunt Phoebe, and toxic licorice tea playing a wild game of tag in her head. Working on her current journal article on advanced art therapy for trauma in preschoolers had proven to be futile. She simply couldn't concentrate on the research she was trying to collate into useable form. She found herself typing, retyping, and deleting the same sentences over and over.

Every time she closed her eyes, she felt Gramma Crawford's imaginary fingers gripping her upper arm and heard ominous words about poisons and people who made deadly mistakes with, of all things, black licorice tea.

She also had an intense craving for fresh snapped green beans and smoked ham with cornbread, but she suspected that was unrelated to the rest of the dream.

Charlie's name flitted through her head once or twice too, but she tried to push him out of the way. Life had been so peaceful without him. So quiet.

She'd followed her first impulse and hadn't even called him about James and his cryptic hymn singing. There wasn't enough in the words *joy* and *morning* to make a decent conversation, much less offer clues. Besides, he hated to be bothered almost as much as she hated to call him.

Her life had settled into such a lovely, boring routine.

Now, with her grandmother's insistence that Charlie needed to hear the words "black licorice," she knew she couldn't put off calling him. But she still didn't know how to bring up the subject of hymns with someone who hadn't set foot inside a church in years.

She and Thomas had their morning coffee on the front porch before he left for the office at a quarter till eight, and Jane got up around eight thirty to dress and have her breakfast. Solomon nibbled from a bowl of dry food at her feet, playing with the little girl's shoelaces and batting at one of the matching stuffed kittens' tails as they hung from under the child's arm.

Marjorie arrived with her usual punctuality just after nine, greeted at the door by a treat-demanding tomcat and a cheerful Jane, then checked off the first item on her Monday morning routine, vacuuming the downstairs and prepping meals for the week.

A normal Monday. Except for the dream. Two dreams now.

Cora sat staring at the computer screen in her office wondering if she should bite her lip and call Charlie, casually bringing up Aunt Phoebe and licorice tea. And dying.

The idea seemed ridiculous, yet she was forced to admit to herself that every time she'd had a dream in the last year or so, there was something in it that Charlie needed to know. Besides, her grandmother had specifically told her to call.

She picked up the phone several times to put it right back down again, telling herself that she'd call when she knew what to say. But that time did not arrive.

She thought of Thomas. What would he think? What would he advise?

Her husband had been much more philosophical about Charlie's place in their lives lately, especially since months had passed since they had last seen or heard from him. Cora made a concerted effort to share more of her thoughts with Thomas and to get outside the house more, if only to the front porch every morning and the backyard to view the garden in the afternoon.

I hope he sees how much I love him, she thought, remembering the frantic visit to his office at Christmas. *He's put up with so much and he asks so little. I wonder what he'd say if I told him about the dream. Maybe I'll ask him what he thinks I should do.*

The ruby stone in the gold ring on her finger sparkled, nestled between the elaborately engraved eagle feathers. She traced the pattern with a loving touch. A curious gift that was so much like her husband in some ways and yet nothing at all like Thomas in others. A conundrum.

Her husband was, much like the dreams, a precious puzzle.

He'd refused credit for the Christmas gift, insisting that Jane had chosen the ring all by herself, that he simply followed his heart and the child's instructions.

Cora felt his love in the respect and consideration he gave her every day. He thoughtfully and patiently allowed for her quirks and fears, the disruption of the dreams in their lives, and Charlie.

Her adoring husband was quite charitable, all things considered, with Charlie's reentry into their world and for Cora, the ring was tangible proof of the depth of his caring.

Cora could still imagine the look of amazement on Marjorie's face and hear the delighted squeals of joy from Jane when she opened the box from Copperfield's Jewelry shop and read the card inside. The gold and the ruby were mined in nearby Dahlonega, and the original design was created by a Native American Cherokee, a handmade one of a kind.

Cora tentatively touched the silver locket and delicate chain at her throat. Inside were oval miniatures of her and her husband's faces. A wedding gift from Thomas.

He had given her only those two pieces of jewelry in the five years they had known each other.

She wore the plain gold band that had been his mother's wedding ring on her left hand. He'd offered to buy her anything she wanted, but she refused, pleased that he had wanted her to wear something so precious and sentimental.

She had no ring for him, but he produced his father's simple band and insisted that it was all he needed.

His parents had a long and loving marriage, devoted to each other, and the thought warmed her and encouraged her.

Marjorie came to the door to announce lunch just as Cora's cell phone vibrated. The housekeeper glanced at the clock over the desk. She knew who it was.

Right on schedule, she thought. *I should know better than to put lunch on the table at noon. She won't touch it until she's spoken to him first.*

"Hello, Thomas," Cora said, waving to acknowledge Marjorie. "No, I'm not having lunch yet. I was just thinking about you."

The housekeeper nodded approvingly, tiptoeing discreetly away and pulling the office door closed behind her.

Ten minutes later, Cora appeared in the doorway to the kitchen, surveying the familiar lunchtime routine. On the floor under Jane's high stool the housekeeper had placed a ceramic cat dish decorated with shiny enamel goldfish and filled with smelly treats for Solomon.

Jane was seated, waiting more or less patiently from her perch at the island in the center of the kitchen, staring intently into a bright blue mug that nested among a sea of Ritz crackers and cheddar cubes.

"Morrie made soup for us," Jane announced cheerfully, her dark dual ponytails swinging back and forth beside her ears. "We have round crackers with cheesy pieces."

"Looks delicious," Cora agreed, giving the little girl a warm hug and taking her place beside the child across from Marjorie. "Thank you so much."

"I know you both like vegetables," the housekeeper said, placing a stack of white paper napkins next to the additional basket of crackers in the center of the island. "Won't be long before we can get them from our own garden."

Marjorie seated herself, balancing on the padded stool top, tucking her sneaker-clad feet onto the cross stretcher at the bottom.

"I've made up some dough for chocolate chip cookies later this afternoon," she said, meeting Cora's eyes over the top of Jane's head. "Maybe there's someone who would like to bake with me. Unless we've other plans for the afternoon."

"No," Cora said, taking a napkin and covering her lap. "No plans at all."

Jane's tiny face broadened with enthusiasm, although her own hands remained folded meekly in her lap, waiting for the blessing over the food and permission to begin.

"Then it's settled," the housekeeper said, bowing her head as the little girl followed suit and Cora watched.

"Thank you for our food," Jane said, her voice innocent and sincere. "Amen."

"Amen," Marjorie added. "Would you two like some freshly squeezed lemonade? Lemons were on the weekly BOGOs at Sanderson's. I just made it."

"I'll get it," Cora said, rising. "I know you two will have fun this afternoon."

"I know you're busy with your book, but you're welcome to join us."

Marjorie picked up her spoon and dipped into her bowl, stirring as the steam rose up and a plump piece of carrot popped to the surface, followed by a sliver of slender green bean. "Many hands make light work."

"Thank you," Cora said, removing three clear glasses, one small and two larger, from the cabinet and placing them on the counter. "Maybe next time. I've an important phone call, and I'd better make it before I talk myself out of calling."

Marjorie shot a questioning look over Jane's head.

"Indeed," she said, lifting a suspicious eyebrow, her voice full of unspoken accusation. "Anyone I know?"

Cora deliberately turned her back and opened the refrigerator.

"Could be," she answered cryptically. "But I've discussed the matter with Thomas and he thinks this particular person is some-one I need to talk to, so I'm going to trust his judgment."

"Indeed," Marjorie said again, a tinge of skepticism in her

voice, stirring absently at her soup. "You'll have to let me know how that goes."

"Oh, I will," Cora said, returning to the island with a cut glass pitcher of lemonade, plump round slices of fruit floating on the surface of the sparkling yellow liquid. She poured the child's glass first.

"Thank you," Jane said, nibbling at a chunk of cheese.

"You're welcome," Cora said. "Marjorie, would you like a glass?"

"Yes, dear," the housekeeper said, biting her lip but unable to resist. "And I won't even make a cryptic comment about making lemonade out of lemons."

"I appreciate that." Cora laughed. "But you just did."

Chapter 18

Simmons' Restaurant was entertaining a bustling, busy Monday clientele.

Sam, darting deftly among the tables taking orders and sharing the latest details of Balfour gossip and chitchat, was enjoying herself immensely.

Even an isolated and uncommunicative Thomas, stoic and silent in his corner booth, couldn't dampen her spirits.

What was being dubbed "the Sunday incident"—the call from the Memphis Police Department to Harry Halstein while he and Susan were having lunch in a front booth—was the most exciting, albeit alarming, event in Balfour since the bizarre Christmas season kidnapping of Marjorie O'Quinn.

Sam wasn't celebrating the tragic events, but the notoriety of the incident brought an increased number of first-time daily customers and curiosity seekers.

In addition, her regular patrons were presented with a novel topic of conversation to add a touch of spice to their placid country life.

The dining area was abuzz with socialization and community.

Grandpa Sam had often called the restaurant "Balfour's front porch," and in times like these his granddaughter hoped that other people felt that way too.

A place to pass by and stop for a spell, to have a cup of coffee with friends, to celebrate with family, and to hear the latest news and the stories of the day.

Fresh country style alongside cosmopolitan food with a side of gossip, and Sam did love a good story.

She was a closet romantic at heart, holding on to hope. Never rejoicing in the heartaches of others, and certainly not in something as tragic as a suicide, she still believed in the power of love, friends, and family. And sharing the load to lighten it.

She lived vicariously through those who came within her circle, welcoming each with her own brand of nosy Southern charm.

Sam's outlook, much like her Grandpa Sam's, tended to be uplifting, positive, and optimistic. Her attitude spilled over to create an atmosphere that drew locals and return travelers into Simmons' Restaurant on a regular basis.

She looked around the room at her current diners.

The Judge and Linda, chatting congenially, arrived shortly after eleven thirty, proceeding straight to the Judge's reserved booth in the back without waiting to be seated. Twice in as many days was not unusual for them. They were avid supporters of the small business community.

A bustling Virginia Evans joined them ten minutes later, followed immediately by a hesitant Katy Wilton.

Sam knew the Judge and Linda's standing lunch order, chef salads with Thousand Island dressing on the side and sweet tea with extra lemons. She wasn't sure about Katy, and to her knowledge she'd never served Virginia Evans at all.

She put two single-sheet laminated menus down on the edge of the table. Her curiosity was clamoring like a litter of mischievous kittens, but she restrained herself.

"Can I take your drink order?" she said, her silky bleached ponytail swinging between her narrow shoulder blades, her tone full of cheery enthusiasm. "Sweet tea? Cola? Lemonade? Coffee?"

"I'd like hot tea," Virginia said, taking the proffered menu and meeting Sam's gaze with a gracious smile. "Any kind will do. And honey, if you have it."

"Of course," Sam purred. "I'll bring the box with the tea choices. I use a local source in Griffith for the honey. The taste is amazing. Local wildflowers make the difference, you know."

She turned to Katy, who had reluctantly picked up the menu and was studying it intently.

"I'd just like water," she said. "No ice, please."

"Lemon?"

"No thanks." Katy looked up, willing herself to explain. "Sensitive teeth."

Sam wasn't quite sure what she should do with that unexpected and unique piece of information, but she dutifully filed it away for future use.

"I'll give you a minute to look over the specials of the day and make up your minds. I'll be right back," she said.

To her surprise, the group was deep in pleasant conversation when she returned, the plain jar of distilled water in one hand and the cup of hot water nestled in a saucer in the other, the floral cup balanced precariously on the top of the hand-carved wooden tea box.

Sam put the Mason jar in front of Katy, then placed the cup and saucer in front of the preacher's wife, who'd taken out a small notebook and ballpoint pen. Virginia was apparently taking notes on the discussion, her elegant cursive writing already filling one page and flowing onto another.

Sam stared for a moment, fascinated by the old-school script calligraphy.

"Have we decided?" she said, opening the tea box to reveal the neat rows of foil-wrapped, mostly herbal selections. "Bill's been working on a California-style grilled chicken salad and several sandwiches using avocadoes. I hear they're remarkably healthy—the avocadoes as well as the sandwiches."

Her quip fell on distracted ears.

"I'd like some sort of soup," Virginia said, pointing to the section of the menu that touted fresh salads and homemade soups. "Something with potatoes, perhaps."

She listened expectantly for Sam's suggestions while she selected a square package of plain orange pekoe tea from the box and unwrapped it carefully, dipping the bag up and down in the hot water.

"How about loaded potato soup?" Sam offered. "Do you like everything? Green onions, cheese, bacon bits, sour cream? Bill can do all sorts of combinations. He's even wrangled a recipe from Darcie's cookbook for a sweet potato soup with nutmeg and toasted marshmallows."

"I love Bill's loaded potato with everything," Linda volunteered helpfully. "Virginia is notoriously easy to please, aren't you?"

"Everything it is then," Virginia agreed. She turned her attention to the younger woman at her side. "Have you decided what you'd like, dear?"

Katy looked slightly uncomfortable, sliding a little closer to the preacher's wife on the booth bench as if for protection from further interrogation.

There had been too much publicity surrounding Steve's murder, even after the Senator had gone back to Washington and the reporters had stopped following her around trying to take her picture. Even now at least once a week or so she was asked what she thought about the Wilton House reopening. She was so tired of answering questions and living under a microscope. It seemed to her that she and Elizabeth couldn't go anywhere anymore without prying or pity.

Virginia reminded her of her grandmother, only younger. Someone safe and nonjudgmental.

"Potato soup sounds delicious," she said. "Just cheese on mine, please."

"Coming right up," Sam said, collecting the menus and closing the wooden box. "I'll refill those sweet teas in just a minute too."

She dashed off into the kitchen to deliver the orders to Bill and collect prepared plates for other patrons. As she returned, she saw that Ellie Sanderson had come in while she was distracted, put on a clean apron, and was talking to Thomas at the cash register, a take-out bag on the counter.

The girl was certainly as dependable as she was independent and strong-willed.

"Is that lunch for Susan?" she said, walking over. "Has she heard from Harry?"

"Yes, it is. And not today," Thomas said as Ellie counted out his change into his palm, which he promptly deposited into the tip jar. "Thanks, Ellie. See you later, Sam."

Seeing that she wasn't going to get any more useful information from Thomas, Sam's attention shifted gears to the corner booth.

I wonder what Katy Wilton is doing with the Judge and Linda. Why in the world is Virginia Evans in my restaurant for the first time, and taking notes?

So many people. So many questions. So little time.

A glint of gratification sparkled in her eyes.

No better place to be than Simmons' proverbial front porch for a bird's eye view of life in Balfour, and Sam was never more grateful for her perch.

Chapter 19

Charlie let his attention sweep the crowd as he spoke, from time to time coming to rest on the FBI agent standing alone and against the right wall, strategically placed between the framed, nondescript artwork so as not to obscure the view of the pastel watercolor flowers.

She'd left before his first presentation was finished, and she'd come back twenty minutes after the second session had begun.

Exactly as she had before, she was listening intently to every solitary word he said. By his count, she'd been standing for the last fifty-six minutes without sitting down, taking a single note, or changing her jaded expression.

Within the first ten minutes of his talk, she had slipped off her dark sunglasses, pushed them carelessly back onto the top of her head, and revealed dark brown, almost black eyes, equally disinterested.

Encased in a professional, nondescript gray suit, no other

muscle in her body appeared to move again for the remainder of the presentation, not even the stern set of her lips, pressed together in what he decided must be critical judgment of his oratorical ability.

He'd reached the section of his presentation that was mostly slides, so his mind wandered to the agent as he clicked through, allowing the participants time to take notes and copy the information.

A sentry on guard duty, he thought. *Guarding what?*

He didn't flatter himself that his near-celebrity status or the subject matter of his lecture had attracted her attention. She looked much too sophisticated and intelligent to be swayed by either his boyish good looks or his adolescent attempts to be clever during his presentation.

There was something in her facial expression that he couldn't quite define, and he wasn't sure he wanted to know what was on her mind. He'd known a detective once who wore sunglasses all the time because the man said people couldn't tell which way he was looking—or who he was watching. Charlie wondered if she wore the glasses for the same reason, or if she was just dramatic and wore them to be intimidating.

A pit bull personality, he thought. *She's on a mission, and I think I'm in her way.*

He'd come to the end of the sequence and went back to his notes, returning his concentration to his audience, taking questions on the material they'd just seen.

At the hour break, he hoped she'd approach the front of the room where he was standing and tell him what she wanted, but instead she took a cell phone from her suit's inner pocket and slipped out as unobtrusively as she had come in.

Charlie was both agitated and disappointed by her exodus. His male ego stung a bit irrationally that after all that staring she wasn't even going to speak to him, and his raw curiosity nagged at her purpose in coming to the seminar at all.

Who is this woman and why is she staring at me as though I'm the prime suspect in her latest investigation? What could she want with me? he thought, peeved with himself that he couldn't read her any better.

He glanced up. An hour to go before the lunch break.

His hotel handler appeared at his left elbow with another large cup of coffee and two glazed donuts perched on a clear plastic plate. She waited expectantly for his approval, holding out the offerings with a bright smile, but he ignored her flirtatious attempt to curry favor and continued to sort his papers, thanking her with a formal nod and tersely instructing her to put them on the table.

She plopped them down with a frustrated sigh and wiggled away.

Not today, sweetheart, he thought, refusing to look up or otherwise encourage her coy advances. *I'm too old for you chronologically . . . and maybe even emotionally. I've got too much on my mind to flirt with you. This is work.*

"Detective Abbott?"

The velvet voice was in sharp contrast to the gray-suited stalker agent.

Charlie came very close to falling off the stool.

"It's Charlie," he corrected her, his mouth uncharacteristically dry. "Just Charlie."

"Of course," she said indifferently. "Detective Abbott."

Charlie had the bizarre sensation that he was in a waking

dream, one of the kind where everyone else was wearing clothing and he was standing in the corner in his plaid boxers searching frantically for the nearest exit.

He stared at the identification lanyard tucked just beneath the lapel of her jacket and could make out a last name—Walker.

An image of Chuck Norris, Texas Ranger flashed through his mind, along with a dozen hilarious irreverent jokes, but he stopped short of laughing out loud.

This Walker would not be amused at this humor, that much he could tell.

She held out a black-bordered business card by way of introducing herself and pushed back the snow-white cuff of her shirt, analytically checking the men's Timex watch on her wrist.

"We need to talk after your seminar concludes today. I understand there is one more break before you can leave. I'll send an agent. You don't have time for lunch."

She was gone before he could formulate a suitable retort, so Charlie stuffed a glazed donut into his mouth, downing it with a satisfying swallow of lukewarm coffee.

Sugar and caffeine. Not the best type of fuel for dealing with FBI Special Agent Walker, but he hadn't been given a choice.

The cell phone in his pocket vibrated, and a third shiver ran up his now-sensitive spine.

He could almost hear Marcie's cryptic explanation for the phenomenon echoing in his head—"*that feeling means that rabbits are running across your grave.*"

Another phrase immediately came to mind, one he had heard on and off his whole life from friends, family, and coworkers—"*bad news and evil omens always come in threes.*"

Charlie made a vain attempt to shrug off his concern.

The cell phone persisted. He checked the caller ID.

Cora.

Oh damn, Charlie thought, stuffing another donut into his mouth. *Just damn. There's my three—the shivers, the FBI, and Cora. Not right now, Cora. I'll have to call you back in an hour. There's a seminar to finish and an enigmatic FBI agent on my back. You'll have to get in line and take a number.*

The cell phone mercifully stopped quivering in his hand.

He grudgingly waved across the room at the blond, who had found a more congenial audience, batting her eyelashes at a trio of middle-aged detectives.

The three amigos, Charlie thought. *Harmless diversion from an otherwise boring Monday and a required meeting. Sorry to spoil your fun, guys.*

She disentangled herself from their fawning admiration and made her half-hearted way to the podium.

"I'll take that water now," Charlie said. "And if you could manage a sandwich and maybe a bag of chips after I'm done, I'd appreciate it."

She flashed him a sparkling artificial smirk.

"Of course," she said. "Anything you need, Detective Abbott."

Chapter 20

"Thank you for calling back," Cora said. "I wouldn't have bothered you, but I think this could be important."

"Sure," he said. "Are you okay?"

"Yes."

He knew she probably wasn't okay. She only called for one reason. He knew it wasn't his place to ask her personal questions, but that didn't stop him from wanting to know.

"I'm guessing you've had a dream," he said, forcing himself to sound objective. "Do you know what it's about?"

"No," she said. "Charlie, are you working a case?"

He eyed the towering male agent that Walker had sent to fetch him, standing impatiently in the doorway to the Hyatt-Regency meeting room as it drained of officers and detectives. Charlie could almost hear the polished black-toed boot tapping against the floor and feel the darts of distain thrown across the room.

He didn't know what to tell Cora, although if his escort was any indication, he was certainly involved in something important.

I don't know if I'm working a case or not, he thought, his mind on the FBI agent who was giving him the evil eye from across the room. *But I'm being summoned. Walker's got some sort of pull to send another agent like a common errand boy to fetch me. I'd be pretty peeved if I were you, sir.*

"Charlie?" Cora's voice brought him back to the present. "Are you still there? You seem to be distracted. Did I call at a bad time? I asked you if you were working a case."

"*You* called *me*, Cora," he said, evading the question and trying not to sound as frustrated as he felt. "I'm not a mind reader. Why did you call?"

He cupped the back of his neck with his free hand and rubbed the sore muscles.

His shoulders slumped slightly, but he straightened them immediately, refusing to give in to his emotions.

Surely she was as tired of riding the merry-go-round as he was. Maybe more. She had more to lose. Now she had Jane.

If word got out that they were working on cases together again, the whole Ed Brackett case would be back in the news and the quiet little world she lived in would be shattered. Reporters would be back on her doorstep, and then someone would begin to dig and discover that she was involved with other incidents, especially Steve Wilton's murder.

In spite of all that, she'd called him. The risk in the end was hers.

There was no going in reverse, so he chose forward.

He turned his back on Walker's vexed henchman and settled himself wearily on the stool again, face to the wall.

Cora's dreams outweighed the FBI any day of the week.

"Tell me what I need to know," he said. "Just know that I've got someone waiting on me, so be as concise as you can."

The whisper of her breathing stroked his eardrum, and he closed his eyes.

He knew she was formulating exactly how to put the vague impressions of her dream into words. Knowing that she was struggling didn't mean he felt more tolerant or sympathetic.

"Help me out here, Cora," he prodded. "Just give me the clues."

There was a sudden sharp intake of air.

"Well, there are actually two dreams, but the first one was too confusing," she said. "James kept singing hymns as though we were in a church service."

"Hymns?" he said. "Okay, then."

"All about understanding things in the future," she said. "Nothing specific."

"I take it the second dream had something more specific."

"Yes. Licorice," she exhaled, enunciating the word. "Black licorice."

"What?" His stomach lifted and dropped, as though he had come over the top of a rollercoaster, gravity tugging at the lower half of his body while his queasy insides remained temporarily suspended in midair.

"Is that all you have?" he said. "Candy?"

What kind of FBI case involves candy? His thoughts trampled each other. *She's a federal agent. I can't tell her that. She'll think I'm insane—or worse.*

"Cora, seriously," he said. "You can't possibly expect me to begin a conversation with the word *licorice*. You're joking."

"You know me better than that."

Charlie heard a confidence in her voice that was unexpected and insistent.

A voice from Cora that he hadn't heard in years. Since before Lonora.

"That's exactly what I want you to do," she said. "I thought at first that it was about candy too, but it's about tea leaves. Black licorice tea leaves."

"Cora," he said, his voice laced with skepticism.

"Either I believe what I'm told or I don't," she interrupted. "Someone's death is related to black licorice tea. I don't know how or why. There's been a murder . . . maybe an accidental murder, but a murder no less. I was told to call you, so I did."

He wanted to ask how many times she'd been wrong, but he knew the answer.

None. Her intuition had sometimes been slightly off—even the best profilers weren't perfect—but Cora had never been wrong about the dreams.

Outlandish. Far-fetched. Bizarre. The dreams had been all of those things and more—but wrong? No, not wrong. Never wrong.

"So you're sure."

"Yes," she said decisively. "I wouldn't have called you otherwise."

What she said was true. Except for the dreams, she had no reason to call him, and that knowledge hurt more than he wanted to admit, even to himself.

"Okay," he said. "Suppose someone died because of black licorice tea. How am I supposed to start that conversation? How am I supposed to know about the person who made the tea, or the person who drank it?"

There was a quiet on the other end of the phone that implied he should know the answer to his questions.

So this is why Agent Walker walked into my seminar, not once but twice, he thought. *This is why I've had chills up and down from my shoulders to my backside since I got here. Darn Marcie and her country superstitions.*

"Forget I asked," he said. "I already know who I'm supposed to tell."

"Thank you, Charlie," she said.

"Later," he said, risking a look over his shoulder, eying the increasingly incensed agent in the doorway. The agent had taken a cell phone out of his suit pocket and was having his own spirited conversation.

The other end of the line went silent.

Charlie picked up his briefcase and backpack, wondering absently exactly how far Agent Walker's power extended and how deep he was in trouble before he even opened his mouth.

Another chill ran down his spine and up again.

That made four.

He wondered what Marcie would make of her rule of three.

Never mind, he thought, waving a good-natured greeting at the fuming agent and striding across to meet him. *I'm pretty sure I know the answer to that question too.*

Chapter 21

Thomas returned to the office a little after two o'clock with one of Bill's famous chef salads for Susan and a side of her favorite creamy Italian dressing, sneaking in and placing the container in the middle of her desk and backing away with polite reserve.

He, for one, was feeling much better after spending time at the courthouse and enjoying a quiet lunch at Sam's. He'd had his own bowl of homemade chicken noodle soup and some crusty fresh baked bread, although when he talked to Cora he'd left out the part about the generous slice of pecan pie with a scoop of real whipped cream at the end of the meal.

His wife never openly expressed disapproval or even remarked about his indulgence in pastries and pies, but he surmised from her own healthy eating habits that she didn't totally approve. Having Jane in the house had given him a new perspective too, and he realized that he should be setting a better example for the child.

Thomas knew he should be more concerned about his food

choices. His sweet tooth, however, was not quite so cooperative. Sam knew his weakness far too well, and he resolved to skip lunch out until Friday as penance for his overindulgence.

After looking at the condition of his office, he was even more certain that he needed to bring lunch from home for the rest of the week.

Susan, in the interim hours, had resorted to moving the furniture and furnishings, free from his watchful eyes and queries.

Maybe I should have just sent her off to the clerk's office, he thought.

Subtle but noticeable changes were everywhere.

The hat rack had exchanged places with the umbrella stand, the two chairs by the window had taken up residence on either side of the pine bookshelf, and the various houseplants had all played some wild game of fruit basket turnover, none in the spot where it had begun that morning.

Thomas was not at all surprised. The decor, including the wall hangings and numerous framed pictures, had been known to roam around the room at will even on the best of days, trading places at the whim of his trusted legal assistant.

Since they'd moved into the newly renovated building, she'd been on a weekly quest to perfect their work surroundings. Today's upheaval was, to his mind, a bit more excessive than usual.

What made him feel even more ill at ease was her abnormal silence.

He thought of his advice to Cora about calling Charlie and realized that he hadn't heard from his wife yet.

Maybe Cora didn't call Charlie after all, he thought. *Maybe Harry didn't have any news for Susan, and she's upset because she's in the dark about what's going on, just like I am. Or maybe she's heard something that's upset her and she doesn't want to talk about it. How am I supposed to know?*

He rose from his chair and strolled casually past his assistant's desk to get himself a cup of coffee. She was alternately picking at Bill's multilayered salad with a white plastic fork and twisting the sequins on her sweater nervously with the tips of her painted nails.

I've never seen her like this, he mused, adding a second packet of sugar along with three of the individual containers of half and half, the bright white milk dissolving in curling swirls against the dark roasted liquid.

Between Susan's nerves and Cora's call to Charlie, he found himself unable to concentrate on any of the mundane paperwork on his desk.

Without Susan's promptings, his mind drifted off.

At a quarter after four, it dawned on him that except for bringing donuts and salads and remembering her on Christmas and her birthday with bonus checks, Susan had been remarkably low maintenance. She'd efficiently carried on the day-to-day routine in his law office without drama or histrionics, with the exception of her mild redecorating fetish and her recent obsession with handmade sequined sweaters.

This situation, and her taciturn behavior, were novel to him, and he had no idea how to deal with her in this present state of uncertainty, but silence wasn't working.

"I've known you for years," he began. "You're independent, confident, and capable. I want to help, but I don't know how."

The legal assistant looked up from her desk.

"I've been horribly useless," she said. "And exceptionally

difficult to get along with today. I've snapped at you and accused you of awful things, and you've been the best boss in the world to bring me food and lighten my load."

"Now, Susan—" he began.

"Please don't contradict me," she said. "I'm trying to apologize."

She stood and picked up her purse, digging for her keys as she spoke.

"I know it's the middle of the day, but I'm going home. If it's okay with you, I'll take your advice and tomorrow I'll see if there's anything I can do long distance for Harry at his farm."

"Whatever you think is best," he said, relieved to see movement toward the Susan that he knew, no matter how small the steps might be.

"And one more thing," she said, picking up the white donut box possessively. "You were right this morning. I'm going to take these home and polish them off for supper. We both know that you don't need them, and I've a strong suspicion they are just the perfect thing to adjust my attitude."

Chapter 22

"I don't know that I've heard of the Evergreen Clinic," Harry said. "And I'm familiar with many of the commercial properties in the area. I'm still not quite clear what this has to do with Dinah."

He'd taken his respective seat in the Germantown PD interrogation room across the table from Agent Walker. On the way over, he'd explained to Jim the rationale for using the interrogation room, and Jim seemed to accept Agent Walker's explanation at face value. The young officer had reoccupied the corner, although this time a helpful fellow officer had provided cups of coffee and sub sandwiches.

Jim thought there certainly was more room, and he didn't have to worry so much about making a mess with the food, so it did make sense.

The FBI agent's demeanor was also considerably more pleasant than the night before, although her expression reminded Jim of the lead coach on the final game day.

Nevertheless, his cop instincts told him to be wary and keep his back to the wall. The Chief had sent him along for a reason, and he didn't want to let anyone down.

This lady's intense, he thought. *Does she ever lighten up? There's obviously more going on here than Harry's sister's suicide. But what? And why does she need Harry? What does she think he knows?*

Jim openly stared at the agent. She saw him, returning his stare with a curious tilt of her head. He didn't want to make her uncomfortable, but he couldn't shake the feeling that the process was a bit peculiar. He hated that he wasn't experienced enough to know when to be suspicious and when to blindly obey. He briefly considered getting out his sketch pad and pencils and doodling faces to clear his mind, but he thought that might be considered rude and as though he wasn't paying attention to what was going on.

The sound of her voice snapped his attention back to the case at hand.

"Varden Bander is the executive director of the Evergreen Clinic," she said, directing her attention away from Jim to Harry. "Your sister had been a patient of his for the past three months."

The front legs of Jim's chair bumped to the floor with a thud.

"Wait. Bander? I've heard that name," he said, hating to call attention back to himself but unable to contain his enthusiasm. "Wasn't he indicted last week, charged with defrauding his patients out of thousands of dollars?"

"More like millions of dollars over the past five years," Walker corrected him. "He's been on our radar since the agency tracked him from California four years ago, where he was running a nursing home scam. Before that, he ran a health spa scam in Oregon. He's been incredibly careful up until now."

"Do you think he had something to do with Dinah's suicide?" Harry said, sliding to the edge of his chair, at last feeling as though he could be part of the solution.

The agent paused thoughtfully, tapping her pen on the folder in front of her.

"This is the first death we might be able to tie directly to his illegal activities. In Memphis, he deviated from his other schemes. The Evergreen Clinic is a specialized clinic for chronic heart patients. He charged exorbitant fees for subpar services. He's escaped the most serious consequences because up until now no one's died due to his actions. He's also been dealing principally with the elderly who don't have immediate families. Most of them are too embarrassed to admit they've been swindled. Until Dinah Browning became one of his patients, all he'd stolen from them was their money."

"He took their dignity," Smith added bitterly from the corner. "Scum of the earth."

"You haven't answered my question," Harry insisted. "Can you tie him to Dinah's death?"

"We're working on that," she said. "We know his MO, to move into an area and recruit locals. Then he leaves his unsuspecting accomplice holding the bag."

"So where's the partner?"

"The joke's apparently on Bander. Seems she skipped town on him before he knew what happened. She was calling herself a mental health counselor and adviser, although we're certain she doesn't have valid credentials for either. She was using a fake name, so there's no driver's license photograph, but several of Bander's patients have worked with our sketch artist. We've got a composite of what they say she looks like. Middle-aged, curly salt and pepper hair, slightly shorter than average. Nothing of note. She doesn't appear anywhere in our databases. Not even fingerprints."

"Can I see the sketch, please?" Jim said politely. "What name was she using?"

"Eudora Ashford," Inola said, checking her notes, slightly puzzled at his request. "She called herself 'Astra' to her clients. I'll have someone get you a copy of the sketch."

"I take it she's gone to ground," Jim said.

Harry looked puzzled.

"Hunting expression," the officer said. "The fox goes to the den to hide when the hounds are out. Most animals are smart enough to seek out familiar territory and relative safety in the cover they know best."

There was a sharp rap at the door sounding simultaneously as it opened.

Charlie Abbott scanned the room, his attention landing on the first friendly face.

"Rookie," the detective said. "You're a long way from home."

A grin of sheer exhilaration burst across Jim's face, his white teeth glistening against the dark of his skin.

"Detective Abbott!" he said, jumping up awkwardly, like a giant puppy with paws much too large for his body, lurching from the corner. "Am I glad to see you!"

"Likewise," Charlie said, unable to forestall the incoming bear hug. He should have known better than to expect anything else from Jim.

Once he'd disentangled himself, he held out his right hand.

"You must be Harry Halstein. I've heard good things."

Harry cast Charlie a suspicious sidelong glance, but his breeding and instinct took precedence and he still shook the outstretched offering.

"Do I know you?" he said, his eyes narrowing in deliberation.

"This is Charlie Abbott," Inola said smoothly, pointedly checking the time on her watch. "Glad you could respond to my invitation, detective."

He matched her gaze silently.

Invitation my hind leg, Charlie thought. *More like a royal command.*

"I thought perhaps you'd all know each other since you live in Balfour," Inola said, watching each man's face in turn. "It's a rather small town, isn't it?"

"Detective Abbott's reputation precedes him," Harry said, his attitude adjusting rapidly, warming to the sight of the detective. "I know of him. We've just never had the privilege of meeting in person."

"I'm sure you've had an earful," Charlie said. "Susan is quite the historian."

The detective turned to the federal agent.

"Mr. Halstein and Officer Smith live in Balfour," Charlie said. "I work with the New Orleans PD when I'm not doing seminars around the southeast."

"I stand corrected," Inola said. "Your Plott hound Elvira lives in Balfour. The Piney Woods Apartments, if I remember correctly, with your landlady Marcie Jones."

Her manner implied that she always remembered correctly.

Charlie's guard went up even further. This agent knew too many personal details, and she talked as if she had a reason to know them.

She's done her homework on me, Charlie thought.

"So is that why I'm here?" Charlie said sarcastically. "You're a fan. You could have just asked for an autograph. I'm flattered that the FBI needs my help, but that doesn't explain why or how you tracked me down."

"You have quite the reputation," Inola said suggestively. "This particular case has some rather interesting characters that have proven to be . . . elusive. You've got a special skill set, shall we say."

Jim Smith took two steps closer to the detective, looming attentively.

"So, are you on the case?" he asked. "Is Cora involved?"

As soon as the words were out of his mouth, Jim could have willingly bitten off his tongue, or at the least inserted his size fourteen shoe into his face. Maybe both shoes.

What's the matter with me? he thought. *I know better than to bring up Cora.*

Chancing a quick glance at Charlie's expression, he was relieved to find that the detective didn't seem at all angry at his indiscretion.

In fact, the detective's face was disturbingly serene and pre-occupied.

Maybe Walker already knows about Cora, Jim thought, hoping for the best. *She knows about Balfour and Elvira and the Piney Woods. She's an FBI agent. I'm sure she knows everything worth knowing about all of us, not just Charlie.*

There was another knock at the interrogation room door, but this time the person on the other side waited for an invitation to enter.

"We're ready when you are, Agent Walker," the uniformed

female officer said. "The Chief says to let her know what else you need."

"Thank you, Officer Hernandez," Inola said. "Give us ten minutes."

The door closed.

"Please resume your seats," the agent said briskly, flipping open the black spiral notebook in her hand. "I only have a few more questions, and then you're free to return to your hotels."

Charlie wiped his unexpectedly damp palms against his jeans and thought of Cora's phone call. He didn't know how Inola would react to hearing the clues Cora gave him without explanation. He knew he had to be careful not to expose Cora's gifts.

Now or never, he thought.

"Could I have a word with you first?" he said. "Privately."

Inola closed the notebook with a restrained slam.

"Step into the hallway with me then," she said without excusing herself to the others. When she had closed the door firmly, she led him halfway down the corridor, away from the other rooms, and tapped suggestively on the face of her Timex watch.

"I'm on a schedule. Are you still wondering why you're here?" she said. "It's painfully simple, detective. You have a file several inches thick and a solid reputation for solving difficult cases. I've got a difficult case. Since that difficult case involves the town where your former partner now lives and two members of that same community, I thought you might be persuaded to help."

"Out of the generosity of my heart?" he said. "What makes you think this involves Balfour? The suicide took place in Memphis. I don't see a connection."

"Well, then," she said curtly. "When you put it that way, you're right and my instincts are all wrong. You've got nothing to offer the investigation, and we won't be requiring your services. Sorry to have taken up so much of your valuable time."

She looked down at her watch and took two steps back.

"I've got an appointment."

Charlie looked up and down the empty corridor before speaking.

"Is your appointment with the coroner?"

"That's how these things work, detective," she said. "I took a chance when I asked you to help, but if you don't have anything to contribute . . ."

"Just that you might want to run additional bloodwork."

Her eyebrows shot up.

Charlie hesitated.

This was unbelievable. It was as though both Inola and Cora had conspired against him to bring him to this point.

He felt like someone with a foot suspended midair about to take the first blind step onto a tightrope suspended across Tallulah Gorge without a safety net of any kind.

He could almost feel an imaginary breeze gusting at his back.

"Detective," she said, the tapping increasing on the face of her watch. "One minute and counting."

He took a breath and steeled himself.

"Licorice," he blurted out, taking a leap of faith and hoping the rope beneath held firm. "Black licorice."

Inola's hand dropped to her side and her mouth hung slightly open, the breath coming in and out like whispers.

"Black licorice," she repeated, putting her hand lightly on the doorknob. "To clarify, I should ask the coroner to test specifically for black licorice? Can I ask how you came up with this idea?"

Charlie didn't answer.

"So it's true then," she said, "what's in your file."

"What's in my file?" Charlie asked, his guard coming back up, his hesitancy moments before forgotten. Her words were all the confirmation he needed that the FBI had been keeping tabs on him.

He wanted to confirm whether they'd been watching Cora too, but he already knew the answer to that question. Of course they had.

"I'll tell the coroner to look for black licorice," Inola said curtly. "You can keep your sources to yourself . . . for now."

Her look bored into him, searching every line of his face, questioning every twitch like a human lie detector.

Charlie steeled himself and returned her stare.

Inola Walker took out her cell phone.

"Tell Mr. Halstein and Officer Smith that they're free to go back to their hotel," she said to him with a dismissive wave of her free hand. "Just don't leave town."

Charlie was uncharacteristically speechless.

"And you," she added, turning and striding away down the empty hallway, "I'd like for you to cool your heels in the interrogation room and have one of those sandwiches on the table. You must be hungry. I don't know how long the coroner will take, but I'd like for you to be here so we can pick up this conversation where we left off."

Charlie watched her walk away, another wave of dread and shivers washing over him. He was being dragged into a whirlpool. He couldn't decide if Inola Walker was more intimidating when she was ordering him about or when she decided to be polite.

Either way, she was right about one thing. Those sandwiches looked good, and he had plenty of time now to enjoy them.

Chapter 23

The coroner was wearing his surgical mask lowered across the fashionable stubble on his chin like a miniature blue hammock, his clear protective face shield pushed up past his forehead. He was taking the sterilized instruments of his trade out of the autoclave, arranging them in neat rows along the rim of the examination table, refusing to hurry for the approval of the antsy FBI agent rapping on her clipboard.

"I sent you my findings earlier this morning," he said, pacing his words. "Then I got the results you ordered from the second blood screen workup. I took a closer look at the internal organs on your suicide. I convinced the lab to run those expedited tests, but I'm a bit baffled about the reasons. What in the world caused you to ask for a more detailed analysis?"

"I want to know how she died," she said, crossing her arms defensively, hugging the clipboard to her chest. "That's your job."

"Well, most agents would have been content with the gunshot

through her head," he quipped. "Standard testing indicated there was none of the usual in her system. No alcohol, amphetamines, cocaine, or opiates. Not even a whiff of marijuana."

"I thought I made myself clear when I called. I'm not interested in the obvious."

The coroner waved off the remark and gestured for her to hand him the clipboard.

"It's all right here in the report," he said. "Her internal organs show progressive congestive heart failure. Not surprising, since according to the records from Evergreen Clinic, she'd been pre-scribed a cardiac glycoside called digoxin. There were acceptable levels in her blood, used to control what had been diagnosed as arrhythmias, or irregular heartbeats."

"Detectives at the scene found a bottle of Lanoxin in her purse."

"That's a brand name of digoxin. It's taken once per day and most effective at the same time, so it's not surprising she had it with her."

"So she was dying of a heart condition."

"Not necessarily. That's assumption."

"What does that mean? Assumption?" Inola snapped. "Either she was dying from heart disease or she wasn't."

"Well," the coroner said, leaning against the metal table and removing his gloves. He ran his finger down the report. "The di-goxin is a treatment that should have worked, under most normal circumstances, to control her irregular heartbeats. There are some common side effects—dizziness, confusion, loss of appetite—but those are generally minor and never fatal in themselves."

"So she had heart disease, but she was undergoing treatment

that should have helped her. Do the side effects include depression?"

"Not from the digoxin alone," he said. "She was, however, experiencing serious side effects from the binary combination with another substance in her system."

Inola tightened her jaw and waited.

"The expanded toxicology report revealed that there were elevated levels of glycyrrhetinic acid in her kidneys, including higher levels of sodium and a notable absence of potassium."

"I thought you said earlier that you didn't find other drugs in her system."

"Not drugs, per se," he continued. "The extreme lack of potassium throws off the ionic balance that's critical to cardiac conduction. She was undoubtedly suffering from fatal ventricular fibrillation."

"Heart disease," she said. "You said that already."

"Yes, but a specific kind of heart disease. She also had high levels of the same acid in her liver, which, by the way, we'd never have checked if you hadn't insisted on a detailed workup. Like I said, the gunshot wound is pretty darn obvious, and her meds explain her heart condition."

"Exactly how does this acid—"

"Glycyrrhetinic acid," he said, his chest puffing out a bit with intellectual pride.

She ignored his arrogance, infuriated by his posturing.

"Get to the point. Explain to me why I should care about this acid."

"Well, considering the high levels that were being recirculated in her liver, I'd say she had been consuming the binary agent on a regular basis."

"She was slowly being poisoned?"

The coroner flashed a look of smug superiority, and Inola braced herself for another avalanche of tech speak.

"Something nonpoisonous that interacted with her regular meds. She probably didn't know it either," he said, thrusting the sides of his white lab coat aside, balancing his hands on his hips with a distinct swagger. "The cases are rather rare, and any medical examiner might have missed it under the circumstances. A reasonably attentive doctor or health professional would have warned her away from consuming the slightest amount in her condition, especially in combination with her prescription meds."

"I can tell you're enjoying this," she snapped. "Get to the point."

"Licorice," he said smugly.

A look of disbelief flooded over her chiseled face.

"This woman died from candy?"

"Black licorice was a major contributory factor," he said. "The side effects of combining licorice with digoxin are extreme, including chronic depression and suicidal thoughts. There was no evidence of excess sugar in her system, so I can't say she ingested the licorice in the form of a sweet, but, in my professional opinion, if she hadn't shot herself, she was on the fast track to a massive, unavoidable, unquestionably fatal heart attack. She died due to the binary interaction . . . in this case the coroner's report will read that she died by suicide that was a direct result of the depression caused by combining licorice with her prescribed meds."

He rebuttoned his lab coat and handed her the clipboard.

"It's all in there, Agent Walker, in black and white," he said. "Don't know how you did it, or how you're going to use it to catch the bad guys, but great work all the same."

Chapter 24

The interrogation room door opened.

"You were absolutely right," Inola announced from the door-way. "Now we really need to talk."

The intensity of her words bounced off the mirrored wall behind him and danced back and forth across the room like a ricocheting racquetball.

Charlie thrust his hands deeply into his jeans pockets, leaning back against the two-way mirror. Several crumpled napkins lay beside the pitiful remains of the sub sandwich plate, accompanied by three oversized cups containing various levels of cold black coffee.

His laptop, the battery long expired, was abandoned on the opposite corner, closed and cold to the touch.

Vindicated, he thought. *Thank you, Cora. I won't doubt you again.*

It was Charlie's turn to inspect his watch.

Walker had been gone for four long hours and a few minutes, more than enough time to discover whether or not Cora's clue was accurate and had any relationship to Dinah Browning's suicide.

The truth of what he'd told Walker was becoming more obvious by the second.

Rather than being annoyed with his long wait, Charlie was amused. He could have left at any time, but she'd more or less asked politely for him to wait, and that seemed like a rather significant concession for her.

"The coroner did a rush blood workup on Dinah Browning and found licorice in her bloodstream."

"Did that contribute to her death?" Charlie asked.

Inola smoothed back a loose strand of ebony hair that had escaped the bun at the base of her neck, tucking it delicately behind her left ear.

"Yes," she said, waving a manila folder in the air. "There's a rather detailed explanation of a rare interaction. You can read it for yourself—on one condition."

Charlie put his hands into his pockets, wondering what stipulation she might put on his reading the coroner's report.

"And what would that condition be?" he said.

"First, drop this hokey country-boy facade," she said. "Don't smirk like that. You know exactly what I'm talking about. You're going to tell me exactly how you knew that Dinah Browning had black licorice in her system."

Charlie uncrossed his arms and leaned over the table between them, bracing himself on the top with the palms of his hands.

"Right now I'm going to remind you that you're the one who dragged me from my seminar today and into the middle of your investigation," he said condescendingly. "I'm not even supposed to be here."

She matched his position, leaning in herself, until their hands were scant inches apart and her nose almost touched his, her breath hot and forceful.

"Indeed," she said. "You're just full of yourself, aren't you?"

"Indeed," he echoed. "You're looking a gift horse in the mouth. If you've read my file, you already know what I'm like and you wanted me here anyway. You must be pretty desperate to solve this case."

Inola leaned back, her hand splayed across her throat in a helpless gesture that acknowledged she'd lost the standoff. With an air of resentful admiration, she took a step back and reassessed her conceited, gloating opponent.

"All right." Her voice took on an unwilling conciliatory tone. "Give me a reasonable explanation for how you knew to look for a substance not even the medical examiner suspected, especially since, as you said, you aren't even supposed to be here."

Charlie bit his lower lip.

"I've read your file. Tell me something I can believe." Her eyes bored into his. "Otherwise you're going to find yourself on the unfriendly side of my good-natured disposition."

She forced herself to lean away, the toe of her sturdy shoe tapping against the concrete slab floor, slowly at first and then picking up both speed and intensity.

Darn, the woman loves to tap on things, he thought. *Repressed anger, I bet.*

Charlie realized that as a federal agent she had a great deal more power over him than he'd like to admit. He needed a bone of truth in order to appease her.

I can't admit Cora's involvement in an ongoing case, Charlie thought. *Up to now there's only been conjecture. No admissions. No confirmations. We're not partners anymore. Verifying that a piece of data came from her dreams will jeopardize her security and her anonymity, not to mention what it could do to my career.*

"I had a gut feeling," he said, keeping his voice level. The tapping stopped.

"That's it?" she said skeptically, irritated by his hesitation, her instincts screaming that he was withholding vital information she needed to know. "Does your gut feeling have a name?"

"No," he lied, swallowing hard and fishing around his pocket for his pack of gum. His lips felt stuck to his front teeth.

The toe of her shoe tapped again, joined by fingers drumming steadily against the suit sleeve covering her upper arm.

"You're lying to me," she said bluntly. "We were getting along so well, and now you've decided to hold out. You've no idea how dangerous it is to lie to a federal agent, especially when you're doing it so badly."

Charlie reconsidered his dwindling options, retreating against the two-way wall, staring up at the clock above the frame. Almost four in the afternoon.

He methodically unwrapped a stick of gum and then rewrapped it.

Cora wouldn't call again until tomorrow morning, if she called at all. The whole situation could change in twelve hours. The sweep of the second hand kept pace with the rapid beat of his heart.

"I don't know what else to say," he said, returning the gum to his pocket.

Keep your mouth shut, he admonished himself. *Stop talking.*

What's the matter with you? She can't make you say anything else. Think about Cora. Think about the consequences.

The cell phone in his back blue jeans pocket vibrated, startling him as he jumped slightly away from the wall. He saw Marcie's name and thought immediately of Elvira, wondering if there'd been an accident and if they were okay.

He frowned, his facial expression betraying his concern both for his friend and his dog. Walker immediately misconstrued what she saw.

"A call from your gut feeling?" Inola asked, pulling out the chair in front of her and making herself comfortable. "How interesting. Do answer."

The cell phone continued to vibrate, a humming call to action.

"It's my landlady in Balfour," he explained, still staring at the caller ID and the blinking buttons. "She takes care of my dog. I don't know why she's calling."

"Then you'd better answer," Inola said. "Tell her to get your room ready and let Elvira and Marcie know we'll be paying them a little visit tomorrow. And you, Detective Abbott, are going to introduce me to your friend Cora Stone. We'll see what she can tell me about this gut feeling of yours."

Chapter 25

Thomas found Cora in the backyard with Jane, walking hand in hand and counting the tiny yellow and white butterflies that hovered around one of the multiple blooming bushes.

Solomon, completely disinterested in the process, yawned from his post inside the sunroom, tiny rows of shark-sharp white teeth lining his pink jaws and mouth.

Upon seeing her foster father, Jane took a running leap and wrapped her tiny arms around his knees, effectively hobbling him and preventing him from moving any further until he reached down and tenderly lifted her up.

"Butterflies eat flowers," she announced happily. "The sweet part inside. It tickles, but you can't hear them laugh. The flowers don't mind."

Cora smoothed the baby fine hair back from the child's forehead and kissed her, then added another kiss to her husband's cheek.

"How was your day?" she said. "How's Susan holding up?"

"She finally heard from Harry. Twice today," he said, hugging the little girl closer and patting her back affectionately. "She talked to him this morning at the office, and then he called her late this afternoon. They're flying back tomorrow."

"The investigation is over?" she asked.

"Not exactly." He rested his chin on the child's head. "Did you make that call we talked about at lunch?"

Cora nodded without speaking.

"Jane," Marjorie called from the sunroom doorway, "come inside, please. Would you help me set the table for supper?"

Thomas knelt to place the squirming girl on the ground.

"So much energy," he said as the child skipped happily away.

The French doors closed, and he turned to his wife.

"I didn't want to say anything specific in front of Jane," he said. "Charlie's coming with them."

Cora searched for a hint of recrimination or irritation in her husband's words and found none.

"It's because of what I told him, isn't it?" she said. "I'm sorry."

There was no point in denying what they could not change.

"Don't be sorry for doing the right thing," he said, reaching around to draw her closer, her head resting comfortably against his chest, her face upturned. "I don't know what's happening except for what I've pieced together from what you and Susan have told me. Harry told her that there's an FBI agent in charge, and she's coming to Balfour to continue the investigation."

"But I thought Harry's sister committed suicide."

"Susan said they aren't questioning that. It's confusing, but this agent thinks there's something else going on. That's where

Charlie comes into the equation."

"Because of my phone call," she said. "Because I gave Charlie clues and now it's coming back to me, to us."

"Harry told Susan that the FBI agent already knew all about Charlie," Thomas said. "It's not your fault he's good at his job. He's got a high profile. And Harry is from Balfour. There could be all sorts of reasons why they'd want to come here."

"That's true," she said, unconvinced.

"I had a piece of pecan pie at lunch," Thomas confessed, searching for any topic he could use to change the subject. "From Sam's."

Cora slipped her arms around his waist, her hands linking together at the small of his back as she tightened her hold.

"Well," she said sweetly, "there's no evidence of your indiscretion here, so you're off the hook. Fair warning, Marjorie and Jane made cookies today too. Temptation and troubles are everywhere."

Yes, they are, he thought, returning the strength of her embrace. *And I'm the one who may have caused the biggest trouble of all.*

Thomas looked down tenderly at his wife.

"I don't blame you, love," he said. "You asked me, and I told you to call Charlie. This is on me too. We'll get through it together."

Chapter 26

The Third Day: Tuesday

Cora opened her eyes and realized she was not in the kitchen.

Instead she was standing in the midway of the Franklinton County Fairgrounds, a vivid and pleasant memory of the annual fall trips she took in her youth with her grandmother. A fall breeze brushed her face.

Beside her in a blur of passing monochrome faces there were families laughing and snacking and couples strolling arm-in-arm.

In the background she could see an enormous creaking Ferris wheel, its decal-covered buckets scraping the darkening sky as it turned, and in the foreground to her left, a merry-go-round full of stampeding wooden horses carrying clinging riders.

The scene might have been enjoyable but for the fact that she knew this was one of the dreams. There were no colors to be found in the scenery or the people.

More urgently, she knew she should be paying attention for clues. But her senses were overwhelmed, hard-pressed to sift the significant from the trivial.

The crowd around her pressed in, forcing her to one side of the midway into the row of sideshows, where she stopped just outside a battered canvas tent.

A cloud of incense, thick and sickeningly sweet, encircled where she stood.

In the draped opening stood a youthful Aunt Phoebe dressed in a peasant blouse and flowing patchwork skirt, rows of shining necklaces around her neck and an equal number of charm bracelets noisily encircling her wrists.

Huge hoops hung from beneath her tousled curling hair.

"Aunt Phoebe?" Cora asked.

Ignoring the greeting, Cora's aunt jumped right to her sales pitch.

"Fortunes," she said coyly, her claw-like nails reaching out, the metal of the rings on her fingers digging painfully into Cora's upper arm. "I can read your fortune."

Cora allowed herself to be pulled into the tent, bumping awkwardly into the small card table and two metal folding chairs just inside.

"Sit here, my dear," the woman murmured, pressing Cora into the seat closest to the entrance and sliding into the opposite chair.

Oppressive autumn heat enveloped Cora as she struggled to breathe.

"I've made refreshments." The ringed hands fluttered, spotted moths around a flickering flame. "Let's get acquainted, shall we?"

Cora's eyes adjusted rapidly to the semidarkness, her pupils widening as she inspected her surroundings.

A pot of tea sat in the center of the dingy lace tablecloth, flanked by a set of delicate floral-patterned cups and saucers amid a sea of lit candles.

Cora wondered, her stomach mildly protesting, how many times the cups had been washed, if at all, between customers. She shuddered, resisting the urge to check for lipstick stains around the rims.

To one side, a worn deck of faded Tarot cards lay fanned facedown in a semicircle. On the other side there was a cloudy crystal ball, the surface oily with the residue of fingerprints, resting on a polished dark marble base.

The fortune teller poured a generous cup of the pungent, cloudy liquid, pushing it gently toward Cora.

"Drink, my dear," she said. "The tea leaves have much to say."

Cora ran a reluctant fingertip down the handle of the cup and considered her options, leaning over and taking a hesitant whiff, struggling to identify the odor.

Her nose wrinkled involuntarily.

The smells of twisted candy vine rope and nasty jelly beans filled her nostrils.

"No?" the woman said abruptly, snatching the tea away so the cup clattered noisily against the saucer, the black liquid splashing out and onto the tablecloth.

"You'd prefer your fortune from the cards then."

That explains the stains, Cora thought. *It's Aunt Phoebe's licorice tea. That's what I'm smelling. So I'm not the only one who's rejected your brackish concoctions. Maybe the cards have a different clue.*

The fortune teller scooped up the deck with the pointed tips of her nails, the messy pile resting against her wrinkled palm.

She held them out suggestively.

"Take them," she said. "Go on, they won't bite you. Astra will read you, if you're not afraid to see your future."

Astra? Cora thought, her eyes darting curiously around the hazy confines of the room. Her mind tried to work out why her Aunt Phoebe would call herself a different name.

"Really now, Aunt Phoebe," she said carefully. "Who is this Astra?"

"She's a fake and a charlatan in another world," the fortune teller whined. "She stole my tea, so I shall steal her name."

Without warning, the cards were pressed into her open hands.

"Shuffle," the woman hissed softly. "Then cut."

Cora complied as best she could, placing the halves side by side, folding her hands in her lap and awaiting further instructions.

"Morning's coming," the fortune teller said. "One more step. Hurry."

Cora's mouth went dry.

By and by, when the morning comes. The words of James's hymn. When the saints of God are gathered home. We will understand it better by and by.

"Take a card," she barked.

Cora flipped over the top card, revealing a drawing of a skull, stark against an otherwise gray background.

The skull was simple and almost comic. Round, spiral circles sat inside the eye sockets above two teardrop-shaped nostril openings. Below them rested a single row of elongated teeth and a slack-jaw bordered by bare bones.

This isn't a Tarot card at all, Cora thought, mystified. *What does a skull have to do with tea or licorice or a woman named Astra who's a fake and a charlatan?*

And Cora was awake, staring at the red clock numerals projected on her ceiling—2:34 a.m.

The numbers winked at her suggestively. All the images she had seen created a checklist in her mind, beginning with the fortune teller.

Licorice, tea, cups, cards, Astra, a strange skull, and a time, 2:34.

She thought about getting out of bed and decided against moving any more than necessary, reaching for the notebook she'd brought up from the office and replaced in its familiar place in her nightstand.

Thomas rolled away from her, blissfully unaware even when she clicked on the dainty lamp beside her so she could see to write.

Well, she thought as she scribbled, *Charlie wanted details. I hope he can make something more out of them than I can.*

Chapter 27

The early morning spring sunlight streamed through the sparkling bay window of the Balfour Bed and Breakfast in cheerful shafts of greeting, but Stewart Wilton was immersed in the screen of his laptop computer, and he barely seemed to notice.

Neither the sprouting tender branches and the expectant, budding blossoms of the dogwood trees just outside nor the warmth of the brilliant rays of light illuminating the chair where he sat could distract the man from his mission.

His aristocratic, patrician face crinkled periodically in concentrated frowns, his white bushy eyebrows knit in a continuous line above his piercing gaze as he scrolled up and down the spreadsheets with methodical precision.

Any other tenant at the bed and breakfast would have been politely chastised and told to immediately remove the offending electronics from the vintage antique dining table. The Senator, by virtue of his social status as well as the duration and purpose of his visit, was being accorded a far wider latitude.

So, despite the formerly unbending rules of the house, Darcie Jones refilled his cup of coffee for the third time, removed the breakfast plate and the uneaten half-biscuit with muscadine jelly, and retreated to the kitchen without her customary critical comments.

Biting her tongue didn't come easily to the innkeeper, even when her silence was in her own best interest.

There was no one else in the dining room except Darcie, and no one in the kitchen except the preoccupied cook, who was washing and prepping the latest spring produce from the garden patch.

The teenage girl who'd been recommended by Ellie Sanderson was busy on the second floor cleaning, vacuuming, and dusting, checking off the multiple items on her employer's demanding list of specifications.

The house was eerily silent—a calm before the onslaught of the weekend guests. Darcie's intention had been to use the time to discuss items she believed to be of crucial importance concerning the upcoming opening, but the Senator continued to wave her away.

She felt stung and neglected. She wanted her opinions heard.

Virginia Evans and her designated representatives had gone over and above expectations, making certain that every adult citizen who wanted to, and some who didn't know they wanted to, would be involved in the process of opening the house.

Consequently, every resident at this point believed that he or she had a right to a freely expressed and open opinion.

Even Quincy, the crotchety postmaster, found himself engaged in the crucial distribution of flyers, posters, bulletins, and mailers to all the surrounding towns, cities, and counties.

"Made me feel darn near as patriotic as I've felt since the war," Quincy loudly announced to everyone who came into the tiny brick post office to buy stamps or mail a package. "Just what this town needed—a common cause!"

No one knew exactly what war Quincy meant, but from his cryptic gnome-like appearance "the war" could have meant anything from the Korean Conflict to Desert Storm and all military operations in between. No one knew for certain. No one was bold enough to ask.

Darcie grew bored with alternately peeking in at Wilton and discussing the virtues of cherry tomatoes with the cook, so she decided to slip up the back stairs to survey her kingdom.

Much to her surprise, she was able to praise the quality of the cleaning the teenage girl had achieved on the second floor, especially the spotless bathrooms.

I need to ask Ellie if she knows anyone else, she thought. *I could use another person like this one. At least someone has respect for a job well done.*

She sent the new hire to the kitchen to help the cook prep vegetables, and descended the stairs with an air of self-pity, racking her brain for an excuse to begin a conversation with her lone boarder.

She was saved the trouble of pretense when the Senator called out her name.

"Yes?" she said sweetly, her vibrantly painted maroon gel nails gripping the white frame of the doorway like cat's claws. "Did you call me, Stewart?"

"Someone's at the front," he said, not looking up. "They've knocked twice."

"Oh," she said, deflated. "It's probably Jenkins here to talk about security for the opening on Saturday. I texted him to come around to the back door, but he obviously didn't get my message."

She started walking to the foyer when Wilton's voice bellowed a second time.

"As long as you're in here . . ."

He didn't wait until she was actually in the room to continue in his strongest tone of disapproval, tapping one of the lists on the screen.

"Why have we contracted with Vicki to supply flowers? The gardens at the house are in full bloom. Why would we waste good money buying something we already have plenty of?"

Darcie's expression froze on her face as she resisted the urge to put her hands on his neck and throttle him soundly with his own necktie.

Men, she thought sourly. *He's been sitting there for over an hour and a half and all he can do is criticize. And it's something he knows nothing about. Flowers, indeed.*

"Well, Stewart," she said, chewing at the inside of her lower lip as the furrows between her eyebrows grew deeper, the barest barbs of sarcasm like an army of tiny stinging fire ants in her tone, "we can certainly cut the blooming flowers outside and move them into vases inside the house, but then there'd be a question about what to do about the bushes in the formal gardens once we've stripped them bare."

Wilton's hand lifted to his smoothly shaved chin and he rubbed it thoughtfully, as if he were applying the logic of Darcie's explanation to his face.

"I suppose barren bushes would be awkward when we are trying to promote the formal gardens for commercial photography."

His patronizing tone indicated that he was still not totally convinced of possible flaws in his thinking.

"So, that's all well and good, but where is Vicki getting the flowers she's using inside the house? Aren't we overpaying for those? It's spring. They should be cheaper."

Darcie bit her artfully painted lower lip a little harder, counted to ten in her head, and reminded herself that she needed to be more tolerant, especially with a long-term, well-paying guest like the Senator.

She reminded herself that she had wanted a conversation with him.

There was another much louder and more impatient knock at the front door.

Jenkins will just have to wait, she thought, increasingly frustrated with the two men who were in this moment complicating her life. *Or maybe he could just check his text messages and show up at the right door.*

Darcie calmed herself and launched into one of her many prepared speeches.

"There are a number of long-established gardeners, ladies in Balfour who have prize-winning gardens and gorgeous yards," she said. "Dogwoods, azaleas, magnolias, irises, violets, wisteria, peonies—most of those are in bloom. Vicki's made a valiant effort coordinating with those women for individual vases of flowers in all the rooms, each with a label containing the contributor's name and the type of blossom written in calligraphy on fine linen place cards. Vicki's saved us enormous amounts of money and hasn't charged us a penny for consulting or arranging. We should be thanking her."

Wilton crooked his head sideways and eyed her with skepticism.

"That sounds terribly complicated and unnecessarily complex," he said. "Is that really the best way to handle this problem?"

Spoken like a man who hasn't lived with a woman for fifty years, she thought. *You've no idea how important flowers are to women and even less how community spirit and pride play into our town. You've no clue how to decorate a home for an open house.*

"I can understand that you don't understand," she said, the words oozing like honey between her recently whitened front teeth and tight lips. "We feel it is important to involve the community as well as give credit where credit is due."

The Senator didn't know it yet, but the generous cup of Darcie's patience was officially drained.

"But what about the flowers that Vicki is bringing?" he persisted. "Why are we paying her? Can't we just get more flowers from the local women and use those?"

Darcie's eyes rolled back into her head.

The fourth pounding knocking at the front door was interrupted by the sound of friendly greetings and jovial conversation on the porch.

Well, thank goodness for whoever intercepted Jenkins, Darcie thought gratefully. *You'd think I was the only one around here who knows how to handle a problem.*

She stared down the Senator, all her ire laser-focused on his face.

"There weren't enough local women to provide all the flowers we needed," she said. "Especially for the individual tables where people will sit during the ceremony and reception. For those, we wanted matching vases filled with bouquets of wildflowers."

"I don't understand how they can be matching if they are all wildflowers."

"Stewart!" she snapped, wondering why she had ever wanted to engage this man in a dialogue. "Wait and see on Saturday."

Striding across the room to his table with deliberation, she snatched up his empty cup and saucer with her remaining tolerance for his shenanigans.

"I'll have Anna bring you a cut-up fresh peach with extra cream and more coffee," she said. "There's still quite a lot to be done before Saturday morning, and I'm expecting other guests for the weekend, so I know you'll excuse me to do my work."

He scratched his head, bewildered at the mercurial changes in her tone and disposition.

What's gotten into her? he thought. *Darcie's usually so accommodating. She's awfully touchy this morning. Must be all the pressure of the opening on Saturday. She's just not herself.*

He looked longingly at the space where his cup had been and then at the kitchen door, still swinging slightly from the landlady's hasty departure.

Sighing heavily, he resigned himself to reviewing the computer files, searching for more ways to improve the budget and streamline the process for maintaining the house once the initial opening weekend was over.

Women are so confusing, he thought. *Here I am helping. She doesn't seem to appreciate what I'm doing. I'm certainly blessed I don't have to live with a woman full time anymore. I don't know how married men manage to keep their sanity.*

Chapter 28

Charlie wiped at his bleary eyes and stared longingly at the one-cup coffee maker in his hotel room, longing for caffeine and wishing he'd stopped on the way back last night and bought a dozen donuts.

Cora's early morning call had disturbed his already uneasy sleep.

"I don't have any idea what you are trying to tell me," he muttered, determined not to share Inola Walker's threats to come to Balfour. There was time for bad news when he saw her later today. "The sun isn't even up yet."

That's fair, Cora thought. *I did wake you out of a sound sleep, and I don't have the least idea what I'm trying to tell you either.*

But that's not what she said.

"Charlie, the dream was at a county fair. There was a fortune teller. That's what I saw. A card table with a tea-stained cloth, several china teacups with saucers, and my crazy Aunt Phoebe wearing some sort of gypsy costume."

"Is there more?"

She read the items from the notes she had scribbled in the middle of the night.

"A name. Astra," she said. "And a time . . . 2:34."

"Astra?"

"Well, it was my Aunt Phoebe who called herself Astra. It's complicated. I think you're looking for a middle-aged, rather frumpy and nondescript woman who wears too much eye shadow and makeup. She's got unkempt streaked hair, and she'll be wearing a peasant skirt and blouse."

"Wow," Charlie said. "That's pretty specific."

"Aunt Phoebe was always memorable in her own right," Cora said. "I felt as though I was watching her give a command performance."

"What makes you think the time is important?"

"Just a strong feeling," she admitted, pulling her robe closer. She didn't want to tell him that she thought the red clock lights were blinking at her. There were some things she didn't want to admit she'd seen, even to Charlie.

"Anything else?"

Charlie was awake now, fumbling through his pockets to find his notebook, and was jotting down what she said.

"Yes," she said. "There was a Tarot card with a skull."

"Which Tarot card skull?" he asked. "The traditional one with the roses coming out of its mouth?"

"You know about Tarot cards?"

He ignored her jibe.

"Seriously," he said. "What kind of skull? A photograph or a drawing of a real skull? Can you describe it?"

She closed her eyes and visualized the skull from her dream.

"Not realistic," she said. "More like the Day of the Dead without the gaudy colors or flowers. Representational. The fortune teller claimed it was a Tarot card, but I looked at examples of decks when I couldn't go back to sleep. If it was a Tarot card, it wasn't from any set I could find online."

Somewhere in his subconscious a seed of memory sprouted.

"Fortune tellers and skulls," he repeated. "Tea and Tarot cards. Could be the words to a rap song."

This sounds so familiar, he thought. *Why does all this sound so familiar?*

"I don't feel like laughing about this, Charlie," she said.

"And I don't feel like apologizing again for trying to make the best of a difficult situation," he said. "So here we are, one more time."

Cora wanted to say she was sorry, but she wasn't.

"I'll call you if I remember anything else that might be useful," she said and abruptly hung up the phone. She'd come back up from her office with her vanilla coffee, hoping to talk to her husband before anyone else was awake.

She reached for her laptop on the foot of the bed, where Solomon now slept only when he wanted a reprieve from Jane's fervent attentions. Thomas was rattling about in the bathroom brushing his teeth, and Marjorie was moving around in the bedroom next to theirs, singing along to Christian music from her CD player.

Jane's door was still closed when she came up.

Cora swung her feet over the side of the bed, letting them dangle for a moment while she considered what she needed to do next.

I'm blessed, she thought. *I need to count my blessings.*

Charlie, however, armed with perplexing clues, wasn't feeling blessed at all.

It wasn't even Wednesday and he was craving donuts. And a hot shower.

Almost an hour later he was shaved, dressed in clean jeans and a dark-blue polo shirt with his favorite sneakers. He'd also polished off the second cup of black caffeine from the foil-wrapped individual packet of ground coffee and the protesting, gurgling coffee maker. He'd get more at the Germantown station, and better, although he knew he wasn't capable of resisting the urge to stop and get donuts on the way.

There was only so much hospitality he was ready to accept from his fellow officers, especially when he had no idea about their regular routine.

He wasn't going to show up empty-handed and expect anyone to share food.

He had no inclination to accept favors from Agent Walker either. He debated whether or not he should share Cora's latest revelations and then realized he might not have anything to lose by naked honesty.

It is what it is, he thought. *She knows what she knows.*

Fortune tellers, tea leaves, artsy skulls, a woman named Astra, and 2:34.

It was the strangest list of leads he'd ever had, but then licorice was ranking up there too.

He wasn't surprised by Walker's mildly irritated reaction when he arrived at the station, three dozen hot donuts in hand, and asked to see her privately.

This woman blew hot and cold like the changing spring weather in Georgia.

One minute she acted like he was the favorite son, and the next she was treating him like a red-haired stepchild. He couldn't tell where he stood, but then maybe that was the point. To keep him off-balance.

"I don't suppose you've got more hunches this morning," she said, refusing his donut apology and closing the interrogation room door firmly behind them.

He shrugged.

"Actually, that's exactly what I have," he said, but she stopped him from going further with a wave of her hand.

"Wonderful," she said. "Tell me what you know that I don't know."

"Does the name Astra mean anything to you?"

Inola's pupils widened, although her expression didn't change.

"Score one point for you," she said. "I'm listening. Anything else?"

Charlie looked longingly at the donut boxes, wiping his palms against his jeans.

"She's not in Memphis anymore," he said, spouting conclusions he'd drawn from Cora's notes in the car ride to the station. He'd found it easier to connect the dots than he'd expected, like skipping stones on a placid pond. "She's a tea leaf, Tarot card reading fortune teller in Atlanta."

"That's pretty specific," she said. "But even if you're right, Atlanta's a big city. She could be there and it would take days or weeks to find her."

Charlie coughed. He wondered how far he could or should go.

He'd no idea whether he could trust this FBI agent not to take what he gave her and run with the clues without him. Especially when he'd remembered where he'd seen the skull.

"Don't think," Inola snapped impatiently. "Talk."

"There's a community in Atlanta called Little Five Points, full of artists and creative people. The perfect place for someone as eccentric as Astra to hide in plain sight. Maybe you've heard about it."

"I've heard. We're still talking about Atlanta. You can't possibly check even one neighborhood in a single day. This woman will see you coming."

"I don't think she'll be expecting me," he said. "Besides, I'm pretty sure I know where she's going to be around two thirty tomorrow afternoon."

"That's not just specific, that's downright prophetic, detective."

"Maybe," he admitted. "You asked me what I know. I told you."

Inola Walker cupped her chin in her palm and pressed her forefinger against her upper lip with ominous deliberation.

She locked her focus on Charlie, and he felt like a specimen pinned to an insect display board.

"I want to talk to Cora Stone."

"No," Charlie said, squirming unpleasantly. "Absolutely not."

"You aren't in a position to negotiate," she said coldly. "I told you yesterday what was going to happen, and I don't say things I don't mean. We—and to be clear, I mean you, me, Mr. Halstein, and his police escort—we are going to fly to Balfour this afternoon on that charter plane Senator Stewart Wilton so graciously provided. You have my conditional permission to take Officer Smith with you in the morning to Atlanta to look for my suspect in Little Five Points. Before you go, however, you're going to arrange a face-to-face with your former partner Cora Stone."

Charlie opened his mouth.

"Stop before you say something stupid," she cautioned. "I'm not in the mood. You don't need to know why. Let's just say I've read her books on childhood trauma, and I'm impressed by her intellect. Let's just say I'd like to get to know your friends and associates a little better. Let's just say that I'm going to be as forthcoming about my reasons as you are about the source of your hunches."

Crossing her arms across her chest, she tapped her fingers against her upper arm.

"Take it, or I take your information and leave you cooling your heels in Germantown while I go to Balfour without you."

The muscles in his jaw clenched until his teeth started to ache.

Here she was blowing hot again. He hated that he could almost see her point. She was curious. It was her job. In her DNA.

Maybe she'd read about Cora in his file and she had some morbid desire to meet the other half of the team that brought down Brackett and his band of serial killers, and this was her thinly veiled excuse.

Or maybe she suspected Cora was his source.

Either way, he had to protect her.

"Then I don't have a choice, do I?" he said finally.

He didn't want to imagine what would happen if an FBI agent showed up on Cora's doorstep without any warning. She thought she was safe. He flattered himself that he would know what to say if he could only get there first to explain, to prepare his ex-wife. If he went, he might even be able to persuade Inola to change her mind. Maybe. He had to try.

"You never had a choice," she countered. "I've got an agent standing by to take you back to your hotel to get your things. You can brief Officer Smith on the plane and discuss how the two of you are getting to Atlanta tomorrow. Hopefully he'll be receptive to your cockeyed suggestions. For whatever reason, he seems to like you."

Chapter 29

The drive through the winding mountain roads was predictably pleasant.

Katy Wilton was relieved. The meeting at Sam's had been much more stressful than she'd anticipated, and she was thankful that Virginia Evans had been there to offer support.

No matter how much Katy wanted life to return to normal after her husband Steve's murder, there were some things about small town life that never changed. She couldn't walk down the street, shop in the local stores, deliver Elizabeth to preschool, even attend the services at Emmanuel without feeling the pity radiating from a sea of staring eyes.

The well-intentioned sympathy overflowed and suffocated her.

Katy's visits with the psychologist had helped her more than she could ever express to anyone. Cora understood how she felt. She knew how uncomfortable and difficult it was to leave the safety and confines of her old room at Amy's house and venture out after the funeral.

It was awkward being the widow of a murdered rapist while also being the sister of that rapist's victim, even if the general public didn't know the full story.

The case had been sensationalized in all the papers and news outlets when it happened, and now that the Senator was back in town on a regular basis because of the Wilton House, reporters were reviving the sordid details. The trial itself was still months away. Dan was filing motion after motion from his prison cell, and she knew that this wasn't at all like the television and movies. Nothing happened that quickly or cleanly. Thomas had warned her that this could drag on for a year or more, becoming, as many things did, much worse before it got any better.

Then there was her complex relationship with Amy as the two of them worked their way through feelings about Amy's pregnancy.

At least the knowledge of paternity was still restricted to those who had actually been in Sam's at the time of the arrest and their spouses. Katy was thankful for that much.

Cora thought most of the problems Katy faced were rooted deep in her childhood, that she needed to deal with those before she could begin to heal from the trauma of Steve's death.

As a result of the hours they spent together, Katy had grown stronger and more confident in her decisions, especially her decisions for Elizabeth's care. She just had no clue how to use that strength in the world outside. Not yet.

The whole situation reminded her of her teenage years. One moment she felt like an adult, and the next she felt like a five-year-old.

Today she was feeling encouraged to step out on her own.

The calm male voice on the GPS called her attention back to the road but could not distract her completely from her thoughts.

She'd never been one for hazarding out on her own, even less since her recent widowhood. She avoided situations where someone might delve into the lurid details of her husband's death.

When Linda called unexpectedly and said that she and the Judge wanted to discuss plans for Katy's part in the opening of the house on Saturday, Katy openly expressed her fears to Cora, who suggested asking the preacher's wife to come along.

Katy's heart was reassured by Virginia's motherly concern and gentle spirit. She felt safe and yet empowered by the older woman's encouragement. The well-respected preacher's wife would make certain that the young widow's ideas were heard.

The Judge, whose presence made her feel like the small child she had been growing up, ate his salad in relative silence, nodding and smiling when Linda nudged him into the conversation, while the two women who had spearheaded the renovation of the Wilton House briefly shared an overview of the opening day for Katy's approval.

Not that anyone needed her approval, she knew that. But the widow was touched that they considered her opinion important. She knew the Senator had left her out of the decision-making process for reasons that were obvious to both of them, but Cora was convinced that her involvement, even in the slightest way, was part of the healing process.

Katy adored Virginia from the first moment they met after Steve's funeral service—her kindness and sensitivity to the situation, her tenderness with Elizabeth, her gentle acknowledgment of Amy.

Most of all, Katy appreciated Virginia's impressive ability to diffuse the Senator's blustering and handle him in the most skillful and unobtrusive manner.

Virginia sensed the painful insecurities that plagued Katy's bruised and battered heart. She insisted that she could be available to spend the entire opening day with both of the sisters, running interference with any and all of the town's well-meaning gossips who might pry or make unnecessary and innocent but hurtful comments.

Amy had declared firmly that she wasn't going, but with the promise of Virginia's support and Katy's newfound courage, she bravely agreed to attend if her sister was going.

All of which had brought Katy full circle to the impetus for her present adventure.

Amy's baby would soon be born, and Katy hadn't yet put a headstone on Steve's grave.

Images of birth and death collided in her mind. Easter seemed the proper time for both welcoming a new life and saying a formal, final goodbye to her husband.

For a rebirth of a sort for the Wilton estate.

She had no idea how to prepare for any of these events, but beginning with the headstone seemed the least challenging. A baby step toward closure.

Katy had no idea how to go about buying a headstone.

The Senator had removed himself from the whole decision-making process. At first that puzzled Katy, but then she realized that putting a stone over his son's body was too final, too painful. He'd put all his hopes and dreams into the grave with his son, and she thought maybe he couldn't take that last step. She understood.

Cora suggested asking local funeral homes and ministers for the name of a suitable company, but neither Katy's preacher, Andrew Evans, or Virginia knew anyone in the area who manufactured and sold headstones.

The funeral home, along with the Methodist minister Reverend Johnson suggested a local monument company located in the nearby mountains. He added that Balfour's UMC secretary, notoriously finicky, had recently contacted the company about providing a preemptive dual headstone for her living parents as an anniversary gift and was pleased with the results, although she complained that the engraver was a bit abrasive and entirely too full of himself.

Katy wondered at the notion of such an odd anniversary gift, but she refused to judge. Balfour residents, as most small towns do, have more than their fair share of quirky ideas and bizarre behaviors. As a native Georgian, she knew that over time the local residents resigned themselves to their neighbors' idiosyncrasies and foibles, settling instead for quiet snickers and hushed tittle-tattle under the guise of conversation.

The Reverend Johnson had assured her that although the memorial stonecutter was rumored to be brusque and a bit crude, he knew for a fact that he was also a decent, hardworking man, descending from a distinguished heritage of blacksmiths and sculptors dating back to the 1850s and whose history coincided with the founding of the town of Balfour itself.

An unmistakably pregnant Amy protested Katy's solitary venture into the narrow, two-lane countryside, but Katy insisted that she was more than capable of programming a GPS and finding her way into the hills and back.

In the end, Amy propped her swollen feet on a padded

footstool in the den with a book and grudgingly conceded that she was in no shape for an excursion on a bumpy country road.

"Besides," Katy said pointedly, "you're due in a little over two weeks. What if you're early? You really don't want to deliver your first baby in the woods north of nowhere out of cell phone reception."

Amy stuck out her tongue, pulled a blanket up to her chin, and took a nap.

Hannah protested as well. But when Katy pointed out that Hannah needed to babysit a rambunctious Elizabeth so Amy could sleep, the housekeeper admitted that Katy was right but still protested that she shouldn't go alone.

She looked down at her faded Levi's, light blue cotton sweater, and her simple flats. She'd removed all her jewelry except a tiny pair of gold hoop earrings. Pulling her dark hair back into a tight ponytail at the crown of her head, she studied her reflection in the mirror.

"You don't look one day older than you did when you started high school," Hannah said. "And you sure don't look like a mama to that baby Elizabeth. Have mercy, sweet girl. Please be careful with all the crazies out there."

All the crazies out there, Katy repeated to herself. *Some people think I'm one of the crazies for putting up with Steve's behavior for as long as I did. I'm tired of following other people's expectations and ultimatums. I want to do what I want to do.*

Besides, she thought, turning the steering wheel lightly under her firm hands, *I shouldn't have to pretend to be someone I'm not with a stranger I've never met. I'm asking him to do a job for me, not be my friend or pass judgment on my behavior or my choices, past or present.*

The woods were dense with fragrant cedars, long leaf yellow pines, and scrub oaks, budding dogwoods and snowy Bartlett pears, fresh with new foliage and growth. Around every turn, pink, fuchsia, magenta, and yellow-dusted white azalea bushes were overgrowing the edges of the road, as spring in Georgia is known to do. Bright green, shiny kudzu vines and wild ivy, along with its sinister poison cousin, crept and crawled onto every available crevice and unabashedly blanketed the landscape in shades of emerald and jade.

The intermittent breeze, filled with the scents of wild honeysuckle and the towering evergreen trees, drifted into the open windows of the silver-gray Lexus, a gift she had given herself for her thirty-fifth birthday from the trust fund her parents had left.

Katy was disappointed when the voice in the GPS announced the last turn onto the driveway of the Balfour Monument Company. She hadn't realized how much she'd been enjoying the drive and the momentary freedom from painful memories.

For several gratifying moments, she'd almost forgotten why she'd ventured out.

Chapter 30

Her first impression of the lone, ramshackle building in front of her was that this could not possibly be a place of business.

The sloping tin roof, rusting in several places, seemed to be holding on to the rafters with not much more than wishful thinking. The doors, mere slats of rough-hewn planks, were hanging crookedly from their hinges, one only slightly more open than the other.

The grounds around the sides and front of the building were littered with bits and pieces of granite in all manner of colors, shapes, and sizes, from finished works of art to misshapen, jagged discards of stone in piles, interspersed with patches of tenacious crabgrass and obstinate dandelions.

Katy parked the car to the right of the building and saw that the makeshift gravel driveway continued on in a sharp curve back to the left. Behind the ramshackle building was a broad open field of switchgrass, and across the sea of green sat a charming wooden house with a front porch swing and hydrangeas in variant shades of purple, blue, and hot pink, blooming rows to either side of the broad wooden steps going up to the front door.

That must be the owner's home, Katy thought. *How inviting! A watercolor picture from an old Country Living magazine cover. It's a shame no one can see it from the main road. But maybe that's the way the owner wants it.*

She looked further past the house and could discern yet another building nestled into the hillside almost directly behind the house but situated on higher ground, a rustic mountain log cabin, unused and abandoned. The grasses were tall and overgrown around the elevated footing. To one side was what looked like a wrought iron fence enclosing a tiny plot of land.

That's the cabin where the original stonecutter lived, she thought. *I wonder if anyone ever uses it for anything. Someone should really preserve it.*

In her distraction, she stepped on a discarded piece of granite and twisted her ankle, her attention immediately back on her own feet. Focusing on where she stepped, she picked her way through the debris to the doorway of the workshop. She didn't know what she'd expected, never having visited a monument company, but she didn't think this was the norm.

The young widow was trying to decide whether the proper etiquette was to knock and wait to be acknowledged or if she should shout out a greeting to announce herself when a friendly voice at her back startled her.

"What can I do for you?"

The pixie of a girl appeared to be around ten or eleven, her pitch-black hair glistening in even cornrows around her friendly ebony face. Her intelligent black eyes twinkled with restrained mischief.

Katy, who was petite herself, saw that she was only a head or so taller than the child, who was wearing fashionably faded jeans and purple high-top sneakers with a long-sleeved lavender cotton sweater.

"I'm looking for the stonemason," Katy said. "I need to buy a monument and have an inscription carved."

"Then you're looking for Zedekiah," she said.

A second voice, deeper and male, startled Katy once again, booming from the doorway of the battered building behind her.

"Naomi, how many times have I asked you not to use my first name?"

"But Father," the child said, cajoling and pleasantly condescending, "she won't know who I mean if I don't use your proper name."

"She has a point," Katy said, admiring the little girl's spunk and teasing logic.

"Please don't encourage her," the man said. "She's incorrigible as it is."

"Incorrigible?"

The stonemason's eyebrows came together in a black, angry cloud above his piercing eyes. His handsome face appeared as hard as the granite around him. She watched as his dark knuckles tightened first around the hammer in his right hand and then hefted the chisel in his left.

"I suppose you think that's a big word for someone like me."

So that's what they meant when they said you're abrasive, Katy thought wryly, noting the similarity in the facial expressions and speech between the father and the daughter. *Maybe that's where your daughter gets her spunky disposition. The apple doesn't fall far from the tree, now does it?*

"I think it's a big word to describe such a diminutive girl," Katy countered, glad she'd had some advance warning about the man's moodiness and refusing to be baited. "My, you are sensitive, aren't you? I suppose that comes with the territory. I hear great artists *are* known for their passionate temperaments."

The color of anger rose under his dark skin, and he made a noise that sounded like a growl.

Katy chose to ignore his reaction, indicating the imposing statue of a sparkling gray-white angel to her right, rising from the granite base like a mighty warrior, sword drawn, resplendent feathered wings a four-foot-wide canopy over the broad shoulders.

"This piece is magnificent," she said. "The archangel Michael?"

"I haven't given him a name," he snapped. "Don't patronize me."

The child who stood between them coughed delicately, her own lips twitching at the corners with barely restrained amusement, before reaching out her tiny right hand to the older woman in solemn greeting.

"We haven't been properly introduced," she said, offering her hand with endearing and unexpected maturity. "I'm Naomi Balfour. This is my father, Zedekiah Balfour, the most talented engraver, sculptor, and blacksmith in Balfour, Georgia. Maybe even all of the Southeastern states. Perhaps we could offer you fresh-squeezed lemonade and molasses cookies while you tell us why you've come all this way to see us."

Katy shook the extended hand warmly, returning the firm grip, swallowing the strong desire to laugh at the child's earnest speech and yet impressed by the young girl's poise and self-assured control.

"I'd love some lemonade," she said, genuinely interested. Something about the relationship between father and daughter was intriguing and honest. Something worth knowing and understanding.

"I've come to select a headstone for my husband's gravesite," Katy offered. "I've heard that your father here is the person who is best suited for what I want to do."

Naomi maintained her grip on the woman's hand.

"I'm so sorry for your loss." She lowered her voice to a sober, sincere murmur that she hoped disguised her age. "How long has it been since your husband passed over?"

What a quaint term from a child, Katy thought. *But it suits her, caring and so serious. There's a precious old soul inside that little girl's body.*

"He died last September," she said. "Rather tragically."

"Do you have any children?"

"Naomi!" the man exclaimed. "You're being entirely too inquisitive. Remember your manners."

"Yes, Father," she said, her bright eyes twinkling, the mischievous lightness returning to her voice. She released Katy's hand. "I've been properly chastised. I'll go and prepare lemonade and cookies."

She looked directly at Katy's face, meeting the older woman's gaze with an expression of polite curiosity that told the adult that the questions were only paused for the moment and had not yet come to an end.

"I'll bring our refreshments out here," she said, calling back as she picked her way skillfully through the workman's granite debris toward the house. "The weather is lovely, and there are quite comfortable stone benches under the pines."

"And Naomi—" Zeke called.

"Yes, Father," she added without turning. "I'll remember to bring the order forms, brochures, and receipt book."

"You have a remarkable daughter," Katy said once the child was out of earshot. "I'm sure you know that."

Zeke Balfour made a gruff mumble of acknowledgment.

"That's kind of you to say so," he said, removing a sweat-stained handkerchief from his back pocket and wiping the powdery granite dust from his dark hands, a film of perspiration forming on his face. "She's always been precocious and bluntly outspoken. Not traits most people can appreciate, especially in a child."

"I find honesty, even the brutal kind, commendable in both children and adults," Katy said, thinking of Steve, of Dan and Amy, of little Elizabeth and the unborn baby girl. Of the pain caused by deception and the potential havoc that could influence the kind of young women they would grow up to be. "I find that truth is always the straightest path in the long run."

She saw the monument maker's curious look, but she found she had nothing more to say, wondering if perhaps she had already said too much.

Chapter 31

Marcie stood with some difficulty, her knees creaking with complaint, and brushed the loose black soil from the legs of her ample overalls. Surveying the neat rows of purple, pink, and red peonies lining the walkway of Piney Woods Building A, she was filled with considerable satisfaction.

She'd waited until the parking lot repaving and repair was done. Just this morning the painters had applied the final fresh white striping and designated blue handicapped spaces, the lines sharp and stark against the shiny asphalt. Recently installed gray concrete bumpers were lined like sentinels along the lower edge of the flower beds.

The construction equipment had been removed, the final orange-yellow dump truck and a lone compactor driven off only this morning, fully exposing the L-shaped woodsy section of land for which the Piney Woods had initially been named.

The landlady inhaled deeply. The fresh spring air was cool and crisp and quiet.

The day laborers had finally gone, along with the temporary construction dumpster and the porta-potty that had marked their first appearance. She felt no pity for them, since there was more than enough work to go around over at the ongoing Wilton House projects.

The two-sectioned parking lot was empty and deserted, only Marcie's lone economy car occupying its customary manager's slot.

Took them long enough, she thought, smoothing her embroidered overalls. *But I certainly can't argue with the quality of the work. Long overdue improvements and well-worth the delays. Add some more flowers and some touch-up paint around the windowsills and doors, and I'll be set for the summer.*

The present absence of cars in the lots didn't concern her. She was completely booked for the weekend for the Wilton House opening. Full capacity, with the exception of Marjorie's and Charlie's suites and her own, of course. Her tenants would begin arriving tomorrow for an early start to the weekend.

A vigorous advertising campaign, word-of-mouth, and the early arrival of spring had combined to create the perfect opportunity for success.

Marcie was feeling productive and content with all the visible progress.

She bent to gather the discarded plastic plant containers littered around her feet and the empty potting soil bags, a tightness to her spine reminding her of her advancing age.

Marcie had been asked to help on Saturday at the Wilton House, but she knew she wouldn't have a second to herself as soon as her own guests arrived. Besides, there were too many annual chores of her own to complete.

"Not that I'm complaining of all the work, mind you," she had said to Darcie in their weekly phone conversation. "I know you know exactly what I mean. I love what I do, but hospitality does have its challenges."

"I do indeed," Darcie said. "Although at least you've been able to do what you need to do in peace. I've had Stewart Wilton underfoot."

Marcie laughed.

"Doesn't he usually stay with those wealthy donors?" she asked, teasing. "What's the draw at the B&B? Maybe I'll have to check out those new amenities you've been bragging about. Or maybe he's just coming to see you."

"Shut up," Darcie snapped. "You're just jealous."

"Not I," Marcie said. "Couldn't pay me enough cash to cater to your high society clientele and hire a cook for fancy food. I'm a country girl at heart."

The line went dead, as it did almost every week, leaving the owner of the Piney Woods listening to her sister's dial tone and shaking her head in sisterly amusement.

Oh, well, Marcie thought. *I guess we all decide what we're willing to tolerate, and my sister doesn't choose to put up with me and my jokes.*

She was considering making another trip to her favorite nursery in Griffith for more plants when she heard Ben Taylor's patrol car coming around the first building and heading for the back parking lot.

The distinctive sound of the Crown Victoria's engine was apparent to her ears. She'd heard it often over the years.

Like any proper Southern woman, she went into her apartment

and checked her refrigerator for sweet tea and cut lemons. Then she thoroughly washed her hands and got two glasses from the cabinet before she heard his car door slam. Ben's hand was suspended for the first knock when she opened the door.

"Fancy seeing you," she said. "Come on in and sit. I'll pour you a glass of tea with extra ice, just the way you like."

"Thanks."

He politely wiped his boots on the welcome mat and took off his police cap before he stepped inside.

"Hello there, Elvira," he said.

The Plott hound lifted her head in sleepy acknowledgment and dropped it again, drooling onto the linoleum in a shiny puddle.

"Sit down," Marcie said. "You're making Elvira nervous."

Marcie put the two full glasses on the table, lemon slices perched on the rims, and then returned to the kitchenette to get a Tupperware container of cookies.

"I just had something to eat," he said, eyeing the treats with suspicion.

"They're Marjorie's," she said. "She baked them on Saturday. Don't think I don't know what you think of my cookies."

He sat down and sheepishly took two of the oversized discs.

"It isn't that I don't like your cookies," he explained, fingering the chunks of chocolate morsels and breaking off a generous piece. "Marjorie's cookies are just—"

"Shut up, Ben," she said. "You'll only make it worse. What's going on? It isn't like you to pay me a personal visit in the middle of the week."

"True," he admitted. "I might as well get to it. Are you booked for the weekend?"

Marcie sat down and took a cookie for herself, crumbling it as she spoke.

"Yes, as a matter of fact, I am," she said. "First time since Christmas. Must be a really important somebody for you to come in person to ask me to take on a boarder."

"No chance of getting a room?"

"Not unless I rent out Charlie's room for the week . . . or Marjorie's."

She saw his hopeful look.

"Don't you even ask," she said briskly. "Marjorie would never give up her privacy and let a stranger stay in her room. You know her better than that."

"Well," he said, clearing his throat, "you can't rent Charlie's room either."

"Of course not," she said. "Charlie's going to be here tomorrow."

He picked up the tea, pushing the lemon away with the tip of his tongue, and drained the icy brown beverage before putting the glass back down, the ice cubes clinking agreeably as they settled against the bottom.

"How did you know? Did he call you?"

"No. I called him," she said, ignoring his scowl. "You're looking for a room for the FBI agent, aren't you?"

"Yes," he said.

Charlie and his big fat mouth. He just doesn't know when to quit sharing.

Marcie felt a sudden surge of sympathy.

"Maybe there's room at the Holiday Inn," she said. "Or over in Griffith."

He bit off another chunk of cookie, his mouth curved upward with satisfaction as he chewed.

"I was trying to keep her with locals," he explained between bites. "She won't have a car, and there's no point in trying to rent a room in Griffith. It's too far. The extra patrol car is in the shop, not that I'd insult her with a police car. AJ says the limo's reserved for Darcie's B&B customers. It's the Wilton House opening, and there's a pack and a half of visitors in town. It's complicated."

Marcie got up to refill his glass of tea, balancing her hand on his shoulder with a friendly squeeze as she rose.

"I get it, Ben," she said. "You want me to offer to be a chauffeur. You're here because you don't want an unaccompanied FBI agent wandering around town without supervision."

"You make it sound like I'm paranoid."

"Aren't you?" she said. "Are you sure she'll see it your way? What if she wants her own car? You could send someone over to get one from Griffith and bring it back to the airport."

"I suppose I could," he admitted. "But I'd rather not. Just doesn't seem too neighborly to me."

"Ben . . ."

He stuffed the last of the two cookies into his mouth and reached for a third.

"Thanks for all the advice," he said. "How about if I just wait to see if she asks for her own car and I deal with it then?"

"How about you remember that I told you that was a crazy idea?"

"Ha, ha," he said. "On another subject, I'm glad you talked to Charlie. He'd be my biggest problem if this other hadn't been dropped in my lap."

"You've got a bigger problem than Charlie?"

"Hard to believe, isn't it?"

She checked his expression to see if he might be joking, but he was as serious as she'd ever seen him. She put a second brimming glass of tea in front of him.

"Okay," she said, suspecting that there was more to the FBI story than he was telling. "I've got your back. Just call if you need me."

"Thanks," he said. "I knew I could count on you."

"Just like I know I can count on you, Ben Taylor," she said with a conspiratorial twinkle in her eyes. "And I'll try not to call you crazy when you do call. Have another cookie and let me get back to work. You and the FBI have soaked up most of my day already."

Chapter 32

The plane ride back to Balfour felt at least twice as long as the initial flight to Germantown, at least for Jim. He was at least twice as restless.

Jim studied Inola Walker, who was seated next to him, staring out the window and casually counting the clouds. The man wondered how anyone could maintain such an impassive, detached expression for such an extended period of time.

"So you know the Senator," Jim said, stretching his long legs out into the narrow aisle and searching unsuccessfully for a comfortable position.

"By reputation only," she answered, pulling her own feet closer, barely missing a collision of long limbs.

He wanted her to clarify what she meant, but she hadn't turned from the window and he couldn't see the expression on her face. He didn't want to pester her.

"Why don't you tell me about yourself," she said. "How long

have you been with the Balfour PD, Officer Smith?"

She was changing the subject, putting the burden of conversation squarely on his shoulders. Shifting his torso and then his focus, he decided Agent Walker wasn't the least interested in the answer to her question, perfectly content to be left alone with her thoughts.

"Not long," Jim said, stifling his inclination to rattle on and on. "It's not really an interesting story, and I don't want to bore you."

He decided it was in his best interest to stop talking, shifting his attention to the interior of the Cessna as he looked across at his other two traveling companions.

The four cushioned, cream-colored leather seats faced each other, a folding table had been removed, and the row of four oval-shaped windows on either side were all curtained and closed, except for Agent Walker's, which she had pulled back herself.

Harry, exhausted from the emotional rollercoaster of his half sister's death and the subsequent investigation, had fallen asleep almost immediately after securing his seat belt in the chair directly across from the FBI agent. The pilot had kindly provided a travel pillow with a fresh case, and Harry had spent the flight with his head propped more or less comfortably between the back of the seat and the window frame, snoring softly and unobtrusively.

Then there was Charlie, brooding silently, slouching across from him.

Beneath the cocky veneer, Jim imagined the detective internally chafing at his second fiddle position, specifically to a woman—an exceptionally tall, attractive, intelligent female.

The signs of Charlie's stress were obvious to the officer—knuckle cracking, bouts of uncomfortable silence followed by random remarks, furtive glances, frown lines around the eyes and mouth.

The most obvious of all was Charlie's unerring deference to authority and stilted polite manners. The detective's withdrawal inside a shell of well-bred Southern chivalry was conspicuous.

The Charlie he knew bantered with all of the female officers in Balfour, friendly and casual. He could make them giggle like teenagers in his own rebellious fashion, the teasing way of a man who admired and appreciated their femininity but who meant them no harm and would defend them with his life.

A doting big brother. A protective, non-romantic best friend. A gallant knight in slightly tarnished armor, his battered blue Volkswagen a further symbol of his revolt against all artificial expectations.

There was not a hint of casual chattiness in his current attitude toward Inola Walker, or, Jim realized, in Charlie's attitude toward Cora. He'd seen the detective interact with his ex-wife on more than one occasion.

Jim had little experience observing divorced couples, but for him it was glaringly obvious that Charlie still cared deeply, his intention that Cora shouldn't know.

He didn't joke with her as he did with others. He didn't tease her. His guard was up. The shell intact.

Like opposite poles of magnets, attracting and repelling with equal force.

A tension not unlike what was happening between Charlie and the FBI agent, although to Jim the conflict here was completely one-sided.

The FBI profiler seemed indifferent to Charlie's presence. She simply sat, her hands folded in her lap on top of her slender gray laptop case, patiently looking out the window of the plane. Her expression never changed, serene and serious no matter what.

Unfazed by the occasional turbulence, she showed no signs of fatigue.

She sat with the detached interest of a professor watching unprepared students taking a final examination, and Jim was completely mesmerized.

He wondered with some morbid fascination if perhaps there was a volcanic explosion lurking just beneath the placid mountain that was Agent Inola Walker, and if he would be privy to the eruption when it eventually came.

He couldn't deny that he hoped so.

A muffled two-way conversation from the cockpit interrupted his thoughts, and he detected masculine voices that could have been Mike or Frank responding to the pilot.

He checked his watch—almost six forty-five p.m. He'd overheard Harry call Susan just before they boarded, and wondered idly what arrangements had been made for the rest of them once they reached Balfour.

He needn't have been concerned. Small town Southern conventions were already in motion. Susan was waiting patiently in the terminal with Ben Taylor.

She'd never exchanged more than a dozen polite words with Balfour's police chief in the entire time she'd lived in the town.

Thomas had expressed admiration for him. He was elected almost unanimously and unopposed every term, but she'd made the assumption that no one else wanted the position. That his longevity was due to blind loyalty rather than ability.

As she watched him interact with the airstrip's two grizzled attendants, she realized that she couldn't have been more wrong in her deductions.

Under the unassuming veneer of a country constable a la Andy Griffith, Ben Taylor seemed to command both respect and admiration.

After Frank had indifferently directed her to a chair in the corner and offered her a lukewarm bottle of Aquafina, which she refused, the two men turned united, undivided attention to their honored male visitor.

Mike produced a frosted white mug sporting the logo of a faded peach from a cupboard in the dingy office, filling it with coffee from a freshly made pot and presenting it to the Chief without ceremony, while Frank pontificated about the merits of the latest Cessna and the new requirements for pilot flight certification.

The three men, armed with caffeine, perched around the massive desk like vultures surveying fresh carrion. They were engaged in an intense discussion on every subject from flying to sports to hunting to politics and back again, all but ignoring her presence.

She was surprised to find herself not the least offended by their behavior.

Susan realized that she had nothing of interest to add to what they had to say, and that was fine with her.

She alternated studying the tips of her recently manicured nails and staring out the picture window at the setting sun, feigning disinterest, although she had to admit to herself that she was greatly entertained by the scene playing out before her.

With all the uncertainly surrounding Harry and the investigation into his half sister's death, she'd been rethinking her place in

Balfour. She hadn't made many friends among the women of the town, and until Harry arrived her life had descended into boring humdrum. She'd come to regard Balfour as a Southern backwater full of good old boys and country bumpkins. Her work with Thomas was the crux of her life.

Seeing Ben with these two men, listening to them, she heard the voices of men of character. Eavesdropping on their conversation reassured her that she was among the most loyal and faithful of mankind. Men who cared. Men like Harry.

She recalled what Thomas had told her about them the day she'd first met them. The day she and Thomas flew in from Atlanta on a chartered Cessna to his grandfather so Thomas could consider an offer to take over the older man's law practice.

She remembered the details well. Details were a vital part of her job description.

Frank, she'd been told, was an A&P certified mechanic who often serviced the planes between trips, keeping them securely in the solitary Anson hanger. Mike was a ham radio operator who had been an air traffic controller at Hartsfield for years before his retirement. Both were licensed pilots themselves, but neither enjoyed flying as much as they liked working as the ground crew and spending time in the Georgia mountains.

Their long-suffering wives, accustomed to having their husbands go off to work every day for years, were pleased that the men had found a useful and productive way to spend their waking hours, going on about their household tasks knowing that the men were equally happy and out from underfoot.

Both Frank and Mike welcomed the breaks in their otherwise mundane and rather lonely routine, spending their days in long games of checkers, endless cups of oily black coffee, tinkering with the inherited planes that had come with the airstrip and the ones that arrived from time to time, and amusing the occasional travelers and tourists who stumbled upon their airstrip.

Between their Social Security payments and the trust fund set up to maintain Anson's, and boosted by the generous fees the Senator paid, both men were living a quite comfortable retirement doing what they had done best before retiring, caring for airplanes, pilots, and passengers.

Susan pulled her attention away from the conversation and checked the time. She'd followed Harry's directions to the letter. She knew the plan.

The plane was scheduled to arrive around seven p.m. Ben was to pick up Jim and Charlie, along with a federal special agent, and deposit them at the police station for a meeting of some sort. She was taking Harry back to his house, then returning to the police station to pick up the federal agent to take her to the Holiday Inn Express, where Susan had dutifully booked a room for the next five days.

Susan had wondered why Harry had asked her to be the designated driver for the FBI agent, but he seemed adamant, so she agreed.

When the plane finally landed at 7:12 p.m. and the passengers emerged, she knew why she had been chosen.

Susan had never seen such a mismatched, ragtag assembly of individuals in her entire life, and the FBI agent seemed to be at the epicenter of the discomfort. The paralegal's feminine intuition drew rapid conclusions as she watched the quartet cross to the building.

Three men, each with his own unique response to Inola, descended from the plane. Jim, in awe of her, loomed behind her like an oversized St. Bernard puppy waiting for permission to be let outside. Harry was doing his best to act like a Southern gentleman without offending her, his expression clearly torn about whether to open the door and offer to take her bag. Then there was Charlie, last off the plane, resembling a rejected suitor who was plotting some trivial revenge.

Susan felt an unforeseen empathy for all three men, but especially Charlie.

I wonder if Thomas knows he's here, she thought. *Surely Cora does. Maybe he's here because of Cora. That would explain so many things.*

Suddenly she was quite ashamed of her snippy attitude toward her boss and her own self-pity. She might be stuck as a chauffeur for an FBI agent, but that meant some other poor soul was stuck with Charlie.

Harry, groggy from his recent unplanned sleep, took his bag from a helpful Mike, shook Jim's hand, and then appreciatively followed Susan to her car.

Jim grabbed his duffel bag and, with a nod of acknowledgment to the pilot and Mike, headed with intention for the front seat of Ben's patrol car, which had been left with the run lock ignition on.

That left Charlie and FBI Agent Walker to share the back seat, hardly a kindness on Jim's part, but at this point he'd ceased to care about anyone's comfort but his own.

Someone else, Jim decided, keeping his vision discreetly forward out the front windshield, could navigate the uncomfortable and generally unpleasant territory reserved for the felonious.

The back seat was made of the traditional easy-to-clean hard plastic and painfully cramped, forcing the unfortunate riders to sit low in the space or bend their heads down. Between the front and back seats, the combination steel mesh and bulletproof glass cage wall was equally intimidating.

Not to mention there were no handles on the inside of the back doors. The occupants were trapped with no way to exit unless they were freed from the outside.

Jim had been in the back seat of a patrol car only once, for the experience of being there, and his oversized frame rejected the notion of climbing back there again.

Jim fancied himself a gentleman, but he wasn't going to play contortionist, even for Charlie or a female agent.

Nonplussed, Agent Walker shouldered her own modest canvas carry-on. She amenably followed Jim, tossing her clothing bag carelessly into the back seat of the police car and gracefully folding her slender, suit-clad body inside, tucking her gray computer case at her side under a protective elbow.

Charlie, last to claim his luggage from the impatient Mike, reached the back bumper of the car just as Ben arrived.

"I guess you won't let me drive," the detective said hopefully.

"I guess you're right," Ben said, chuckling. "Hop in the back, son. If it's good enough for the fed, it's good enough for you."

Charlie meekly leaned down and in, pushing Walker's canvas bag to make room, and slid over, wedging his own flight-approved carry-on onto the narrow floorboard while cradling his backpack in his arms.

Ben inserted the key in the ignition, still amused and a bit distracted by Charlie's unexpected compliance and the equally unexpected aura surrounding the federal agent. His foot slipped on the accelerator, and the police car lurched forward as the unprepared Charlie bumped his head on the reinforced rear window with an audible thud.

"Sorry," Ben mumbled without turning around.

He adjusted the rearview mirror, looking first at the FBI agent, who had secured her own seat belt and was patiently watching the sun set out her window, and then readjusting to come eye to eye with Charlie.

"Buckle up there," he advised. "No one to blame but yourself."

Sure, Charlie thought, rubbing his throbbing forehead and searching for the elusive shoulder strap. *I'm not blaming you. I'm not blaming anyone.*

He stared pointedly and uselessly at the back of the FBI agent's head.

There will be plenty of blame to go around before we're through, he thought. *But if Inola Walker has her choice, I'll bet most of the blame for anything that goes wrong eventually lands on me. I might as well get used to it now.*

Chapter 33

The Fourth Day: Wednesday

Cora opened her eyes. She was sitting in her usual ladder-back chair at her grandmother's kitchen table. The other chairs around the table were empty. The air in the room was chilled as it almost always was, however an odor of decay—a stale and musty scent she could not identify—hung heavy where she sat.

One of her grandmother's antique coal oil lamps glowed from the center of the table, the wick turned low and the light falling in a narrow, pale pool.

Cora was holding a curious object in her hands, the size and weight of a gallon- sized stoneware container, like Gramma Crawford used for pickling cucumbers in the summer, only with a narrow opening like a jug. This jar was unlike any she'd ever seen, a misshapen oddity, striking to the senses and grotesque in its form.

The entire peculiar object, from the cork-sealed opening in the top neck, down the uneven curved sides, and circling the bottom edge, was covered with a thick coating of earthy Georgia river clay into which a bizarre collection of bits, pieces, and random objects had been pressed to dry.

The base was coated with a thinner layer of clay, flat and smooth, cool to her exploring touch.

Cora turned the jar upside down. Scratched almost imperceptibly into the even coating across the bottom was a year—1861.

She righted the jug in her hands, taking inventory of the trinkets and broken baubles littering the surface, tracing them individually with morbid fascination.

Into the hardened clay were pressed fragments of porcelain doll faces, chipped lips and vacant eyes, and a half dozen cloisonné beads with tiny gold wires and enamel, creating intricate patterns.

Between the larger pieces there were multiple transparent glass beads, in black and white so she had no idea what color they might be, and children's cat's eye marbles. Bits of broken chains from necklaces filled in the remaining vacant spots. One tiny tarnished, twisted brass safety pin rested, like an afterthought, near two random buttons.

The seal was an aged, stained cork with a single dark bead pressed into the center, held in place by a rusty straight quilting pin with a glass ball on top. A thin line of wax around the outer edge completed the closure and ensured the security of the contents, and Cora had no clue as to what those contents might be.

One round glass eye, deeply socketed into a rim of white and larger than the others, stared out blindly, the iris swirled like the center of a hurricane. Disjointed lips, cracked and pouting, were pressed just below the eye and to the left, off-center.

Cora's analytical mind attempted to make sense of it, to piece together what had once been the whole. A porcelain doll's face that was once quite lovely now spoke of a melancholy sadness spilling over in waves of anguish.

From the darkness at the edge of the room came a halting voice.

"Do you know what you have there?" Gramma Crawford asked, the creaking of the ancient oak rocking chair in time with the cadence of her words. "My grandmother, your great-great-grandmother Nancy, called them gypsy jars."

Cora, her eyes adjusting to the semidarkness, searched for the source of the sweet sound, reassured to find someone who belonged in the room.

"You've seen one of these before?" she asked the shadowed outline.

"Yes, sweet girl," her grandmother said. "The oldest ones come from country tradition. That one looks authentic."

"Yes," Cora agreed. "1861."

"Sorrow finds us all." Sadness and sympathy flowed from the quavering voice. "A battered heart, a lost baby, a mourning mother. Shattered pieces and broken dreams pressed into cold wet clay."

The lamplight on the table brightened of its own accord, further illuminating the details of the jar she cradled.

As she watched in disbelief, the hardened clay fell into pieces, breaking in half first and then into smaller parts, each section crumbling further between her fingers until the entire object became little more than an irritatingly fine dirt powder full of bits and pieces, a palm-sized partial face and eyeball remaining eerily intact.

The dusty remains, tiny beads, buttons, and bits of glass glittered and winked at her. She ran the tips of her fingers through the dust and found the contents, a small handmade linen bag tied at the top with a faded satin ribbon.

She pulled at the ribbon and poured the meager contents into her palm—a thin gold wedding band, an engraved oval locket on a serpentine gold chain, and a curling lock of fine dark hair tied with another sliver of satin ribbon.

Near the row of windows in the opposite corner of the room, at the edge of her vision, Cora saw her grandmother's shadow rise and stand.

"From what you've got there, looks like the baby was a girl," the old woman said compassionately. "The wedding ring's there too. I'd say her grieving mother scarcely had time to finish before she joined her."

"The jar was in memory of a baby?" Cora said, prying apart the locket to reveal two faded portraits of a man and a woman.

"Yes." Gramma Crawford nodded, a lilt in her voice that seemed to contradict the gloom of her words. "I never made one myself, but I've known women who did. A gypsy jar of remembrance. A story of love and family. A tale that was meant to be told."

Gramma's piercing gaze met Cora's over the top of the glasses through the semidarkness of the room.

"The woman would want someone to know," she insisted. "Cora, the man should know the truth. He doesn't know the truth."

"Charlie?" she said, genuinely bewildered.

"You'll need Charlie later," her grandmother corrected her gently. "No, this time you should speak to another mother. Someone who knows the man. Someone who can reach the man and make him understand. You'll know when you should tell her. She'll know what to do."

And Cora was awake.

Chapter 34

Charlie woke with the full weight of Elvira's fifty-two Plott hound pounds lying horizontally across him, pinning both his knees to the queen-sized bed they shared.

He slapped irritably at the beeping alarm on his cell phone and sat up and stretched, pushing her drooling head aside. A glimmer of sunlight filtered in through the venetian blinds, and he squinted.

"I missed you," he said, flexing his joints. "And I'd love to sleep until noon, but there's not much chance of that with Agent Walker in Balfour."

Elvira yawned with a long, whining yelp, rolling aside, shifting her substantial weight with a thump, and landing parallel to the man, still pressed against the lower half of his body.

"I know," he said. "My thoughts exactly."

He cradled her head in his hands with tender camaraderie and looked into her brooding, sad eyes.

"Don't be pitiful," he said. "I'll make you a fried egg and bacon before I leave. It's better than you're going to get from Marcie. Appreciate me while you can."

An hour later, Elvira had returned to her extended napping on the unmade bed, half-covered by the quilted blanket. Her soft skin was crisscrossed by beams of warm sunlight from the now-opened blinds, and she was snoring contentedly as playful squirrels and chattering chipmunks filled her doggy dreams.

The dispatcher at the Balfour Police Department greeted him with an expected lack of enthusiasm. He was, after all, disrupting her quiet, uncomplicated life and adding to her workload. He never came unless there was trouble, and she knew it well.

At least Burton and Dalton are already in the middle of their shifts, he thought. *I'll be spared their arrogant attitudes and snide remarks.*

"Morning, Charlie," she said without looking up from her paperwork. "Chief's waiting for you in his office."

"Good morning, Jennifer," he said politely. "Did you cut your hair? Attractive."

She grabbed a pen from the collection of pens in the cup at her elbow and wielded it like a small sword, scribbling with apparent irritation.

"Yes. It's Wednesday," she snapped. "The donuts will be here in a few minutes. Running late because *someone* had to pick up a federal agent at the Holiday Inn Express this morning before he could go by the bakery."

Ah, he thought. *You're missing your sugar rush, are you? No wonder you're cranky. Bet that someone drives a shiny red pickup truck and goes by the name Jim Smith.*

"Didn't mean to upset your schedule," he said.

"Oh, didn't you?" she said, finally meeting his boyishly handsome face, her tone saturated with sarcasm. "That would be a first now, wouldn't it?"

The outer double doors opened, a rush of fragrant, cool, early morning air at his back, and her gaze shifted over his shoulder, her demeanor changing instantly.

"Good morning, Officer Smith," she said sweetly, standing to walk briskly around the counter, reaching out for the stack of white bakery boxes.

"I'll be happy to take those from you," she gushed. "The Chief is waiting for you and Agent Walker in his office. I can bring you some coffee when you're ready."

"Good morning, officer," Inola said. "Thank you."

"I've got them," Jim said awkwardly, lifting the boxes away from the young female officer's hands, his gaze avoiding the detective's curious stare. "I'll put them down in the break room while you get the Chief's coffee. I know he likes to wait until the donuts get here to have the first cup."

Inola stood by, her agitation evident in the drumming tips of her fingers on the countertop, until the two officers were out of earshot.

"Hello, detective," she said, lowering her sunglasses and inspecting him with casual disdain, as though he were a bug she had found attempting to enter her house by the front door. "You've made my appointment?"

"No," he said, returning her look of calm cool. "I haven't."

Her eyebrows rose.

"You haven't spoken to Cora Stone about an appointment?" she repeated.

Charlie shook his head, shrugging his shoulders.

"We don't stand on formality in Balfour," he said. "How Cora treats you and what she says won't change, whether she knows you are coming or not. She may be seeing someone for counseling, but Marjorie will give you a cup of coffee and a cookie on the porch or the front room and you can wait for a few minutes until she's free to talk."

"That sounds very—"

"Cora," he interrupted placidly. "It's Cora. It's how things are done in Balfour."

She stared at him quizzically, unconvinced.

"Are you sure this isn't Charlie being Charlie?" she countered. "Maybe you'd just rather not call her and make the appointment for me. That's a distinct possibility, isn't it Detective Abbott?"

Charlie bit down hard on the inside of his cheek to keep from responding. Profilers were like mind readers. All tainted with the same brush.

Jim returned.

"Ready?" he said. "The Chief's got his coffee and a bear claw. We're good to go."

"A bear claw?" Inola said.

"And you call yourself a law enforcement agent," Charlie said, hooking his thumbs into the loops of his jeans and risking a jest at her expense. "I'd take you for a plain glazed. Am I right, Agent Walker? Jim there is a jelly donut man all the way, and I'm just happy with whatever no one else wants."

Jim wasn't sure how to take Charlie's attitude, although he'd been expecting the detective's respectful reserve to crack, especially when he was back on familiar ground.

The dispatch officer returned to her desk.

"The coffee's getting cold," she announced, taking her seat. "But that's none of my business."

Jim spun on his heel and Inola followed, with Charlie blowing a noisy unwanted kiss into the air at the still-disgruntled dispatcher.

It's not her fault, he thought charitably. *The only time I come around lately is when I'm disrupting routines and rural life. I'm a royal pain and everyone knows it. Gotta blame somebody. I'm the face of the problem.*

Ben was wiping the last of the creamy pastry filling from his chin, picking at the bits of slivered almond on his napkin and savoring the final sips of his first cup of coffee when Charlie entered the cluttered office.

Two other cups, obviously meant for Jim and Inola, sat untouched at the edge of the desk, as they stood to one side in mute expectation.

There was no cup for Charlie. He wasn't a regular officer and he wasn't a guest, so Jennifer apparently thought he should fend for himself.

Ben Taylor rolled his eyes under his bushy brows and groaned.

"Let me get this straight, Charlie," he said, leaning back, the ancient wooden office chair matching his grumbling. "You're taking one of my best officers to Atlanta for the day based on one of your hunches, looking for a person of interest who was last seen in Tennessee almost a week ago? Do I have that right?"

Charlie opened his mouth, but Ben interrupted by dramatically clearing his throat.

217

"Agent Walker here is evidently in favor of this unorthodox expedition, so I don't know how I'm supposed to object, although I do."

He patted the badge on his left pocket emphatically, paused, and tossed the crumpled napkin into the trash can.

"Furthermore, Officer Smith has his own duties to catch up with around here," he said, the chair groaning under him again as he leaned backward. "He's been in Memphis and now you're taking him off again before his heels are cool? Are you paying his salary?"

Charlie stared longingly at the coffee cups and kept his mouth shut.

He almost wished he hadn't antagonized Jennifer. But not quite.

"I've reached the critical point in my agenda, Detective Abbott, where your very presence involves altering my plans." Ben tilted the cup and drained the last drop. "So, I'm open to your views and suggestions."

"I—" Charlie said, but Ben continued talking as though he had not asked for an opinion and he were the only person in the room, locking his fingers in a cradle behind his head.

"You'd think," he said, "as the elected executive law enforcement officer, that I'd have some say-so in what goes on in my department. But no. Charlie's in town, and here we go again."

"Chief, I—" Charlie started to say, but he saw Ben's expression and wisely bit his tongue.

Experience with Ben had taught him to let the tirade run its full course. This time Charlie sensed the police chief was nowhere near fully vented.

Out of the corner of his eye, he saw Walker step forward to

the desk, tapping the edge, blocking Ben's view of the detective, commanding his full attention. Her elegantly impressive stature required that the chief of police lean further back in his chair to look up at her formidable presence.

"Excuse my interruption," she said evenly. "Thank you for your cooperation, Chief Taylor. Your concerns are duly noted. Detective Abbott is acting at my behest."

She pressed her slender hands together under her chin and tapped them together lightly as she spoke.

"There is certainly no intention to supersede your authority nor to omit you from the decision-making process," she said, her alto voice steady and soothing. "You're a vital part of our efforts. The agency has reason to believe that one of the prominent members of your community, Harry Halstein, would be benefited by the outcome of our current investigations. Our goal is to do that quickly and efficiently, with as little disruption to your routine as possible."

"Sure," Ben mumbled, a bit overwhelmed by the steady stream of soothing, agreeable words combined with her confidant tone. He lifted his empty mug. "Could someone please get me another cup of coffee?"

"I've got it," Jim said, reaching across the desk, blinking his eyes. "Be right back."

Charlie was thoroughly delighted by Inola's mysterious ability to take charge and placate the Chief in the same breath. He stuffed his hands in his jean pockets and leaned out of the way against the doorframe as the Rookie darted past and returned seconds later.

Hot glazed donuts, she's smooth, he thought. *Credit where credit is due. I could be offended that she's in charge, but I'm not. Ben's not only eating out of her hand, he looks like he's going to grocery shop, cook dinner, and wash the dishes too. He's good, but she's better.*

The Chief took several more sips of hot coffee, digesting the agent's speech, before considering the clock on the wall.

"I suppose if you two are going, you'd better get on the road," he said, sighing. "Do you need a patrol car?"

"Rather not," Charlie replied. "A bit obvious for undercover."

"My truck's not exactly inconspicuous," Jim said, remembering his last rather uncomfortable road trip with Charlie. "But it's available, and I don't mind driving."

"That just leaves you, Agent Walker," Ben said. "I'll get you rides with locals if you don't mind."

"I'm used to Lyft and Uber," she said.

"Sure," Ben agreed, clasping his second cup of coffee like a life preserver in white water. "Don't have much call for those in Balfour. I could also send for a rental car over in Griffith. I could get one delivered to the station by midday."

She closed her eyelids, apparently running through the options in her mind.

"That long? Midday?" she repeated, opening her eyes. "Is there a map of the town I could use to navigate? I suppose I could always use the GPS."

Ben looked sheepish.

"Don't have much call for maps either," he admitted. "Most people in Balfour just know the landmarks for where they're going, and I don't know about the GPS with all the trees around town. We don't get a really clear signal up here in the mountains."

"I see," she said, although she was clearly baffled.

"How about I get a volunteer to drive you where you need to

go?" he asked, repeating his previous suggestion. "I've got just the right someone in mind."

"That sounds like an imposition."

"Not really," he corrected her. "But please, do me a favor and sit in the front seat, and for goodness' sake, don't offend the locals by trying to pay for gas or, worse yet, tip. Balfour folks won't take kindly to being offered money for being neighborly."

"I'm really more used to driving myself, Chief Taylor. I—" Inola began. She was cut off when the desk phone buried amid the stacks of paperwork and folders rang.

"I'll make that call for your ride in just a minute," he said to Inola as he dug through the manila folders and files. "Make me a list of where you want to go today, who you want to see, and in what order."

Inola took a breath and resigned herself to being chauffeured around town. Maybe it would even be better this way. Travel in Balfour seemed too complicated when the rest of the situation was complicated enough as it stood.

He found the receiver.

"And you"—he pointed specifically at Charlie as he picked up the phone—"stay out of trouble and keep in touch with Walker here. I'll see you when you get back."

Chapter 35

"I'll get you out in just a second," Katy reassured the squirming, giggling child in the car seat behind her. With a self-conscious touch-up to her lightly tinted peach lip gloss, she tightened the ponytail at the back of her head. Hannah's words about her youthful appearance echoed in her head, telling her that no one would take her seriously because she looked too young.

Why should I try to look more mature when I don't feel old? she thought. *She and Amy both worry too much.*

Elizabeth kicked the back of the seat in front of her, her sparkly pink and purple sneakers pounding a rhythm. She squealed with typical childish impatience, a Cabbage Patch doll beside her bobbing up and down as she shook the doll by one plump leg.

"Mommy!" she said, her voice rising. "Mommy! I want to be out!"

"Yes, little Lizzy," Katy said. "Right now just be sweet to Dolly."

Katy looked forward to seeing Cora every week for a number of reasons, not the least of which was the growing friendship between their young daughters. From the beginning of their sessions, Cora had encouraged the widow to bring Elizabeth with her.

Elizabeth was enthusiastic and loud, typical for a child her age. Having spent her formative years in the Methodist church nursery and preschool, she was accustomed to interacting with other children and enjoyed their company.

Jane, having never had a playmate her own age, was fascinated by anything and everything Elizabeth did, watching with intense admiration. Despite her quieter, less rambunctious behavior, she too delighted in these times.

The therapy playroom was amply supplied with an ever-changing variety of toys, but Katy made certain that Elizabeth arrived with her well-loved Cabbage Patch doll.

Both girls, despite the differences in their personalities, had in common their generous, kind hearts. Under Marjorie's attentive eyes, they were provided living and stuffed toys alike, with an ample supply of tea party treats and personal attention.

The session today began much like all the others. The two little girls greeted each other as if they hadn't seen each other in weeks, as though they hadn't spent every Wednesday morning since the second week in January in the sunroom of Cora's house under the watchful gaze of Marjorie and Solomon, the cat.

Elizabeth, the younger but more vocal of the two, danced through the hallway, Dolly securely tucked under one delicate arm, her destination clear. Jane, her own two stuffed black kittens in hand, dutifully followed.

Katy stopped apologizing for her three-year-old's boisterous enthusiasm after the first week.

"Marjorie adores spending time with Elizabeth," Cora had insisted. "Jane enjoys having a playmate who comes on a regular basis. They all have such fun together."

Katy agreed, though from time to time she insisted that it was an imposition to bring her daughter along, no matter what Cora said.

She tried to increase Cora's weekly fee, but the therapist wouldn't hear of it.

"Why should you pay me for a playdate?" Cora had said. "You're doing me a favor, you know. And I appreciate having another child in the house. Jane needs a friend."

This morning as Cora closed the office door, muffling the echoes of hilarity coming from the back of the house, she and Katy could hear Marjorie's musical voice join in the merriment.

"Lizzy is in rare form today," Katy said, taking her usual place on the sofa. "She's getting excited about the house opening on Saturday. I wasn't sure she should go, but the Senator really wants her there to be part of the children's storytelling sessions."

"How do you feel about that?" Cora said, taking a seat behind her desk. "Have you decided to go?"

Katy folded her hands and settled against the soft cotton cushions.

"I've thought about it," she said. "Virginia Evans has offered to spend the day with me and Amy."

"Are you comfortable with that?"

"I'm getting there," Katy admitted, picking up a nearby pillow, hugging it to herself as she spoke. "Amy even agreed to go when she found out that Virginia would be with us."

"That's a brave decision."

"I don't feel particularly brave," she said. "I don't know if I could even think about it without someone like Virginia. Going back into the house is going to be hard no matter how different it looks after all the renovations."

"You haven't been there at all?"

"No," Katy said. "The Senator offered to let me get anything I wanted, but I just couldn't go myself. I made a short list for Hannah and her sister. They went for me and packed up our clothes, some special toys, and a few personal books and pictures. I left everything else. It never felt like my house anyway."

"So Senator Wilton has been supervising the changes?"

"Yes," she said. "He seemed pleased with everything when we all had lunch on Sunday. I know he's trying to come to grips with the whole situation. His relationship with Lizzy was never particularly warm, and now he has no idea how to relate to Amy's pregnancy and a second grandchild."

Katy began to pick at the cuticles around her fingernails.

"Do you want to talk about that?"

"Not really," the young woman said. "No one knows. I mean, outside the people who were there the day they arrested Dan. Everyone just assumes the baby is Dan's, and it's better that way for everyone concerned."

"Healing is hard work," Cora said. "What do you want to talk about?"

"There's something I did yesterday, and I'm rather proud of myself," Katy said, slipping to the edge of her seat. "I'd like to talk about that."

"Of course," Cora said, leaning forward. "Tell me about what happened."

"I went to order a headstone for Steve's grave."

Cora took out a folder and her pen.

"That's a major step," she said. "How did that go?"

"I really enjoyed the drive into the country," Katy said. "I felt happy riding out in the mountains all by myself. As though I had a great adventure. I felt more assertive than ever. Is that strange?"

"No," Cora said. "You're finding yourself. Did you find a monument company?"

"I found someone who owns one. His name is Zedekiah Balfour."

"Balfour?"

"Isn't that interesting? One of his ancestors was a founding father of the town. A settler before Balfour was established in the 1850s, or so Hannah says. She says her grandparents told all sorts of stories about those early years. There's a tragic history of what happened, but Hannah insists it was a long time ago and most of it's just gossip. She's sensitive about spreading rumors."

"I can understand that."

"Zeke is really gifted. He has a precious daughter named Naomi. She's one of the brightest, most intelligent children I've ever met."

Katy paused, and Cora looked up from her note-taking, nodding her head in encouragement.

"The father's nickname is Zeke. Don't know how anyone gets that from Zedekiah, but apparently someone does. He's got a chip the size of a yellow pine on his shoulder," Katy explained. "But the work I saw scattered around was amazing, and after meeting his daughter, I'd say he's doing a pretty good job as a single parent."

She paused.

"I don't want to be critical," she said. "About his attitude, I mean."

"You're one of the least critical people I know," Cora assured her. "I'm glad you've found someone you feel you can trust to do the work."

The therapist leaned forward.

"Putting up a gravestone is a huge step toward closure and healing."

"I hope so," Katy said, shifting her delicate form in the chair and twisting her fingers together. "It's easier than dealing with the Wilton House opening. I guess it all comes back to that."

Cora lingered over her notes, waiting for Katy to continue.

"Oh," she said, playing absently with the multicolored circlet on her finger, twirling and fingering the stones. "I'm fine with what-ever happens to the house and the material possessions. There was part of me that felt as though nothing there really belonged to me anyway, or to Lizzy. Except for redecorating one of the bedrooms as a nursery, I didn't change anything after I moved in."

She thought about the abandoned cabin behind the stone-mason's house and the beautiful child and her father.

"I guess I envy someone with a family home. And roots."

She hesitated.

"I think I know what is really bothering me. I grew up in Balfour. Everyone else is helping. I feel as though I should be helping. Not because I'm Steve's wife, but because I live in Balfour and I want to be a part of the community again. I want Lizzy to be part of all this too."

Cora resisted the urge to chew on the end of her ink pen.

She knew what Katy meant about wanting to be part of the

community and not knowing how. This session was about Katy and not about her own feelings, but there was something heartening about knowing she was not alone in how she felt.

"There's enough funding," the widow said. "The Senator has graciously seen to that. Everyone else has found a gift or ability to share. Vicki is helping the gardeners with flowers and arrangements. Local artists have talents in sketching, painting, pottery, even handmade jewelry. There are sewing circles and quilting groups who've made curtains and crafts. Even Darcie has her jams and jellies, not to mention the rest of the cooks and all the specialty food and pastries."

Katy's eyes reddened with unshed tears, and her soft soprano voice trembled.

"I've never been able to do anything except attract photographers."

Cora considered contradicting the young woman, but words wouldn't change Katy's feelings. There was some measure of truth in what the widow said.

Cora held out the tissue box, and Katy pulled several in rapid succession.

"You're expecting a great deal from yourself," Cora said gently.

"I just feel useless," Katy said. "I haven't the gifts or talents the other women have. I've never had the time or the need to explore who I really am or what I might be gifted at doing. Maybe if I'd listened to Amy and gone on to college instead of marrying Steve, things would have been different."

Cora kept silent, letting Katy's thoughts and voice drift away, waiting until the younger woman came back to reality.

"I just wish I could find something, anything, to show

everyone that I want to be involved too. I'm so thankful for Lizzy. At least I can say I'm a mother."

Katy wiped at the corners of her swollen eyes and sniffed.

"That's a lovely thought," Cora agreed. "You're a wonderful mother."

The widow sighed and looked down at her hands.

"Everything I can think of has already been done, and much better than I could ever attempt. I don't really want to call attention to Steve or the Wilton family per se. I want something to celebrate Balfour . . . the history of the town."

"Balfour's history," Cora repeated. "That could be a fascinating research project."

Thomas knows about that, she thought. *He's talked about those times often. His great-grandfather came about the time of the railroad. What was the date? 1873? 1874?*

A vision of the gypsy jar flitted through her mind's eye, and she batted it away.

"I know Balfour's history extends to the 1850s, before the Civil War," Katy continued, her enthusiasm growing. "My parents said there wasn't an actual town until the railroad came, but before then there was already a small settlement named for a blacksmith named Balfour."

Her pale face lit up, and she clapped her hands in pure joy.

"Zeke! His name is Zeke Balfour. If he's related to the original Balfour, maybe I could persuade him to make a statue or sculpture to display at the Wilton House. It wouldn't be ready in time for the opening, of course, but it's an idea."

Katy stopped, remembering the man's arrogant attitude.

"No," she said, pulling the reins on her enthusiasm. "He

didn't seem to be too pleased with outside interference. Maybe he wouldn't listen to any suggestion I might make."

"You're persuasive, Katy," the therapist said firmly. "Maybe if he isn't willing to design an original piece then he has something of historical value he could donate."

The image of the gypsy jar flashed through Cora's mind again, but she resisted the urge to share anything so vague, especially not with anyone except Charlie.

"I'm sure you'll think of something."

Katy's forehead furrowed in thought.

"Now that you mention donation, there's lots of land around the main house. I know they're planning on a parking lot, formal gardens, and a children's playground with walking trails, but all that still leaves acres and acres. What if there were a log cabin that belonged to an original Balfour? What if it could be moved to the Wilton property?"

"A log cabin?" Cora asked.

"Yes, there's an old cabin on Zeke Balfour's property," Katy said, her enthusiasm mounting. "And it would be just perfect. When I saw it I thought immediately that it could be the cabin owned by the original Balfour who founded the town. That would be such a great addition to the Wilton House grounds!"

Katy pictured Zeke's log cabin, no longer abandoned and neglected but settled peacefully into a garden setting, a docent in a ruffled pinafore on the porch waving to visitors who could admire the rustic charm and beauty of the place where Balfour originated.

Cora considered the idea, turning it over in her mind.

"Preserving a building that significant seems like a good idea to me," she said. "But could it be something else? A slave cabin? You'd want to be sure."

"No, that's not what it is at all," Katy said. "I'm sure of it. Based on my interactions with Zeke Balfour, I can tell you plainly that he'd have torn it down long ago. He'd never let his daughter grow up with a slave cabin in the backyard."

Cora sat speechless, wondering at the transformation from quiet church mouse to outspoken advocate that was taking place before her.

"I wonder how much it costs to move a building," Katy continued, lost in her own creativity and passionate imagination. "And who would do that, and how long it would take."

"Katy," Cora said, a warning note in her voice, "maybe you should slow down and take things a little more carefully. Perhaps Zeke Balfour won't want to move his family homestead. It's his building after all. You said he's proud."

"I said he's arrogant," Katy corrected, her enthusiasm waning as quickly as it had come. "But you're right, of course. I got carried away."

"Maybe there's still some small item he'd be willing to loan for display," Cora said gently. "Or you could do that research about Balfour's history. This doesn't mean there's nothing for you to contribute."

"I suppose," Katy said, unconvinced, her shoulders sagging. "I just thought for once I'd had a good idea all on my own."

Chapter 36

Marcie decided that riding the elevator two floors up to knock on the door of Inola Walker's hotel room was rather presumptuous and she wasn't going to do it, no matter what Ben Taylor said when he gave her the room number.

She told herself that she didn't really mind waiting in the Holiday Inn Express lobby for her passenger to come down, even if the whole process was disconcerting and foreign to her experience.

Much like the temporary discomfort during her weekly visits to Darcie's Bed and Breakfast, she felt insecure. Darcie never let her forget that she was the country mouse, the plain one. That the Piney Woods belonged to a bygone standard of roadside motels.

I am who I am, she thought. *Ben asked me to do this for a reason. He could have asked someone more sophisticated. I'm not going up to the agent's room. Besides, what would I do if she isn't ready? What's the etiquette for that? Does she invite me into her room? That's awkward.*

Where would I sit? On the corner of the bed? No one in her right mind would do that.

She took in the gleaming fake wood laminate floor, the faint scent of cleaning supplies, and the uniformed desk clerk with her superior, inquisitive stare.

Part of her wished she hadn't offered to help, but she'd never been able to resist Ben's reasonable requests. They were, after all, few and far between.

She jumped twice as the elevator doors opened and closed, disgorging a variety of hotel guests, before the solitary stairway door opened and Inola Walker appeared, computer bag slung over her shoulder.

What has Ben gotten me into? she thought, immediately recognizing the agent by her professional demeanor, her height, and the impressive cut of the gray tailored suit and slacks. *This woman doesn't need a driver. She needs a Secret Service detail.*

"Good afternoon," the landlady said, standing, overcoming her natural tendency to informality and extending her right arm. "I'm Marcie Jones."

Inola gripped the landlady's hand with a firm, brief shake.

"I know you'd probably rather have your own car," Marcie began, thinking of her conversation with Ben. "There's a rental agency one town over, and I could take you there. You could have your own car in less than an hour."

"That's very considerate of you," Inola said. "Chief Taylor seems to think that imposing on local Balfour residents is a more acceptable means of getting around."

"Ben does have some rather quaint ideas," Marcie agreed, finding she liked the agent more than she expected. "That offer to get you your own car still stands."

"Thank you, but if you don't mind taking the time to chauffeur me," she said, "I'm in your debt."

Marcie couldn't think of a suitable response, so she said the first thing that came into her head.

"So," she said awkwardly, "have you had lunch yet?"

"Thank you for your concern, Miss Jones," Inola said politely. "I'm fine. Officer Burton was going on duty. He gave me a lift back here after my meeting with Chief Taylor. I'm ready to get to work."

Marcie noticed that the list of names didn't include Jim Smith or Charlie.

This woman doesn't take prisoners, she thought. *Underlings and those deemed unworthy are not worth mentioning.*

Inola deliberately pushed up the starched cuff of her tailored shirt and inspected her watch for the second time.

"I tried to call Mrs. Stone to make an appointment for today," she said crisply. "I was only able to reach an answering machine. I'd prefer to notify her before I appear at her home."

"Ben . . . er, Chief Taylor . . . didn't share where you wanted to go when he called me," Marcie said. "You don't need an appointment to see Cora on a weekday. Marjorie's there."

Inola looked as though she might ask for clarification and then didn't. "If you're certain that this isn't a wasted trip," she said. "I'll trust your judgment."

Marcie jingled her keys as she pulled them from her oversized purse.

Well, after Ben talked you out of getting a car, I'm surprised you trust anyone's judgment in Balfour, she thought sympathetically.

"I can promise you that Cora will be at home when you get there," Marcie said. "You may spend a few minutes waiting if she has a client, but she'll certainly see you."

Marcie jingled her keys again.

"My car is just outside," Marcie said. "We can be there in ten minutes or so."

"Oh," Inola said. "That quickly?"

Marcie pulled the straps of the floral Vera Bradley purse over her shoulder and tucked it under her ample arm.

"Oh, everything's only ten minutes or so away in Balfour," she said cheerfully. "That's part of our charm."

Chapter 37

There were no vacancies for the weekend at the Balfour Bed and Breakfast, and Darcie was exceptionally pleased. Not since the Christmas bazaar weekend had she had a full house, and there was nothing Darcie loved more than being surrounded by people she could make happy, or do her best to try.

But after her ten-round verbal boxing match with the Senator on Tuesday, Darcie was doing her best to keep her disposition sunny and her attitude positive.

After all, she reminded herself, *the Senator's booked the most elaborate and expensive suite in the B&B for the entire week. He could just as easily have stayed with his old family friends on the outskirts of town, and I'd never have gotten the opportunity to talk to him at all.*

Darcie, selected as the financial liaison and budget director for the entire project, relished her position and contact with Stewart, whom she considered a longtime close personal friend in spite of his reputation as a notoriously difficult man.

She couldn't deny that she loved the challenge and the detailed work involved, relieving Linda Candler and Virginia Evans so they could focus on multiple other areas of planning and organization.

This last week had plunged everyone into the final preparations, and Stewart's critical gaze repeatedly focused over Darcie's ample shoulder as he questioned each of the detailed spreadsheets of inventory and cost projections.

The Senator accepted Darcie's business acumen, but they both knew he trusted nothing that he himself had not approved. And there was still quite a lot that he wanted to approve.

Darcie made herself a cup of coffee with a slender slice of spinach quiche and slipped out to the front porch swing to fully anticipate her upcoming guests.

The Wilton House opening had attracted a number of visitors, both former and first-time, each of whom had distinctive needs and wants.

The two spinster sisters who loved research and all things historical had reserved their favorite floral room for the entire weekend, hoping, as the elder sister had confided when she booked the room, to learn a clandestine secret or two about the early history of the settlement.

A member of the Griffith Historical Society had also reserved a room for the weekend for much the same reason, although Darcie suspected that he was more interested in writing some salacious version of Steve Wilton's murder. At least, those were the rumors swirling around when it came out that he had been selected to write an article.

He'd better keep a civil tongue in his head while he's in Balfour, Darcie thought. *I don't want to be in his shoes if he decides to step on*

Stewart Wilton's toes and dig up dirt on Steve and, by association, Amy and Katy. The whole town is behind those girls. No questions asked or expected from either of them.

"I can't believe you're going to let him stay at the B&B," Marcie had said in their most recent weekly conversation. "You saw that nasty piece he wrote for the *Griffith Gazette* two years ago. He criticized everyone. The mayor, the police department, Sam's, every little shop on Main Street, even the town council. He trashed the whole town of Balfour and insulted every single one of us."

"You're just angry because he called you a 'buxom bumpkin' and said the Piney Woods was a throwback to the worst of roadside motels."

"So you *do* remember," Marcie snapped. "Do you want me to repeat what he said about you? Because I remember that too."

"It's not necessary to be mean," Darcie said loftily. "I'm well aware that he's too pompous and full of himself, but you know what I always say—"

"Yes," Marcie interrupted, sniggering. "The only thing worse than being talked about is *not* being talked about."

"Shut up, Marcie," Darcie said. She hung up the phone.

Still, she knew there was truth in what Marcie said.

I hope the people over in Griffith know what they're doing sending this man, Darcie thought, enjoying the last bite of quiche and making a note to compliment the cook on the trial recipe. *They'd better understand the weight of the Senator's reputation. That historical society will never survive an attack on Steve Wilton's memory or his young widow and their daughter. The Senator will chew them up for breakfast and spit them out at suppertime with no one the wiser for it.*

Darcie felt confident in the dignified behavior of her other weekend tenants, two recently retired couples from Atlanta traveling together for a celebratory empty-nest minivacation and a doting mother and her only daughter scoping out the venue for a possible site for a summer wedding.

Thank goodness for Ellie Sanderson, she thought.

Torn between her commitment to Sam's and her occasional holiday work with Darcie, Ellie had enlisted the aid of two of her roommates from college and convinced them to come spend the spring break week with her in Balfour. Both had been splitting their time between the restaurant and the B&B, serving and cleaning on and off for the last three days.

Even the cook had found two vintage recipes for the buffet breakfast, one a flaky butter pastry full of local pecans and glazed with honey, and the other a healthy quiche full of fresh local vegetables and free-range eggs.

Darcie had spent the last week alternately working on the financial books and dealing with the Senator before moving room to room inspecting, approving, checking, and rearranging until the first of the guests arrived.

To say she was in her element as a central pin in the social circle of Balfour was an understatement.

Darcie drank the last swallow of coffee.

Time to print out the most recent spreadsheet.

She was ready for anything, even an irritating, disagreeable reporter and an equally annoying, distrustful senator.

Chapter 38

"Tell me again why we're here," Jim said, coughing discreetly into the crook of his elbow. His eyes were burning, squinting through a lightly drifting fog of cigarette smoke emanating from the fenced area around the outside corner of the building. "Are you sure this is even legal?"

Charlie shrugged, his nostrils twitching with the odor of nicotine, covering his own urge to cough. He pushed up his sunglasses and checked his watch.

They'd been standing in a steadily moving line for ten minutes, and the Rookie's stomach was growling so loudly that other patrons were beginning to notice.

"They've got a great air handling system," the detective reassured him. "There's no smoking inside. Get out your ID. You've got to be twenty-one to get in. Fair warning, though, I want to be able to see the register and the walk-ups, so if we have to sit in the playpen, then that's where we'll sit."

"The playpen?"

"That's what it's called, the outside area where smoking is allowed while eating," Charlie said patiently. "Don't ask me why."

"Sure," Jim said, shifting from one size fourteen foot to the other and back. "Can I at least ask why we're here?"

I guess you deserve that, Charlie thought. *But I'm not sure I can explain.*

Charlie looked up at the creatively bizarre exterior of The Vortex.

Plastered around the doorway in spectacular 3-D was a giant, stark-white skull with red swirling lines for eyes and a row of even white teeth, a gaping jaw supported by two white stucco bones, the opening beneath the means by which the patrons entered.

The art deco, Day-of-the-Dead-looking skull of Cora's dream.

He knew the area well from his time with the Atlanta PD. He knew exactly where to find the skull once he recalled where he had seen it.

A one-of-a-kind landmark for the quirky inhabitants of Little Five Points, located near an equally historic, sensational tourist destination called Junkman's Daughter.

Moreland Avenue boasted eclectic shops, charming restaurants and bistros, coffee shops, and vintage clothing stores, completed by apartments, condos, lofts, and cozy homes.

If Cora's clues were right, and he had no reason to doubt her, Astra was a self-professed fortune teller who would go back to her larcenous roots in Atlanta.

And why not?

Metropolitan city. Multiple hiding places.

If she wanted to disappear in a crowd and to feel comfortable and safe among her peers, there was no better place than Little Five Points and no more varied, diverse, accepting people than the ones who lived in the bustling, inclusive community.

Live and let live.

A party of four was called, and the pair found themselves at the front of the line.

"Inside or out?" the host asked. "Booth or table?"

"We're expecting someone," Charlie said, placing a twenty dollar bill under his ID as he passed it over for the T-shirt-clad young man's inspection. "Any place with a clear view of the door."

The man discreetly took the bill, slipping it into the front pocket of a black half-apron tied around the waist of his fashionably torn jeans and shifted the menus from one arm to the other.

"There's an empty booth right by the front doors behind you," he said, returning the ID. "Will that do?"

"Sure," Charlie said. "Thanks."

The detective slid across the leather-covered bench facing the door, motioning for Jim to take the opposite side with his back to the entrance.

"Your server will be here in a minute," the host added, placing the laminated menu sheets on the table. "Thanks for your patience. We're busy for a Wednesday."

He dashed away to greet another group of patrons.

"Since I can't see the door and I don't know who I'm looking for, I'm going to have food," Jim said. "Is there a specialty? Anything especially good?"

"Everything," Charlie said.

An attractive young woman appeared at their table.

"I'm your server," she said. "Can I get you drinks from the bar?"

"Not today," Charlie said. "Just iced tea, please. As sweet as it comes with lots of lemons on the side. And we're ready to order."

"We are?" Jim waved the menu suggestively. "I haven't been consulted."

"I know what you want," Charlie said, taking the menus and returning them to the server. "We'll start with Dixie Wrecked Taters."

"Whole or half?"

"Oh, whole." Charlie winked broadly, much to the young woman's delight. "Then I'll have the Diablo with fried plantains. My grumpy friend will have the Double Coronary Bypass Burger with fries. Both medium rare, please."

"All right," she said admiringly. "I'll get that right in."

Jim turned to watch as she maneuvered gracefully away. When she was out of sight, he leaned over the table, his elbows and forearms taking more than his fair share of the space.

"How did you know I want medium rare?" he said. "And not to sound ungrateful, but what did you just order for me? What in the world is a fried plantain?"

"You can try one of mine. Don't worry, you'll thank me later."

Charlie tilted his sunglasses down and scanned the room, traveling from one table to another, from face to face, with unobtrusive deliberation.

"What time do you have?" he asked.

Jim checked his cell phone.

"Almost two fifteen," he said, his elbows moving even further across the table, his voice thick with concern. "I understand you want to keep things close to your chest here, but you haven't shared the time table either. I don't know what's going on."

Charlie folded his hands on the table.

"Feels like it should be later," he said.

"Yes," Jim replied. "Time's a funny thing, isn't it? Some days, like right now actually, I feel like I'm caught in a loop. A never-ending Six Flags Cyclone rollercoaster hugging the rails, jerking side to side in the sharp curves, dangling upside down through the gravity-defying, back-breaking track, but sooner or later coming right back to the beginning in the same cramped car with the same screaming co-riders."

Their server put two oversized Mason jars of mahogany-colored sweet tea on the table with a generous bowl of freshly sliced lemon wedges.

"Food will be out in a minute," she said, tossing down two straws and a stack of paper napkins. "You okay for now?"

"Fine," Charlie said, staring slack-jawed at the Rookie, momentarily speechless at the unexpected outburst.

He dug a pack of chewing gum from his front jeans pocket, slowly unwrapping the foil, sliding the stick into his mouth before speaking, purposefully pressing the gum between his molars as he spoke.

"That's pretty profound, Jim," he said. "I'm not sure what you want me to say."

"Nothing, really." Jim reached into his knapsack and pulled out his sketchbook, flipping halfway through the pages. "Just sometimes I get these crazy thoughts in my head and they've got to get out."

Charlie felt an unexpected stab of pity for the hulking young man.

Crazy thoughts, indeed.

Charlie knew that rollercoaster feeling well, to be trapped in a day-to-day routine that held scant joy or personal fulfillment, and certainly not much hope for anything beyond the mundane pseudo-thrill of small town police work.

The Daltons and the Burtons of the world couldn't understand. They'd escaped. They had chosen to return to Balfour with their bios and their resumes full of praiseworthy military exploits, proud of their world travels and their Marine Corps pedigrees.

Men of integrity and honor, nonetheless full of their own self-righteous egos.

That's not really fair, Charlie corrected himself. *Dalton's okay. He spends too much time with Burton, that's all.*

Ben Taylor, on the other hand, had found his purpose in dedication and duty to a place he'd never left, loved and respected by the people he served. Honor above all. The unsung hometown hero of Southern folklore.

But for Jim, things were different.

Charlie watched the nimble artist's strong fingers remove a sooty black charcoal pencil from a leather pouch, check the point, and begin to sketch. The Rookie was in many ways different from the regular small town police officer. Charlie could clearly see his younger self in the officer's size fourteen shoes.

Wanting more. Understanding that there was more to be had for the taking.

"Wish we had a photograph or maybe even a sketch," Charlie said, admiring the detailed drawing, amused at the incongruity of the brawny, masculine former linebacker and the delicate lines the man drew. He took a swallow of his tea, trying to remember Cora's description of the fortune teller.

"Now that you mention it," Jim said, flipping a page back and sliding the book across. "Would this help? Probably should have mentioned it sooner. I got a description and a rough copy from the sketch artist in Germantown. Agent Walker said you had everything covered. I didn't want to insult you. I redrew it myself from the original."

Charlie bit his tongue, sheepishly recalling his recent words to Inola about looking gift horses in the mouth. He deserved this. Better late than never.

He pulled the sketchbook toward him. Against the creamy white of the paper an image, harshly feminine and brooding, stared back. Eyes like bottomless empty pits, heavily painted lids and arched artificial brows, the whole pulled together in frowning judgment. Bitter lines at the mouth lay like irrigation trenches extending from the hawkish nose to just under the curve of the cheekbones and in rings around the throat.

Salt and pepper colored hair framed the whole with tangled, uneven strands.

"That's not a happy woman," Jim observed.

She's a thoroughly unattractive woman, Charlie thought. *Downright intimidating and foreboding. No wonder she had a strong influence over Dinah Browning.*

"I don't think I've heard her given name," Charlie replied, having no problem reconciling Cora's clues with the image before him. "Only her alias, Astra."

"Eudora Ashford," Jim said, shading the jawline absently. "Not sure that's even her real name, since there's no fingerprint record. FBI's still working on that."

A platter of food hovered just above the table, suspended in air by the patient server. Jim hurriedly removed the sketchbook and dropped it on the seat beside him, making space for the generous appetizer.

"Good golly," he exclaimed. "I've never seen tater tots that looked like this! Is that gravy and cheese?"

"Glad you approve," the detective said. "Sausage gravy, to be specific. Grab a fork and help me before she gets here."

"Before who gets here?" Jim said, taking a huge bite and savoring the chunks of meat amid the creamy gravy and cheddar cheese sprinkled with bacon bits. "Sorry, this is so good. I wasn't thinking. You mean before Eudora Ashford gets here."

"Eudora?" the server repeated. Neither man had noticed that she had remained, standing slack-jawed at the end of their table, her curious gaze locked onto the open sketchbook lying on the bench.

"Were you talking about Eudora Ashford? That looks just like her," she continued, then hesitated. "Nothing personal if she's a friend of yours, but she's darn scary."

"No problem," Charlie said, putting down his fork. "Does she come in often?"

"Every day for the past week," she said. "She just moved or something, and we're within walking distance. She picks up takeout like clockwork between two thirty and three in the afternoon. Always uses a credit card and shorts on the tip. She likes her burgers rare with everything, but why not? We're the best."

"Yes, you are the best," Charlie agreed, taking out his wallet. "Can you get us the check, please?"

"But your food isn't here yet," she protested. "And you haven't even started the Wreck."

Her brow furrowed, her expressive eyes wide with sudden concern.

"Wait," she said. "Is she in trouble? Maybe I shouldn't be talking to you. You don't look like cops. I don't want to stick my nose where it doesn't belong. I'm not a snitch."

Charlie pressed a twenty into her hand and closed her fist over the money.

"No, nothing like that," he assured her, handing his Visa credit card to Jim as he met her gaze with boyish innocence.

"My colleague here is going to finish this amazing appetizer, and then if you'll put the rest in a couple of take-out boxes, that'd be great. He'll make sure you get at least a twenty percent tip on the charges too."

He glanced over his shoulder, motioning with an index finger for her to lean in closer, tucking back a strand of her wispy blond hair and patting her arm as he whispered into her multipierced ear.

"Feature story on the occult influence in Little Five Points," he lied effortlessly, tossing a cautionary glower at Jim. "Freelance journalist writing for the *Atlanta Journal-Constitution*, exclusive Sunday magazine edition. Don't want to broadcast we're here and scare away the primary source. Sensitive topic, you know how it is. Sources say she's got a mystical coven somewhere off Moreland Avenue."

Her pupils widened as her mouth formed a bright pink oval of surprise.

"You mean she's a real—"

She gasped with a mix of horror, awe, and disbelief.

"Shhhh," he said, pressing the tip of his index finger to her lips. "We try not to say her name out loud."

He hesitated dramatically.

"Reports are that she's incredibly powerful. Who knows what other dark spirits she might conjure."

Jim covered his face with his broad hands and stared down at his lap, his appetite eclipsed by his surge of wonder at Charlie's never-ending skills.

"This is the sketch artist for the article," Charlie went on, pointing at Jim. "No cameras, you know. She doesn't allow photographs. Superstitious and private."

"I get it," she said, pulling back slightly, fascinated. "Ah, there she is!"

Charlie casually peeked around the server's head to the cash register and take-out pickup station near the door. There, dressed in a flowing patchwork skirt and ruffled peasant blouse, was Eudora Ashford. Even the floppy cloth hat bordered with faded silk flowers and rhinestone-rimmed sunglasses could not disguise her profile.

She was rummaging through an oversized quilted bag.

She does look like the sketch Jim drew, Charlie thought. *And she's dressed exactly the way Cora described the fortune teller in the dream. Score another one for Cora. Game on, Astra.*

Charlie took advantage of Eudora's distraction to rise from his seat.

"Thanks," he said, pressing past the young girl, quickly replacing his wallet in his pocket and striding to the front door. "Thanks for everything."

Chapter 39

Marjorie knew, looking out the kitchen window to the flower beds behind the house, that something remarkable was about to happen. Sweet, fresh spring air hesitated just outside the screened back door. The scent of blooming flowers, mostly tea roses, wild purple violets, and pink and red honeysuckle banked by snowy white gardenias, all combined with a faint smell of rich, fertilized earth, drifted expectantly in the humid air.

Marjorie knew.

Her senses felt sharper, smells seemed stronger, and the light was brighter.

She told herself that it was probably only the time of year, only the anticipation of Resurrection Sunday, but there was something else she could not deny.

Maybe it's because there's a child in the house, she thought. *Maybe it's Jane. Maybe it's because Cora told me this morning that the dreams have returned. Maybe because Charlie's back in town. Maybe.*

Marjorie wiped her hands on the corner hem of her flour sack apron as she considered the ingredients for her buttermilk biscuit dough.

No sense, she said to herself, *in wasting time just fretting away the day when there are things to do. Songs to sing. People to feed.*

The rhythmic motion of the curved pastry cutter blades made their way back and forth, back and forth, over and through the creamy shortening and powdery flour as they combined, blending into chunks and crumbles.

A cup of cold buttermilk sat at her elbow, waiting patiently to take center stage, the primary role in her recipe.

As she was prone to do, she hummed contentedly as she worked. Hymns ambled through her memories like faithful friends coming to call in leisurely succession.

She had flipped the lump of dough onto the floured table when the doorbell rang. She dusted the white powder from her hands over the sink and grabbed a clean dishcloth before she headed for the front door.

In spite of her premonitions, she was completely unprepared for the sight of Marcie on the porch accompanied by an impressively elegant Native American woman wearing a tailored pantsuit and carrying a briefcase.

"Hi, Marjorie," Marcie recited, as if from a prepared script. "This is Inola Walker. She's a federal agent come to Balfour to investigate what happened to Harry Halstein's half sister Dinah in Memphis. She'd like to talk to Cora."

"I was given to understand this wouldn't be an issue," Inola interjected, her voice sounding less apologetic and more accusatory. "I tried to call and make an appointment for today, but I was unable to get through to a human being."

"No problem," Marjorie said easily. "Cora's in her office. Jane's playing hide and seek in the backyard with Solomon."

She looked past the agent.

"Time for coffee in the kitchen?" she asked Marcie. "Just took lemon pound cake out of the oven, and Jane would love to see you."

"Sorry," the landlady said. "Two weekenders coming early. I need to get back and get them settled. Rain check?"

"Absolutely." Marjorie nodded, wiping her hands on the dish-cloth. "Step on inside, Agent Walker."

Marcie turned to the agent, relieved to be passing off her charge to Marjorie, at least for the time being.

"Just give me a call when you're ready for your next stop," she said pleasantly. "Marjorie's got my number. What I've got to do won't take long, and I can be back—"

"In ten minutes," Inola interrupted dryly. "Yes, I know. Thank you."

"I'll call you," Marjorie promised. "Come on along to the den, Agent Walker. I'll get you settled and let Cora know you're here."

Inola was facing the fireplace with her back to the doorway when Cora entered. She'd been taking mental inventory of the items on the mantel.

Normal, nondescript, she thought, creating a mental picture of the owner, since for some reason there had been no photograph attached to this woman's file. *The decor of her home and her possessions should give me an inkling of who she really is.*

An anniversary clock under a dome of clear glass. Several small white candles in crystal cut holders. No photographs or memorabilia of people. Nothing remotely warm or personal. No knickknacks or clutter. Simple. Unadorned.

She was taken aback, however, at the sight of her diminutive hostess in baggy black pants and an oversized blue dress shirt, the sleeves rolled to her elbows, her long, dark hair pulled into a careless messy bun at the back of her head.

Cora's fingernails and toenails were as absent of polish as her face was of makeup.

"I'm Cora Stone," the therapist said, extending a hand in friendly greeting. Her voice was cordial and accommodating. "You must be Inola Walker. I understand you want to speak to me."

Her arm hung midair as Inola, moderately stunned, studied the gold ring on Cora's outstretched hand with unabashed concentration, the red stone winking between elaborately carved feathers, the unique pattern disconcertingly familiar.

She hesitated before she regained her professional composure and met Cora's open expression, grasping her hand with equal firmness.

The two women stood, one towering over the other, eyes and hands locked in questioning greeting until Marjorie appeared with two tall glasses of ice water on a simple wooden tray.

She placed them on the low table in front of the overstuffed chairs and pretended not to notice the gathering clouds of apprehension in the room.

"I'll be right back with lunch for the two of you, then I'm going to the backyard with Jane," she said. "We're having a snack picnic with Solomon and the kittens."

"Thank you, Marjorie," Cora said, releasing Inola's hand but maintaining eye contact. "Please sit down, Agent Walker."

"Solomon?" Inola asked, her mind whirling with contradictions between the person she'd expected Cora to be and the person she had met.

Her body refused to relax, bend, and sit.

"The cat," Cora explained, amused but not particularly surprised at the look on the agent's face. People with preconceived notions were forever being taken aback by her appearance. It was as though they expected her to be taller and to look older, and when they saw just how petite she was they didn't quite know how to react.

"Solomon's a rather typical example of his breed, a Maine Coon. He's been a family pet for years and quite the accomplished therapy feline in his own right. Jane's our foster child."

Inola's first impulse was to say that she knew all about Jane, but she stopped.

What's the matter with me? she thought. *I don't volunteer vital information. When did I lose control of the situation? Who is this woman?*

"I can tell by your expression Charlie didn't adequately prepare you for our meeting," Cora said, dropping into her customary chair and folding her bare feet under the folds of fabric. "I'm afraid I'm not meeting your expectations."

"On the contrary," Inola said. "I believe I may owe you an apology. I came here with preconceived notions."

Marjorie reappeared with a platter bearing triangular quarters of crustless sandwiches and cubes of assorted cheeses surrounded by bunches of green and red grapes.

"Pimento and cheese on wheat, or turkey on a potato roll," she said. "Jane and I have settled on our usual peanut butter and grape jelly, if you'd rather."

"You're very kind," Inola said, taking her seat in the opposite chair, crossing her long legs at the ankles, and placing her computer case across her knees. "This is quite lovely. Were you expecting me? I didn't expect to be fed."

"In the South we're always expecting someone," Marjorie said. "It's tradition to break bread together, especially when people arrive around mealtime."

Inola looked up to see if the woman was being sarcastic or critical, but Marjorie's expression was one of serene observation, nothing more.

"Anything else before I go?"

"You've outdone yourself," Cora said. "Thank you."

Inola's gaze followed the older woman out of the room, waiting until the slam of the back door to give Cora an openly questioning stare.

"Your housekeeper didn't answer my question. Did you know I was coming?"

"Marjorie's much more than a housekeeper," Cora said, selecting a plump pimento and cheese and wiggling herself down into the cushions. "Please don't give us so much credit for preplanning. I didn't even know your name until you arrived in my den. Charlie suffers from impaired communication skills. He rarely shares vital information with anyone until he thinks it's absolutely necessary, and sometimes not even then."

Inola crossed a self-conscious arm over her rumbling stomach and reluctantly took a pimento and cheese for herself with the other hand.

"I agree," she said between satisfying bites. "Charlie plays close to the vest, doesn't he? . . . When he deigns to play at all."

Cora's laugh, a deep, rich laugh of appreciation, startled the reserved agent, who made an impulsive decision to deviate from her standard procedure.

"I've seen your file," she admitted bluntly, watching for signals in the therapist's response. "You're nothing like the person I've read about."

"Really?" Cora finished her sandwich and casually collected a handful of grapes, placing them one by one into her mouth. "Should I be concerned?"

Inola swallowed a last bite of sandwich and took a sip of water.

"No, I wouldn't be the least bit concerned if I were you," she said, wiping her fingers delicately on the paper napkin, her profiler's mind in a state of controlled confusion and disorder, working rapidly toward understanding.

"Now that I've met you, I'm finding so many obvious fallacies in the report," she continued with a tone of growing camaraderie. "It's obvious to me that whoever wrote about you wants to prevent anyone else from meeting you."

"And you suspect Charlie?" Cora said. "Why do you think he would do that?"

"I have my suspicions," Inola said, reaching for another sandwich and beginning to relax. "I've seriously misjudged Detective Abbott."

"You're not the first who's underestimated Charlie," Cora said. "And I can assure you that you won't be the last."

Chapter 40

Andrew Evans felt he was finally making progress with the Easter Sunday sermon. At least, until he reread what he'd spent the entire morning writing.

The world is full of individuals and events that alter our preconceived notions.

The more he looked at the opening line he'd written, the more pompous and self-serving it sounded, but he had nothing else. He was stuck with his own beginning and not much notion about where to take it from there.

Not even a meaningful scripture verse.

He had writer's block.

He'd been sitting in his office with cold coffee and a half-eaten slice of vanilla pound cake since Ginny had come by with a leftover meatloaf sandwich for his lunch. She'd been suitably sympathetic to his plight, but she had also recognized the utter futility of any further action on her part.

She did what she could. She dropped by midday with food, encouraging words, concerned embrace, and fervent prayer.

She was gone, and he was left staring at his yellow legal pad full of haphazardly scribbled notes, surrounded by a mountain of theology books.

At least she didn't bring up Jack again, he thought. *I don't need another glowing report of how useful he's being to the Wilton House opening. Why doesn't the boy just get a paying job and a real profession? How hard can that be?*

Alice's sharp knock at the door brought his frustration up short.

"Sorry to disturb you," she said insincerely, taking in the chaos of the room with one disapproving glance. "There's a deacons' meeting in the conference room at two this afternoon. You asked me to remind you that Frank wants to talk to them about the funds for tuning the piano before Sunday morning services."

"Does Frank remember?" he said.

"I do."

A balding head with thick round rimmed glasses perched on a hawkish nose appeared over the top of Alice's heavily hair-sprayed, coiffured blond hair.

"I've been waiting in the office here to talk to you for almost twenty minutes," he announced, "but Alice said you couldn't be bothered."

"It's been ten minutes, Frank, and that's not exactly what I said," she corrected.

"No," he said petulantly. "Your clock is slow. You told me I was early, so I should just shut up and sit in the corner until a quarter till. That's what you said. Ask Donna. Same thing."

"I'll be right there," Andrew said. "Give me two minutes."

Children, he thought. *They are rambunctious children, and I'm a tired parent.*

He stuffed his most recent attempts at a sermon under his open Bible.

Out of the way of prying eyes, he thought and pressed his palms into the desktop, heaving himself slowly from the leather office chair.

"Now, about this piano tuning for Sunday," he said. "I have questions. You have a qualified someone in mind? Isn't this rather a late date to make that decision? Wasn't the grand piano just tuned at Christmas?"

"Temperature and humidity," Frank chanted, his nose twitching. "The changing of the seasons, Preacher. And moving. The children's choir moved it for that Valentine's Day program. If you remember, I opposed that. Can't haul a delicate instrument hither and fro and expect it to hold the tuning."

"I'm not arguing, Frank. I'm trying to understand."

"Sure thing," he said, his nose twitching from the scent of hairspray and his proximity to Alice's hair.

"You have someone in mind then?" Evans asked. The preacher took his suit jacket from the back of his chair and pulled it on over his short-sleeved shirt, tugging at the lapels. He straightened his tie.

"Same guy we've used for years," Frank said. "He sells and services out of Griffith. Already contacted him, and he's set aside time on Saturday morning. Everybody else will be at that Wilton House wingding."

"I'd hardly call it a wingding," Alice said. She sniffed, refusing to give up her sentry post in the doorway between the preacher and the minister of music, accustomed to fulfilling her secretarial duties no matter the preacher involved. "This event is bigger and much more important than a wingding."

"Okay," Frank said petulantly. "Whatever you say. No skin off my nose."

"If you've already scheduled him," Andrew said, rubbing his throbbing temples, "why are we going to the deacons with this?"

"Because I can't pay for it out of the music department budget, Preacher," he said, his voice rising. "These things cost money, you know, and we just had the choir robes professionally cleaned. Besides, it's Resurrection Sunday, and the music won't sound nearly good enough for that if the piano is off-key."

Evans's mind returned to his sermon notes.

Well, he thought, *at least I'm not the only one under pressure to perform.*

"I understand," he said. "Thank you, Alice, for the reminder about the meeting. Come on, Frank. Let's go have a talk with the deacons. At least you have a problem we may be able to solve this afternoon."

Chapter 41

"I haven't even started on your headstone."

Zeke Balfour wiped the dripping perspiration from his forehead and stuffed the red bandana into the back pocket of his overalls.

"You were just here, and I told you that I couldn't get to it for at least a week, maybe a week and a half. I guess you rich folks don't have anything better to do than gallivant around the mountains harassing hardworking folks."

Naomi's slight form appeared around the corner of the workshop building.

"Did you call for me?"

"I did *not*," Zeke barked, brushing his dust-covered hands against each other. "Why can't you get on about your business and let me get on about mine?"

"I can understand that you're working. I just need a few minutes of your time."

Katy tucked her purse under her upper arm, planting her

sneakered feet firmly into the ground. Her whole body was trembling, and all she could think about was Saturday and the Wilton House opening and how useless and ornamental she felt. Cora had advised her against talking to Zeke again so soon, but she needed some sort of victory over her fear. She also knew if she waited she might never talk to him at all.

She'd been thinking all week about Naomi and how the child handled Zeke. She found herself admiring the child's sweet yet strong attitude, and she was inspired to step up and speak up for herself. If Naomi could find her own voice, then she could too.

Katy bit her lip hard to steady herself before she spoke.

"I have something I'd like to discuss with you," she said. "Please if you could spare just a little of your time."

Zeke turned away from his persistent customer and addressed his daughter firmly.

"Naomi," he said, "I need to discuss business with Mrs. Wilton. Go back into the house and read, please."

"I read four chapters."

"Then read five," he said. "Or finish your math lesson."

"I did my math lesson. It was too easy. It's just review. I learned fractions when I learned to cut up apples and peaches to make pies."

"Naomi."

"Yes, sir."

She obediently retreated a half dozen steps toward the house but not out of earshot.

"I want to talk to you about your cabin in the back," Katy said, making no effort to keep her words from reaching the listening child and throwing all caution and Cora's warnings to the fragrant wind.

"My cabin is none of your business," he said, bristling.

"The cabin is an important piece of our history—Balfour's history," she said, her voice cracking despite her resolve. "I noticed that you don't seem to use it for anything specific. I wondered how you feel about it."

"That isn't your business either," he continued. "But if I did try to use it, exactly what would I use it for? It isn't fit for human habitation. Hasn't been in decades."

"Did the original Balfour live there? Was it his home? He was a blacksmith too, or so I've heard, and a stonemason as well."

Katy knew she'd begun to babble, but the words wouldn't stop coming.

"Well, it's just standing there neglected," she continued, trying desperately not to offend him and knowing that was impossible. "Without care, it's going to collapse and decay. Would becoming a pile of rubble improve what it is now?"

"What are you suggesting? That I repair it and do something with it? I don't have that kind of money."

He was clearly aggravated with being interrupted in his work, shifting the hammer and chisel from hand to hand, sweat accumulating and dripping down his dark temples and forearms.

Katy sensed something else beyond the annoyance and the resistance. There was another emotion she couldn't quite define.

"I'm sorry to bring all this up now," she said. "I really am."

"If you were sorry, you'd go away and leave me alone," he said. "You're still standing in my yard and wasting my time."

"Then I apologize," she said. "I didn't mean to waste your time. I just had an idea. I'm not creative or gifted in making or doing anything. I've been reminded that I'm good at being a mother, and of all the things I do for my daughter. And I think I'm good at being an encourager."

"None of this feels very encouraging," he said. "Could you find a point?"

"Well, as I see it," she said, summoning all her courage, "I'd like to encourage you to repair the cabin as a historic site."

The hammer slipped from his hand to the ground.

"I'd pay for it, of course," she said quickly, taking a step back at the stunned look on his face. "Then later on we could possibly move it where more people could see it and appreciate it as the true beginning of Balfour."

"Have you lost your mind?" he shouted. "I don't want people tramping all over my privacy! If you're so keen on moving a building, you can go pick up your own house and carry it off down the road."

"Daddy!" Naomi interrupted, skipping up to Katy's side, her eyes sparkling with childish enthusiasm and mischief. "We could be part of history!"

Zeke made derisive snorting noises.

"I see that I've upset you," Katy said. "I'm sorry."

"I'm not upset!" Zeke exploded, his arms flailing at his daughter. "I thought I told you to go inside the house."

Naomi took another step closer to the woman's side in pure defiance, and Katy's knees almost buckled under her as she leaned against the child.

Cora tried to warn me and I wouldn't listen, she thought. *And now look what I've done. I wasn't ready for this. Not for any of this. I'm causing a scene and coming between a father and daughter. What if someone did that to me and Lizzy?*

A silent tear slipped from the outer corner of her eye and slid down her face.

"Are you crying?" Zeke shouted again. "Is that how you handle all your problems and win arguments?"

"Oh, Daddy," Naomi said. "Let's be kind. We aren't really using the cabin, are we? It is a piece of history."

"I told you to go inside the house," he said. "This is an adult conversation."

Katy pulled her arm away from the child and wiped the tear from her own cheek.

"I was wrong to come here," she said, steadying herself and searching her pocket for her keys. "I apologize for trying to push my idea on you, Mr. Balfour. The cabin is obviously very important to you, and I had no business asking you. Please excuse me."

She turned quickly to hide the second and third tears that slid down her face after the first.

What a mess you've made of this, she scolded herself as she stumbled toward the car. *You're not as strong or as clever as you think you are.*

Behind her she could hear low murmuring, but she kept going.

"Wait," Zeke's voice bellowed behind her.

She stopped but didn't turn.

"Tell me exactly what you want," he said harshly. "I don't have time to waste. The truth. What's in it for you?"

She faced him and saw that he'd run a hand through his close-cropped wiry black hair, leaving a trail of gray granite powder from his forehead to his crown. Naomi stood at his side, her hands now gripping her father's forearm.

"Okay," Katy said.

She had nothing else to lose. She'd driven all the way up here to have her say. She needed to finish what she'd started.

"The truth is embarrassingly simple." She moistened her lips with the tip of her tongue. "The Wilton House is opening this weekend and everyone is doing something to help except me."

"Isn't it your house?"

"Not really," she said. "It belongs to my father-in-law."

"The Senator?"

"Yes." Katy looked him in the eye. "And I'm expected to be there. I thought I'd be okay about it, but I'm not. I'm not okay about going without something to add. I feel like I'm attending a birthday party without a gift. It's humiliating."

She stopped and let the words sink in, averting her eyes and pretending not to notice the thunderstruck man and the sympathetic little girl.

"Almost as humiliating as right now," she added, "explaining this to you."

The breeze blew again, and she looked to see their reaction. She saw what she'd expected—pity. Again. The same pity she'd seen on the streets, in the stores, and throughout the church.

Poor Katy. Poor little Katy.

"So you see, I came here with selfish intentions," she said. "I came to ask you to help me give a gift. I thought about a sculpture of some sort, but then the cabin kept coming to my mind. It was a selfish, ridiculous, impulsive, impossible idea, and I regret it."

"Why my cabin?"

There was genuine curiosity in his voice and the slightest hint of amusement, although she couldn't imagine what he found humorous.

She knew what she wanted to say.

Because it's still standing. Because your cabin encourages me to believe that no matter what happens to me, I can be still standing too.

"Because it's Balfour's beginning," she said instead. "Because it's Balfour's home as much as it is yours."

"That's without a doubt the most absurd thing I've ever heard anyone say."

Zeke shook his head in disbelief as he patted Naomi's hands and removed them from his arm.

"You are a strange, strange woman, Katy Wilton, and you don't make a tinker's damn of sense either."

Naomi whispered in his ear as he bent down to pick up his hammer.

He touched his daughter's hair gently.

"I heard you the first time," he said quietly before turning to Katy. "You don't have to remind me."

"Naomi had a suggestion," he said straightening. "I'm not ready to sign over the cabin. I may never be. But maybe there's something historical inside it that you'd like to use. I can't imagine there's anything of worth, but you can try."

It was Katy's turn to ask the question.

"Why would you do that for me?"

"Since we're being totally honest," he said, "because my daughter asked me to do that for you and not another reason on God's green earth."

Katy took a tissue out of her purse and delicately blew her nose.

"You're going to be disappointed," he warned her. "Probably just rotted wooden furniture and a rusted iron pot or pan. Will that satisfy you? Will you keep off the property and leave me alone?"

"I promise not to come back and irritate you myself."

"I suppose that's the best I can expect," he said. "And no more talk about moving the cabin."

"I promise that too."

"Daddy?"

"Yes, Naomi."

"Can I see what's inside the cabin before they take it?"

Katy felt a pang of sadness and guilt at the shocked expression on Zeke Balfour's face.

"It's just a cabin," he said. "What do you think is in there?"

"I don't know," she said. "That's the adventure, isn't it? Please?"

He looked at Katy.

"Oh all right," he said. "As long as it's safe. I'll go inside too."

Naomi embraced her father, her arms wrapping themselves around his waist and her dark head resting on the bib of his overalls.

"I'm all dusty and sweaty," he protested. "Your clothes are getting messed up."

She hugged him more tightly, her face beaming with unrestrained joy.

"I don't care," she said, releasing him and skipping back to the house as she called over her shoulder, "I'll do more math now, and reading too. I love you. Thank you, Daddy."

"I love you too," he called after her, exhaling heavily before he turned on Katy. "I'm never going to get that work done for you if we spend the rest of the day out here gabbing. Send anyone you please to empty the cabin, but I take no responsibility for broken necks or legs from exploring."

"Thank you," Katy said, playing absently with her car keys. "I'll let you know who's coming as soon as I can figure that part out."

"Oh, really?" Zeke said, hefting the hammer from one hand to the other. "At this point, I can't imagine anyone refusing to do what you want, Mrs. Wilton, if only to get you to stop talking and just leave them alone."

Katy disregarded his snide innuendo. She knew she'd been too pushy and gone too far. She had no idea what Cora would say, but Katy certainly felt as though she'd reached up and grabbed a handful of stars.

"Well, there's just one more thing," she said. "I almost forgot the main reason I came out today. I never told you the exact wording for Steve's monument."

"You gave me all the vital information," he said, folding his arms across his chest, the hammer clutched in his muscular left hand. "What else do you want?"

"Steve was never one for Bible verses," she continued. "But I want one on his tombstone. Something I believe with all my heart."

She walked the narrow distance between them and tucked the folded paper nonchalantly between his clenched right fist and his chest.

He stared ahead without meeting her eyes, unmoving as she made her way to her car without looking back.

When the taillights of her car rounded the far turn of his driveway, he uncrossed his arms and looked down at the handwritten words, her husband's epitaph.

"And do not let me be ashamed of my hope . . ." Psalm 119:116

Chapter 42

Charlie could not, would not admit fear.

Former law enforcement partners and surveillance teams might debate his unorthodox attitude about rules and regulations of procedure, but never his ability to handle dangerous situations with common sense and good-natured wit.

He seldom resorted to violence, proud he could count the times on one hand that he'd taken his sidearm, a glock, from its holster, except when he lovingly cleaned and serviced it.

With his cocky attitude a major sticking point, Charlie often found himself alone in his duties, which suited him well on virtually every occasion.

He was not a team player.

He was the tom cat with nine proverbial lives who always landed on his feet. The lone hero on a quest for justice and truth.

Charlie seldom hesitated, except for today.

Today, after surreptitiously following an unsuspecting Eudora

Ashford from The Vortex clutching her takeout, he was standing across the street from a modest rental house, reevaluating his one unconfessed, irrational dread.

Those who possessed the powers of perception made him nervous. Profilers and fortune tellers terrified him.

More than that, they were the stuff of his nightmares. The kind that found him standing in his boxers, his deepest thoughts and feelings exposed for the world to see and be amused. Dreams that rivaled Cora's in their detail and frequency.

His vulnerability to their prying certainty was his kryptonite, his weakness.

In the short block sprint from The Vortex, his imagination had launched into overdrive, picturing a Halloween-style haunted house, cracked windows, and dilapidated, run-down wooden steps and shutters. Peeling paint and overgrown bushes and vines. A spooky, spectral-ridden antebellum mansion.

His dread had worked his psyche into something of a frenzy before he arrived at the naked truth.

He was wrong.

The yard was lushly green, neatly manicured, and recently edged. The windows were sparkling with reflected sunlight and curtained with tiers of white lace, friendly eyes ridiculing his cold sweat of unreasonable apprehension.

Beneath the double front windows on either side of the entrance were charming rectangular redwood flower boxes containing a 64-Crayola-box-colored assortment of blooming wildflowers, flanked with wooden sky-blue shutters.

The rest of the bungalow-style house was painted a discreet, warm beige, and the wooden steps leading up to the small landing of painted concrete were well-tended and sturdy.

The latest of many coats on the front door was also painted a cheerful darker shade of the same blue, adorned with a crafty burlap wreath decorated with perky silk flowers in similar sizes and colors to those growing under the windows.

In the center of the wreath hung a simple, hand-lettered sign: *Fortunes.*

Charlie argued with himself one last time. The optimistic appearance of Eudora's residence did nothing to dispel his feeling of intense dread. But there was no valid reason that he shouldn't do what he had come to do—interview Eudora Ashford.

After three quick raps the door opened, and the colorful figure from The Vortex emerged, her laugh a musically derisive cackle.

"Yes," she said pleasantly, swirling the hem of her skirt and fingering the ruffle at her shoulders. "I'm Astra, reader of the stars. How may I be of service to you today?"

Charlie managed a stilted hello before he tilted his head sideways, his ingrained training overtaking his momentary shock. He studied the salt-and-pepper-streaked mop of hair trapped beneath a sheer pale blue veil trimmed with tiny gold stars. There were myriad crinkles at the corners of her pitch black eyes, which peeked over frameless, square, rose-colored spectacles, replacing the gaudy sunglasses on the end of her sharp nose.

On closer inspection he could see that her eyelids were painted with shades of glittery bronze eye shadow and outlined in charcoal, skillfully applied under spikey false eyelashes. Several thick layers of peach rouge and powdery foundation had settled deeply into the wrinkles and creases of her angular face.

She's trying to distract by slathering herself with makeup, Charlie thought. *She's a caricature of what she thinks her clients expect. The bone structure is there. Her hair hasn't been colored. The eyes are the same. She's counting on smoke and mirrors.*

"Did you have a specific question, young man? Love? Finances? Employment?"

Her voice carried more curiosity than impatience.

You're not much of a clairvoyant, Charlie thought. *You don't have the slightest notion why I'm here or what I'm doing. Cora would have nailed me at the door.*

"I saw your sign," he said, pointing. "Do I need an appointment?"

Eudora's orange acrylic nails fluttered among the folds of the flamboyant fabric as she stepped back for him to enter.

"Come in," she said. "Don't be shy."

Charlie willed his body across the threshold into her lair. He had the disquieting feeling of having interrupted a Grimm's fairy tale evil queen in the process of casting a horrible spell on an innocent princess.

"I'm looking for Eudora Ashford," he said simply, surprised that he sounded so normal. He pointed a second time to the painted wooden sign above her doorway that read *Fortunes.*

"Call me Astra." She flashed a toothy smile, so blindingly white and perfect between her shiny, copper-colored lips that Charlie had the sudden thought that they were probably dentures. "There's something familiar about you. Do I know you?"

"No," he said, reaching unconsciously for his badge and flipping it open in a burst of honesty. "My name's Charlie Abbott."

"A police officer," she said, her eyes narrowing to glittery slits. "My permits and papers are in order, I assure you."

"That's not quite why I'm here," he replied.

She took a sweeping step back into her den and waved him inside.

"Well, let's just ignore your faults, dear," she purred. "I'm sure you must have other questions. You're too cute for this to be all about business."

Stepping from the sunlight into the dimly lit front room, Charlie stood two steps in across the threshold, allowing his pupils to adjust to the semidarkness.

The space itself was a shabby-chic, country-clutter of confusion. Decades of collectibles and bric-a-brac covered every flat surface and filled the multiple wooden shelves that adorned the walls.

Two equally overflowing curio cabinets sat against the wall, their dim back lights illuminating the thrift store array of contents. An oversized leather chair occupied the space between them.

Directly in front of the armchair sat a heavy, dark-stained desk with two smaller, antique gentleman's chairs out front, tops adorned with intricate rose carvings and their back and bottom cushions covered in faded blue velvet.

Charlie took in all the finer details of his surroundings with forensic precision as he moved between the two gentlemen's chairs, trying not look as uncomfortable as he felt.

She makes my skin crawl, he thought. *This whole house gives me the creeps.*

He had a sudden vision of an old Cary Grant movie he had watched once with Cora, *Arsenic and Old Lace,* and he reminded himself of the dangers of elderberry wine and other beverages offered by lonely little old ladies.

Astra, enjoying her victim's discomfiture, closed the door firmly and then slipped gracefully behind the enormous desk. Seating herself delicately, she propped her silk-covered elbows on the edge of the polished surface, placed her rather pointed chin in her hands, and leaned forward amid the sea of floral fabric, oozing saccharin.

"Young man," she twinkled. "Do sit down. Tell me why you've come. I don't bite."

Charlie tore his gaze from the room and stared at the toes of his new black and white Converse high-tops, stark against the faded red Chinese rug, and felt much like a scolded schoolboy. The silence hung for a moment in the incense-scented air as he marshaled his mutinous thoughts.

Charlie could hear his heartbeat pounding in his ears.

Odors that went beyond the first whiffs of smoky incense assaulted his sense, a cacophony of smells his mind could not readily separate and identify. He looked around the cluttered room once again, his interest landing on the front windows.

I know that smell, he thought. *Or something like it. Earthy. Damp. Dense.*

The space in front of the double windows, separated from the glass by the wall of lace curtains and bathed in sunlight, was blocked by two sets of wooden shelves, each bookcase laden with fifteen or more painted ceramic pots of all shapes and sizes.

Each pot held a different kind of plant, a mad horticulturalist's delight, and each emitted its own unique aroma into the stale, uncirculated air of the crowded room.

Cora's sunroom, he thought suddenly. *That's why I know this smell. Full of plants. Not the same kinds, but plants nonetheless. The hothouse smell of fertilizer and green growing foliage and herbs.*

The image of Cora righted his mind and quieted his heart.

This woman wasn't Cora. She would never come close to Cora's talents and abilities.

Charlie took a long moment to study the pots, speculating that the plants had come with her, and wondering how much of the other bric-a-brac besides the furniture had come with the rented house.

Astra misunderstood Charlie's interest in her horticulture, sighing audibly, her hands flitting vaguely toward the collection.

"Those are my medicinal herbs," she explained. "All perfectly legal, I assure you. Now, you must sit down. I can't answer the questions you don't ask."

Charlie took the chair on the right and leveled his gaze into the quasi-gypsy's exotically painted face, summoning all his resolve.

Cora thought he should be here confronting this woman, so here he was.

Astra reached across the desk, extending her puffy, multiring-clad fingers and gestured for him to surrender his hands to hers.

"Perhaps you'd like a reading?" Her warm voice was soft and soothing, hypnotic. Her lengthy nails tapped gently on the wood in invitation. "We can get to know each other."

Instead Charlie took his notebook from his jacket pocket, along with his ink pen, and clicked the pen firmly. This woman was mesmerizing.

Astra gave a rich, throaty laugh that held mockery.

"Tea, then?" She gestured toward a sterling silver service on the desk at her right elbow. "I made a fresh pot just before you knocked."

"Because you knew I was coming?" he said skeptically.

"Of course," she retorted.

Charlie shook his head slightly side to side, wrinkled his nose, and made a note.

"So, you were sent to meet me." Her mouth took on an unpleasant twist. "You aren't here of your own accord. What do you want?"

"I just wanted to meet you," Charlie said. "See your operation, as it were."

She was still unrattled, that same disturbingly odd smile on her face, the same shining lips tight and curled over her white teeth.

"I'm an entertainer." She shrugged nonchalantly, folds of fabric rippling around her thin shoulders and down her arms. "An experienced reader of people. Much as you as a policeman must read people. I tell people what they want to hear, or maybe what they think they want to hear, about their boring little lives."

"So you claim to know about other people without being told?"

"That's for other people to decide, now isn't it? At any rate, I cannot and will not be held responsible for fortuitous guessing, or for other people's interpretation of my gifts and talents."

"I'll bet you've never guessed about anything in your entire life."

Cold darts of angry irritation shot from Astra's eyes.

"So you're suggesting that I actually can tell the future?" Her teeth had taken on the look of a cat's glistening pointed canines. "I should charge more."

"You admit that you charge, then?" Charlie made a note. "By the hour or by the premonition?"

"I take donations," she countered. "Purely voluntary."

"Like the church?" He summoned his best wide-eyed innocence. "Do you also promise salvation?"

"You are a wicked, wicked boy." Astra stood abruptly, her friendly mood soured, her expression squinting. "What did you say your name is? I want you to leave. Now."

"Before you collect the offering?" It was Charlie's advantage. "That's not very Baptist of you, dear."

"Show me your badge again!" she snapped.

"Charlie Abbott," he said. "You're under investigation for your association with Dr. Varden Bander in Germantown, Tennessee."

"I don't know what you are talking about."

He detected a quiver in her voice, a faint tremor in her hands, fear in her eyes.

"Oh, you know exactly what I'm talking about," he countered, standing. "Like you said, I can read people too."

Astra gritted her teeth together, and she bit into her lower lip.

"You're just harassing me." Her voice had lost the sweet, persuasive tone and gone to sarcasm. "What do you want?"

"Oh I have what I came for."

He closed the notebook, clicked his pen, and slipped both into his jacket pocket. With an equally casual movement, he extracted his wallet from his back jeans pocket and removed a crisp twenty dollar bill, which he placed under the crystal ball in front of the fuming impostor.

"Don't bother seeing me to the door," he said over his shoulder as he turned. "I can see everything quite plainly from here."

As Charlie closed the door behind him and started down the steps, he heard a crashing thud inside the house behind him. He wondered absently which of Astra's china curiosities had fallen victim to her frustration.

He realized with relief that he didn't care, already dialing Jim to meet him at the truck.

He had another, equally important call to make.

A new and improved apprehension had taken him over, and he felt a sudden need to talk to Cora.

Chapter 43

As soon as she could no longer see the detective's retreating form from the safety of her lace-curtained window, Eudora callously swept the fragmented remains of her shattered thrift store teacup and matching saucer into a dustpan. She dumped the shards into the trash along with the remains of her uneaten Vortex hamburger and cold fries and got out her laptop, resolved to thoroughly research her would-be nemesis and latest opponent, Detective Charlie Abbott.

What she found left her cursing furiously under her breath.

The word Balfour hit her directly between her painted eyes.

There was a patient who mentioned that town. Eudora dug into her memory, struggling to find the name. Dinah Browning. That was who it was. She said she had family in Balfour.

Realization began to tease at the edge of her mind.

The family must have hired an investigator to look into the suicide. But they'd been estranged for years. She remembered that part. Who could have predicted that anyone would care about that woman, or keep in touch?

Eudora forced herself to breathe deeply and slowly.

They can't prove a thing, she assured herself. *I didn't do anything. So what if she came to me for readings? So what if she gave me money and jewelry and signed over property? There's nothing illegal about that.*

Varden said Dinah was an easy target from the minute she came into his clinic. She was wealthy, isolated, and her condition totally treatable. He claimed he could control her meds to milk her treatment for a whole lot of money, especially if they added the additional costs for Eudora's biweekly readings and consultations.

A simple scam so beautiful in its design.

Eudora still didn't know what had gone wrong, but she was experienced in knowing when to leave. That stupid doctor. She'd gotten to the clinic that morning in time to see them hauling him away. Then the evening news talked about indictments, and she knew to save herself.

Of course, there was no time to let the clients know, not that she would have let anyone know where she was going. Not that she actually cared about Dinah as a person. She'd been an easy mark. As entertaining and profitable as any Eudora had fleeced over the years.

Dinah was the most transparent kind of victim—a public figure, much of her life an open record. Background was just straightforward research. Even the gruesome details of her father's suicide and her mother's remarriage to a business partner had been detailed in multiple newspaper and magazine articles.

Eudora understood human nature. A master of filling in the blanks, she knew how to dangle the prospect of speaking to a loved one from the beyond, offer glimpses of the future disguised as hope, and keep the mark coming back again and again as she worked to make and keep herself indispensable to Dinah Browning's happiness.

She had no way of knowing the woman would go off the deep end and shoot herself. Bander was the medical doctor, the trained physician. He was supposed to know these things. Anticipate the pitfalls.

What a fraud, she thought. *He was just plain stupid and overconfident. He deserved to be caught. He wouldn't listen to me when I told him to slow down and be careful. He thought he was so smart. No foresight. No long-term planning.*

Eudora retrieved the half dozen papers from the printer tray.

Varden Bander and Charlie Abbott. Two of a kind. Poking their egotistical noses into her business. No idea what they were doing or who they were dealing with. Bander might be able to name her as an accomplice, but she couldn't do anything about that now. She doubted the police in Memphis knew where she was.

But Abbott could be a potential problem. He did know where she was.

But he was from New Orleans. What was he doing in Atlanta?

Working. That was obvious. But for whom? And why?

What did he want from her?

She thought about all the other cases she worked on, the scams she'd run. People who would want to find her.

Come on, she snapped at herself. *You can put two and two together. Figure out how this man found you in Atlanta and who helped him do it.*

She studied the pages and saw one name repeated over and over on every page. Cora Stone. Formerly Cora Abbott.

She ventured back to the computer and printed more pages.

The search for information about Cora proved enlightening. She was a former profiler. A psychologist who worked with the police to analyze and solve crimes.

As far as Eudora was concerned, a glorified psychic with a diploma on the wall.

More importantly, Cora lived in Balfour, Georgia.

Dinah Browning had mentioned the small town before—her brother lived there.

Was that the key? The common denominator she was looking for?

Had Dinah Browning's brother hired this Abbott to find her? Had Abbott somehow used his profiler ex-wife to track her down?

It was fanciful. Ridiculous. Beyond any rational logic.

But Abbott and Cora had been partners at one time. Married, too. Were they working together to find her? Balfour wasn't far from Atlanta.

No. It was too crazy. It couldn't possibly be. She'd been so careful.

The uncertainly made her head throb more violently.

She'd spent years convincing people that she could do what she thought was being done to her now—that someone had pulled her location out of thin air.

No. Not thin air at all.

Abbott and this woman had solved some incredible crimes together, that much was true. The facts were clear. She shuffled the papers.

If she waited for the detective to return, he might bring the Memphis authorities with him, and she couldn't have that.

If they'd found her once, they could find her again wherever she went.

Were they working for Dinah's brother? She needed to know.

Her frantic mind could think of only one course of action. She would ask them.

More specifically, she would ask Cora Stone. Not outright, of course, but in her own way. Using her own wit and cunning to find answers. She wasn't safe in Atlanta. She wasn't safe anywhere.

Abbott was a moving target, but she knew where to find Cora.

Maybe she could find the brother too. Convince whoever it was that she had been Dinah's friend and confidante. That she could tell him things about Dinah that he'd want to know. She could find out how much they knew about her.

But all that was secondary to the question of how Abbott had found her in the first place. When she knew that, she would know what to do.

She couldn't ask Abbott how he'd done it, but she could do the next best thing—she could ask Cora Stone.

She made herself a cup of tea to calm her nerves and told herself that she didn't have a choice. Going on the offensive was the only way.

Balfour was the only clue she had, and a little day trip to the North Georgia mountains seemed preferable to waiting in Atlanta and wondering about what she didn't know.

Besides, she was Eudora Ashford, psychic.

She'd solved mysteries and murders herself with far less than this. She'd do it again.

Chapter 44

The Fifth Day: Thursday

Cora stood at the kitchen sink in the semidarkness, filled with cautious curiosity, anticipating the inevitable message.

Then she realized that something was disturbingly different.

There was no shelf over the sink, nor any sign of a window in the wall. The chipped enamel pan to her right was empty of dishes, as was the sink, except for a lonely cup and saucer that she didn't recognize.

The faucet had been replaced by a heavy oaken bucket filled with stagnant water sitting on the rough-hewn floor, a crude pottery pitcher and ladle to the side.

This is a dry sink, she thought. *No plumbing. This is an old house. Where am I?*

There was no rug beneath her feet.

Cora looked down and saw that she could not actually see her feet at all, hidden beneath folds of flowing fabric that rippled in a flood from her shoulders.

Her arms were covered past her wrists to the tips of her fingers, and as her eyes reached her hands, she stopped in wonder.

In place of her simple, self-manicured fingers, she found that her hands were calloused and cracked, the nails chipped and broken.

The hands of a farm wife, hard work taking its toll.

As she felt the weight in her hands and arms, the heaviness spread throughout her entire body, as though her tiny frame might drown in the clothing she wore.

Turning awkwardly, she searched for something concrete, her mind refusing to clear, unable to absorb an avalanche of unexpected feelings careening through her.

Fear, pain, frustration, and anger shot out in all directions, as if several minds were all at war within her, fighting for her attention. Struggling to be heard, to get out.

She shifted her focus back to the odd room.

The stove had been replaced by a fireplace with an empty cast iron pot on the edge of the hearth, embers burning low amid the mounds of ashes. A stack of cut firewood lay nearby, as if waiting for someone to prepare an evening meal.

Her head had begun to throb, and her midsection felt bloated and swollen.

She had no idea which details were important and which weren't.

Why am I dressed like this? she thought. *This doesn't have anything to do with fortune telling. What am I supposed to see?*

Two rough-hewn benches shoved against an equally primitive table had taken the place of the ladder-back chairs, and in the far left corner was a humble rocking chair.

To the far right, in the corner of the room, was a simple double bed covered with faded patchwork quilts and two scant pillows too flat for any useful purpose.

At the end of the footboard to the bed was a carved wooden cradle, vacant except for a folded wool knit blanket. A baby's long christening gown and cap were draped over the side.

Stacked beside the bed was a pallet of blankets and in the center was a book that looked remarkably like Brother James's preaching Bible, only slightly smaller.

The wooden plank floor was bare—unlike her grandmother's floor, which was covered with linoleum and braided rugs. The ground beneath was visible in the spaces between the slats of rough-cut lumber.

There was no glass in the windows. No curtains. Just wooden shutters, folded together and latched from the inside.

Cora reached out a trembling hand to steady herself against the table, the pain in her abdomen increasing.

No coffee. No food. No visitor. No clues.

Not even a hint of the cryptic messages that she had come to expect from the dreams, except for the warring emotions inside her head and the pain in her middle.

There was an urgency to do something. She was supposed to know what to do. She had no idea what it was she was supposed to see.

Tentatively, she slid her bare feet along the floor beneath the swirling fabric and maneuvered herself to the bed and sat down.

Waves of cloth enveloped her slight frame as she struggled to push the material back from her hands, finding her struggles almost useless.

Only when she leaned back and stopped moving did she notice

that there was another movement that was not fabric around the bottom folds of the caftan. Lifting the fabric up and away from the floor, Cora saw her feet and stopped breathing.

A baby ball python, slits for pupils, tongue dancing in exploratory searching, was coiled around her ankles, kissing at her calves and joining her bare feet in living handcuffs that denied her the ability to run.

Her body froze in terror.

The warm roughness of the scales caressed her ankles as the snake moved, slithering across the floor.

Cora watched in horrified fascination as the reptile disappeared beneath the sagging bed frame.

Without her permission, her own body slid from the bed and onto the floor as well, flattening herself as best she could to peer through the darkness to follow the path of the python.

To her surprise, the snake had disappeared and in its place was the gypsy jar from her previous dream. Behind in the shadows she could see a medium-sized trunk—cobwebbed, battered, and sporting a gleaming padlock winking from the curious hiding place.

Every nerve in Cora's body was electrified and throbbing.

And she was awake.

Chapter 45

Every possible surface area of the florist's workshop was covered with bits of pastel-colored ribbons, rolls of sticky green tape, metal-tipped floral picks in multiple lengths, flecks of snow-white baby's breath, stems of shiny greenery, assorted vases, clear glass beads, and pastel ceramics empty, half-empty, and brimful with fragrant arrangements.

Darting around the counters were three agile, accomplished women in fashionable blue jeans and matching long-sleeved jerseys, their hands fluttering like frenetic butterflies over a massive field of variant blooms.

Vicki, on a rare break from supervising her well-trained crew, was talking on her phone on the other side of the dividing curtain in the relative peace and calm at the front of the shop.

"Miss Vicki," a lively voice called from behind her. "The rose order is here. Do I put them in the cooler and keep working on the table arrangements? Do you want to check to make sure the greenhouse sent what they promised?"

"Are they shades of pink, yellow, and red?" she asked, covering the phone with her hand. "As long as they aren't all the same color, I think we're good."

"Right," the voice responded. "Are you okay?"

"*Tres bien, cherie,*" she said, her Cajun French accent melodious and smooth. "The wildflowers need to be sorted and tucked into the second cooler, then you can take off for the afternoon. We'll put the vases first on the agenda tomorrow. They'll keep until the weekend. I'm going to need all your help with the local arrangements on Thursday and Friday."

"Of course." The voice disappeared behind the curtain.

Vicki returned the phone to her ear, avoiding the multiple dangling chains and decorative enamel hoops in rows down the outer edge of her lobe.

"I'm sorry for the interruption," she apologized. "There is so much still on the list before Saturday. I know you understand. You've got even more on your plate. . . . Don't be silly, *cherie,* you wouldn't call if this weren't urgent. What do you need me to do?"

The florist listened intently as she watched the traffic move back and forth in front of her shop window.

Cars, trucks, and pedestrians made their way around the town. Everyone with somewhere to go. Something to do.

Being in the center of the activity was a blessing to her heart.

She brushed at the flecks of white baby's breath littering the front of her colorful embroidered caftan with the tips of her enameled nails.

"Of course," she said finally. "No, you don't need to say anything else. I see why you called me. I can certainly do that. I'd be happy to do that for you."

She listened again, the corners of her deep-red lips curving upward.

"Yes, *cherie!*" she said. "You have asked, and I will not fail you. I promise."

The voice called from behind the curtains.

"Until Saturday," Vicki said into the receiver. "*Bon jour, mon amie.*"

She slipped the cell phone into the pocket of her caftan and turned.

"Coming, little ones," she answered the voice cheerfully. "I'll be right there!"

Chapter 46

Cora had some reservations about the trappings of Easter, especially bunnies that delivered candy-filled plastic eggs and shredded cellophane grass in multicolored wicker baskets.

She wanted Jane to enjoy holidays, but she also knew the discussions around Easter often turned to more serious, deeper religious conversations for which she felt radically unprepared.

Just as she'd felt unprepared for Inola Walker's recent visit.

Cora tried to push all the contradictory thoughts steadfastly out of her mind, along with the details of last night's dream. She'd made copious notes, but she still had no idea what any of the symbols meant.

The empty cabin, the python, the burdensome swelling of her hands and body, or the reappearance of the gypsy jar and a dusty trunk under a tumble-down, quilt-covered bed.

She had no clue who to tell or what to say.

Her head hurt, and all she could manage was thankfulness for

Marjorie's arrival and the soothing melodies she could be counted on to share throughout the day.

Marjorie, on the other hand, had seemed nonplussed about the appearance of the FBI agent. She was also perfectly comfortable with her own relationship with the Almighty. She could, and did, freely reconcile the dying of Easter eggs with the dying that came before the Resurrection and the joy that came from an empty tomb.

This morning the kitchen island was littered with a collection of coffee cups and mugs half-filled with brightly colored liquids. A stinging smell of hot white vinegar clung to the inside of her nose, hanging like mist in the air above each container.

Jane, wearing an oversized, once-white T-shirt rescued from a donation bag in Thomas's closet, sat on her customary stool. The white fabric, spotted and stained with various primary colors, had begun to resemble a tie-dyed explosion of messiness.

With the intensity of a mad chemist, Jane moved from one cup to another, stirring the liquid in each container, rolling each single, submerged boiled egg in turn.

At the apex of the semicircle of dyed eggs was an egg carton containing a half dozen eggs in bright shells, still damp, awaiting the next stage in the official decorating process—stickers, paint markers, glue, and copious amounts of colored glitter.

Marjorie never did anything by halves. Easter eggs were no exception.

Among the tinkling of the spoons and cups came the sound of the doorbell. Cora and Marjorie exchanged inquiring glances over the top of Jane's head.

"I'll answer," Cora said, sliding nimbly off the stool, pleased with a temporary reprieve from the smell of vinegar.

"Are you sure?" Marjorie took a spoon from Jane's hand and wiped the child's stained fingers. "We aren't expecting anyone, are we?"

"I don't think so," she said. "Maybe Agent Walker has more questions."

"I wouldn't be surprised," Marjorie agreed. "Call if you need me, please."

Cora could tell by glancing through the oval-shaped insert in the center of the door that the visitor outside on the porch was a man.

A man in a suit on a weekday in Balfour. A puzzle.

Andrew Evans and Thomas wore suits, but the shadow was too short and a bit wide for either of them. She thought about Charlie and his puzzling phone call about meeting Eudora Ashford, alias Astra.

This can't be Charlie on the porch either, she thought. *He always said the only time he'd be caught dead in a suit would be if I dress him in one for his funeral.*

The doorbell rang again more insistently.

Stop overthinking, she told herself. *You'll know what to do, you always do. There's nothing to be afraid of. Marjorie's right there in the kitchen. Don't be so silly.*

Harry Halstein seemed as startled as she was when she opened the door.

"Hello, Harry," she said, thinking he looked rather like a sheep waiting to be sheared.

A self-conscious silence floated between them as the businessman searched for words and found none.

"I'm Cora Stone," she said, extending her hand in greeting. "I recognize you from your picture on the cover of the *Griffith Gazette*.

I enjoyed reading their piece on your retirement and resettling in Balfour."

"You have an excellent memory," he said, shifting uneasily, looking past her into the house. "I don't want to bother you. I'm sorry I didn't call for an appointment. Susan seemed to think you wouldn't mind. I can see this wasn't the best idea. I can come back another day if you're busy."

You obviously don't want to be here, Cora thought.

"Not at all," she said. "I'd love to have an opportunity to get to know you better. Come into my office where we can talk. Marjorie and Jane are in the kitchen decorating Easter eggs. I'm sure you can smell the vinegar from here."

Cora could tell by his response, or rather his lack of response, that he was barely listening to her at all. He'd stepped over the threshold far enough for her to close the front door behind him, but he came to a standstill and she saw what had his attention.

Solomon was sprawled across a stair halfway up the staircase, his enormous black plume of a tail swishing back and forth, his green eyes blinking, and a tip of pink tongue visible through his bone-white teeth.

"Magnificent cat," he said, showing no sign of moving from the foyer except the constant shifting of his weight from one foot to the other.

"He certainly thinks so," Cora said. "You're not allergic, I hope, or ailurophobic. Solomon's harmless, but I can also put him upstairs if you'd like."

"No, I'm good with the cat," Harry said absently. "Are you sure you're available to talk? I didn't even ask about your fees."

"We can discuss that after we see if I can help," she said,

stepping aside, hoping to encourage him to precede her down the hallway.

Harry took a step toward the staircase, and Solomon poked his head through the railing, presenting himself to be petted. Harry obliged.

"I'll let Marjorie know you're here," she said when she reached the door to her office. "Would you like some coffee or lemonade?"

"Yes, please," he said, giving Solomon a final chin scratch. "Coffee, although I probably don't need the caffeine. I'm a little nervous about being here."

Well, keep talking, Cora thought. *That's a start.*

She found it interesting that Solomon, who generally preferred children over men, also liked Harry.

"Have a seat in the office and I'll be right back," she said.

When Cora returned from the kitchen, she found Harry staring at her newest framed picture of Jane's artwork, proudly displayed to the right of her desk.

Solomon had joined him, curling around the man's legs and purring contentedly, but Harry's attention was firmly fixed on the picture. He rubbed the palms of his hands together as if to remove something sticky.

A stick figure family of four—two adult women, a man, and a girl—stood beside a two-story white frame house surrounded by trees laden with oddly shaped fruits that might have been peaches or apples.

Even the cat, a ball of black scribbles with a wild feathered tail, had put in a comic appearance beside the feet of the stick-figure girl, whose huge red hair bow identified the artist. The entire artwork was ringed by rampant, wild-looking flowers.

It was a typical crayoned picture, the upper half filled with billowing white clouds partially hiding a shining, smiling yellow sun.

"Jane drew that the afternoon we came home from the court hearing in Atlanta," she explained. "The day we filed preliminary paperwork to set the adoption in motion."

"It's very good," Harry said, finally reaching down and petting Solomon's head. "She's got talent."

Deflection, Cora thought. *He's finally making small talk. He's probably come to talk about his half sister's death and just doesn't know how to begin. Maybe the picture makes him think about family.*

"Thank you," she said gently. "She loves to draw, like most children her age. You're very kind."

She motioned him toward a chair and took her place behind her desk, taking out a pad and pen.

"Why don't you tell me why you're here," she said. "And maybe why talking to me makes you feel nervous."

Harry leaned back in the chair, unsuccessfully attempting to relax. He unbuttoned his suit jacket and fiddled with the faux silk handkerchief in the pocket.

Cora thought he looked even more ill at ease than he'd been at her front door.

She assumed her most congenial counseling pose, summoned her most encouraging facial expression, and waited.

A brief knock at the office door broke the surface tension.

Marjorie, neither speaking nor acknowledging the business-man's presence, entered and placed a tray on the front corner of the desk. She was gone before Cora or Harry could express appreciation, rushing back to her young charge and the assorted cups of food color and boiled eggs.

"Thank you for your time," Harry said, running a hand through his meticulously groomed hair and playing with the collar of his shirt. "And for the coffee and the snack. Those are Marjorie's famous chocolate chip chunk cookies. I recognize them from the last bake sale."

Cora poured a steaming cup and held it out hopefully. He took the cup and blew away a white wisp of steam, watching as it dissipated into the cool air.

"Cream? Sugar?" she offered.

Harry liberally added both, stirring as the dark liquid faded to a light beige.

Pen in hand, Cora maintained her silence.

Until her visitor made the difficult decision to tell her what was on his mind, she was not in a position to help him. Half a cup of coffee and a cookie later, her patience was rewarded.

"You are the only one I know who might understand," he said, putting down his cup and resuming his palm-rubbing. "Susan suggested I talk to you about my half sister Dinah's death, especially in light of the ongoing investigation. The more people dig and the more they find out, the less I feel I knew my half sister or anything about her life."

He paused, encouraged by the open expression on Cora's face.

"I'm not much for talking about myself," he said, self-conscious and not too surprisingly shy. "My mother wasn't a believer in therapy and such. More a doer than a talker. We shared the same house for most of my life, but we never really discussed emotional issues. Feelings weren't something we shared. No offense to therapy or you."

You have a kind face, Cora thought. *No wonder Susan is attracted to you.*

"No offense taken," she said. "Everything you say is in confidence. Sharing isn't simple, nor is it painless. You should know that I'm only taking notes so I remember exactly what you tell me. No one else will see what I've written."

Harry stared down at the half-empty cup and began to toy with the handle.

"I suppose I feel guilty," he said. "We weren't at all close, Dinah and I. Maybe I could have helped her, been more of a brother to her."

"Many people experience strong feelings of regret at the suicide of a loved one," she assured him. "Guilt is a normal emotion under these circumstances."

Harry coughed to clear his throat in embarrassment.

"That's just it. I don't know if I'd call Dinah a loved one. We barely knew each other. I suppose I feel a bit guilty about that too. Time slipped away."

He stopped again, pulling nervously at his shirt collar under the edge of his tailored suit, perspiration gathering on his forehead.

"Maybe what I feel is angry," he admitted. "Angry with Dinah for calling me when it was too late. Angry that she didn't even give me a chance to know what was going on or offer to help her. I'm used to running a corporation and managing committees. I hate to admit that I'm not in control of any situation or even the master of my own feelings."

Cora nodded, waiting for him to organize his thoughts.

"Maybe I feel guilty for being angry with a dead woman," he said, reaching over and taking a tissue from the box on the desk.

"That doesn't make any sense at all, does it? I just keep saying the word *maybe*."

"Everything you've told me so far sounds perfectly normal," she said. "You're going through the stages of grief."

"I just hate not knowing what really happened to Dinah." He touched the tissue to his forehead to mop at the perspiration.

"Susan said your half sister had a heart condition," Cora said. "Was she under a doctor's care? In pain? Perhaps she wasn't thinking clearly. She might have been suffering the side effects of medications. It's quite possible her death had nothing to do with you at all."

"She was under the care of a doctor," he said, "though no one seems to believe he was a competent physician. He's under indictment right now. The FBI have hinted that she was under the influence of someone else, a fortune teller, a charlatan named Eudora Ashford who called herself Astra."

Only a slight widening of her pupils gave away Cora's response, which she covered quite effectively by pouring her own coffee and lifting the cup to her lips.

So the clues have been useful, she thought, allowing herself a moment of satisfaction, knowing she'd helped.

Harry drained his cup and resumed talking.

"The FBI found Dinah's journal among her personal posses-sions in her hotel room," he said. "I haven't even told Susan. Agent Walker let me read it after they'd gone through looking for clues about her state of mind. This Astra told her so many things that Dinah believed to be true about what her father supposedly said from beyond the grave. Nonsense like that. She convinced Dinah to sell her estate and all her assets based on these lies. In her final days, Dinah liquidated her entire life and signed it over to a foundation that this Ashford and Dinah's doctor controlled."

Cora sighed.

So, that's another thing that's bothering you, she thought. *Besides believing that your half sister's financial matters have been mishandled, now you're wondering about whether mediums and psychics are real.*

"She told Dinah things that *appeared* to be true," she corrected him firmly. "There are logical, reasonable, rational explanations for the vast majority of what are claimed to be psychic phenomena. Mentalists and mind readers are adept at taking bits and pieces of truth and weaving a believable narrative. This woman tricked your sister."

"With the help of that crooked doctor," he said, crumpling the used tissue in his fist. "I wish I knew what that charlatan told her that made her give up hope."

"You want to understand how that happened," Cora said. "That's normal."

"Can you help me?" The businessman's face reddened but his voice remained even. "How can a rational person like Dinah be convinced of such ridiculous nonsense?"

I wonder what you'd think of my dreams, Cora thought. *Ridiculous nonsense? I suppose that's what they'd look like from where you're sitting. Maybe from where Inola Walker's sitting too, if the true be told.*

"Is that what you really want from me?" she asked. "For me to explain how the human mind can be deceived by a trained mentalist? I don't know Eudora Ashford, but I've met many individuals like her who trade on human frailty, loneliness, and need."

Cora waited for Harry to digest what she was saying.

"I'm not sure what I want," he said sadly, rolling the ball of tissue in his hands. "I just wish I'd kept in touch with Dinah. Maybe if she'd had someone to turn to rather than this woman, she'd still be alive."

"None of us grow old without regrets." Cora tried to sound reassuring. "Judging ourselves through the lens of the past is unfair, to ourselves and our memories."

"I don't know what to think," he said. "Dinah never went to church, though my mother said she tried once or twice to talk to her about her relationship with God. I've got no idea if Dinah even believed in life after death. She must have, right? She sought out this woman who claimed to give her a connection with her dead father."

"Many people feel there's a spiritual outside of the religious. That the occult's a shortcut to seeing the future and taking a walk on the other side."

"And what do you believe, Cora?" he asked, picking up a napkin and wiping the crumbs from the corners of his mouth. "About the occult? About seeing the future?"

She lifted the plate of cookies and offered him another one, which he accepted.

"I believe you came to me for a solution to a problem and not my opinions on religion or the occult," she said, replacing the plate on the tray, turning her notebook to a blank page, and clicking her ink pen.

"Let's begin with your relationship with your mother, her influence on your life, and how that may affect what you're feeling about your half sister's untimely death."

She paused briefly.

"And then maybe we can talk about what you expected to

accomplish from today's visit with me. I'd like to help you, Mr. Halstein, I really would."

Chapter 47

"I don't want to be disturbed," the man said, his designer fountain pen flowing smoothly over a blank signature line in Darcie's guest register. His obnoxiously rude and condescending behavior grated on her nerves, but what was worse for Darcie was that his portly bulk kept blocking her view of her own sign-in table.

As though he were keeping some sort of secret.

There wasn't much Darcie despised more than people who weren't honest with her. And this man was not being honest with her. She could tell from the moment he'd sauntered into the front foyer, preceded by a pungent wave of Old Spice aftershave.

"I assume as a reputable bed and breakfast that there will be a breakfast served," he said. "But I'm not interested in all the additional frills and niceties. Just expresso and whole wheat toast."

"Would you like homemade jam or jelly with that?" Darcie asked, summoning her most accommodating hostess skills. "We've got a wide assortment of local preserves from which you can select, and I can make certain your choice is readily available."

"I'd also rather not eat with a crowd," he added, ignoring her offer and tugging at the bottom of his tailored brocade vest, adjusting his teal and pink polka dot bow tie with chubby pink fingers. "Do you provide room service?"

Darcie shot him a withering scowl. He'd crossed a line and he knew it.

"No," she said.

"All right then," he said petulantly. "What is the optimum time for privacy in the dining room?"

Darcie swallowed her exasperation. She told herself that she should feel sorry for him. The pitiful man looked like a lost member of a barbershop quartet, or an over-dressed collectible doll, his blustering ego inflated beyond his intellectual capacity.

He has no fashion sense at all. That's a costume for a vaudeville show, she thought, watching him preen in the mirror beside the hall tree. *And that aftershave. His sense of smell is gone too. I don't know how anyone can be that self-absorbed and tone-deaf.*

"I asked about the schedule," he snipped. "You do have a schedule, I presume."

She took a deep breath.

Well, with that attitude, you and the Senator will make excellent breakfast mates, she thought. *He doesn't want to come down until everyone else is gone either.*

"We normally serve from seven until nine on weekdays, and seven thirty until ten on the weekends," she said. "I really can't accurately predict when the other guests will come down to breakfast."

She reached past him to turn the guest book around to see what he'd written.

John Smith, she thought. *I knew you were up to something. You've got to be kidding me. Do I look that gullible?*

"That's hilarious, Daryl," she said. "The Griffith Historical Society may be paying for your room, but that doesn't change the standard policy. I know why you're really here. You're doing an article for them on the Wilton House opening. I don't care who's picking up the tab for your room, I'm still going to need a credit card for incidentals. Your credit card. With your real name, please."

"Is that absolutely necessary?" he said stiffly. "I'm here representing the society, and I do not want to broadcast my presence in Balfour."

"Of course, Daryl," she said. "I'm not surprised you're trying to keep a low profile after that hit piece you wrote about us. But honey, you've got to be more imaginative with your disguise than a handlebar mustache and a cheap gaudy suit doused in cologne. Folks around here have known your family for years. For heaven's sake, you were only two years behind me in school."

"Please lower your voice," he said, adjusting his heavy rimmed glasses and brushing at his substantial mustache. "I'm incognito. I'm doing in-depth research."

"Once a whiner, always a whiner," she said. "We all remember Ben Taylor had to walk you home every day in fourth grade to keep the bullies from beating you up and taking your book bag. I like you, Daryl, in spite of that horrible article you wrote about Marcie and me, our family, and our town. I don't hold grudges."

"I was only being honest." He sniffed defensively. "People want to read the truth about history."

"What you mean is your truth," she said. "And any nasty little innuendos you can find to spice up the story. I'd be ashamed of myself if I were you. Raking up red Georgia clay and smearing it all over your neighbors. Why don't you take some English classes at the community college and improve your writing skills so people will read your work because you have something worth saying and not just for the bits of sensational drivel?"

"All the same and your opinions aside," he said loftily, snatching up his battered Samsonite suitcase in one hand and his computer case in the other, "I'd like the key to my room now, and I'd like to remain undisturbed for the next twelve hours."

"Fine with me, Daryl," she said. "You just do you, honey. But if you want a key to a room in my bed and breakfast, I'm still going to need to see a credit card. With your name on it. Please and thank you very much."

Chapter 48

The Sixth Day: Friday

Cora felt a cool spring breeze blowing against her skin and rough boards of hand-hewn wood underneath her bare feet. Looking down, she realized she was wearing a simple cotton sheath, her upper arms wrapped in a cotton knit shawl, and her silky hair pulled back at the base of her neck with a grosgrain ribbon.

She inhaled the scent of wild honeysuckle and a forest of pines.

The last rays of light were fading behind a cluster of hills to her right, and black and white dusk reflected on the porch of the log cabin she recognized from the previous night.

The image of the python and the persistent slithering about her feet and legs drifted through her mind and was quickly gone.

From the primitive building behind her, she heard the muffled sound of a man's booming bass voice and a woman's heartbroken weeping.

Cora hesitantly pushed open the unlatched door, greeted by the odor of burning logs and coal oil and the musty smell of earth and old quilts. And death itself.

The same room from the night before was now occupied by the residents of the past.

The meager stone fireplace, down to glowing coals and embers, illuminated the one-room cabin, throwing shadows and shafts of gray light into the gloom. In the center of the room a second source of light, a burning coal oil lamp, made a dim pool on the square handmade table, flanked by two long benches, and a crude three-legged stool.

Within the circle of gray light sat the unsealed gypsy jar she had already seen. Beside it, a leather-strapped wooden chest and an open, palm-sized padlock.

Cora saw something else that hadn't been in the first dream.

A small oval wicker basket with a scrap of cloth draped across the top sat on the corner of the table. She looked closer and realized that the material was an unfinished baby gown, half-sewn and hand-stitched, straight pins still holding together the bits of delicate gossamer fabric.

And Cora knew without being told.

The gown was waiting for the sewing that would never come. A baby it would never adorn.

An anguished cry rang out in the semidarkness.

In the far corner she saw the source of the weeping, a humble bed containing a slight figure, her face a mask of pain, her agonized cries bubbling up from some infinite pool of suffering. At the foot of the bed was a rough-hewn wooden cradle.

A diminutive bundle lay unmoving within.

Standing beside the bed were two figures—one the ominous shadow of a slump-shouldered man and the other a smaller, wiry shadow, that of an adolescent boy trembling as he gripped the man's much larger forearm.

Cora watched as the heart-wrenching drama played out before her. The woman took her last sobbing breath, uttering a hushed plea to the shadow-man, reaching out a thin arm and pointing to the table and the gypsy jar with the last strength in her frail body before the hand dropped lifelessly onto the quilt at her side.

The boy wept uncontrollably, but the man made no move to comfort him.

Instead he detached the boy's hand and pushed him away, reaching down the brief distance to remove the simple wedding ring from the woman's still-warm finger.

With a snort of distaste, he drew the blanket over her lifeless face, whirling angrily to the table.

As Cora stood helplessly by, he snatched the jar from the table and tossed the ring into a small leather bag from the tabletop, then into the gypsy jar.

Cora knew the bag's contents.

The lock of a baby's hair from the bundle in the cradle. From the woman's infant child.

The man took a roundish stained cork from his trouser pocket and pressed it roughly down into the neck of the bottle, sealing it tightly.

Then, in a rare moment of emotion, his glance fell on the pin-cushion lying atop the wicker sewing basket. He pushed aside the unfinished gown and removed a single glass-topped quilting pin, stabbing it into the center of the cork.

As the boy's crying subsided, his shoulders still shaking and his eyes fixed forlornly at the draped form, Cora could almost feel the agony of his pain, as if he knew the man would demand he regain control and the time of grieving come to an end.

The man sniffed, wiping his broad nose with the back of his hand before he roughly tossed the jar into the open trunk, slamming and locking it securely without so much as a cursory glance at the boy or the body.

Snatching up the box with one calloused hand, he hefted the key in the other hand and stomped to the front porch into the gathering nightfall.

This is not her husband, Cora thought. *This is not his son, nor his dead baby daughter in the cradle. A father couldn't be so cruel. So heartless. He must be her relative. A brother? An uncle? Where is the baby's father? Why is this man so angry?*

Cora could feel the rush of damp night air as he swept past her. For a moment she debated staying with the boy, but as the fire burned lower and the coal oil lamplight faded, she sensed that she should follow the man, although her tender heart ached with sympathy for the scene she had witnessed.

She could do nothing to change the past, and for that she grieved.

Shadowing the enraged man out onto the porch, she watched him stumble down the narrow steps into the darkness at the edge of her vision.

He dropped the trunk on the ground and strode further into the yard, just to the edge where the faint light blended into pitch black. His powerful arm drew back and he threw what she could only surmise was the key into the dense forest.

Then he returned to the cabin, picking up a weather-beaten shovel leaning against the corner of the steps, and thrust the tip of the iron into the rocky earth.

"No," a pleading voice protested. "No, Uncle. Please don't put it in the ground. Mama wouldn't want you to bury it. You know she wouldn't."

The man looked up begrudgingly and grunted.

"She finished the dry cellar," the boy continued between ragged breaths, fighting to maintain composure. "You know why she did. Please put it there where it's safe."

The man leaned on the shovel, making a pretense of paying attention.

"You know she'll have to go in the ground," he said unkindly. "And your baby sister too. Even if it was big enough, the dry cellar is no place for dead bodies."

The boy squared his shoulders with a glint of raw defiance and a prophetic spark of manhood. This child was resolute that his mother's last requests should be honored.

"Then that's enough burying in the ground," he said simply, firmly. "Please, Uncle."

Uncle, Cora thought. *The dead woman's brother. Or her husband's brother.*

The dank, dark humidity suspended between the two of them as they stood, dancing between the adult's cold logic and the child's love for his mother. The older man looked away first, taking out a grimy handkerchief and wiping the sweat dripping from his forehead and neck.

"Then you can take that back inside yourself," he snapped, carelessly kicking the side of the trunk. "I'm done with the whole business. I'll put them in the ground tonight, but if you want anything else, you'll be the one to do it. There's nothing left for me here. You think you're a man, then be a man."

The boy descended from the porch, self-assurance and conviction increasing with every step. With a sweeping motion, he picked up the trunk and walked back into the cabin, the transition from youth to manhood complete.

Cora followed to see what he was going to do with his newfound responsibility and his self-imposed burden, but she already knew.

In the dimness, he struggled to push aside the bed frame, still laden with his mother's body, revealing the outline of a slightly lighter square of fresh-hewn wood planks about two feet by three feet wide. The boy's hand slid across the boards and found a crude latch, tugging at it until the top creaked to expose a hidden cavity.

With a labored sigh, he reverently lowered the trunk inside and closed the wooden floor top with a thud.

From outside the open cabin door, Cora could hear the muted hiss of the shovel as the steel bit into the graveled ground. Again and again. Hiss after hiss.

Cora thought of the python wrapped around her ankles and shivered.

Outside in what would become the fenced graveyard, the bitter uncle was digging the final resting place for the two bodies inside the house. But thanks to a ten-year-old boy who'd become a man, the chest that contained their heritage and hope was hidden inside the house for posterity to find.

And Cora was awake, staring into the red numbers of the time blinking beneath the blades of the ceiling fan as it turned—4:20 a.m. Two hours until daylight.

Beside her, Thomas made a soft snoring noise and restlessly rolled away from her onto his side, taking most of the bedcovers with him as he turned.

Cora took her chenille robe from the foot of the bed and slipped out from under what was left of the sheet on her side. Her feet searched the floor for her soft slippers.

There was no question for her now. She knew the reason behind this particular dream and the story that needed to be told. The hissing crunch of the shovel in the ground and graves that held voices from the past reverberated against her doubts.

A mother who had lost a child so long ago and who was reaching out to her, pleading that her story be told. That her son and his descendants know the truth.

Cora knew exactly what she had to do, and who she needed to tell.

Chapter 49

Cora waited until almost eight that morning to call Katy on her home telephone. Hannah answered with her usual cheery enthusiasm.

"Yes," the talkative housekeeper said, "Katy's been up since seven. She's taking Elizabeth to preschool this morning to drop off the Easter eggs for the hunt today. Then she did mention something about errands. I don't remember. She walked out of the house about five minutes ago. I'm sorry you've just missed her."

"Do you know what time she's dropping off Elizabeth?"

Cora wanted to have Katy's full attention while she determined how to bring up the subject of searching for a hidden trunk in Zeke Balfour's cabin.

"Classes start at eight thirty," Hannah said. "Katy likes to be the first in line even if she has to wait."

Cora could hear Amy in the background asking something about breakfast.

"Thank you, Hannah," she said quickly. "I'll just try to catch her on her cell phone."

Now I have time for coffee with Thomas, she thought pleasantly. *I'll give Katy time to drop off Elizabeth, and I'll also have a little more time to decide how to broach the subject of searching the cabin for the trunk.*

The image of the cabin that Katy had described during their therapy session was vivid in her mind, as well as the gypsy jar that Katy had not described. That a trunk could be hidden somewhere under the bed inside seemed perfectly reasonable and logical.

Cora was certain the trunk would contain the secrets to a story that she knew needed to be told. Not a secret about a crime so much as a heartache and history that was in some way connected to Katy.

The cabin, the gypsy jar, a hidden trunk, a devoted son, a mother and child, and an angry brother digging graves. How to communicate to Katy, and where things should go from there, she had no idea. She resisted the urge to share the dream with Thomas, or even with Marjorie.

No sense muddying the waters until she could see things clearly for herself. She was still trying to sort through the dreams about dear old Aunt Phoebe and licorice tea and cope with Charlie's annoyance at being drawn back into their old alliance.

She'd just finished making her vanilla coffee when Thomas appeared in the kitchen doorway, suited and ready to leave for the office.

"Marjorie left almost a full pot of your coffee," Cora said. "She's gone upstairs with Jane so she can help her dress in play clothes. They have a garden date with Marcie to plant flowers in the window boxes at the Piney Woods."

"Sounds like fun," Thomas said, because he thought it sounded like the right thing to say. Gardening was not something he especially enjoyed, and besides, his mind was on Charlie. He poured his mug full and turned. "Did you have the dream last night?"

Cora pressed her cup between her hands, appreciating the heat, and knew that her husband was wondering if she was going to call Charlie. And if she was going to ask his opinion about calling. Some days Thomas was painfully obvious.

"Come to the front porch," she said reassuringly. "Nothing much to share with Charlie. Just jumbles for now. I'd rather talk about something more pleasant like Jane's latest favorite book, whether or not to plant okra and squash in our vegetable garden, plans for the Wilton House, or juicy gossip from Susan."

Thomas glanced at his watch and immediately regretted his decision when he saw the disappointed look on his wife's face.

"Unless you're in a hurry," she added quickly. "It's Friday and I thought we could talk about normal things for a change, but just if you have the time. I don't know what's on your calendar for today."

He loosened his tie and unbuttoned the top button of his shirt.

"You're right," he said. "It's Friday. Almost the weekend of a really stressful week. Of course I have time. There's nothing on my calendar more important than talking to you. I'll just tell the boss I had a critical meeting with my best client."

He held the steaming mug slightly away, reaching out to take his wife's hand in his and squeezing her palm possessively. "I've got a great boss. I'm sure she'll understand."

"You do know that you're the employer and she's the employee, right?"

Thomas kissed her lightly on the forehead and turned, leading her behind him down the hallway to the front door, still holding her hand.

"Don't tell Susan," he said over his shoulder. "She thinks she's in charge. Makes for more peaceful and productive days at work."

Twenty minutes later Thomas was gone and Marjorie was preparing a grocery list at the kitchen island with eager input from Jane.

Still not quite certain about how she was going to approach the subject of finding the mysterious trunk, Cora prepared another cup of vanilla coffee and went into her office to call Katy on her cell phone.

The widow answered immediately.

"I know this sounds unusual," Cora said. "And I hesitate to interfere, but I wanted to talk to you before the Wilton House opening tomorrow."

Katy interrupted her almost immediately.

"I was going to call you," she said, suddenly embarrassed that she'd gone so diametrically opposite to her counselor's directions. "I know you told me it wasn't a good idea, and I know I should have listened to you, but I went to see Zeke Balfour again."

"Oh," Cora said. "How did that go?"

"Better and worse than I expected," she said. "Worse because I made a complete idiot of myself in front of a total stranger, and better because his daughter persuaded him to let me have something from the cabin for the opening day."

"Of course," Cora said, weighing her words. "I'm happy you've found something to contribute. I know that's important to you."

"Yes," Katy said meekly. "I'm not sure I'd have considered stepping out and asking for what I want without your encouragement over the last few months. I know this isn't what you meant for me to do, but you've helped me so much."

There it is, Cora thought. *The opening to suggest something. To hint at the trunk in the cabin. Stepping out indeed. Katy's not the only one in uncharted water.*

She'd shared her dreams reluctantly with Charlie, Marjorie, and Thomas. And Ted Floyd, of course. He'd tried to help her after the first dream with James, but she didn't count him with the others. They were her family. They believed, or they let her think they did. The psychiatrist viewed her nocturnal visitor as a clinical sign of her past break with reality, her ongoing depression and phobias. A manifestation of her mental illness. He would have scoffed if anyone had suggested they were anything more than that.

Sharing with Katy felt risky and uncomfortable, yet right at the same time.

"That's great news," Cora said, summoning her courage and trusting her instinct. "You know, it's interesting that you said Zeke is willing to give you something from inside the cabin. I had a thought last night while I was doing research for my book. There's always the possibility that what's inside the cabin might be useful and valuable. Something you could put on display."

Katy laughed, delighted that Cora was on board with the plan.

"As I said," Cora continued, meticulously walking a line between fact and fiction, absolute truth and lies, "I do quite a lot of research on random subjects that come up while I'm writing. We assume that before bank deposit boxes and safes that items of value were always buried when they were often hidden inside older homes to protect them from the weather or theft."

Katy was momentarily puzzled by the turn in the conversation, and then an idea came to her.

"Speaking of buried," she said. "Not that I'd know what to do about it, but there's a gated graveyard just to one side of the cabin. Two old graves with granite headstones inside a rusty iron fence. One is larger than the other. I tried to read what's carved on them, but it's no use. The words are just a blur with what looks like a crude cross etched into the top of each marker. Zeke claims he doesn't know who's buried there. I don't think he'd care if he did know, but I'm sure there must be a story about those people. Maybe the Griffith Historical Society has some information I could research."

Cora bit her tongue until it hurt.

"Now if you're talking about the inside of the cabin," Katy continued, "I chanced a peek through a window on the porch. There's nothing except some rustic handmade furniture, a table with benches, and a rope bed. Are you saying you think there might be something else there, just hidden?"

"Maybe," Cora said cryptically, mentally trying to separate what Katy had told her about the cabin from what she had seen in the dream, trying to keep from mentioning some detail that she couldn't possibly know.

This is harder than I expected it to be, Cora thought.

"Yes, there could also be something hidden that isn't obvious at first sight."

"But where would I look?" Katy asked. "Are you thinking they might find something in the walls or floor? Do you really think there's a chance of that?"

"I've heard that valuables are often put for safekeeping in trap-doors in the floors," Cora said. "Often under pieces of furniture."

"Ah," Katy said. "Under rugs? There might have been a braided rug in front of the stone fireplace. I don't remember."

"Or beds," Cora countered. "I was just thinking you could check. Or if you're busy with Elizabeth this afternoon, maybe have someone check for you."

"Thank you," Katy said, feeling further emboldened. "I'll be at Lizzy's preschool Easter egg hunt at noon. Besides, I promised Zeke that I wouldn't show up and annoy him again. Did you have someone in mind? Zeke Balfour has a mighty strong personality."

Charlie's going to argue with me about this, Cora thought. *But who else can I ask? Who's going to believe me? Who's going to accept the clues in a dream without question? Who's going to know someone in Balfour who can open a hundred-year-old lock without a key?*

"Charlie's in town," Cora said. "You know how he loves a local mystery."

Katy imagined the spunky, spirited detective in a toe-to-toe confrontation with the sulky sculptor.

"Yes, you're right, Cora!" she said. "You have the best ideas! Charlie's perfect for the job. Are you sure he'll be willing? If there's something hidden anywhere around that cabin, who better than a clever detective like Charlie to find it? And he won't have any problem dealing with Zeke either. I had no idea he was back. I never got to really thank him for all he did for us when Steve died. He just disappeared. Do you want to call him, or should I?"

Chapter 50

Eudora Ashford slipped into the Salvation Army thrift store around the corner from her rental house without attracting undue attention and purchased a classic grandmotherly dress from a sales rack. Plain and simple with generously unflattering lines, it accentuated the frumpiness of her middle-aged figure.

She zipped the navy-blue dress and surveyed the tiny white floral print and crisp white Peter Pan collar and cuffs in the full-length mirror. She was pleased.

Directly under her artfully painted face was a cheap cameo pin, and clipped to her ears were marble-sized, single faux pearl earrings from the local dollar store. Her streaked hair had been captured into a tight, tidy bun at the base of her neck and was covered by what appeared to be a hand-crocheted snood of snow-white lace.

Even her pudgy, lily-white hands, bare of any trace of nail polish, were absent of her customary rings.

One single gold wedding band, kept at the bottom of her jewelry box for just such an occasion, had taken up residence on her left ring finger, proclaiming discreetly that once, perhaps, she had been married to an equally simple and honorable man.

The drive to Balfour had given her plenty of time to think and plan what she would say and do and what part she would play to get the information she thought she needed.

Keep things simple, she told herself.

She just needed to be able to answer the questions the other woman would ask without giving away too much information of her own.

She would say that Dinah was a dear friend and had told her there was a brother in Balfour. That she wanted to meet him and offer words of consolation.

She'd say that she'd only looked up Cora because of the detective. Maybe that she knew they'd been married before. That she was looking for a contact person and thought that a psychologist would be willing to help her.

She would say that he had asked for her help with the investigation, as she was Dinah's close friend and had experience helping law enforcement.

The trickiest question of all might be why she hadn't contacted the detective directly, so she would have to say he didn't leave his card with her.

It all sounded so right, so logical in her head.

She would use Cora Stone to find the detective or the brother—it didn't matter as long as she was safe in the end.

When she arrived, Eudora parked her car respectfully at the end of the driveway and turned off the engine to the car. She dropped the keys into her fake leather purse and surveyed the house.

Typical, she thought. *Victorian. Traditional. Old South. How precious.*

She opened the car door and gathered her wits.

Stay calm and remember why you came, she told herself. *You've rehearsed your lines. Stick to the script.*

Marjorie was watching from the kitchen window as the woman got out of her car and started up the steps. She dried her hands on the cotton dishcloth and took her time answering the knock on the front door.

No sense getting in any kind of hurry. She knew from what Cora had told her over coffee that morning the identity of the woman coming up the front walk. They'd talked about it and made plans for what they would do when she arrived.

Eudora Ashford, she thought. *It's about time.*

Agent Walker had called them early with the news. She'd put a surveillance team on Ashford's house to see what she'd do after Charlie's visit, and this morning Inola called to let Cora know that their suspect was on the move. They'd tracked her north toward Gainesville, and their best guess was that she was headed to Balfour. They'd followed her all the way just to be certain and stayed the rest of the afternoon in town at Sam's for good measure.

Marjorie had been considering what she should or could do to help while she washed the breakfast dishes, and a mischievous, rather deceitful idea had popped into her head.

She knew better than to share her plan with Cora. Cora would not approve, but as far as Marjorie was concerned, Eudora Ashford deserved exactly what was going to happen to her and more.

Cora heard the louder-than-usual hymn humming before she heard the doorbell ring, coming down the stairs just as Marjorie pulled the door open to reveal their guest.

Framed in the doorway, Eudora Ashford assumed a practiced pose, like an aging actress auditioning for the ingenue role in a British drawing room drama—out of her time and well out of place.

In spite of the meticulous veneer, Cora recognized the woman for who she was. Eudora Ashford might be a gifted chameleon, but Cora had the edge. Not only was she a trained profiler, but she had a loyal partner in Marjorie, who was no less proficient herself in the art of assessing human nature.

Even a proverbial horse of a different color, Marjorie thought smugly, *is still, after all, just a horse. And you, Eudora, are woefully underprepared.*

"Good afternoon," Eudora offered quickly, making good on her decision to go on the offensive. She extended her hand, and Cora took the last few steps down the stairs to meet the much taller woman.

"Hello," Cora said, giving the woman a firm handshake, her smaller hand encased completely in the woman's grip. "I'm Cora Stone. How can I help you?"

"Eudora Ashford. I was wondering if you could spare a few moments for a conversation about a mutual friend," she said, looking pointedly at Marjorie. "A private conversation."

"Did you want a counseling session?" Cora asked. "Or a consultation?"

"Neither," Eudora said.

She gave the waiting Marjorie another harsh stare.

"I really would rather discuss this in private," she continued. "It's personal."

"Then perhaps we should go into my office," Cora suggested. "Please come this way."

As per their hastily made plan, Marjorie dutifully waited until the office door closed, and then, deviating slightly from the design, made her way quickly out the sunroom into the backyard.

"It's really quite a lovely home you have here," Eudora said, eyeing the two chairs in front of Cora's desk and then sweeping her gaze around the remainder of the room with a practiced inspection.

"Thank you," Cora said. "Won't you have a seat?"

Eudora put her hand on the back of one of the chairs and waited for Cora to sit first, sizing up the situation as a large cat might contemplate a tiny mouse. Hoping that by standing the smaller woman would feel intimidated.

But Cora recognized the tactic for what it was.

A sudden inspiration hit Eudora. There'd been no mention of children in anything she'd read about this woman, but by the artwork on the walls she was clearly invested in work with children. She could use that as a starting point.

"I see you work with children," Eudora said. "Do you enjoy your work?"

Cora ignored the question.

"You said you had something personal to discuss," she said sweetly. "Is this about a child?"

"Not really," Eudora said, feeling unexpectedly awkward.

She leaned over and placed her hand on Cora's desk as if reaching out to offer help.

Time to be blunt.

"I've come about Dinah Browning," she said dramatically.

The woman studied Cora's face intently, searching for some

reaction to hearing Dinah's name, but she was sorely disappointed.

"Dinah was one of my dear friends," Eudora said, persistently watching for a reaction from Cora and finding none.

"Why would you think I'd know anything about a woman named Dinah Browning?"

Maybe she isn't working with the detective, Eudora thought, realizing suddenly how tenuous the connections were and struggling with her own logic. *Perhaps she can still help me find the brother.*

"Detective Abbott came to see me. He wanted my help with the investigation into a death—Dinah's death," Eudora said. "He's from Balfour, isn't he? And my dear friend Dinah told me that she had a brother here in Balfour. I don't know how to get in touch with Detective Abbott again, and I would love to reach out to the family. I simply thought that since you and the detective had once been married, and because Dinah's brother lives here now . . ."

Her voice trailed off, and she hoped Cora would pick up the thread of thought, but the psychologist remained quiet, waiting for clarification.

"I'm a psychic, you know," Eudora announced as though her occupation explained everything. "I have a gift."

"I've never met a psychic," Cora admitted. "Please tell me what it's like."

"It's been with me since birth." The older woman sniffed with a touch of arrogance, unable to resist the urge to talk about herself to an avid listener. "A valuable gift to law enforcement. Perhaps you yourself are familiar with those who make themselves available to assist in investigations."

"Really?" Cora's eyes widened artlessly, determined to keep the woman talking until Marjorie came in with the tea and cookies.

"You've assisted in police investigations? That's impressive. Please elaborate."

"Well," Eudora said, preening proudly, "I've had premonitions and visions of missing children, serial killers, and of course murder cases."

"In Atlanta?"

Eudora hesitated, trying to puzzle together how Cora would have known about Atlanta if she wasn't working with the detective.

The broken threads of connection between Cora Stone and Charlie Abbott began to weave back together in her mind.

She knows more than she's saying, she thought. *Was I right to come here?*

"No, not Atlanta."

For the first time since she sat down, Eudora twisted uncomfortably in her chair and stared down at the floor, inspecting the toes of her navy pumps.

At that moment Marjorie, who had been monitoring the time on the kitchen clock, entered the office with the freshly polished silver tea service and two elegant porcelain silver-rimmed teacups with tiny fluted saucers. Delicately positioned on the silver tray between the cups were a half dozen silver-dollar-sized raspberry thumbprint cookies, resting like tiny bright red eggs in a doily-lined crystal nest.

Cora's eyes met Marjorie's and she tried not to laugh out loud.

A virtual celebration of silver.

Marjorie never brought out or polished the silver service for people she liked and respected. The housekeeper felt that such showiness was ostentatious and crass except under the most formal of circumstances.

She decided to show her distain for this charlatan with a show of opulence and artificial fine breeding. To Marjorie's mind, only the shallowest and weakest minds were taken in by a show of wealth.

While the cookies were indeed delicious, Cora knew that these, unlike many expensive handmade delicacies, were store-bought and prepackaged. Cheap, generic, and not even a name brand.

Poor Eudora had no idea she was being mocked.

Marjorie had also chosen a pretentious local blackberry tea, strong and pungent, the darkness swirling against the sides of the cups as she poured. A tea the housekeeper knew should be taken in careful moderation since it was well-known locally for its mildly laxative properties.

With a flourish worthy of a grand English butler, Marjorie shook out a lacy linen napkin and draped it elegantly onto Eudora's lap.

Solomon, with his own sense of pompous grandeur, padded into the room at that moment and eyed the dangling corner of the napkin closest to him with understandable curiosity, his feathery black tail sweeping like a bridal train behind him.

The fortune teller had been watching the presentation in stunned silence. With a thick gasp of displeasure at the cat's arrival, she flicked the napkin up and out with sudden, flourishing fanfare. The tip of the napkin struck the air slightly in front of the cat's whiskers, barely missing his sensitive pink nose.

Solomon hissed and retreated.

Marjorie, quaking with repressed fury, lifted the cup in its saucer and placed them into Eudora's waiting hands.

"Would you like a cookie, Ms. Ashford?" Marjorie offered through her clenched teeth, lifting the cut glass nest with both hands. Eudora looked down at the cup in her lap and hesitated.

"Maybe in a moment," she said blankly.

Cora covered her mouth to prevent herself from giggling at the look on the woman's face.

Marjorie poured the second cup without asking and placed it on the desk before Cora, just out of the therapist's reach, while Cora deftly picked up a cookie and popped it into her mouth, waiting for her urge to laugh to subside.

"This is delightful tea," the fortune teller said, sipping the hot liquid and looking up through slightly steamed glasses. "Enchantingly bold flavor."

"I thought you might like it," Cora replied, ignoring her own cup. She preferred coffee or herbal tea, and it was time to play the final card in her hand. "I was given to understand from Detective Abbott that you're something of a connoisseur of homemade teas and herbal remedies. That you use them regularly in your prognostications."

Eudora's cup and saucer made a tiny, tinkling clatter as they came to rest on the edge of the desk.

The detective! her mind screamed at her. *So they are working together! What game are they playing?*

The woman wiped her lips hastily with the napkin as she tried to regain her composure.

"Interesting that you'd bring up the subject of homemade. I sometimes grow my own leaves, that much is true."

"Marjorie learned to pick her own leaves and brew from her great-grandmother in the mountains of Tennessee," Cora offered helpfully.

Both Marjorie and Cora could not help noticing the rapidly changing reactions on Eudora's face and the rash of color that flashed up from her white collar.

"Actually," Marjorie corrected, thoroughly enjoying her key role in the charade, "I learned from my crazy Great-Aunt Flora in the heart of the Mississippi Delta. I even have her handwritten recipe book from the 1920s. Her scrawling spider writing is so hard to read, not to mention those scribbled illustrations of which leaves to pick, and when, and where. She was no artist, I can tell you. Most of what Flora did was medicinal, anyway."

"You brewed this yourself?" Eudora was running her tongue over her perfectly polished teeth and scrubbing her lips with the edge of the napkin, searching for an aftertaste she might recognize. "Could I have a glass of water?"

"Maybe you would like more tea?" Marjorie reached for the silver pot, but Eudora waved her arm away and searched around her feet for her oversized purse.

"Or perhaps we could offer you some licorice tea?" Cora suggested. "Marjorie discovered one of her Aunt Flora's recipes only last week. It's inspired."

At the mention of licorice tea, Eudora knew it was finally time to leave. That there was nothing to be gained and everything to lose. The women knew too much.

"I just realized that I need to go," she managed through a strangled breath. "I have an afternoon appointment."

What have I drunk? she thought wildly. *Some insane concoction of weeds? A toxic tonic of some sort? I need to get back to Atlanta and pack up again. This was foolish of me. Much too foolish of me to come here.*

"So soon?" Cora stood. "But we've only begun to get to know each other. I'd hoped you'd spend the entire afternoon with us.

I'd love to hear more about your exploits with the Memphis PD. Marjorie was going to prepare lunch too."

Eudora found her purse and clutched it to her bosom as she stood, almost tripping over the chair as she stumbled to the door.

"Perhaps another time," she called back, Solomon hissing from the staircase as she disappeared down the hallway to the front door.

"I'll see you out," Marjorie offered, but Eudora Ashford had ungracefully bolted, neither slowing nor acknowledging the house-keeper. If she'd bothered to look back into the room, she'd have seen Cora lift the used cup with the corner of a napkin and artfully pour the remaining blackberry tea back into the silver pot.

The front door slammed firmly before the conspirators burst into uncontrolled laughter.

"You offered for me to feed her lunch?" Marjorie said, feigning irritation.

"I'm sorry," Cora said through her own giggles. "You wanted her to leave, now didn't you? Where is that evidence bag Inola gave us? She wanted a clean set of prints and DNA for the FBI database, and if I laugh any harder I'm going to drop this cup."

"In the kitchen." Marjorie said. "I'll get it."

She paused in the doorframe.

"Now, admit it, Cora, wasn't that fun? That look on her face when you offered her licorice tea was priceless!"

"Yes," Cora said. "Yes, it was. Maybe too much fun. I hope she's okay."

"Oh, she'll have a tummy ache for sure, but nothing serious. No such thing as too much of this kind of fun." Marjorie chuckled. "We can finish those cookies when Jane gets up from her nap.

They're rather good for being so cheap. I'll run that woman's cup over to Agent Walker at the station and be back in a snap."

"You're remarkable, Marjorie." Cora took another cookie and let the sweetness melt in her mouth, the raspberry jelly dissolving on her tongue. "I have to agree with you. These really aren't half bad for store-bought cookies."

"Maybe so," the housekeeper admitted. "But don't touch that tea all the same."

"Marjorie?" Cora sat up straight in her chair. "What did you do?"

"Nothing really wicked," the housekeeper responded artlessly. "Or at least, no more wicked than making the blackberry tea a little stronger than usual . . . and I might have accidently on purpose put in a few pine needles for added flavor."

"You're awful." Cora took another cookie. "Simply awful."

"Yes, I am," Marjorie agreed, suddenly sober. "After what she did to poor Dinah Browning, someone needs to give that woman a dose of her own medicine."

Chapter 51

Charlie hadn't been prepared for Cora's call, much less her insistence that he should find someone who could pick locks and wasn't afraid of crawling under dubious bed frames in some godforsaken cabin in the Balfour woods.

He was even more stubborn about agreeing when she said it had nothing to do with Eudora Ashford and everything to do with Katy Wilton.

He had better things to do, or that's what he told himself. Things like spending the day with Elvira, hiking the trails behind the Piney Woods, having a leisurely lunch at Sam's, and an entire day away from Walker's eagle eyes watching his every move.

I've done enough, he thought. *My fair share and all that.*

He'd already said no to Inola Walker, who hadn't been too pleased when he announced that he was unavailable to consult with her or chauffeur her around after he and Jim returned from Atlanta, but then her attitude was as inconsistent as spring rain.

One minute she was breathing down his neck and the other she didn't want him underfoot.

He couldn't tell what was going on with her.

She blew hot and cold at the same time.

Charlie had no problem telling Inola he was done with her, but he decided not to argue with Cora. At least, he wasn't going to argue with her right now.

He was tired of being at odds with her, and she seemed to think the clues in this dream were at least as important as finding out what happened to Dinah Browning.

The truth was, he did know someone who could pick locks at a moment's notice, and he did feel an obligation to Katy Wilton, who called right after he talked to Cora.

Katy had assumed the best and thanked him profusely for being willing to help.

Charlie wasn't used to people who thought the best of him, and he wasn't sure if he liked the pressure that put on his behavior, but he couldn't say no to Katy either.

"Sorry, Elvira," he said on his way out the door. "I'll make it up to you with a special canned chili dinner tonight and a long walk in the woods tomorrow. Promise."

Quincy, the one-named postmaster and resident locksmith, brought his own grumpy attitude and resistance with him to the cabin on Zeke Balfour's property. The man's thick, curly white mane flowing over the straps of his faded overalls and his equally snowy beard in a fringe around his chubby red face made him one of the town's more photogenic citizens.

Naomi decided he looked like the original ancient troll inhabitant of a rustic mountain cabin, or maybe a hillbilly Santa in search of an elf-infested Southern toy workshop.

The locksmith eyed the dust-encrusted, leather-strapped trunk with suspicion and gave Charlie another hard stare of mistrust.

"How did you know this would be under the floorboards under the bed?" he snapped disagreeably, his hands tucked into his armpits and his shoulders squared defiantly, a mirror of Zeke Balfour's confrontational stance in the opposite corner of the one-room log cabin.

Bookended by bad attitudes, Charlie thought from his precarious middle position between them. *How do I let Cora talk me into these situations?*

He looked at the eleven-year-old girl across the rough-hewn wooden table.

At least there's one person who's glad to be here, he thought.

"You dragged me away from breakfast at Sam's," Quincy barked. "Putting it in a box and eating it in the car doesn't count. A hungry man deserves the answers to his questions. How did you know where to look?"

"Mr. Charlie said Miss Katy told him where to look," Naomi offered helpfully. "That's what he said when you got here. Don't you remember?"

She looked at Charlie, her dark eyes bright and naive.

"Isn't that what you said?" she repeated. "Miss Katy said there might be a trapdoor or something like that under the bed."

It's what Cora told me to say, he thought. *Cora told me to say that it was Katy's idea. Not sure why I'm lying. I didn't think to ask.*

"And how did Miss Katy know where it was?" Quincy persisted, still glaring at Charlie, a distracting bit of biscuit crumbs with blackberry jam caught in his beard.

Naomi looked from one man to the other in puzzlement.

"We don't need to get into the weeds here, Quincy." Charlie tapped the postman sharply on the shoulder. "Doesn't matter how we found it. Let's just say it was a hunch."

"Funny things, those hunches . . ." Quincy paused and met Charlie's warning look. "There's a lot of those going around lately. More than the usual if you ask me, which you didn't."

Charlie dug a napkin from his pocket and handed it to the postman, gesturing to the man's white beard.

Then the detective deliberately let his gaze drop to the top of the chest.

I know that look, Quincy thought, swiping at his beard as the crumbs fell. *Only Cora puts that look on your face. Something in this box must be a mystery that needs solving. Of course it's about Cora. That's why you won't talk.*

"Never mind," Quincy said grudgingly. "We can discuss the lunch you're buying me later. There's a stagecoach strongbox here. Might as well open her up and see what's inside."

"Step back, Naomi," Zeke said, reaching out a protective hand to his daughter's shoulder and giving her a firm paternal tug backward. "Let Mr. Quincy work."

"Just Quincy," the old man corrected him, winking broadly at the curious girl. "And the child's welcome to watch. She might learn something useful."

"I'm not sure lock-picking is useful or morally suitable for children," Charlie said dryly, leaning back to enjoy the performance.

"Neither am I," Zeke agreed.

Quincy took a temperamental step back and held out the slender leather tool case in his left hand, waving it with an air of challenge.

"Get off your high horse, Charlie," he said gruffly. "You called me for this little rodeo. You're welcome to do this yourself, if you think you know how."

"Katy doesn't want the trunk damaged," the detective said. "Otherwise . . ."

Teasing implications hung in the air for a moment before Charlie knew he had pushed too hard. Quincy didn't venture far from the post office except on his delivery routes, and never socially. Everyone knew he was a crotchety recluse who considered himself the town's historian, resident Santa Claus, and keeper of all secrets.

Everyone also knew that underneath the beard on his chest beat a heart of genuine Dahlonega gold and the rough exterior was all bark and no bite.

He was doing Charlie a huge favor, especially since his leisurely breakfast had been spoiled.

"I apologize," the detective said meekly, putting his hands into his jeans pockets. "Lunch on me. Your choice at Sam's. Please continue."

"That's what I thought," the old man said, temporarily mollified. He put the long tool case down on the table next to the trunk. "Maybe you're the one who should get out of the way and let me work. At least the young lady knows how to behave."

He winked at Naomi again.

"You can see better if you pull up that stool over there and take a seat," he offered. "Your daddy can sit too, if he likes."

"I'm fine," Zeke said stiffly, refolding his arms and frowning.

Naomi didn't move, looking eagerly at her father for his approval.

"Yes," he said with a resigned sigh. "By all means learn something, but I'll decide if it's useful or not."

She happily dragged the stool from the corner and perched at the end of the table, her sneaker-clad feet dangling a few inches from the wooden plank floor, elbows resting on her knees and eyes intent on the prize before her.

"Thank you," she said sweetly. "Thank you, Daddy."

"This," Quincy said, reaching out and cradling the lock in his weathered palm, "is an antique Yale lock. Linus Yale was a bona fide, one hundred percent genius, a pioneering mechanical engineer in the early 1840s."

Naomi nodded.

"That's why it says Yale on the front," she said.

"Indeed. A lock like this would have rusted outside in the elements, but this one's in great shape for the age. I'd say it's well over a hundred years old. That shine on it, that's called a patina."

"That's why it's greenish."

"Yes, it's made of brass. The patina forms from oxidation."

"Will being old make it harder to open?" she said, moving closer to get a better look. "It doesn't look like any lock I've ever seen before."

"Not at all harder to open," the old man said confidently, warming to the interest of his young observer. "You're right, the early locks were made a bit differently from locks today. This one is a lever lock, made before pin tumblers. Notice how the opening for the key is on the front and not on the bottom?"

"Yes," she said, pointing at the tool case. "How will you open it? Do you have a skeleton key in your kit?"

"Ah," he said, untying the strip of leather that wound around the outside of the case and rolling the flap open. "That would be too simple with a key, but not too difficult without one, if you know what you're doing. These are my lock-picking tools."

"They look like bent wires," she said.

"Indeed," he said. "That's exactly what they are. They're very strong and made of steel. Different lengths and widths, all bent at the end at different places. We will simply insert the wires into the place where the key would go and push the levers out of the way."

"How do you know where they are? The levers, I mean."

"That's another smart question," he said, pointing to the lock in his palm. "Do you see those little round bumps in the metal?"

"The three on the outside edges? Yes," she said, touching them tentatively with her index finger. The metal was cold and smooth. "Why isn't there one in the top left corner?"

"Ah, clever girl," Quincy said admiringly. "That's because the release is there. That's where the lock hinges open. We'll look for the levers on the left side. From the looks of this, there are probably four levers, and we just need to pop them up in the right sequence."

"And the lock opens like magic."

"Hardly magic." His kindly reproof was accompanied by yet another friendly wink. "More like common sense, skill, know-how, and a little patience."

The old man picked up one of the wires and skillfully inserted the bent end into the lock, twisting and turning until there was a faint but distinct click.

"One down, three to go," he said. "Hmmm, next let's try a little longer wire."

He exchanged the wire in his hand for another.

"Should be spring-loaded and self-tensioning," he observed,

trying the second wire. "We are basically forcing all the pins up the way a key would, but one at a time instead of all together."

"I see," she said. "So when all the pins are out of the way, the lock will open."

"Indeed," he said, almost effortlessly continuing to twist, turn, and push. There were several more distinct clicking sounds, and then suddenly the hinge released and the lock opened.

Naomi gave an audible gasp of delight.

"Nothing to it," Quincy said, rightfully proud of himself. He removed the lock from the trunk and placed it triumphantly into the girl's waiting hands. "Nothing to it."

"Can we open the trunk now?" Naomi looked up at her father's face. "Please?"

Zeke shot a look of momentary concern at Charlie. He hadn't expected any of this. He'd had no idea there was anything in the cabin. Certainly not a hidden trunk.

Whatever this box is, it once belonged to Balfour, he thought bitterly. *The man who'd built the cabin.*

Stories he'd heard from his youth overwhelmed his senses.

Balfour. The man who'd founded this town. The man he firmly believed owned his ancestors, his great-grandmother and his great-uncles. The man who'd escaped to Texas just before the Civil War, leaving his cursed cabin and his name behind him.

He wanted no part of any tainted thing that belonged to that man.

Naomi had to be protected from whatever ugly truth lurked in that chest.

"Take it," he said to Charlie. "I told Katy Wilton that she could have what's in the cabin."

"But—" Naomi said.

"I said you could watch them open it," Zeke said sternly. "You're going back to your lessons now."

She saw the determined look on her father's face and the stern set of his lips. She knew that look too well. This was not an argument she could win. Anything else she might say would only make the situation worse.

Her father held out his hand, and she dutifully placed the lock into his palm. Zeke waited until Charlie picked up the wooden box from the table.

"I'll see that Katy gets this," the detective said.

"I don't care who gets it," Zeke retorted bluntly.

He tossed the lock onto the table with a thud and reached for Naomi's hand.

"Now if you will excuse me, I've got to make a living, and you've got what you came for. You can close the door behind you when you leave, or not. I don't care what happens to any of it anymore."

Chapter 52

The preparations for the opening of Wilton House were going more smoothly than either Linda or Virginia had anticipated, and that bothered each woman for her own very different reasons.

Linda, a devotee of all things theatrical, held to the director's adage that polished dress rehearsals predicted disastrous opening nights. She feared that overconfidence would lead to neglecting some vital part of the preparations and cause a calamity of omission.

Virginia, on the other hand, was more concerned with Stewart Wilton's recent mercurial disposition and his vacillating attitude toward the project. One minute the man was intensely interested and involved, and the next he was ignoring calls and texts requesting his opinion and input.

She most feared a scene of epic proportions involving the Senator's famous temperament and any one of a number of vendors, townspeople, and contractors.

Both were thrilled that at least the financial issues were out of their hands and into the capable hands of Darcie Jones, and that she'd taken over personal supervision of the Senator for the week. Neither envied Darcie her responsibilities.

They sat across from each other in the garden of the Wilton House, the most recent spreadsheet from Darcie, lists of vendors and participants, and sticky note reminders for last-minute needs littering the tabletop between them.

Both knew the countdown had officially begun.

"I can see you're still concerned," Linda said soothingly, sipping at her iced tea. "We've gone over the check sheet twice in the last hour. The workers and servers have confirmed they'll be here by seven thirty in the morning. The committee chairs have all called in, and their areas are ready to go. The musicians have rehearsed, and the pictures, pottery, and crafts are in place. Vicki's delivering the flowers for inside the house tonight and will deliver for the tables first thing in the morning. Except for an impulsive emotional outburst from Stewart, I can't imagine what's still bothering you."

Virginia picked up her own glass of tea, wiping the condensation from the side with the tip of her finger.

"To be truthful, I was just thinking about what we're doing here," she said sadly. "I was just wondering if opening up the house will dig up unpleasant memories for Katy and especially for Amy. Whether or not the family can ever get past what happened here . . . and why. Whether we've done the right thing turning the study into a library for children. If anyone will want to spend the night in the upstairs rooms or take wedding pictures in the gardens."

"Oh my!" Linda reached over and grasped her friend's hand. "You *are* worried! We've gone through this over and over since the beginning."

"I know it sounds silly to still be concerned at this late date, after all the work we've done. Last-minute jitters, I suppose. But I'm the one who convinced the Senator to put a ridiculous amount of money into this project. Then I turned around and asked Deborah's Daughters to invest so much time and effort into my own vision about what we needed to do . . . I suppose I'm just feeling insecure when I ought to be praying."

"You're right that this started with you, but we're all with you. I hope you know that. You're an inspiration. You've done so much more than pray, Virginia. You've put feet on your prayers and encouraged the rest of us to do the same. To give ourselves. You've been such a blessing to all of us."

Virginia, embarrassed by her friend's praise, tentatively nodded her head.

"Darcie seems to think there's a reporter from the Griffith Historical Society who's going to do a negative story about the house and the Wilton family," she said, changing the subject. "That he'll use the opening as an excuse to dig up dirt and rumors. Turn it into some sort of expose on Steve's death and make a name for himself."

I really do need to have a word with Darcie about gossiping, Linda thought. *She's got no business frightening people with her drama.*

"Daryl Miller," Linda said. "Poor little man. I've known him all his life. Success runs from him like a frightened rabbit. He's spent his whole life pretending he's more important than he actually is. I wouldn't be concerned about him."

"Really?" Virginia asked. "But what about the negative publicity?"

"Dear," she said, "Daryl couldn't influence his own mother to read his articles. He's so full of himself there's no room for an interesting thought, much less an expose. Please don't fret about anything he might do."

"Are you sure?"

"Yes, I'm sure." Linda picked up the spreadsheet closest to her and smoothed it with the palm of her hand. "Now, if you'd like to go over this list of the participants one more time, let's do that. But do put your mind to rest about the Griffith Historical Society. If all else fails, Darcie and I already have a plan in place to deal with him. I made a call to Vicki about it this morning. Daryl Miller doesn't know who he's up against."

Virginia patted her friend's hand warmly.

"No, twice through the list is enough," she said. "You're a wonderful friend. I'm so thankful for you. I just need to have faith."

A breeze blew past, the scent of wildflowers, gardenias, and yellow pines in the cool air. From inside the house behind them came the sounds of bustling movement and enthusiastic conversation.

"You've got plenty of faith, Virginia," Linda said. "But just like the rest of us, some days you just need to be reminded. Have another cup of chamomile, dear. We've done our part. God's in control now, and I'm certain He knows what He's doing."

Chapter 53

"I wasn't sure you'd open the door," Katy said, clasping the heavy canvas bag closer to her torso, wondering if anyone else could hear the pounding in her rib cage.

Much like Zeke Balfour, she couldn't believe she'd had the nerve to return to Zeke Balfour's house, much less knock on his front door and ask to speak to him.

"I'm not sure why I did," Zeke said sourly. "Are you looking for Naomi?"

"Not really. I wanted to talk to you."

She shifted from one foot to the other, wondering if he would invite her into the house and off of the front porch and hoping he wouldn't.

"Well, Naomi's gone over to spend the afternoon with a friend," he said. "She's still angry with me, thanks to you and that blasted trunk."

"Speaking of the trunk," she said, ignoring his accusation,

which she found justified but his tone rather rude and uncalled for. "I think you need to see what we found inside it."

She reached carefully into the top of the bag and brought out what looked like a thick cardboard frame, the yellowed edges embossed with faded red scrollwork. She held the envelope-sized rectangle out expectantly.

Zeke Balfour scowled.

"What's that?" he said.

"A tintype," she said, pointing to the photograph that was mounted in the center of the paper. "Otherwise known as a ferrotype. I did some research. This one's a half-plate, probably taken by some traveling photographer who came through with one of the Georgia public county fairs. Tintypes were very popular in the 1850s mainly because they were cheap and fast to make. The most common size was smaller than this. This one is about four by five inches. Large enough to see some of the details."

"I don't really care that you know how to google," he said. "Do you have a point?"

"Well, tintypes are mostly associated with the Civil War," she said, warming to the topic and pleased with herself. "They were used to document battle sites and soldiers, famous people, and those who weren't so important to anyone except the people who loved them. Many of the soldiers even carried gem tintypes of their loved ones in their pockets, tiny ones maybe an inch or so square."

"So that's a picture from the Civil War," he said flatly. "Are we done here?"

"No, I'm not done," she said. "Not until you look at this picture and listen. It's been remarkably well-preserved from humidity and bright light in the trunk, so there's really no rusting on it, and it's hardly deteriorated at all. You can see the faces clearly. All three of them."

For the first time, Zeke looked closely at the picture she held. It was nothing like any photograph he had ever seen, a monochromic brown with milky-white highlights, yellowed in places and with flecks of silver scattered about the image.

The three faces were almost stoic, although a wistful smile played about the lips of the woman in the center. Pale colors had been hand-added to the chocolate and sepia tones. The cheeks of the man were tinted a pale peach, and there was a tinge of light blue in the shawl the woman wore around her upper arms. The boy at the man's side held a red-tinted bandana.

It was a portrait of a family.

The man, tall and athletic, had shoulder-length white hair flowing down around his broad shoulders and bristling whiskers reaching to the center of his suited chest. At his side, his right arm protectively encircling her upper arm, stood a round-faced, charming black woman, swollen with pregnancy. The man's left arm was placed paternally around the shoulders of a gangly boy who was leaning affectionately into the man's ribs, a mop of unruly dark curls framing his handsome dark face.

"There's an inscription on the back of the cardboard," Katy said. "February 1861, and three names. You should read them for yourself."

Zeke finally took the photograph and turned it over.

Daniel Ezekiel and Celia Elizabeth Balfour, and Ezra Elijah Balfour.

"Ezra was my great-great-grandfather's name," he said. "I don't understand."

"I didn't either, at first," she said, indicating the rockers on the front porch. "Can we sit down maybe? There's more you need to see."

He nodded mutely and waited until she took a seat, although he continued to stand stiffly, still gripping the edges of the cardboard frame between his thumb and forefinger. She opened the bag in her lap, rummaging again, and removed a stained, leather-bound journal thick with parchment pages and tied with a strip of rawhide.

"This belonged to Celia," Katy said. "You said I could have whatever I found, so I read through it. The writing's faded, but the calligraphy is beautiful. And the words, well, she has an enchanting way with words."

He frowned but didn't interrupt, so she went on.

"The journal is a record of the major events in her life, from the time she married in January of 1852 until the second baby was born in January of 1864. It's her diary. The first entry is the night before her wedding day. Daniel Balfour gave her the journal as a wedding present. The last entry is the day the second baby—a little girl—died."

"I'm still not following you," he said, clearly shaken, leaning against the porch post for support. "What are you trying to tell me?"

"The truth about who you really are," she said. "You must have heard stories about Daniel Balfour when you were growing up."

"None that I'd care to repeat," he said. "He owned the cabin and built the settlement they called Balfour. When the Civil War broke out, like a coward he deserted his slaves and his land and ran to Texas, where he presumably died. Good riddance."

"Celia has a different story to tell," she said, cradling the journal like the priceless treasure that it was. "She loved him and bore his two children, only one of whom survived. The son in the picture, Ezra, was barely ten years old when his baby sister died."

"So?" he said, tossing the photograph back into her lap. "What does this have to do with me?"

"They were married," Katy said. "Daniel and Celia. They planned to move to Texas with their son. They'd been able to live in the mountains together undisturbed for years, but the Civil War was brewing. Celia convinced Daniel to go on without her, that it wasn't safe for a white man to be married to a black woman in Georgia with all the conflict and the soldiers traipsing through the countryside. That they'd both be found, along with their son, and she was afraid. She told him that when the baby was born she would follow him just as soon as she could travel."

"Travel? Alone?" For the first time Zeke appeared shocked, the disbelief evident in his voice. "How was she supposed to cross the country with a boy and a baby?"

"She had a brother who lived with them," Katy said. "He was older than she was. Apparently he never liked Daniel and never approved of the marriage. The brother was supposed to take her, the newborn, and Ezra to Texas to meet Daniel."

"That's all in that book?" he said skeptically.

"Yes, Zeke, it is," she said. "Along with other artifacts in the trunk that prove and substantiate her story. Not that you'd really need anything except the journal."

"But she died?"

"Shortly after the baby died."

"Maybe you're just seeing things because you want to see

them," he said. "Maybe you're making more out of that journal than is really there. It could just be fiction."

She reached into the bag and reverently removed an object wrapped in chamois cloth. With delicate care, she folded back the fabric to reveal a reddish clay-covered jar, encrusted with bits of pottery, buttons, broken jewelry, marbles, and toys.

"Didn't you ever wonder about the two graves?" she said softly. "About who's buried there and why they aren't with the other family members? Celia had time to make this before she died. Do you know what it is?"

Zeke sat down in the second rocking chair and took the jar in his hands, turning it as he inspected the curious objects pressed into the sides.

"No," he said. "I've never seen anything like this before."

"I've been told it's a gypsy jar," she said. "A remembrance made while mourning the unexpected death of a family member, often a newborn who doesn't survive. Celia talks about making it in the journal, but she doesn't say what she put inside."

"So you didn't open it," he said.

"No," Katy said. "I'm not sure anyone should open it."

She watched as the anger on his face softened ever so slightly into a glimmer of perception and conjecture.

"I suppose I'd always assumed my name was Balfour because we were slaves," he said. "I thought my great-great-grandfather took the name when Balfour left so he and his descendants could lay claim to the property. That they didn't have names of their own before he bought them."

Katy reached into the canvas bag for the third time.

"There are other things too," she said. "There's a Bible that records their names and the date of the marriage. The preacher's name is there, along with two men who were witnesses to the ceremony, a Candler and a Stone. In those days, recording events like birth, death, and marriage in the family Bible was all the legal proof anyone needed. The two births are recorded there along with all the dates."

"You're telling me that my great-great-grandfather Ezra was the legal son of Daniel and Celia?"

"Yes."

"And you're telling me that Celia wasn't his slave."

"No, she wasn't. According to Celia, Daniel never owned slaves at all."

She watched the successive emotions sweep across his face as he attempted to merge the stories he had been told with the reality of what he held in his hands.

"There are details about Celia's life before she married Daniel in the journal." Katy held up the yellowed volume. "She was owned and educated by a family in South Carolina. The eighteen-year-old daughter, a secret abolitionist, taught her to read and write and then helped her to get away when Celia was only fifteen, along with Celia's brother, who was also a slave and had been taught the blacksmith trade."

"And Balfour?"

"I only know what Celia's diary says. Daniel Balfour was a blacksmith and stonemason by trade. He was born and raised in Tennessee and came down to Georgia looking for gold, but by the time he got here in 1840 the rush was over. He picked up this land from a prospector who was eager to move on to California. Working as a smithy, he came in contact with bounty hunters searching for runaway slaves. He was asked to shoe their horses and repair the bridles and bits, but he found he had no sympathy for what they did. Eventually he became a noteworthy but covert contact on the early underground railroad through Georgia on the way to Mexico, where slaves already had their freedom. Celia and her brother stopped here for food and rest and to hide from their pursuers. Daniel and Celia fell in love with each other, and her brother wouldn't go on without her."

Katy held out the journal, but he ignored her offer.

"You really should read this for yourself," she insisted. "Celia was remarkable."

"What happened to her brother?"

Katy had tried to prepare herself for this. She knew there were questions she wouldn't be able to answer without further alienating this man who was so sensitive about his past.

She thought of the stories Hannah had told her about Balfour's early history. Colorful stories passed down for generations about the origins of the town. Katy decided that like most stories repeated through the ages, they'd been told through the lenses of the story-tellers. Some of them were outright fabrications, but some, based on what she knew now, were probably true.

She had no idea if Zeke had never heard the stories, or, if he had heard them, whether he'd simply chosen what he did and didn't want to believe.

"He was older than Celia," she said, picking her way through the minefield of words. "She didn't say much about him in the diary. Only that he didn't like Daniel and that he was a blacksmith and stonemason too. I think we could assume that he taught his nephew to work the forge and handle a chisel and mallet. Ezra, in turn, passed those skills on to his son, your great-grandfather, and eventually everything they had learned came down to you."

"So my great-great-great-grandfather was a white man," he mused, wiping a thin sheen of perspiration from his face and setting the gypsy jar down on the porch. He finally took the journal. "I suppose you find this entertaining."

"That's not the word I'd use," Katy countered. "To discover there are good people of all races who've loved and protected each other . . . no, that's not entertaining, and it's not surprising either. In my experience, prejudice, like hatred, is taught."

"This isn't going to change anything," he said.

"Not many things we discover about the past do, although maybe they should. That's your choice." She dug back into the canvas bag all the way to the bottom.

"There's just one more thing," she said.

Zeke eyed her guardedly.

"I told you I didn't want anything in that trunk," he said. "You can take all this back with you today and do whatever you want with it. It isn't going to make a difference in how I live my life."

Katy shrugged.

"I'll eventually put it all on display," she said. "I'll need to do some more research and find a curator who's skilled in preservation."

She drew out a weathered leather pouch and held it in the palm of her hand.

"This is the last thing I found. I think this is too personal to put on display," she said. "You should have it."

"What is it?" he said.

"You'll have to open it yourself," she said. "The journal says it was Daniel's parting gift to Celia before he went to Texas. I think you ought to give it to Naomi."

He untied the cord that held the pouch shut and poured the contents into his palm. Inside was a simple gold oval locket on a thin chain and a woman's plain gold wedding band.

Zeke inserted his thumbnail and pried the locket open to reveal two tiny portraits of a man and a woman. Daniel and Celia.

Chapter 54

Inola found she was much more comfortable in Cora Stone's homey den than she really wanted to be. She'd also surprised herself with how cheerfully she'd endured Detective Burton's incessant complaining about absolutely everything on the ride over from the station, just so she could have another opportunity to talk to Charlie Abbott's ex-wife.

Inola had resolved to come to Balfour with an open mind about Cora, never anticipating that she would like the woman. Much to her own chagrin, she found herself not only liking but admiring Cora very much.

I don't have problems being objective, she thought. *What's wrong with me? I'm getting personally involved, and that won't do at all.*

Unfortunately, Eudora had raised questions for which Inola was obligated to find answers, no matter her personal feelings in the matter.

She knew she had to follow the evidence.

"So I can assume that you two did nothing that might harm our suspect," Inola said, getting right to the point. "Nothing that might cause her physical problems of any sort?"

"No," Cora said, avoiding Marjorie's intense gaze. "Why do you ask?"

"Well . . ." Inola shifted her attention from one woman to the other, searching for signs of a guilty conscience. "We took Ms. Ashford into custody as she was leaving Balfour, and she seems to be under the impression that she was poisoned by some tea she drank when she visited you. She's complaining of stomach pains."

Marjorie made an involuntary noise of distaste.

"Did you put something into her drink, Ms. O'Quinn?"

Marjorie didn't flinch.

"It was strong blackberry tea with a dose of pine needles," she said boldly. "Cora had nothing to do with it and knew nothing about what I did at all. I made the hot tea, and Eudora drank the whole cup. She said it was delicious."

"Pine needles can be quite toxic," the agent said matter-of-factly. "May I ask what possessed you to do that?"

"These are harmless," Marjorie retorted. "Come and see the trees for yourself."

The housekeeper turned and led the way out into the sunroom. Cora remained in the kitchen as the agent followed Marjorie out the back door, across the grass, and around the garden to the far corner of the yard.

The older woman proudly indicated a row of three graceful, slightly rounded, pyramid-shaped pine trees across from the fence to the right side of the yard.

"I asked Thomas if I could have a corner of the garden to

myself," she explained. "Planted them there about three years ago as a windbreak and for summer shade. Bought them from a nursery over in Griffith. Special order. They've gotten big enough to use for Christmas decorations, and the pine cones are lovely too. Never really thought I'd have a need to use them in tea."

For the first time, Marjorie thought the agent might burst into laughter.

"Ah," Inola said knowingly. "Eastern White Pine. They don't usually like Georgia red clay. You're fortunate that they're growing so well. I assume you know to keep them well-pruned."

"Yes," the older woman said. "My husband and I had quite a stand of them on the land around our home in Ohio. They remind me of him. They're magnificent trees when they're allowed to grow free, although I must say they're also messy."

Inola turned around and they walked back to the house, where Cora waited for them to rejoin her inside.

"So Ohio is where you learned to make pine needle tea," she said. "Interesting."

"My husband had lung cancer," Marjorie said. "His doctors suggested that the tea might help him, but Marshall thought it was just a placebo. I think he just didn't like the taste, but he drank it because I made it for him."

"My Cherokee grandmother called them the 'tree of peace.'"

Inola recalled the blue-green needles, five to a bundle, like a fan at the ends of the branches. Just like the trees planted in Cora Stone's backyard. Inola remembered being sent to gather them, the minty odor and wood flavor ingrained in her childhood memories.

"There was always a pot brewing in the fall and winter months. She made us drink cup after cup when we had colds or the flu."

Cora, who had followed the women into the yard, heard a wistfulness in Inola's voice.

No wonder we get along so well, she thought. *She sounds as though she loved her grandmother the way I loved mine.*

"My grandmother always claimed that Eastern White Pine had a medicinal purpose as an expectorant," Inola said. "Her description of the process was less scientific and not for sharing in polite society."

Marjorie and Inola exchanged a knowing look before the agent finally broke eye contact and cleared her throat.

"Then that's settled," she said. "There was no intention to harm. Did she eat or drink anything else while she was here?"

"Only some really cheap imitation raspberry cookies," Cora said. "We ought to apologize for those."

There was a momentary awkward silence.

"Maybe you'd like a bite to eat before you go," Marjorie suggested. "I can't imagine you've had much time to have any proper meals since you arrived, and we were about to sit down ourselves."

"I wouldn't want to impose again," Inola said. "This is the second time I've dropped in without warning this week."

"Nothing of the sort." Marjorie bustled past the agent and into the kitchen, patting Cora's arm as she made her way to the refrigerator. "Jane won't be back from her playdate at Katy's until almost bedtime, and I'd planned homemade tomato soup and garden salad for us. There's more than enough for three."

Inola looked at Cora, who shook her head and shrugged.

"You'd do well to agree," she said. "You've probably discovered that eating places in Balfour are few and far between, unless you count Sam's, and that's going to be packed with the afternoon locals and out-of-town visitors for the Wilton House opening tomorrow."

"Sam's?"

"Simmons' Restaurant," Cora explained. "Downtown Balfour, as it were."

"Yes," Inola said. "I recognize the name now. That's where the agents who followed Eudora from Atlanta spent their afternoon. They were very complimentary."

There was a pleasant clatter of pots and pans behind them, accompanied by the muted melody that Cora recognized as one of Marjorie's favorite hymns, one of the ones she hummed when she was especially happy or pleased.

"She'll have the food ready before you're finished arguing with her," Cora said, gesturing helplessly. "I learned long ago that resistance to Marjorie is futile. You might as well enjoy a meal with us, unless you have more work you need to do this afternoon."

Inola's shoulders relaxed, her tension and her pretense gone.

"I'd enjoy that," she admitted, closing her notebook and tucking her ink pen into the bun at the base of her neck. "Thank you."

Following Cora back into the den, she made herself comfortable in an overstuffed chair and openly studied her hostess.

She took in the simple clothing, Cora's lack of makeup, and her two rings—one a plain gold band and the other with carvings and a blood red stone.

A sudden and quite unexpected revelation came to her.

Charlie doesn't understand who you are, she thought. *I don't think you know either, Cora Stone. Maybe someone should tell you. Maybe that's really why I'm here.*

Chapter 55

"I never meant for her to shoot herself."

Eudora's wail reached a shrill, painful pitch, bouncing around the walls of the newly renovated Balfour Police Department interrogation room.

From behind the mirrored glass, Perkins was quietly reading the directions to the dispatcher, and the two were making the first use of their updated recording equipment. Agent Walker had insisted that they didn't have time to call in a technician from Griffith and needed to make do with what the two of them could figure out on their own.

"You can't blame me for what she did to herself!" Eudora shrieked.

Inola watched the woman across from her pounding her plump fists on the table, her hair slipping down in disarray and her upper lip beaded with perspiration. She glanced at the mirrored wall with a question.

Overconfident Astra was no longer anywhere to be found, and a panicked Eudora Ashford was clearly rattled to her core. Inola hoped that Perkins and the dispatcher were getting all this on tape, even though she strongly suspected that there would be more and more hysteria as Eudora's situation became clearer to her.

"But Dinah Browning did shoot herself," Inola said. "Let me explain how this works, Ms. Ashford. You gave Dinah Browning black licorice tea. That tea interacted with her prescribed heart medications, and she became extremely depressed. You poisoned her. Because of that poisoning, she committed suicide. Legally speaking, you contributed to her untimely death through deliberate lies and demonstrable negligence."

"I was only her spiritual adviser."

"You underestimate your influence. You took advantage of Ms. Browning's heart condition and exploited her pain for your own personal gain."

"You cannot charge me with her murder. She killed herself."

"Ms. Browning's death resulted from the vilest form of malpractice. I certainly do intend to charge you and Varden Bander as coconspirators in her murder."

"You can't keep me here!" Her voice reached a crescendo. "You've got no evidence and no witnesses!"

There was a sharp knock at the door, and the dispatcher's curly head popped into the room. She met Inola's eyes and winked discreetly before vanishing.

Inola nodded at the mirrored glass.

"In addition," Inola said pointedly. "You're being charged with federal theft, which is the taking of property belonging to another person without authorization and crossing state lines with said property through multiple states. You're in possession of items of value belonging to the deceased."

"Those were gifts she gave me, only trinkets. You can't prove I stole anything!"

"Furthermore, there is irrefutable evidence of theft by deception which, as I'm sure you well know, is a general criminal act of theft that entails plotting to take and coming into the possession of Ms. Browning's property with the added caveat of trickery, lies which were claimed as truth."

"I have no idea what you're talking about . . ."

"Then let me rephrase. You will be charged with intentional misrepresentation of your abilities and the omission of the facts concerning drug interactions, which were directly caused by the victim's consumption of products provided exclusively by you."

"I never prescribed anything. That was Varden Bander. He's the one you want. He's the one who said he knew what he was doing!"

"Furthermore, since this is a federal matter, there are penalties which may be more rigorously enforced as well as added to those already imposed by the state of Tennessee under O.C.T.N.16-8-3."

"What does that even mean?"

Inola sighed. "It means you knew that Dinah Browning had every possibility of recovery, yet on the numerous occasions of contact with her, you intentionally failed to disclose that information for the sole purpose of attaining her property in the event of her death."

"That's not true," Eudora whined. "I didn't want her to die."

"But you had every intention of taking her money under false and dangerous pretenses. You promised performance of services that you didn't perform nor had any intention of performing, and that deception led to Ms. Browning's death."

"You can't prove that."

"I'm in possession of proof. There are federal prosecutors whose sole mission is to take that evidence and exact the just consequences for your behavior in a court of law. There are judges in courts whose job is to make certain you spend an appropriate length of time in a federal prison facility. The entire process is a well-oiled machine, powered by the hands of justice."

Inola walked over to the two-way mirror and nodded. She hoped they were getting all this on the recording. She found all this conversation repetitive. She knew she had to do it, but she was getting tired of listening to herself and she was really tired of hearing Eudora's twangy voice.

"I didn't make her decisions for her."

"Ms. Browning relied upon you for counsel. Without your intervention she would, in all reasonable probability, still be alive today."

"You can't be serious."

Eudora slapped her hands on the tabletop.

"I'm always serious."

"What if I could tell you about the doctor? He knew what I was doing. He told me what to do. He should've known what would happen."

"The doctor's already in custody in Germantown," Inola said, sitting on the edge of the table, "and he's had a most interesting story to tell my colleagues. He's given considerable insight into your participation in the process."

"He's a liar!"

"Well, that remains to be seen, doesn't it, Ms. Ashford?"

Inola stood and went over and rapped on the door. When it opened, she turned back to Eudora, who was radically subdued and huddled down.

"We'll be leaving in the morning for the airport in Atlanta," she said crisply. "From there we'll take a flight back to Memphis for your arraignment. I suggest you get a good night's sleep. You're going to need all that energy to find yourself a competent lawyer before Bander lawyers up and beats you to a deal with the federal prosecutor, if he hasn't already."

Chapter 56

The Seventh Day: Saturday

The room was cold and ordinary, but at least she was back in her grandmother's kitchen wearing her own familiar jeans and one of Thomas's oversized sweatshirts and not a nightgown. She was standing over a drip pot already full of fragrant coffee, her bare toes visible and cool against the linoleum.

Two familiar cups, her floral cup and the mug James always used, sat empty and waiting.

Cora was relieved. She was overfull of crying and sadness, drama and death, snakes under the hem of her clothes, and pain around every corner.

James cleared his throat from his seat at the table.

"Come and sit with me for a while," he said. "Bring the coffee and let's talk."

Obediently, she prepared the cups and brought them to the table, sitting down with a heavy exhale.

"James," she began, "I'm tired."

"Yes, Cora," he said gently. "Tonight I'm here for you. You have questions."

She searched his weathered face. She knew every line and every wrinkle well. The twinkling warmth of his expressions. The kindly twitch in his smiling mouth. He was the grandfather she'd never had, and she trusted him.

Even before the dreams, he'd been a friend, a counselor, a mentor, and a comforter in the days following her grandmother's death. His death had been almost as difficult for her to accept as her grandmother's had been. There had been years in which she'd come to rely on his advice, as she did now.

When he and her grandmother reappeared in her dreams after Lonora died, she'd welcomed both of them back even though James especially brought disturbing messages that reconnected her to police work. To death and dying. To Charlie.

Now she was doubting not only the dreams, but herself as well.

"James, how am I different from Eudora Ashford?"

He sipped his coffee thoughtfully.

"I don't understand the question."

"If people knew about these dreams, what would they think?" she said. "People who don't know me and love me, well, why wouldn't they believe that I'm just like she is? She claims to know the future. She claims to speak to the dead."

"By people who don't know and love you, I can assume you mean Harry Halstein," he said. "And Inola Walker."

"I mean them, but other people too," she said. "The only ones who really know about the dreams are Thomas, Marjorie, and Charlie . . . and Ted Floyd. You know as well as I do that I tried to talk about all this in the beginning, after Lonora died. Ted told me I'd been under tremendous stress. That I'd had a psychotic break. He said you were just a figment of my imagination and a product of hysteria."

"We won't go into what I think of Dr. Floyd," James said, repressed amusement in his deep voice. "He's got that psychiatrist's god complex that I find ironic at best."

"I can see your point," Cora said, picking up her own cup and taking a sip. "But that doesn't change the facts. I can't prove you exist."

"Do you believe that I exist?"

"That's not fair," she said. "Ted would say that mentally ill people don't always know they are mentally ill. Besides, you haven't answered my question. How am I different from Eudora?"

"Well," he drawled, "let's begin with the most obvious differences that are not facts in question. You didn't submit a resume. You didn't ask for this job."

"I don't understand. You know I didn't ask to have dreams with messages."

"That's my point, dear," he said. "Neither did any other major or minor prophet in the Old Testament. They were chosen. A fortune teller chooses her profession. On the other hand, a true prophet is chosen, often against his or her own judgment and will. They'd rather do almost anything rather than what they are called to do."

Cora warmed her hands around her cup and listened.

"I'm telling you what you already know, Cora, but you need to hear it from me," he said. "That woman wants money for what she does, lots of money. Her only interests are finding profit and fame with a heaping helping of control over other people's lives."

He reached out and thumbed the pages of his Bible, which was lying on the table just inside the pool of light emanating from the single coal oil lamp.

"And of course the main difference is the source of her information."

He paused, sliding the book closer to her across the oilcloth.

"Fortune tellers have to cheat to give the correct answers," he said. "They can investigate, they interpolate, they guess. Research skills, body language, and intuition are all clever substitutes for truth. But in the end fortune tellers are all cheaters."

"And I'm not a cheater?"

"Not in the least," he said. "Not in the least, sweet Cora. The fact that you'd doubt yourself is the greatest proof of all. That you'd choose not to be here if you could."

"James, I wish I could believe you," she said. "I'm trying to believe you."

He picked up his mug and took a long, satisfying swallow.

"Then that's a beginning," he said. "I'll leave the rest of this conversation to someone else. Someone whose opinion might carry a bit more weight than mine."

And Cora was awake, more questions on her mind than when she fell asleep.

Chapter 57

"I thought you'd have gone back to your hotel by now."

Agent Walker looked up from her computer screen and the piles of paperwork to survey the gentle giant standing over her shoulder.

"Just waiting on a fax," she said, sniffing delicately at an intriguing aroma she could not define. "What are you eating?"

Jim Smith carried a double handful of individually cellophane-wrapped discs balanced precariously between his forearm and his uniformed chest.

A second unopened box was tucked under his upper arm.

"They're MoonPies," he said gleefully. "They're buy-one-get-one this week."

She closed her laptop and hesitantly took a MoonPie from him, inspecting the snack.

"What flavor is this?" she said.

"Banana," he said. "Mind if I sit down?"

"Not at all."

He pulled out a chair, lowered himself, and quickly changed his mind.

"Don't open that yet," he said, pointing at her snack. "I'll be right back."

Inola watched as he tossed his provisions and the unopened box onto the table in a heap and disappeared, returning with two brightly patterned sixteen-ounce Dixie cups, the inky liquid visible just under the rim of each.

"They're better with black coffee," he explained. "Sorry, I don't have time to make a fresh pot."

"Thank you," she said, not at all certain what she should say as he put the offering in front of her and seated himself. "And they're better with coffee because . . ."

"They're really sweet," he said, popping open the wrapping with a snap and removing a waxy-looking pale yellow sandwich cookie. "These are minis, if you're concerned about the calories."

She turned the wrapped oddity over in her hands, wondering about preservatives and ingredients but not wanting to hurt Jim's feelings by reaching over and inspecting the content list on the box.

"Should I be concerned about the calories?" she said.

Jim put an entire MoonPie into his mouth and chewed thoughtfully, embarrassed that he had mentioned anything about counting calories or gaining weight. He took a tentative swallow of hot liquid before he answered.

"Sorry, I didn't mean you should watch what you eat. What I'm saying is that it's really none of my business what you eat." He knew he was babbling but couldn't seem to stop. "To be totally honest,

I've never looked at the calories. I mean, you can if you'd like, but . . . not that you need to look at the calories. I mean, it's not like you're overweight or anything, since . . . because . . . you're just not."

"Relax," she said. "I understand what you mean."

You've got potential there, she thought. *A kind heart and an awesome skill set. I hope Ben Taylor appreciates you.*

She made an impulsive decision.

"Okay," she said. "I'm game. I'm hungry, and I'm going to assume there isn't an apple or a granola bar hidden around here anywhere that would give me a choice."

"There might be some leftover donuts from yesterday," he said, starting to rise. "I can check if you want."

Inola reached out and grabbed his forearm, surprising even herself.

"Seriously, officer," she said. "Sit down and relax, please. I'm sure this is fine. I've just never seen a MoonPie before, much less a mini MoonPie."

"I grew up with the chocolate ones," he said, settling back and opening another disc with a pop. "But the banana ones are my favorite. The minis are best. More of the outer coating and less cookie underneath."

She picked up the coffee and took a preparatory sip of the bitter brew.

"I see," she said, amused as he put another whole cookie into his mouth with obvious childlike enjoyment. "Banana, you say."

He watched as she guardedly opened the MoonPie, pulling at the edges until the crackling wrapping opened. She left the bottom half covered, holding the circle between her thumb and forefinger, and took a tentative bite from the top.

"Well?" he asked.

Inola picked up the coffee and sipped again, allowing the hot liquid to swish around in her mouth, dissolving the waxy crumbs.

"This tastes nothing like a banana," she said, unable to restrain herself from blurting out with blunt honesty. She rubbed her sticky front teeth with the tip of her tongue. "Am I tasting graham crackers with a marshmallow in the middle, all dipped in frosting?"

"Yes," he said cheerfully, reaching for his third. "It's great, right? What do you really think?"

"You're right, it's very sweet," she conceded. "And the coffee's good."

Jim reached over and grabbed the remaining snack from her hand.

"Please don't eat it," he said. "I can tell from that look on your face that you don't like it. The coffee's stale, so don't fib about that either. We can make a run to Sam's and get you a salad or something healthy when they open at eleven."

"No," she said, trying to take the MoonPie back, but she was no match for Jim's long arms. "I want to eat the rest."

"No you don't," he said, crumpling the remains into a sticky ball and chucking it over her head into the trash can with a flourish. "No need to humor me, Agent Walker. I'm not a trained profiler, but I'm pretty good at knowing when I'm being lied to."

"Fair enough," she said admiringly.

Jim Smith, she thought. *You are a man of many talents.*

Ben Taylor appeared in the doorway with a single sheet of paper in his hand.

"MoonPies," he said, scanning the mound on the table. "Banana, right? Aren't those your favorite, Jim? Henderson's have another two-for-one sale?"

"Plenty to go around, Chief," Jim said agreeably. "I was just having a snack before my shift starts."

"I've got that fax you were expecting," Ben said to Inola. "Let me know what you want to do from here."

She took the paper and quickly scanned the information.

"Just a confirmation that I'm to take our detainee here back to Memphis for more questioning," she said. "Nothing new. Any ideas about how I should go about doing that from Balfour?"

"Several," Ben said, shaking his head at Jim, who had jumped up expectantly. "No, son, you've had enough excitement for the week. I'll ask Dalton or Burton. They've both got the time and either one is more than capable, although Dalton might be a better fit. I'll check the roster to see who's on for the weekend."

"What about transportation?" she said.

"There's a police van on the back lot. I can have it serviced and ready to go by two this afternoon, if that works. Dalton can drive you to Hartsfield and you can fly out tonight, assuming there is someone who can meet you in Memphis."

"That works for me," she said, taking out her cell phone. "I'll let them know to book the flight and arrange for an escort to meet us. Thank you."

Jim gave the remaining MoonPies a last longing look and thrust his right hand out toward Inola.

"Great to work with you, Agent Walker," he said, shaking her hand with vigorous enthusiasm. "Hope to see you again."

He excused himself from the room without waiting for her to respond.

"I'll be in my office if you need anything else," Ben said. "I'm sending out for lunch in about an hour, so let me know if you've got a preference."

A salad sounds good, she thought, *but maybe I ought to use the time during lunch for a different errand.*

"Can I let you know later?" she said. "I might need a ride before I go back."

"Got it," he said, stopping to look back when he reached the doorway.

"So, I'm curious, did you actually eat one of Jim's MoonPies?" he asked.

Inola looked Ben directly in the eyes.

"I liked it," she said without flinching. "It was delicious. I ate two."

"Really?" he said doubtfully. "I'm surprised. Jim's got some pretty strange taste buds and a frenetic metabolism."

"Chief Taylor," she said, "he's a fine officer, and you're lucky to have him."

"That he is," Taylor said. "Let me know about that ride and whether or not you want something from Sam's."

"No hurry," she said, reopening her laptop and tucking her ink pen into her hair. "I'll be ready to go in about thirty minutes or so, and I'm not the least bit hungry."

Chapter 58

All the available potential drivers were busy at the Wilton House opening, so Ben Taylor dropped Inola off in Cora's driveway on his way to pick up lunch for the station dispatcher, Dalton, and Officer Perkins, who was making sure the van was serviced.

"I thought you'd already spoken to Cora," he said, trying not to sound as though he was prying. "I was going to bring lunch back from Sam's. Don't you want to eat?"

Everyone is obsessed with food, Inola thought. *My mouth is still protesting the wax cookies and stale caffeine.*

"I still need a few details for my report," she lied. "Is that a problem?"

"No, no," he said. "I'll drop you off and have Dalton come back and get you when you're ready."

Neither one of them spoke again until she thanked him when she got out of the patrol car.

Marjorie didn't seem at all surprised to see the agent standing outside the front door. She greeted Inola warmly and led her directly into the den, where Cora sat curled on the loveseat with Jane reading *Green Eggs and Ham.*

"Hello, Jane," Inola said, nodding at Cora and waiting for an invitation to sit down. "How are you?"

"Hello," Jane said shyly, hugging her stuffed kittens more closely and attempting to hide under Cora's arm. "Who are you?"

"This is one of Charlie's friends," Cora said easily. "Agent Walker helps people like Charlie does."

"Charlie!" Jane's eyes sparkled, her face reappearing. "I like Charlie. Charlie gave me my kittens."

"Those are beautiful felines," Inola said, bending down to the child's level. "Do they have names?"

"This is Kitten, and this is Sister," Jane said, indicating the one with the red ribbon first, followed by the kitten with the pink ribbon.

As if on cue, a yowl sounded from the kitchen.

"And that is Solomon, of course," Cora added. "Marjorie, could you please—"

"Jane," the housekeeper interrupted, "let's go get Solomon a treat, shall we? Then I'll bring some iced tea and cookies for our guest."

"Yes," the child said agreeably, sliding from Cora's arms and onto the floor. "We'll be right back."

"Of course," Marjorie said. "We'll be right back."

The pair dutifully delivered a tray with two sweet teas and a small plate of leftover raspberry cookies, to which Marjorie had added freshly baked sugar cookies.

Jane gave Cora another hug, and she skipped from the room to follow Marjorie.

The front door slammed before either Cora or Inola spoke.

"I'll answer one of your questions," Inola said, hands folded patiently in her lap, deliberately ignoring the treats, "if you'll begin by answering one of mine."

Cora couldn't tell whether the question was professional or personal from the impassive look on Inola's face.

"Go on," she said quietly. "I don't know that I have any questions for you. What do you want to know about me that we didn't discuss yesterday?"

"May I see your ring?"

"My ring?"

Cora twisted the thick gold band around her finger, contemplating the other woman with a hearty measure of misgiving. She had not taken it off since Thomas put it on her finger at Christmas. Not so much out of sentimental attachment, though there was that. But because Solomon had a feline penchant for shiny objects and had been known to take various objects in the past and hide them away.

At one point when she was vacuuming, Marjorie found a cache of silver-coated twist ties from the bread loaf bags and a solitary sequined button that had popped off one of her Sunday sweaters, along with one of Jane's sparkly hair ribbons, all neatly stashed under the sofa. The pirate rascal had picked them up with his pointy canine teeth like treasure and had made his own personal pile of booty.

Cora wanted no such adventure for her anniversary ring.

Inola was still watching her, expressionless, and Cora felt the strange sensation that she was being profiled—a feeling she had not had the previous day.

She slipped the ring from her finger and held it out in her palm.

Inola took the circlet respectfully and held it to the light, the tip of a finger tracing the design.

"I noticed this yesterday," she said. "I had to think about whether or not I should say anything to you. I wasn't sure how to ask, and I don't want to offend you."

"What's your question?" Cora said.

"Was this a gift from Charlie Abbott?"

"An anniversary gift from my husband," Cora said. "Thomas found it at a church Christmas bazaar this past year. It's one of a kind, handmade by two young artisans who are renting a space at a local jewelry store called Copperfield's. Why do you ask?"

"Is one of the creators a Native Cherokee?"

"I think so," Cora said, trying not to appear as mystified as she felt. "Why is that important? I'm not sure why we're talking about my ring."

"You don't know what it signifies," Inola said simply, returning the ring to Cora's palm. "Please put it back on. I'm sorry I asked you to remove it."

"I don't understand your apology."

Cora slipped the circlet back on.

"Why would it matter if I take it off?" she continued, absently rotating it around on her finger. "Surely as an FBI profiler you aren't superstitious."

"Tradition is too often mistaken for superstition," Inola said, refolding her hands and placing them on her knees. "I came to Balfour for a number of reasons we don't need to go into here. Let's just say my job involves finding the answers to difficult questions, and I had what Charlie calls a hunch. Charlie presented me with clues, but I knew that they weren't originally, shall we say, from Charlie. No matter how charming he may be at convincing other people of his hunches, some things simply are not possible in this world. I'd read his file, and yours, too, by the way. Specifically about the Brackett case. And I wanted to meet you. To see if the rumors might be true. I was going to leave today and honor your secrets, but I've realized that you weren't just a mystery to me. You're a mystery to Charlie, and even, I believe, to yourself."

"I don't know what you mean."

"Whether or not your husband knows what your ring means, I cannot say. I suspect the young woman who created the design may have tried to tell him, but we all don't have the gift of understanding. And that is as it should be."

"I'd like to understand."

"Yes, you should," Inola said. "I can tell you from my unique experiences as a profiler and my heritage and culture what I believe to be true."

The FBI profiler leaned toward Cora, her gaze fixed on the ruby stone.

"The design you wear is an honored one. You did not choose the ring. The ring was chosen for you."

"Thomas insists that Jane picked it out," Cora said, wondering why she felt the need to explain.

"A child," Inola said. "Yes, a child would know the ring should belong to you."

"I don't understand," Cora said. "The design is supposed to mean something?"

"The whole of the design defines the one who wears the ring," Inola said. "White bald eagle tail feathers symbolize ultimate power and spiritual purity. The eagle is a sacred messenger between the earth and the sky. The ruby is the stone of prophecy. Only a Clan Mother, chief, or medicine man would be allowed to wear any one of these symbols, and only a chosen one would be allowed to wear all three."

Cora's pupils widened into black discs. Her face tensed as she listened, and her shoulders hunched as she wrapped her arms around herself.

Inola paused for a moment to allow the gravity of her words to sink in.

"Charlie hasn't told me anything specific about you or your relationship to him or the cases," Inola admitted. "I've done all I can to make him talk, but he's doggedly loyal and protective. I admire that in him. I've been forced to do research on my own and come up with my own conclusions."

Cora nodded without speaking. She refused to consider where the conversation was going.

"As a profiler you're gifted in perception and analysis," Inola said. "You're trained professionally, and your books are brilliant. Your work with both adults and children is well-recognized and respected."

"Maybe you could write the forward for my next publication," Cora suggested, finding her voice and blushing self-consciously from the unexpected praise. "What does that have to do with my ring?"

Inola pressed her palms together and rested her forefingers on her chin just beneath her narrow lips, her brows knit thoughtfully.

"Even Charlie can't protect you from the rumors," she said earnestly. "People are going to talk. The wrong people will make seemingly wild claims and charges about you. Eventually all the denials in the world won't hide the obvious facts or the connection you have with each other."

There was a long, quiet pause. Outside the far kitchen window, Cora could hear the birds chirping cheerfully, and she watched as slivers of sunlight pierced the patterned brick floor of the sunroom.

"I knew when I saw the ring you're wearing. You're a chosen one," Inola said. "You have the dreams."

Cora drew a deep breath but said nothing.

"When I was a very young child my Cherokee grandmother saw in me some of the same gifts you have," Inola continued. "The perception, an ability to see straight through people to their souls and the truth of who they really are. She encouraged me to study and make the best use of what I'd been given to serve and protect others. My grandmother was a tribal Clan Mother. She told me fascinating stories about the really gifted ones, the rare and chosen ones. The dreamcatchers."

Inola relaxed back into the chair and tugged at the hem of her suit jacket.

"That's how you knew about the licorice," the agent said bluntly. "How you knew about Eudora. You have the dreams."

She studied Cora's face.

"You can't act on them. You aren't supposed to. That's not your job. But Charlie can, and he does."

The sound of Jane's laughter drifted in from outside.

"You don't have to say anything," Inola said. "I don't know how this came to be. Someday you may trust me and tell me the story, but you should never try to explain. Not to me. Not to anyone."

The agent stood and laid a black-bordered business card next to the untouched iced tea glasses and cookies on the table.

She tapped the rectangle deliberately.

"I won't take any more of your time," she said. "I just wanted you to know that if you ever need anything, and I mean anything at all, I'd be honored to do whatever you ask of me. My grandmother would expect it, and I can do no less. Please don't hesitate to call me."

Marjorie shouted a friendly greeting from the hallway as Jane skipped into the den, two long black braids swinging wildly, kittens dancing in her arms. She darted directly into Cora's lap.

"I missed you," she said and giggled, wrapping her tiny arms around her foster mom's neck and nuzzling down into the welcoming hug.

"I missed you too," Cora said, tears beginning to form in the corners of her eyes as she looked over the child's dark hair into Inola Walker's serene, serious face.

"I'll see you to the door," she said, struggling to rise, the child still clinging to her side, but the agent waved her back.

"Marjorie can see me out," she said, adding from the doorway, "I'm privileged to have met you, Cora Stone. May you and your house be blessed. Your secrets are safe with me."

Cora had no idea at all how to reply, so she simply wrapped her arms more tightly around Jane and exhaled, fighting back tears of astonishment and wonder.

Inola Walker went out onto the front porch and called Ben Taylor to ask someone to come and pick her up.

It shouldn't take long, she thought. *This is Balfour. He can't be more than ten minutes away.*

Chapter 59

"Everything seems to be going rather well, don't you think?" Betsey Anne waved her recent manicure in the air as though she was still trying to dry the polish, gesturing enthusiastically toward the pairs of French doors leading out onto the veranda. "We couldn't ask for a more perfect day to show off what we've accomplished."

The scent of the blooming roses, fragrant wild violets, azaleas, and gardenias drifted through the room and mingled with pleasant voices and the low melodies from a string quartet gathered from the local high school. Actually, the misnamed group was made up of two violins and a cello accompanied on the recently acquired baby grand piano by Miss Lavinia Toney, Emmanuel's pianist.

Betsey Anne had insisted that since the piano was essentially stringed, that calling them a string quartet was technically true and sounded more elegant on the printed program.

No one was in the mood to dispute her claims, so they humored her.

Someone can just sue me, she thought, feeling rather proud of herself. *Besides, no one in Balfour is going to know the difference anyway.*

Zedekiah Balfour was standing awkwardly off to one side of the gazebo, his freshly starched white shirt buttoned and secured around his neck with a green and blue patterned tie whose colors matched his daughter's equally crisp pinafore.

Naomi was bouncing happily from one foot to the other, one hand securely clutching her father's elbow and the other swinging a white wicker basket full of silk wildflowers and ribbons.

Katy excused herself from Amy's side.

"Well, hello there," she said, extending a hand to the enthusiastic girl. "Don't you look absolutely beautiful! I love the basket!"

"Miss Vicki gave it to me," Naomi said proudly. "She said every young lady should have flowers on certain momentous occasions."

"She's right." Katy smiled, turning to the grim guardian. Zeke was rooted and standing at attention. "And don't you look handsome in your suit."

Zeke made a disgusted face and muttered some indistinguishable, complaining noises.

Naomi leaned over and mock whispered, "I made him buy it. Don't you like the charcoal gray with the pinstripe? We went all the way to the Mall of Georgia to buy it. We walked around the mall for hours. It was so much fun. We bought my dress and his tie too."

Her expression had grown animated with excitement and joy.

"Of course," she added, rolling her eyes dramatically, "he says wearing it makes him feel like an undertaker."

"I believe what I said was that you are going to be the death of me yet," he corrected. "I still don't see why it's necessary for us to be here."

"Please try not to mind him," she said to Katy. "He's missing his nap, and that makes him cranky. He doesn't even want to have any food, although everyone keeps offering."

"Naomi." His voice rose. "We've had this conversation."

"See what I mean?" she said as though he had not spoken. "I think a chicken salad sandwich and a chocolate chip cookie would do him a world of good. I was just reading an article the other day about low blood sugar—"

"Naomi!"

She stopped, her expression that of a mischievous, chastised sprite.

"Yes, Daddy," she said meekly.

Katy's lips twitched with the irresistible urge to laugh. She chanced a quick glance at Zeke's face and saw that he was biting his lower lip, a spark of reluctant laughter in his dark eyes.

Precious, beautiful child, she thought, an image of Elizabeth popping into her mind. *How anyone could abandon you is beyond my comprehension. I feel so sorry for the mother who is missing out on the absolute delight of knowing you.*

Before Zeke could form a response, Ellie Sanderson appeared at the corner of the house carrying a tray of assorted sandwiches in one hand and a small glass of pink lemonade in the other.

She walked directly to the little girl and stopped.

"Mrs. Virginia said that I was to find you and offer you sandwiches," she said, lowering the tray so Naomi could see the selection of tiny, delicate squares and triangles. "I brought you something to drink. There are napkins on the table over there."

She indicated one of the garden tables nearer the house.

"If you and your father will take a seat, you can make your

choices. I'll bring you cookies after you've eaten."

Naomi tugged at her father's arm again, and this time he didn't resist.

"Thank you so much!" she said, pulling the man along as she followed Ellie. "You are very kind."

Ellie blushed at the child's unabashed gratitude and looked back at Katy, who was watching the pair with unapologetic amusement.

"You're adorable," she said sincerely, placing both the platter and the glass on the garden table Naomi selected and looked at Zeke, who was awkwardly standing behind one of the two wrought iron chairs. "I can get you something to drink too, if you'll tell me what you'd like."

"He's going to tell you that he doesn't want anything," Naomi said, seating herself gracefully and removing three petite sandwiches of different sizes and types placing them on a napkin for herself. "But he really wants sweet tea with extra lemons."

Zeke shook his head in surrender and watched helplessly as his daughter chose three more sandwiches and placed them on another napkin.

"Daddy, please sit down," the child said gently. "If you stand you are certain to spill something on your nice new suit."

Katy suppressed another urge to laugh out loud as Zeke sat down and Ellie retrieved the platter of sandwiches, retreating the way she'd come back to the kitchen.

"I'm going to save you the indignity of an audience while you eat," the widow said. "I've got to go and check on my sister, but I'll remind Ellie about the cookies. I'm glad you came."

"Thank you," the little girl said. "I'd appreciate that. I'm glad we came too."

On the other side of the gazebo, the music from the quartet had garnered a modest but substantial crowd who were enjoying their refreshments from the comfort of folding chairs arranged in a semicircle on the stone patio. The completion of each piece was rewarded with a light but gratifying smattering of applause.

Standing beside Linda Candler, Betsey Anne was feeling exceptionally vindicated in her choices and her contributions to the day. She had opened her mouth to announce that everything was progressing nicely when there was a sharp, sudden scream and the sound of china crashing to the ground just beyond where they stood.

Chapter 60

Linda and Betsey Anne rounded the corner of the patio as Ellie and another one of the teenage serving girls scampered past, murmuring vague apologies for the haste and disappearing in the direction of the kitchen.

The two women exchanged puzzled glances.

Almost immediately after the girls went into the house, a determined Virginia came out of the house followed by a less mobile Hannah waving a dishcloth.

"I thought you were supervising the trays of pastries and fruit in the kitchen," Betsey Anne said. "What's going on?"

Virginia didn't answer, sweeping past them, her head lowered, her face intense.

Hannah, noticeably heavier and a bit out of breath, came next, waving the pair to follow her further into the garden to the source of the sounds.

Amy McInnis, her arms and legs like toothpicks around her

blossoming midsection, was sprawled awkwardly on one of the garden benches. Fat beads of shiny perspiration dotted her forehead and had glued her bangs to her skin.

Katy, the color drained from her already-too-pale face, sat on one side holding her sister's hand while Darcie Jones sat on the other, clucking and coaxing the pregnant woman to take a sip of water.

"Oh my goodness!" Virginia exclaimed, watching as Hannah bent over and picked up the larger pieces of the broken cup and saucer, tucking the shards safely into the folds of her apron. Ellie and the other teenager appeared at her elbow with a broom and dustpan.

"Did you fall, dear?" Virginia said. "What happened?"

Amy opened her mouth to speak, but another moan of pain escaped instead. She ran her hands down and pressed them against the bottom of her bloated belly, cradling and soothing the unborn child as best she could.

"I think it's the baby," she managed. "It's time for the baby."

"Now, let's not be hasty," Betsey Anne said firmly, crossing her arms defensively. "Just sit for a minute and see if the feeling passes."

"I don't know why you think you're in charge," Linda observed dryly.

She turned to the girl who was sweeping while Ellie knelt on the patio, holding the dustpan full of the remaining tiny white shards of porcelain.

"Quick thinking, ladies," she said approvingly.

"There's a list of local emergency numbers in the kitchen posted by the wall phone," Virginia added. "Be the sweethearts you are and call Lisa, then the fire department. Let them know that Amy's in labor. We'll take whoever shows up first, but it wouldn't hurt to have both. And please find my son, Jack. The last time I saw him, he was helping direct traffic in the parking lot. He's wearing olive green scrubs."

Virginia had restrained herself from commenting on her son's odd choice of apparel. She had no idea he owned scrubs, but this was not the time to ask.

"I'll call Dr. Lisa and the fire department," Ellie said, standing up with the full dustpan, balancing it tentatively as she scampered off to the kitchen.

"I'll get your son."

The other girl darted toward the front of the building, broom still in hand like Joan of Arc with her sword darting off to battle.

"Don't you think you're overreacting?" Betsey Anne looked around, slightly disconcerted by the gathering crowd of onlookers but unsure how to shoo them away without attracting even more attention. "I'm sure we can just get Amy into her car and she can rest comfortably in her own house. And what do you expect Jack to do?"

Amy gave another explosive gasp.

"I think the baby disagrees with you," Hannah said reprovingly, clucking in displeasure at the woman's haughty attitude.

She's not the maternal sort, the housekeeper thought, trying her best to be charitable. *Not much sympathy for a first-time mama or a baby that disrupts her tidy plans. At least Linda and Virginia know what to do. And Ellie. God love them.*

"I don't think Amy is in any condition to ride in a car," Linda said. "Jack is a strong young man who's strong enough to carry

Amy if she isn't able to walk."

"Walk where?" Betsey Anne sputtered.

"I'll get some clean towels and the first aid kit," the housekeeper said, clutching at the corners of the apron to prevent the pieces and shards of cup from falling as she maneuvered her way around the swarm of spectators who had gathered.

"There's a room off the kitchen area set up with a twin bed for overnight security," Virginia said. "It's simple and clean with no stairs to climb."

She paused, noticing Betsey Anne's discomfort and choosing to ignore her.

Amy made another pitiful groan.

Linda and Virginia exchanged concerned looks.

"Do you think you can walk just a little, Amy?" Linda asked gently. "Darcie and Katy can support you. It isn't far. Lisa's on her way."

Amy nodded, damp tendrils of hair curling as she pushed them behind her ears.

Her face grew taut, her body tense, anticipating the next wave of contractions.

Katy and Darcie gripped her elbows and waited until they sensed her rising before they added to her effort and steadied the struggling woman to her feet.

"Go with them, Virginia. Show them the room," Linda said, taking the glass of water from Darcie's free hand. "Betsey Anne and I will be happy to carry on from here."

"We will?" The blond scowled, irritated not only with the change in plans but with her own irrational dislike for anything painful or messy. She didn't want to be included in the birthing process, but she was equally displeased at being left out of the inner circle.

"Indeed we will," Linda retorted, surveying the group of curious visitors and locals who parted to make way for Amy and her entourage as they made their self-conscious trek into the house. "It isn't every day a new business venture is christened with a birth. I can't imagine anything more fitting."

Betsey Anne made a grunt of decided disagreement.

"Let's go get the refreshments from the kitchen then," Betsey Anne said, more or less reconciled to her place as a supporting player in the current scenario.

"We'll be right back with plates of sandwiches and pastries," Linda assured the group of concerned bystanders. "Please continue to enjoy the gardens."

Across town in the Balfour Clinic, Lisa cut short her stern talk with Quincy about his latest weight gain and the resulting high blood pressure. She grabbed her medical bag, leaving directions with her nurse practitioner to cancel her afternoon appointments.

She arrived at the Wilton House to find that the paramedic had beaten her by a little more than ten minutes and was at work making her job easier.

"I didn't expect to see you here," she said cheerfully. "I saw the fire department ambulance outside. I thought Dave was on call this weekend."

"He is," Casey said, continuing to take Amy's vitals with practiced ease, his gloved hand on her wrist as the second hand swept by on his watch. "I just completed the fire department EMT certification and got driver's certification on the ambulance on Wednesday. I'd dropped by the station to pick up a uniform, and Dave offered to let me take the call."

"How very thoughtful of him," Lisa said skeptically, politely acknowledging Katy and Hannah, waving them out of the way toward Virginia, who was hovering in the far corner of the room.

"How far apart are the contractions?" she asked.

"Four or five minutes," Katy offered, glancing quickly at Casey, who confirmed with a nod of his head.

Lisa looked around the room.

"We're a little crowded in here," she said quietly.

"I was just waiting for you to get here," Virginia said. "Darcie's gone to get a terrycloth bathrobe from one of the suites upstairs. I'll go see what's keeping her."

Casey released Amy's wrist and straightened, closing his tech bag.

"I didn't mean you," Lisa corrected him. "You're our ride to the hospital. I may need some of the specialized equipment you have in the ambulance too."

"I suppose you're talking to me then," Hannah said, trying not to let her hurt feelings show, her shoulders slumped with worry.

Virginia took the woman's arm in a firm, friendly grasp.

"Come with me," she said warmly. "I could certainly use your expertise in the kitchen, if you'd be willing to help with the food and managing the servers. Our doctor here and her able paramedic have everything well under control. All they really need now are our prayers."

Katy smiled gratefully.

"What about me?" she asked. "Should I wait outside?"

Another agonizing cry rose from the bed.

"Please let Katy stay," Amy gasped. "I want Katy to stay."

"Then Katy stays," Lisa said, wrapping her stethoscope

around the back of her neck and pushing her sleeves up to her forearms as she pulled on a pair of gloves.

"Keep breathing, Amy. I need to check to see how far you're dilated. We're here to help, but most of this is up to you and the baby."

Amy nodded, the beads of perspiration forming more heavily in the creases of her forehead and across her upper lip. Her face was quite ashen and strained. Katy freed one of her hands from Amy's grip and tenderly smoothed back her sister's hair, her eyes meeting Lisa's eyes with an unspoken question.

"Everything is going to be just fine," the doctor said reassuringly as Amy moaned and shifted her weight, struggling to find a position without pain.

Lisa turned to Casey, who had reopened his bag and was methodically arranging instruments and supplies. The paramedic waited until the two women were gone and Katy had taken a seat on the other side near the head of the bed.

"I've got the Ambu bag and a pediatric mask ready, just in case," he said. "Her water broke right after I got here. I propped her up with pillows. I've heard it eases the pressure and relieves pain. I checked her once. She's dilated to ten centimeters with the urge to push. No crowning yet."

"Alright, no time to get to the hospital then," the doctor said, pleased with the information and with the paramedic's efficiency. "You've delivered how many babies?"

"My first solo delivery," he said. "There were a few others in training, with supervision of course."

There was a faint knock at the door. Casey automatically moved to block the view of the semi-reclining Amy.

"Yes," he said. "Come in."

Hannah's pleasant face, still wrinkled with worry, poked around the half-opened doorframe.

"I brought a few things," she offered. "A cup of ice chips, a blanket from upstairs, some clean towels, and the bathrobe from Darcie."

"Thank you, Hannah," Lisa responded from behind the paramedic sentinel. "I knew I could count on you."

"Heavens yes!" The woman chuckled softly. "Nothing like a birthing to put a perspective on life."

Amy moaned again.

"I really want to push," she said through her teeth. "I really, really do."

"Here." Hannah thrust the cup and linens into the paramedic's waiting hands. "You've got more important things to do."

Katy reached over and took the cup of ice chips from Casey and held a piece to her sister's dry lips.

"Deep breath," Lisa encouraged. "Let's get you out of this pretty dress and cover you with that robe. Baby girl's in a hurry, so it won't be long now."

Chapter 61

Zeke Balfour glared across the broad gravel driveway at Katy Wilton as the ambulance pulled away from the parking lot.

"You're not going with your sister to the hospital?" he asked as she came toward him with a look of determination on her face.

"She's going to sleep for a couple of hours, and the baby needs to be checked out by a pediatrician," she said. "I'm going home to pick up the hospital bags Amy already packed for both of them. I'll take them to her later. I'm glad I caught you before you left. I wanted to talk to you for a minute without Naomi."

"We don't have anything to talk about," he said disagreeably. "I give up. Naomi convinced me, and I'm sick of looking at it anyway. The lawyers can send me the papers about the cabin. I'll sign. You can have it."

"Thank you!" Katy stammered, shocked by Zeke's unexpected change of heart. She could only imagine what Naomi must have said to him.

She could think of nothing else to add, painful thoughts over-taking her. She'd stood in this same spot just months ago, watching the body bag holding Steve's lifeless form as it was loaded into the ambulance. She wondered if she had the courage to say what she wanted to say.

"I hope you don't think anything's changed because of what was in that trunk," he said. "Because it hasn't. Not for me, and not for Naomi."

"If you say so," she said. "You would know."

"That's right," he said, his eyes turning uncomfortably toward the house as though he expected his child to suddenly appear at the mention of her name. "I told her she could thank people before we left, so if you've got something to say that you don't want her to hear, you'd better spit it out."

The swagger of his attitude and the squaring of his broad shoulders told her that he was nearing his limit of patience, but a persistent voice inside her told her that if he'd listen to anyone, he'd listen to her.

"You know that you're going to have people coming to see you because you've given me the cabin. They're going to ask questions. Not just about your family history, but also about you. About Naomi."

The pupils of his eyes widened, and his jawline grew taut.

"Are you *trying* to talk me out of giving you the cabin?" he said. She ignored his taunting.

"People in Balfour can be proud of the story." She paused and lifted her chin. "You should be proud of the story you have to tell."

He exhaled, the formal clothing like a suit of armor as his body straightened and his demeanor tensed defensively.

"I don't care what people think," he said. "I don't care what you think."

"You shouldn't lie to yourself." Katy bit her lip. "We all care, one way or another, whether we want to show we care or not. If you don't think you care for your own sake, then I believe you care for your daughter's sake."

Zeke folded his arms defiantly across his chest, his fists clenched, and she knew she'd struck a sensitive nerve. The knowledge didn't make her happy.

"We do things for our children, you and I. For our daughters. Things that we'd never do for ourselves."

She took a step toward him, fighting the urge to retreat from the fight, knowing there was more that needed to be said before she walked away and kept her promise to leave Zeke alone.

"There's a particular verse in the Bible that always troubled me," Katy continued, swallowing her discomfort. "I can't quote it, but I know what it says."

The man stood like one of his own granite statues, feet planted apart like deep roots into the ground, his expression unchanged and unmoving.

"Jesus is teaching the disciples," she said, disregarding his apparent disapproval and distain. "They've been talking about forgiveness. He tells them that they're going to be forgiven in the same way that they forgive others."

She paused to see if her words were having any effect on him, and she couldn't tell. But he seemed to be listening, his angry stare fixed firmly on her face.

Go on, she prodded herself. *Finish this, and you won't have to talk to him anymore. Just say what needs to be said. He needs to hear.*

"You're making my husband's headstone," she said. "You may not know that he was murdered by my brother-in-law."

Zeke hadn't moved, but she thought the expression on his face had softened just a tiny bit.

"No," he said. "I didn't know."

"Good Christians forgive. I've heard it over and over, but I didn't want to forgive. I wanted to be angry. I thought I had a right."

He opened his mouth to speak and then reconsidered.

Katy pushed on.

"I finally decided that the hate is too heavy. I was weighed down and held back, and I'm no use to my daughter if that is what I teach her. That other people can control our lives that way. That other people can determine whether or not we go on."

The man made a derisive snorting sound.

"So you're not a saint." Zeke made no attempt to keep the sarcasm from his tone. "I suppose you're going to tell me about your Jesus and how He makes life perfect."

Katy shook her head sadly.

"Life is never going to be perfect," she said. "I just got tired of pretending. Of hating. I finally took the whole mess to my knees in prayer, and I realized that if I believe in God—and I do believe there is a God—that someday I'll stand in front of Him and He'll judge me."

"So?"

"He'll judge me the same way I judge other people," she said. "He'll forgive me the same way I forgive. And in that moment, I realized that I have a choice."

For the second time since the conversation began, Zeke looked away toward the house.

"I can't tell you it's easy," she said. "I can't tell you how to do it. But I can tell you this one thing. Every day I look into my daughter's eyes and tell myself that love and forgiveness are the better way."

"Why are you telling me this?"

Katy could hear the hurt and grief, the anger and bitterness, in his question.

"Because I think you understand," she murmured. "Because you need to know that you're not alone. That there are other people in this world who are still living life in the shadow of what's happened to them in the past. And they've come out the other side. You can come out the other side."

An unexpected spring breeze swept past, and Naomi's voice called out.

Katy slipped her hand into her jacket pocket and retrieved her car keys.

"Please tell Naomi that I'm sorry I have to run," she said. "I need to get Amy's bag and see Lizzy for a few minutes before I go to the hospital. I hope I can spend some time with Naomi when the work starts on the cabin. Maybe you'll consider letting her come here to see what's going on."

Zeke lifted one hand and covered the lower part of his face, wiping his upper lip roughly with a gruff noise of assent, hiding his mouth.

"Thank you again," she said, waving to Naomi as she got into her car.

As she pulled away down the driveway, she refused to look in the rearview mirror.

She preferred instead to hold onto the last distinct impression in her mind, the tiniest glimmer of acceptance in Zeke Balfour's dark eyes.

At least, she was going to pray that's what she'd seen.

Chapter 62

Katy was not the only one who had been waiting all day for an opportunity to talk to someone.

Across the parking lot, hidden among a gardenia hedge row, Daryl Miller had been watching the widow's exchange with intense journalistic curiosity. He'd been following her, taking surreptitious photos with his cell phone for documentation.

At first he'd been keen on talking to both the sisters, but that darned Baptist preacher's wife had kept too close to the pregnant one. She was persistent, that woman. He had a strong suspicion that he wouldn't have gotten the first question out before she'd have had him thrown out of the Wilton House completely. And he couldn't afford to go back to Griffith without a story of some sort.

So he'd contented himself with following the younger one until both of the sisters disappeared together into the house.

Then the fire department ambulance showed up with the local Balfour doctor close after. What he was able to gather from eavesdropping was that the baby, a healthy girl, had been born in one of the rooms off the kitchen in the house, which could have made for a great story.

But some hotshot kid in scrubs with a ponytail was standing guard outside and wouldn't let him get close enough to take a picture of anything or get within shouting distance to ask questions.

Daryl twisted his mustache and tugged at the bottom of his vest.

There's got to be a story around here somewhere, he thought sullenly. *I never get any breaks. If I don't come back with something juicy, I'm going to have to pay for my own room. I can't mess up this opportunity.*

He considered trying to get close to the Senator to extract a comment from the newsworthy politician.

If he just gives me one comment, one sentence or maybe two, Daryl had thought. *I've made do with less. I can just elaborate. Add details. Draw conclusions.*

But even Daryl Miller had heard stories about what happened to people who crossed Senator Stewart Wilton. Hassling a couple of defenseless women for an article was well and good, but he was a coward when it came to pestering grown men and anyone who might be able to fight back. Or sue for libel.

Besides, the Senator had spent the day glued to Darcie Jones's side, and she'd made it absolutely clear how she felt about him.

Daryl had to content himself with following Katy Wilton.

So when the ambulance pulled away and the younger sister didn't leave, Daryl thought his luck had finally turned.

Then he saw her with the angry man in the parking lot.

Darn, darn, darn, he griped to himself. *That guy could snap me like a toothpick. Who is he anyway? Why is she talking to him? What's that story?*

He lifted his cell phone to begin taking more pictures, and a heavy hand landed on his shoulder.

He squealed like a piglet for its supper.

"Daryl," Vicki's soft Cajun accent rang out. She'd just finished carrying the last of the floral baskets to the van and was returning to help move the vases on the outside tables into the main house. "God loves you, *être ami*, but you need to decide whether or not He's going to be happy with you."

To his credit, Daryl had never met Vicki, much less heard of her. He found her appearance truly astonishing.

The sight of her warrior Amazon frame swathed in an ankle-length purple caftan, gold leaves of jewelry dripping from her ears, arms, hands, and neck, with her face elegantly painted in glittering greens, lavenders, blues, and golds set his heart to thumping like bongos in his head and chest.

He was as startled as if he'd flipped on a blindingly bright light switch and found himself squinting at his own clownish reflection in a full-length mirror.

Vicki pressed her clear advantage.

"My friend, you are in search of a story, yes?" she purred. "Do not deny it, little man. You must stop this skulking in corners and behind the greenery. You must listen to Vicki. I know. There is a better way."

"What are you talking about?" he said, regaining some of his limited composure and brushing away her hand. "I'm only looking at the scenery."

"Tsk, tsk," she chided him. "You, *être ami*, my friend, must know how foolish you sound, and how you look. I know who you are, you silly, silly man."

"Well, I don't know you," he said boldly. "Who are you to tell me what to do?"

Vicki's hand fluttered out before Daryl knew what was happening, and she gripped the lower half of his earlobe with a vicious pinch. His chubby hands flew up to disengage her, and she snatched his phone.

"Ouch!" he shouted. "Let me go! Crazy woman!"

She released him, and he backed quickly away, rubbing his injured ear while she systematically and quite efficiently began to erase all the pictures he had taken.

"That's personal property!" he said. "You can't do that!"

"You've no signed releases for these pictures," she said, taking no more notice of his complaint than she would an annoying housefly. "You cannot publish without permission. You are not the only one who knows the law, my friend. I didn't believe them, but they are right. All of them. You're a whiner. You don't listen."

"You'll be sorry!" he threatened. "I'll tell everyone what you've done!"

"Ha!" she said, tossing his cell phone back at him. "Write a story about me, little man, and see what happens. I am the florist, no? I will put flowers on your grave and then I will dance!"

Daryl clumsily caught and held his phone against his brocade-vested chest, inhaling a pitiful, ragged sob. Vicki felt a stab of sympathy and realized that he was close to crying.

Now you will listen, she thought. *Now you are paying attention. Darcie and Linda said I must be firm with you, so I have been firm. I don't like being firm, but you gave me no choice.*

"We can be friends now, yes?" she said, tossing an affable dark arm around his shoulder. The flowing sleeve of her purple silk caftan draped over him like a superhero cape, and she dazzled him with a display of her glistening teeth. "We can make peace and find a story that you can write. A happy story. I know a story like that. I know many stories like that, my little friend."

"Why would you do that?" he said, attempting to pull away and failing to escape her vise-like hold. "Why would you help me? You're angry with me."

She took and tucked his cell phone into his front jacket pocket, hugging him zealously to her side as though they'd been comrades in arms, fighting in some long-fought foreign campaign, returning triumphantly to the homeland.

"Because I like you, *être ami*," Vicki declared. "This is my way. You will learn."

She planted an ardent kiss in the center of his forehead, leaving a bright orange lip-shaped stain on his pasty white skin.

Daryl Miller's jaw dropped open, but no words came out.

"You'll see," she said, closing his mouth with the palm of her hand and tweaking his cheek. "We're going to be great friends! I just know we are!"

Chapter 63

The Eighth Day: Sunday

The kitchen was colder and the coffee was hotter than she remembered, even from the night before. But James was still wearing the same baggy suit he always did and was sitting in his same chair, his gnarled hand resting on the same weathered leather-bound Bible on the table.

The coal oil lamp burned a little brighter, and the gypsy jar was back at the edge of the circle, the shiny objects embedded in the sides sparkling in the half-light.

Nothing ever changes, she thought, her heart filling with a burdening heaviness. *I'm here, and I don't know why. Maybe I'll never know why.*

"Everyone leaves a legacy, Cora," James announced, as though beginning one of his masterful sermons from the country church pulpit where he'd stood for almost twenty-five years. "Everyone who ever lived leaves footprints behind. No one lives his or her life in a vacuum. We're all created for a purpose and with the free will to accept or reject the direction God has set for our lives. You've been chosen too."

She looked longingly at the gypsy jar, her inquisitive fingertips tracing the trapped objects as her thoughts turned to the dying woman who had created the memorial to her child. So much grief and sadness. So much death and despair.

What about the ones who never live at all? she thought. *What about the ones like this baby girl? Like Lonora?*

"They live, Cora," he said compassionately, reading her thoughts as easily as he did the expression on her face. "They live in the hearts of the mothers and the fathers who love them. They live forever with their Creator."

Her heart ached, unconvinced.

Just say you can't tell me why because you don't know, she thought. *You don't know why, do you?*

"Faith is a decision, sweet one," his voice continued. "A daily choice. We learn, step-by-step, to walk on."

She thought about Harry's half sister. About Harry's questions. Harry's pain.

"What about the ones who try to change their destiny?"

James reached out and covered her hand with his in a gesture of condolence and sympathy.

"I'm not going to take up residence in the judgment seat of the Almighty, Cora, and neither should you." His tone was kind. His touch was gentle. But she knew she was being chastised. "I believe that *all things work together* and that it's a choice to keep walking in faith and trust."

"Is that really necessary where you are? Aren't you beyond all that now?"

"I'm talking to you, Cora," he said. "None of this is about me."

He released her hand, pushed his thick glasses up on his nose, and drained his cup. Cora knew the conversation was almost over.

"When will I talk to you again?" she asked.

"That's not up to me." He balanced himself on the corner of the table as he stood, picking up his Bible and touching the glass pin in the center of the cork on the gypsy jar. "I'm a preacher, dear one, not a prophet."

"I'd like to be ready for the next time." Her voice drifted off, knowing that she was asking the impossible, or, at the very least, the unlikely.

James laughed, a musical vapor that reached out and touched her soul with a soothing balm she had not expected.

"None of us is ever truly ready, Cora," he said. "We may think we've packed for the journey—that we understand the path. But there are always going to be unexpected detours along the way. We do the best we can with what we've been given."

What we've been given, Cora thought, remembering her earlier conversation with Inola. *Or maybe what has been chosen for us. I'm a dreamcatcher.*

"So you aren't going to give me a hint as to when I'm going to see you again?"

"I cannot tell you what I do not know," he said, pushing the chair forward until the back was flush against the edge of the table top. "I can quote you some scripture references about not knowing the time or the place. Maybe over in Corinthians, or one of my personal favorites found in the book of Revelation."

Small shivers like electricity ran through her body.

"All things for His good purposes," he said.

And Cora was awake and staring at the ceiling of her bedroom, the blades of the fan over her head turning silently and tiny waves of fresh air drifting down across her cool face. The red numbers of the clock glowed against the white of the ceiling—five forty-five in the morning.

For a moment she thought the numbers might have flickered in the darkness.

What does James know about time anyway? she thought as the tremors ceased in her physical body and her natural cynicism and frustration returned. *It's no longer any concern for him. It's all well and good to tell me not to worry and just to trust. It's harder than it looks.*

Beside her, Thomas lay sleeping, his dark hair dusted with the first signs of silver and tousled against his pillow, his breathing full and regular.

His expression was as it almost always was, peaceful and calm. The earthly keeper of her heart. He believed. He trusted. He had faith.

Whatever happened next, and wherever the dreams led, Thomas was God's gift to her.

I never wanted, never asked to be a dreamcatcher, she thought, her eyelids heavy with fatigue.

Names and faces of people she had never met, thoughts and visions of places she had never seen, gypsy jars and Tarot cards, tea leaves, and disembodied skulls drifted in and out of her semi-consciousness.

Cora brushed the damp frustration of tears from her face.

Then, overcome by the weight of uncertainty and the burden of purpose, she pressed herself against her husband's back and drifted to uneasy but dreamless sleep.

Chapter 64

Marcie couldn't decide who was drooling more over the aroma of her waffles, Charlie or Elvira, but it didn't matter to her. Flattery was flattery whether it came from sleepy man or faithful dog.

Both the man and the dog were following her movements around her kitchenette with intense interest. Charlie was slouching in his customary chair at her table, his hand resting between Elvira's velvety ears. The dog's huge jowls pressed down into his blue-jeaned thigh. From time to time she rolled her soft brown eyes and tilted her head to assure herself that, for the moment at least, he was indeed still here.

Neither Charlie nor Marcie had the heart to say aloud how short-lived her time with him really was, although the Plott hound knew.

She'd seen him pack his duffle bag upstairs. She'd watched him toss it into Marcie's trunk when they trotted side by side down to the manager's apartment just after the first glimmer of dawn.

413

Charlie had wanted to leave as soon as the sun came up, but unfortunately for his plans, Marcie stubbornly refused to drive him over to Griffith to a car rental until he had eaten a leisurely breakfast and spent the morning with Elvira.

As she chattered away with juicy bits and pieces of the local gossip, most of which involved his most recent visit to Balfour, he suspected that Marcie was glad to spent time with him too.

"Don't you have breakfast with Marjorie on Sunday morning?" he said, sipping at his coffee and tugging affectionately at Elvira's ears. "Where's she?"

Marcie eyed him suspiciously.

"She went to the sunrise service prayer breakfast," she said. "She's spending the afternoon with Jane, so she'll meet Thomas at services and go home with them. Don't change the subject."

"What are you talking about?" he said innocently. "I was just thinking that you didn't have to go to all this trouble. You could drop me off in the rental company parking lot in Griffith and be back in time for church as usual. Elvira could ride with us, and we could grab fast food on the way."

"Elvira is riding with us anyway," Marcie said much too loudly, pans clattering and silverware clinking against the dishes. "Fast food isn't real food, and the church isn't a building."

"I don't want to be a bother," he said. "And I especially hate that you're missing Easter services."

"Too late. The ox is in the ditch, Charlie."

She leaned around the doorframe and waved a spatula.

"Don't you fret for my salvation. There's plenty of provisions in the Old Testament for situations like this. You'd know that if you went to church more."

"I'm not sure how I like being called an ox," he joked. "Or being preached to."

"I don't particularly care," she said, refilling the coffee cup in his hand. "Waffles are almost ready. Now that you mention being concerned about me, you could always hitch a ride with your friends from the police department and that nice FBI woman they're taking down to Hartsfield today. She's impressive, that one. You could spend more time with that fortune teller too."

"You're a great cook and a good friend, but you've got a mean streak the width of I-285," he retorted. "Don't try to pretend you don't. Makes me feel sorry for Elvira."

"She's got nothing to worry about," Marcie said, sliding a heaping plate of waffles dripping with strawberries and whipped cream in front of him. "I wouldn't think of holding the dog responsible for the sins of her owner."

Marcie leaned down and patted the Plott hound's huge head.

"Your food's in the dish over there, dog," she said. "Something special. Get along and let Charlie eat in peace."

The Plott hound moved, limb by giant limb, ambling into the kitchen. They could hear her throw her face into the dog bowl and begin to chew.

"Eat up, Charlie," Marcie said. "I prayed the whole time I was cooking, so the food's been amply blessed. I knew you were in a hurry. I threw in a couple of extra requests for you while I was at it."

"Do you really think prayers can help me?" he asked, cutting into the enormous stack with the side of his fork and stuffing the food into his mouth.

"Not sure," she said. "But you aren't dead yet, so maybe my prayers don't hurt either."

The sounds of chomping and slurping floated in from the kitchen, matching the sighs of satisfaction from Charlie as he ate his own meal. A few scant moments later, Elvira reappeared in the doorway, flopping herself across the laminate floor and yawning, a high-pitched yelp escaping her jaws, her eyes drooping in sleep.

Charlie scraped the last of the strawberries and cream from his plate and polished off his coffee.

"I'm going to miss you, Charlie," Marcie said, rising. "I'll put the rest of the coffee from the pot in a thermos for the road."

He wiped at the corners of his mouth with the back of his hand.

"I'm going to miss you," he said. "Thank you for everything."

"Shut up," she said cheerfully. "Bring your dishes to the sink, and don't step on my dog. And for goodness' sake, stop being maudlin. If you don't get that rental car and get out of Griffith by ten, you're going to miss your plane."

Chapter 65

The choir's rousing rendition of "He Lives" brought the packed congregation to their collective feet, raising their arms in praise with a unified gasp of approval and unexpected Baptist applause. Frank beamed joyfully and seated the choir with an enthusiastic wave.

Andrew Evans stepped with confidence to the pulpit to begin his sermon.

The preacher opened his Bible, removing the copious yellow legal pages of notes for his four-point sermon on the true meaning of Resurrection Sunday, when his eye caught the expression of absolute and unabashed boredom on Marjorie O'Quinn's face.

He hadn't meant to look at her. He hadn't meant to make eye contact with anyone at all, much less a woman he believed to be one of his harshest critics.

His momentary confidence evaporated, settling like the fine yellow pollen of the Easter lilies that decorated the windows of the sanctuary and lined the edges of the speaker's platform.

He'd taken a second dose of allergy medication as a precaution, but he knew what he felt had nothing to do with his sensitivity to blooming flowers.

All his insecurities flooded back. He knew that he wasn't the most inspirational of speakers, but he had shored himself up with justifications. He'd prepared. He'd planned. He'd prayed.

Ginny's face, radiant in the reflected light of the stained glass windows, beamed at him from the front pew, but even Ginny's encouragement seemed too far away to reach his misgivings. He tried to remind himself that he did, from time to time, speak to the needs of his modest, conservative congregation.

But today, as he looked out over their faces, he knew Marjorie was not the only one who doubted his ability to inspire. Today, he was forced to confess, he was as distracted and discouraged as the members he saw looking back at him from the pews.

In what appeared to his flock to be a dramatic pause, his attention deliberately moved from pew to pew, searching out others.

AJ Lee was struggling to stay awake after spending the last two days chauffeuring tourists and locals around town nonstop for the Wilton House opening. The poor boy was clearly exhausted.

Ellie Sanderson was doodling absently on the margin of the bulletin. She was attending a community college and had talked to Virginia about changing her major to nursing but worried where she would find the money for tuition.

Doctor Lisa had been up all night delivering twins over in Griffith after delivering Amy's little girl at the Wilton House. She had completely given up and was napping, chin to chest, on the back row, a soft splash of light from the stained glass window like a night-light illuminating the fatigue on her face.

Even Bill's taciturn expression was more blank than usual.

Quite suddenly, Evans realized what his congregation needed. They needed what he needed. He closed his Bible and took a slow step to the right of the pulpit.

"I'm sorry," he said earnestly, catching his wife's eyes and seeing the quizzical look on her face. "Sometimes when I prepare my sermon for Sundays, I stop listening to God on Friday afternoon."

There were nervous, random twitters of expectation. The sudden departure from the normal Sunday sermon routine seemed to snap the congregation back into the present. As people shifted in their seats and their attention came back to the pastor, hands reached out to subtly shake and wake those who were still sleeping.

Collective confusion settled like early morning fog as they waited to see what Andrew would do next.

"I've been thinking about why we're here this morning," he said. "Resurrection Sunday, of course, is a special celebration with glorious music and fellowship. As your pastor, there's quite a bit of pressure to say something that you haven't heard. Something uplifting. Something inspirational. Something that might help you in your lives."

Evans took a deep, brave breath. This kind of improvisation was not like him. This was the stuff of resignations and removals, and he knew it well.

He'd seen it happen to others, and he had no desire to join their dubious ranks.

"I will begin with saying that I'm sorry, because I have failed you. I confess. I don't know exactly what to say to any of you."

Evans reached over and gathered his Bible from the podium, cradling it into his elbow and pressing the worn leather book into his suited chest, letting his unfamiliar words sink and soak. He looked down at his wife's glowing face and felt encouraged to go on, her steady challenge to him to forgive their son on his mind.

"Life is short. We all have words that we ought to say, people we ought to seek out. We come every year to an empty tomb and look for an answer that isn't there because the One who saved us isn't there."

Some of the congregation began to nod in agreement, but the vast majority maintained puzzled looks of bewilderment and uncertainty.

"We've been given a gift of forgiveness, but the proof of our forgiveness is in our own ability to give it to others."

Around the room, more heads began to bob up and down as the undertones of approval rose.

"What I have to say to you is simple, maybe too simple."

Evans motioned for the pianist to take her seat at the freshly tuned baby grand piano. She began to play a familiar hymn softly, an undercurrent of soothing tradition and calm beneath the preacher's words.

Beams of the midmorning sun illuminated the stained glass windows around the edges of the room, and some in the membership searched around for their belongings, although the vast majority were riveted by their pastor's words.

Evans descended the long, broad steps from the platform and extended his free hand toward his wife, who rose to join him before the communion table.

"What I do know and what I can declare as truth"—his voice was firmer now—"is that our little town has endured a great deal of heartache and healing in the past six months. I know that we should join hands to encourage those both inside and outside our walls to join with us. We cannot and should not hide our love and forgiveness. Not because of who we are, but because of who He is."

Two or three scattered but forceful amens sounded and echoed from the back pews of the building, moving forward until the entire sanctuary had risen.

"Find someone," he continued, "someone who needs to hear what it is you need to say. That's all. Today you should be the Resurrection sermon."

He avoided the pointed stare of the chairman of the deacons seated on the front pew to his right and put his arm around Virginia.

In the choir loft behind him, a woman's soft, throaty alto voice took up the chorus of the hymn as other voices joined and blended together. Hands reached across the aisles to join other hands, moving together, singing in harmony as they filled the empty spaces between the pews, the aisles, the nave.

Andrew Evans looked at his wife's face and then out into the congregation at a sea of contentment. Although he couldn't see from where he stood, on the back row Marjorie O'Quinn was smiling.

Epilogue

Cora was resting in the swing on the front porch when Thomas and Jane arrived home from services, the pale lavender silk of her floral print dress flowing around her calves and one bare foot tucked up under her as she used the other to push gently back and forth.

The blooming roses and the scent of pines drifted around her, and the light spring breeze lifted the dark strands of hair that flowed loosely over her shoulders.

Her upper arms were wrapped in a frothy white shawl Thomas had never seen.

He also saw that her lips and cheeks were a darker rose color than usual. It took him a moment to realize that she was wearing makeup.

She had never looked so lovely to him, or so precious.

"You're home early," she said, looking at her watch. "Is everything okay?"

Jane bounded up the steps and climbed amid the cushions on the swing to nestle beside her.

"Morrie's coming over today," she said cheerfully. "After I take a nap."

Cora looked at Thomas over the enormous bow on the child's head.

"Jane," she suggested, hugging the wiggling child to her and rubbing her cheek against the little girl's smooth hair, "why don't you go up and change into play clothes before lunch? I've already set out the plates for our spaghetti. You don't want to get sauce on your Easter dress."

Cora stopped the movement of the swing with her foot while the agreeable child hopped down and danced off through the front door.

"Thomas," Cora said earnestly, "why is Marjorie coming over? I thought she was having lunch with Marcie. What's wrong?"

"Nothing at all," he said, taking the place beside her, settling into the cushions and beginning to push the swing back and forth again, his feet flat against the planks. "A change in plans. No worries."

"You're still home very early," she said, trying not to sound suspicious.

"Evans had a different kind of sermon this morning," he explained. "I don't think I've ever heard one quite like it."

She tilted her head, hair falling into her face as she brushed it back over her shoulder, questions running rampant through her mind.

Her husband reached across and spontaneously took her hand in his.

"Cora, I'm so incredibly proud to be your husband."

She had no idea at all how to respond, so she didn't.

"You're a remarkable woman," he continued. "You solve hundred-year-old mysteries, heal four-year-old hearts, bring closure to wounded souls, and soothe angry spirits. You always seem to know what to say and exactly how to say it. As a lawyer, I both envy and admire that quality in you."

He cupped her chin in his hand and brought the swing to a standstill.

"I'm sorry for all the hurt in your life, for all the pain these dreams of yours bring you. But I can't be sorry for the good they do, and I'll never be sorry that it was that hurt that brought you to Balfour and into my life."

"Is that what you'd call a closing argument?" she quipped through trembling lips.

"That's what I call a witness statement," he said. "The truth, the whole truth, and nothing but the truth."

Cora felt the tears gathering in the corners of her eyes.

I do wish I didn't cry so much lately, she thought. *I really do.*

"I like your dress," he said, fingering the ruby in the ring on her finger. "And you put on makeup too. I noticed."

"Yes," she said shyly, feeling remarkably self-conscious. "I thought about coming to church, but I only made it as far as the front porch. I'm sorry."

He took her left hand and pulled it through his elbow, tucking it under his arm and against his rib cage.

"That's an excellent beginning," he said, leaning down to brush the top of her head with his chin. "I love you, Cora Stone."

She tilted her face up to his.

"I love you too, Thomas."

Jane's head, minus the bow, appeared in the doorway. "Can I have spaghetti now? I'm hungry, please."

"Yes, of course," Cora said. "We'll be right there."

"Yes, we will," Thomas agreed, pressing a loving kiss into his wife's temple. "Yes, indeed. We'll be right there."

to
Wilton Estate

Sheland to Piney Woods
Lake

Cemetery

Miss Bessie's House

United Methodist Church

Cemetery

Hanson's Pharmacy

Emmanuel Baptist Church

Florist's Shop

Park & playground

Parson's Funeral Home

Balfour Elementary School

Nursing Home

Stone Law Firm

Post Office

Balfour, GA est 1818

to Anson's

Dreamcatcher: Daughters

Book 4 in the Balfour Mystery Series

Summer's been here and is almost gone. Lazy mornings and long afternoons give way to dog days and the scorching heat of the Georgia sun. Cora's content spending time with Jane and Thomas, closer than ever to venturing out of her house. Charlie's avoiding Balfour and his birthday as best he can, busy with travel, lecturing, and writing his latest book about cold case criminals and their crimes.

But there's an assassin in Balfour, and Inola Walker has her own plans for the detective and the dreamcatcher.

And who is Charlie to argue with the FBI—especially now that Cora is involved?

There's no escape for either of them until yet another mystery's been solved, but what could any of it have to do with a dream about groceries in Gramma Crawford's kitchen?

* * *

Cora's cold, stiff hands, which had been automatically unpacking the grocery bags, stopped as she reflected on yet another unexpected situation. James, too, had paused, a generic can of mixed vegetables in his hand, and was watching her intently.

"Sorry," she said. "I let my mind wander."

"I was there with you," he confessed. "I hope they're good thoughts. Happy memories."

"They were," she said. "But what you've come to tell me isn't pleasant at all, is it?"

He shook his head sadly.

"No, Cora, it isn't."

"What am I supposed to do?" she said.

"Unpack your bags, dear," he chided. "I'm already finished with mine."

She turned to the last bag on the counter and reached inside, but her hands touched something ice cold and oddly shaped.

Not a can or a box or a bag.

Her fingers closed around the object and lifted it cautiously over the serrated edge of the heavy paper. She placed it carefully on the countertop.

For all her work with the police, Cora knew very little about firearms. She used two hesitant fingers to rotate the cold tip of the barrel away from where she and James stood, running a cautious fingertip over the metal in an attempt to memorize any details that might identify what she was seeing. Sleek. Modern. Not a revolver. Some sort of patterned grid on the grip. She tried to decipher letters and symbols engraved into the steel.

She wished she could tell if there were any color to the weapon at all.

Charlie would want to know all the details.

Charlie, she thought, the inevitable inching its way up like a calming warmth from somewhere buried inside her. *I'll have to call Charlie. He'll know what to do. He always knows what to do about these things.*

Quiet confidence settled over her, and she absently picked up the last bag to fold it. As she turned the crinkling paper upside down, a small white business card fell out and landed on the linoleum at her feet.

Both she and James stooped at the same moment, but she, being younger and more agile, reached the card before he could bend his aged ethereal frame to the floor.

There were only two words printed on the card.

A name she didn't immediately recognize.

She had a split second to memorize the name before the preacher took the bag and began to fold it himself, a cryptic grin on his wrinkled lips.

And Cora was awake.

ABOUT THE AUTHOR

KC Pearcey has spent much of her life reading and writing, telling her own stories as well as encouraging others to share the stories of their lives over a cup of coffee, a tall glass of sweet tea, or a homemade lemonade.

Through the years, she has written, directed, and produced numerous original plays, skits, essays, poems, children's programs, and murder mystery dinner theatres for churches, schools, friends, and family—for enjoyment, entertainment, education, evangelism, and sometimes profit.

After forty years of teaching people of all ages how to write, perform, communicate, and think, she retired to travel with Darling Husband, enjoy time with her grandchildren, and write the books she always promised herself and her students she would someday write. So far, she's had more excellent adventures than she ever hoped to have.

Dreamcatcher: Fortunes is the third installment in a series of cozy mystery novels about the town of Balfour, Georgia, and its quirky inhabitants—their secrets, their struggles, their successes, and the strangers that come into their lives.

She hopes you enjoy getting to know everyone who lives there just a little better. They certainly are looking forward to sharing another story or two with you.

Email: dreamcatcherkcp@gmail.com

Made in the USA
Columbia, SC
02 July 2024

37993347R00241